SIMPSON

IMPRINT IN HUMANITIES

The humanities endowment
by Sharon Hanley Simpson and
Barclay Simpson honors
MURIEL CARTER HANLEY
whose intellect and sensitivity
have enriched the many lives
that she has touched.

The Cleaving

CRITICAL REFUGEE STUDIES

Edited by the Critical Refugee Studies Collective

1. *In Camps: Vietnamese Refugees, Asylum Seekers, and Repatriates,* by Jana K. Lipman
2. *Networked Refugees: Palestinian Reciprocity and Remittances in the Digital Age,* by Nadya Hajj
3. *Departures: An Introduction to Critical Refugee Studies,* by Yến Lê Espiritu, Lan Duong, Ma Vang, Victor Bascara, Khatharya Um, Lila Sharif, and Nigel Hatton
4. *Suspended Lives: Navigating Everyday Violence in the US Asylum System,* by Bridget M. Haas
5. *Lived Refuge: Gratitude, Resentment, Resilience,* by Vinh Nguyen
6. *Almost Futures: Time, Dispossession, and the Haunting of Vietnamese Refugees,* by Nguyễn-võ Thu-hương
7. *Emergency in Transit: Witnessing Migration in the Colonial Present,* by Eleanor Paynter
8. *The Cleaving: Vietnamese Writers in the Diaspora,* edited by Isabelle Thuy Pelaud, Lan P. Duong, and Viet Thanh Nguyen
9. *The Black Muslim Refugee: Militarism, Policing, and Somali American Resistance to State Violence,* by Maxamed Abumaye

The Cleaving

VIETNAMESE WRITERS IN THE DIASPORA

*Edited by Isabelle Thuy Pelaud,
Lan P. Duong, and Viet Thanh Nguyen*

UNIVERSITY OF CALIFORNIA PRESS

University of California Press
Oakland, California

© 2025 by The Regents of the University of California

Cataloging-in-Publication data is on file at the Library of Congress.

ISBN 978-0-520-41035-0 (cloth : alk. paper)
ISBN 978-0-520-41037-4 (ebook)

Manufactured in the United States of America

34 33 32 31 30 29 28 27 26 25
10 9 8 7 6 5 4 3 2 1

The publisher and the University of California Press Foundation gratefully acknowledge the generous support of the Simpson Imprint in Humanities.

CONTENTS

Foreword ix
Viet Thanh Nguyen
Acknowledgments xvii

INTRODUCTION:
A CLEAVING, A LEAVING, A HEAVING 1
Lan P. Duong

1 · On Violence: There and Here 8
Kim Thúy and Ocean Vuong 12
Doan Bui and Beth (Bich) Minh Nguyen 21
Bao Phi and Dao Strom 29
Cathy Linh Che and Diana Khoi Nguyen 39

2 · Authorship and Authority: The Americas and Việt Nam 46
Monique Truong and Viet Thanh Nguyen 49
Lan Cao and Vincent Lam 58
Amy Quan Barry and Thanhhà Lại 66

3 · Writing Feminism and Disobedience 74
Hoai Huong Aubert-Nguyen and Vaan Nguyen 77
Abbigail Nguyen Rosewood and Violet Kupersmith 87
Thi Bui and Thảo Nguyễn 97
Nguyễn Phan Quế Mai and Hoa Nguyen 105

4 · Representation, Writing, Reception   114
Le Ly Hayslip and Dương Vân Mai Elliott   118
Anna Möi and Aimee Phan   126
Andrew X. Phạm and Marcelino Trương Lực   134
Tracey Lien and André Dao   143

5 · Form and Future   151
T.K. Lê and Duy Đoàn   155
Hieu Minh Nguyen and Matt Huynh   162
Philip Nguyễn, Paul Tran, and Minh Huynh Vu   169

Conclusion: On Being a Writer at the Border   179
Isabelle Thuy Pelaud

Coda   186
Viet Thanh Nguyen, Lan P. Duong, and Isabelle Thuy Pelaud

Notes   191
Works Cited   203
About the Contributors   207
Index   219

FOREWORD

It is an incredible moment to be a Vietnamese diasporic writer. Four decades ago, when I was first fantasizing about the possibility of being a writer, very few Vietnamese writers were publishing in English. I knew about this scarcity because I haunted the aisles of the San José Public Library in California, reading anything that intrigued me, including any book that might tell me more about where I came from and who my people were. I was an American, but I was not American-born, and the reminders of my other country were ever present in the 1970s and 1980s, when the United States was fighting its war in Việt Nam again in memory. In 1982 the Vietnam Veterans Memorial was constructed, honoring the more than fifty-eight thousand American soldiers who died in the war but forgetting to mention the more than two hundred thousand South Vietnamese soldiers who died, or the hundreds of thousands of Vietnamese civilians who perished, or the Laotians and Cambodians who were also lost, both as soldiers and civilians. By now it is a cliché among Vietnamese in the diaspora to say that Việt Nam is a country and not a war, but in my childhood and adolescence, war was almost the only association in English with the name of the country of my birth.

I yearned to hear the voices of Vietnamese people because, as an American, I understood how Americans saw and heard, or didn't hear, Vietnamese people. I watched almost all of Hollywood's Vietnam War movies, an exercise I recommend to no one, especially if you are Vietnamese. Whether Americans meant the war or the country when they said Việt Nam, "Vietnam" for Americans was an American drama, an American civil war, a conflict in the American soul in which we were the extras. This was our country, and this was our war, and yet our only place in American movies was to be killed, raped, threatened, or rescued. All we could do was scream, cry, beg, threaten, or curse, and if we could say anything at all, it was either "me love you long time" or "thank you" for being rescued. Of course, we were never so rude as to mention, at least in English, that we wouldn't have needed to be rescued by Americans if we hadn't have been invaded by Americans in the first place.

Perhaps I intuitively understood that this American understanding would have global significance. The United States was a world power, and its memories of the war and the country that both had the same name would influence how the rest of the world saw these things. American memories certainly influenced me, but they also confused me, because they were not the same as the memories of my parents or, so far as I could tell, the memories of thousands of other Vietnamese people in the refugee community of San José, one of the largest outposts of the global Vietnamese refugee diaspora that sprang into being in the wake of the war. Back then, that diaspora numbered in the hundreds of thousands. Now the number is roughly four million, relative to a Vietnamese population in the country of origin that is more than ninety-five million. The global diaspora is a minority but a significant one. When it comes to literature, for example, it's possible that more non-Vietnamese people have read books by diasporic Vietnamese authors than have read books by Vietnamese writers from the homeland. The names of some of the writers in this volume—Kim Thúy of Canada and Ocean Vuong of the United States, for instance—would likely be recognized by their national literary audiences more so than their contemporary postwar equivalents in Việt Nam.

The reasons for this are complex and perhaps have something to do with the Vietnamese government's highly restrictive attitude when it comes to free speech, artistic freedom, and cultural production, which has prevented many diasporic writers from being translated and published in Vietnamese. For those refugees who fled to countries like the United States, Canada, France, Germany, Australia, and Israel, the situation we find ourselves in is contradictory. Unlike in Việt Nam, we are generally free to say what we like, which has undoubtedly spurred literary, cultural, artistic, and political expression. But we also reside in countries shaped by some mix of past and present imperialism, colonialism, and racism, where our presence as refugees and immigrants, Vietnamese and Asian, brings mixed results. Sometimes we are the evidence of our countries' tolerance for diversity. Other times, we are treated as the Yellow Peril, as was the case during the global COVID-19 pandemic.

The importance of literature specifically and writing in general is magnified in these kinds of moments, especially as we look back on the war in Việt Nam and other episodes in our countries' histories of maltreatment toward people of color, minorities of various kinds, Indigenous peoples, and others who were colonized. For many immigrants and refugees, writing and storytelling became some of our most important tools, methods, or weapons for fighting back against racist erasure, sexual exploitation, and imperialist manipulation. In my adventures in the San José library, what I discovered was that the books about Việt Nam were mostly about the war and therefore mostly about Americans. I found one well-intentioned children's book about a Vietnamese refugee, but I didn't recognize myself in its world of rice paddies, water buffalo, and half-naked peasant boys, even if others might have. I finally stumbled on the novel *Blue Dragon White Tiger* by Trần Văn Dĩnh, a diplomat writing about the war from a South Vietnamese point of view and perhaps the first Vietnamese writer to write fiction in English. He said, "I am a Vietnamese by birth, an American by choice." An echo of this must have stuck in my head, for decades later I wrote, "I was born in Việt Nam, but made in America." His novel put another thought in my head: we could write about our own experiences, in English, which was an adopted tongue that felt like my native tongue.

Others did not see this tongue in my mouth as my native tongue. Another cliché of the Asian American experience, perhaps applicable to other countries where Asians find themselves to be a minority, and where they find themselves seen as foreigners, is the question: "Where are you *really* from?" And the statement: "Your English is so good!" Now that there are more of us writing in English (and French and German and other languages), perhaps these kinds of questions and comments are rarer in countries with white, or at least non-Asian, majorities. But even after I published my first novel (written in English), a white American editor asked me if any of my work has been translated into English. I am not convinced we in the diaspora have won the battle against our perceived foreignness and our lack of legitimacy in speaking the master's various tongues, but if we have made progress, much of that credit is due to our storytellers.

Writing is perhaps the art with the lowest price of entry. All that writing costs is a writer's time, and some portion of their life and spirit. TV and the movies would allow us to make a much larger impact, for even a bad TV show or movie will be seen by millions, whereas a good or great book would be lucky if it sells hundreds of thousands of copies. But TV and the movies are the slowest to change, being so expensive to create, finance, and produce. Vietnamese diasporic writers have seized on the more readily available literary medium, in poetry and prose, fiction and nonfiction, to tell our stories. I say "our" with the awareness that there is an oftentimes ambivalent relationship between a so-called minority writer and their community, the infamous burden of representation where a so-called minority writer is expected to speak for their entire community. That burden is imposed by the so-called majority and also by the community, and the result is that sometimes the community groans at a writer's inaccuracies while the writer sighs in exasperation and demands simply to be seen as a writer.

I hope one thing this book demonstrates is that to be a diasporic Vietnamese writer and to be *just* a writer are not mutually exclusive choices. They are mutually exclusive only in the sense that dominant societies built on legacies and realities of racism, sexism, and colonialism have imposed such a binary on us, and not on writers of the majority, who have the freedom to be *just* writers. These unmarked writers rarely have to question their individuality and their freedom. That in itself is a privilege of race, gender, class, ability, and sexuality, and is not something that we who have not been so privileged should yearn for. Instead, we should be working to create a world where such an advantage is questioned, where we should ask why some writers (and people) have adjectives put before them, like "Vietnamese American writer," and other writers do not. I have no problem with adjectives and with being a Vietnamese American writer, but there should be adjectives for all or adjectives for none. Call me a Vietnamese American writer so long as you call a white American writer a "white American writer."

Adjectives and identities such as "Vietnamese American" are symptoms of deeper structural inequities. Instead of treating "Vietnamese diasporic" or any identity like it as a problem or a pejorative, we should be asking why a need for such an adjective or identity exists in the first place. Attempting to answer that question from many different perspectives, this book is also an effort to reach what I call "narrative plenitude." Narrative scarcity is when almost none of the stories are about us, which is why any time a story by one of us appears, an unfair burden is put on that story and its creator that would hardly ever be put on a white writer, a white male writer, a white straight male writer. Narrative scarcity is only a symptom of structural inequity, a sign of other injustices throughout a society that have stifled us in many different ways historically and in the present. In contrast, narrative plenitude is when there are many stories about us. When no one story or one person has to carry the burden of representation. When there are so many stories we cannot keep up.

Narrative plenitude cannot be achieved without social and economic justice. We still live in unjust times, and we have not reached narrative plenitude when it comes to diasporic Vietnamese people. Even when it comes to the largest such community, Vietnamese Americans, we are not there yet. But in the realm of literature, signs of hope flash. In the 1980s and 1990s, when Le Ly Hayslip and Andrew X. Pham were publishing, I read their books right away. Even as recently as ten years or twenty years ago, when I first encountered the works of Lan Cao, Monique Truong, Dao Strom, Bao Phi, Thanhhà Lại, Aimee Phan, Beth (Bich) Minh Nguyen, Amy Quan Barry, Hoa Nguyen, Vincent Lam, and Dương Vân Mai Elliott, I could still keep up. But now that's no longer possible. Partly this is because I've become more aware of writers writing in other languages besides English, like Hoai Huong Aubert-Nguyen, Doan Bui, Vaan Nguyen, Anna Moï, and Marcellino Trương Lực. And partly this is because there are so many writers publishing their first books in English over the past few years at a rate I could only have fantasized about decades ago: Thi Bui, Nguyễn Phan Quế Mai, Hieu Minh Nguyen, Duy Đoàn, Cathy Linh Che, Diana Khoi Nguyen, Violet Kupersmith, Abbigail Nguyen Rosewood, and Paul Tran. There are many more Vietnamese diasporic writers not included in this book. The increasing diversity of such writers means that the war and colonialism and history are no longer the only preoccupations, even if they still are the most prominent.

When it comes to our domination by the past, I am reminded of the ending of Toni Morrison's *Beloved*, when she says this about slavery: "This is not a story to pass on."[1] The implication is twofold: don't ignore this story, and yet don't keep telling this story. Both can be true at the same time, because history is not done with us, even if we are sick of history. In the case of Vietnamese diasporic writers, a horrific past of colonialism and war has killed millions and has produced the diaspora. No wonder some writers want to take a pass. Must we always be defined by horror? And no wonder some writers refuse to pass on by. If we do not write about this horror, won't we be defined by a history written by our colonizers?

This edited volume dwells on both questions and includes some newer voices like André Dao and Tracey Lien in Australia and T.K. Lê and Duy Đoàn. There are also arts activists Philip Nguyễn and Minh Huynh Vu as well as visual artist Matt Huynh and musical artist Thảo Nguyễn in the United States who gesture toward what a new generation might think. Narrative plenitude is also about the need for new voices, new writers, and new ideas to take the stage and have their turn. We have more than one generation and more than one voice, and this book collectively makes that claim. No more voices for the voiceless, which was never a title that many of us wanted to adopt or have placed on us. We could sense that when any of us were called a voice for the voiceless, what others really wanted was to have just one of us speak in place of the chorus or the cacophony of our communities, who were never voiceless. Rather than seeking voices for the voiceless, abolish the conditions of voicelessness instead. Literature and writing, storytelling and art, cannot accomplish that abolition on their own. Only social and political movements, motivated by utopian dreams, can abolish these conditions of mass inequity and injustice. But literature and writing, storytelling and art, can illuminate the way.

Viet Thanh Nguyen

ACKNOWLEDGMENTS

Building on the feminist anthology *Troubling Borders: An Anthology of Art and Literature by Southeast Asian Women in the Diaspora* (edited by Isabelle Thuy Pelaud, Lan Duong, Mariam B. Lam, and Kathy L. Nguyen, published by the University of Washington Press in 2014), *The Cleaving: Vietnamese Writers in the Diaspora* is a project of the heart. This edited volume could not have been possible without people believing in its importance and creating the conditions to bring it to fruition. As with every project, *The Cleaving* has an origin story. It started on a sunny day in San Francisco, when two community organizers met over a home-cooked dinner and did what they always did: talk shop and dream up ideas on what could be done to shed light on the invisible barriers diasporic Vietnamese writers encounter and to promote their work at the same time.

"I just read a dialogue between writers in a magazine. What if we gathered dialogues between the writers when we invite them to our residency?" asked Anh Thang Dao-Shah, one of the organizers of the first diasporic Vietnamese writers retreats in California, held at the Djerassi Resident Artists Program in 2018. In response, Isabelle Thuy Pelaud, founder of the Diasporic Vietnamese Artists Network (DVAN), said: "I am reading *The Children of 1965* by Min Hyoung Song. One of my professors from the French department at the University of California–Berkeley once told me that what writers think about their work is irrelevant and what matters is the literary critics' interpretations of their works. I disagree. What writers think about their work and their place in society is relevant and helpful to know. Yes, let's do it!" This project eventually grew too big for Thang to stay on board, but we acknowledge her crucial role in igniting this work.

We take a deep breath here to wholeheartedly thank all the writers, poets, and artists for entrusting us with this project in a spirit of collectivity and collaboration. That so many responded to our invitation fed our passion to continue fighting for diasporic Vietnamese artists' voices and stories to be heard and read.

We are grateful to the Critical Refugee Studies Collective and Yến Lê Espiritu for helping us shepherd the manuscript through the University of California Press. We are indebted to UC Press executive editor Naomi Schneider for seeing the value of this project and working with us to make this book possible. DVAN staff Minh Huynh Vu and Philip Nguyễn were instrumental in scheduling the planning sessions, organizing the writing drafts, and proofreading the first round of dialogues, while research assistant Fiona Martin Tran contributed references for the conclusion. Titi Nguyen helped with assembling the release forms from our writers.

We appreciate the leadership and staff of the Djerassi Resident Artists Program for hosting the first DVAN residency where we invited ten Vietnamese writers from Australia, Canada, France, and the United States, to write and engage in dialogues either in writing or verbally with one another in 2018, and organize them loosely by themes. These dialogues were so invigorating for the writers, and so rich in their content, that we decided to expand the project and include more writers in the assembling of this book. Our next set of dialogues were collected in New York, at a reading organized in collaboration with the Asian American Writers' Workshop. We thank former executive director Ken Chen and his staff for going out of their way to provide us the space and time to conduct these dialogues. Two additional sets of dialogues (a writing retreat in Vézelay, France, and a large public event in Seattle) were unfortunately canceled due to the COVID-19 pandemic. Although these gatherings could not take place, we invited writers who would have joined us to be part of *The Cleaving* by facilitating remote conversations.

Introduction

A CLEAVING, A LEAVING, A HEAVING

Lan P. Duong

> an engine crossing,
> re-crossing salt water, hauling
> immigrants and the junk
> of the poor. These
> are the faces I love, the bodies
> and scents of bodies
> for which I long
> in various ways, at various times,
> ...
> eager to eat
> four kinds of meat
> prepared four different ways,
> numerous plates and bowls of rice and vegetables,
> each made by distinct affections
> and brought to table by many hands.
>
> —LI-YOUNG LEE, "THE CLEAVING"

Li-Young Lee's poem imagines the immigrant body and its desires to eat and be eaten. The meat of this stanza speaks to being famished among your own and of feasting among your own; it is a kind of loving devouring that in "crossing and re-crossing salt water" is "talkative," "voracious," and "eager." In naming this edited volume *The Cleaving*, we recall this poem and its visceral imagery of meat, face, and bone to bring home the ideas that a cleaving bursts open for us. More precisely, the word "cleaving" alludes to the formation of a diaspora, one that has been separated not so cleanly from its homeland and yet nonetheless cleaves closely to this origin. A cleaving, a leaving, a heaving. All of this brings to mind the Vietnamese diaspora's leave-taking from Việt Nam throughout the twentieth century, a cut and a break from the homeland that represents a metaphysical and psychic hewing to the country at the same time.

The Cleaving mirrors Lee's ode to face (and familiarity in providing readers) an encounter with the many faces and facets of Vietnamese diasporic literature and art. In the poem Lee identifies with a butcher who is responsible for the violent severance, concluding the poem with: "this immigrant / this man with my own face." Similarly we see our faces and voices throughout this book. Collected here are the conversations among Vietnamese artists who are located in Australia, Canada, Germany, France, Israel, Kyrgyzstan, and the United States, and everywhere in between. Together these artists speak to the impetus of "eating as reading" and "reading as eating," as Lee states in the poem, and of consuming the Western canon to take it in and take it apart.

This book embodies other communal aspects of eating. When we brought writers together at the Djerassi Resident Artists Program in 2018 and in San Francisco and New York in 2019, we spoke over food in the era before COVID-19. Eating together in Vietnamese culture is not only about relationship building, it is also an act of care and love. Put simply, to eat is to commune. Gathered to eat and talk, we asked a group of writers across several oceans, ages, and experiences to discuss topics that concern them and us. But in 2020 the pandemic had different plans for us. Instead of meeting in Seattle (Washington), and Paris and Vézelay in France, we had to change directions completely and instead facilitate email and virtual conversations. Moreover, we had to shelter-in-place, homeschool our children, and organize virtual events and lectures during the writing and editing of this book, made especially surreal when it felt like time was a river in which we found ourselves almost drowning.

Ironically, throughout *The Cleaving*, we discuss the importance of human contact and communication, of having communal exchanges in the making of community; and yet, during the process we had very little human contact and in-person interaction with each other. While facilitating these conversations, we also bore witness to the devastating effects of the pandemic and white supremacy in the United States and in other parts of the world. The pandemic clearly demonstrated the deleterious ways that racial capitalism produces structural inequalities, with the disproportionate number of Black and Latino people dying from COVID-19—a direct result of how racism and violence have affected health treatments and outcomes. It was also during this time that anti-Asian racism reared its ugly head again, especially with Donald Trump's labeling of the disease in 2020 as the "kung flu" or "Chinese virus."

Compiled during such historic events, this edited volume testifies that Vietnamese diasporic writings have changed the literary landscape in the Global North fifty years since the war ended in Việt Nam. The contributions bridge the wide range of experiences of the diaspora, of those who left Việt Nam before and after the war ended in 1975 as "immigrants" and "refugees." Indeed, some of the artists identify as immigrants, some as Asian American, some as refugees or national citizens, which is to say that these identificatory modes are fluid and historically specific, depending on where the authors are located and the audience to whom they choose to speak.

The book's larger framework relies on a specific formulation of diaspora. Leaning on the word's Greek etymology (*dia* means "across," while *speirein* is "to scatter"), we use the word "diaspora" to describe the populations that originate from Việt Nam and have been geographically dispersed all over the world for much of the twentieth century, motivated by an overlay of political and economic factors. This is certainly the case for the Vietnamese diasporic community in France who migrated to the colonial motherland from the 1920s onward as scholars, soldiers, and laborers. Such communities are highly diverse in terms of immigration histories, class status, economic and symbolic capital, and political affiliations. This diasporic lens allows us to capture the experiences of these populations and the displacements that they have experienced in straddling multiple subject positions and histories at once.

The Cleaving understands the diasporic condition as crosshatched by the affective textures of grief, alienation, ambivalence, nostalgia, and exilic longing. The varied contributions show that conditions of diaspora are rooted in the entanglements of war and imperialism and fundamentally shape the diasporic writer's voice and persona as well as aesthetic and political style. Being in the diaspora, far from "home" and yet longing for it, produces the possibility of nostalgia but also critique, whose edge we sharpen here to draw attention to the nation-state and its mode of statecraft, whether this is the country in which the writers presently live and/or Việt Nam itself. A category container and method of analysis, diaspora encompasses the subjectivities and affective states that come with being transnational, an immigrant, and a refugee at various moments in diasporic time and space.

The term "immigrant," however, is freighted with pejorative and positive connotations of foreignness, class, and mobility, often used in the Global North to describe migrants who move and permanently resettle in other countries. If "immigrants" also "do the job right," as the American librettist Lin-Manuel Miranda wrote in the US context, then the word encapsulates some sanguine connotations about the country and its constitution. Similarly, "refugee" is rafted with meaning, owing to its legal and political lineage as a result of the United Nations's 1951 Convention Relating to the Status of Refugees, undertaken in the wake of World War II, and its massive displacements of people. As the Critical Refugee Studies Collective pointed out in its book *Departures: An Introduction to Critical Refugee Studies*, there are serious limitations to the UN formulation, which pertain to refugees before 1951 and "those already considered refugees under the 1926 and 1928 Arrangements and the 1933 and 1938 Conventions."[1]

The Refugee Convention also deploys the language of pervasive fear in offering restrictions on why and how might refugees move and leave. Leaving a critical refugee studies critique of the Refugee Convention aside, in this book we use the term "refugee" to describe the Vietnamese and ethnic Chinese Vietnamese who left the country after Communists claimed victory in 1975 and who fled to many neighboring countries outside of the West to refugee camps in Hong Kong, Indonesia, Malaysia, Singapore, Thailand, and the Philippines (with some of these refugees stranded and stateless in the same countries for years on end). Being an immigrant or a refugee, we underscore, is an experience that has no expiration date in terms of temporality and can shift depending on the spaces one inhabits.

Following the end of the Vietnam War, Vietnamese refugees also permanently resettled in Australia, France, and the United States, among many other countries. Our use of the word "refugee" signals the ways that these Western countries in particular have politically and militarily intervened in Việt Nam's struggles for national independence and reunification throughout most of the twentieth century, which resulted in the displacement of millions of people. Following sociologist Yến Lê Espiritu's foundational work in *Departures*, we intentionally use the sign of the "refugee" to mark how US militarism and imperialism both unsettled many Vietnamese people and provided the transpacific and transregional routes of flight and resettlement through which Vietnamese refugees have traveled (with the same American military bases that launched US bombers over Southeast Asia later hosting refugee camps). Each of these appellations of "diasporan," "immigrant," and "refugee" speak to the diverse experiences that impact how one is seen and treated in the public as a public persona and writer, and how one views and feels oneself and makes artistic decisions about one's work as a result.

Finally, in pairing "diaspora" and "dialogue," we emphasize the power of discourse to lend complexity, nuance, and a sustained critique to the ways in which "Vietnam" has been apprehended in the Western imaginary—too often as a country of war, at times a leftist revolutionary fantasy, and now a viable site for capitalistic investment.[2] Viewing texts in dialogue with each other, and as that which emerges out of specific historical, geographical, sociological and cultural contexts, remains at the heart of what this book offers. Writers conversing with each other about the process of creating opens valuable windows into the "in-between spaces" that exist across several texts. This call for self-reflective reasoning and investigation into how intersubjectivity works is pertinent to artists, writers, readers, and critics alike. It moves away from the problematic viewing of a narrator as the universal representative of a people or a community. By centralizing discussions of diasporic Vietnamese writers with each other, we hope to shed further light on the dynamics of identity formation for the Vietnamese diaspora.

A multivoiced plurality underlies *The Cleaving* in terms of language, aesthetics, themes, styles, and genres. The eighteen dialogues converse with readers to enrich their understanding of Vietnamese diasporic literature, in which writers express a keen understanding of their roles in the ever-evolving debates around the dominance of the white gaze, the forces of history, and the politics of representation. The exchanges between writers articulate how questions of literacy, literariness, and industry structure the ways in which the writers' works are published and received, circulated and produced. By way of these dialogues, an array of critiques and positions emerge in the writers' discussions about writing for the self and community or writing in the service of archiving (familial) memory and of creating work that operates against whiteness. The writers' polyvocality highlights the diversity that inheres in Vietnamese diasporic voices. Oscillating between text and context, author and audience, the book shows that identities across transnational borders are shaped through the very processes of telling, withholding, and reinventing.

By asking writers to engage in dialogues—to speak *for* themselves *about* themselves *with* one another—concerning the issues that interest them most as writers and us as readers and critics, we move the focus more forcefully from these (self-)imposed issues to diasporic artists, centering their creativity and ideas first and foremost. In short, we begin with their centrality a priori in the field of artistic production and in the debates about the art and politics. From there we consider how the themes of war and displacement as well as the social constructions of race (among other vectors of identity that are shaped by a history marked by colonialism and imperialism) influence the form and content of their work.

The questions framing this book are interlinked between writing, reception, and representation. What are the mechanisms by which a dominant culture manages questions of literariness and literacy, and how have these mechanisms affected Vietnamese diasporic writing? How do writers see, imagine, and write about homeland and diaspora? For those who write in French or Vietnamese or English, how do issues of language and translation materialize in their writing and writing practices? How do the intersectional vectors of identity (including race, gender, sexuality, ability, religion, age, and class) figure into their work? Who is their chosen audience and why?

In addition, we've provided commentaries and more context for the dialogues to situate the writers and their texts within a continuum of themes. In pairing the writers, we matched them according to their aesthetic and thematic concerns and backgrounds. We provided prompts such as those found above in advance of their conversations, but their interactions (in person, by recording, and/or virtual means) have also been improvised and blend well with the themes we envision for the book. Besides novelists and poets, we have included graphic novelists, visual artists, and musicians in these dialogues, among both emerging and established writers.

We invite readers to reflect on the words and thoughts of Vietnamese diasporic artists, but *The Cleaving* holds clear to the idea that we have always discoursed—both extravagantly and necessarily—about war and history, otherness and art, as well as our colonial past and imperial present.[3] To return to Lee's words, we have eaten words with one another for years, and now we are ready to share our feast with readers. Dialoguing with one another across regions, languages, memories, and experiences affords us the ability and privilege to remake a community of readers and writers in our own likenesses. It is no coincidence that this hunger and aspiration for a collectivity profoundly reflects Lee's words about seeing in the other a mirror of ourselves.

ONE

On Violence

THERE AND HERE

Wars, genocide, enslavement, organized terror, population displacement, and sexual assaults are traumatic events that create cumulative emotional and psychological injury over a lifespan and across multiple generations.[1] Historical traumas cannot be empirically measured through conventional forms nor rational representation. They are marked by various forms of forgetting and dissociations. Trauma does not have to be located or contained in one event that one remembers; it can be compounded by daily cultural practices that send the message that one does not belong.

Given Việt Nam's long history of war and migration, it is not surprising that at times historical trauma surfaces in diasporic Vietnamese literature. The people of Việt Nam have fought and resisted against one thousand years of Chinese control and aggression and one hundred years of French colonization and expropriation. Over the past century, Việt Nam was at war with France, the United States, Cambodia, and had intermittent military border conflicts with China. This history of foreign occupation, war, and civil war has formed a Vietnamese culture rife with stories and legends of warriors and resistors such as the legend of emperor Lê Lợi and that of the Trưng Sisters. It may not be a coincidence that although the country is two-thirds the size of California, Việt Nam has an army that is among the ten largest armies in the world.[2] Referring to the Vietnam War, Vietnamese American scholars, poets, and writers have told us that although Việt Nam is so much more than a war, this "history still demands an ongoing engagement with what that war meant" and that we must be "concerned with its meaning to revisionist, [and] nationalist agendas."[3] Poet Barbara Tran is correct when she states that "for too many of [us] ... the past has gouged too deep a hole in their lives. They keep falling back in."[4]

Aggression and daily forms of microaggression due to racism in the countries of resettlement are not commonly considered to be a source of trauma. However, early Asian American writers such as Carlos Bulosan, John Okada, and Maxine Hong Kingston have explicitly denounced some of the ways racism exerts psychological costs.[5] Although it is not the responsibility of an author to represent a whole community, Asian American writers have played (and are continuing to play) a significant role in social justice work and in empowering Asian Americans in all realms of the arts. How one copes with the impacts of racism is not something we are born with but rather shaped by how we as a minority are represented, looked at, and subsequently treated.[6]

Such a gaze is reflected in mainstream cultural productions through stereotypes that are deeply ingrained in our social, legal, and political apparatuses—and in American culture in general—to an extent that cis-heterosexist and patriarchal white supremacy, to quote the late bell hooks, can be difficult to see, identify, and critique. Not only are stereotypes not true; they are dangerous because they have the power to alter people's feelings and behaviors, including whom one finds desirable, who can speak up, and who can fights back.[7] The internalization of stereotypes is a process that regards these stereotypes as true; they have the power to impact our self-esteem and how we relate to the world around us. To feel invisible or too visible because of race, these writers and many who came after them have shown repeatedly and consistently, creates real psychological wounds.

It is thus not surprising that destructive emotion such as self-hate is found in Vietnamese American literature—for instance, in Andrew X. Pham's *Catfish and Mandala* (1999), Lac Su's *I Love Yous Are for White People* (2009), and Bao Phi's *Sông I Sing* (2011). These writers make visible in their work that intergenerational trauma *and* racism toward Vietnamese Americans both impact their relation to self and identity, which in turn produced a strong desire to hide, fight, or run when faced with the desire or demand of wanting to belong.[8] When Vietnameseness is rendered or perceived as anomalous and worthy of social stigma, one can unconsciously wish to be white.[9] This is understandable given the fact that for a generation, the Vietnamese as the enemy of war, who are not allies or whole subjects to Americans, have been depicted in television and movies not as full human beings but as subjects to be killed, pitied, or saved.[10]

Diasporic Vietnamese writers in this chapter have written books about the human impact of violence in both Việt Nam *and* in the country of resettlement. They have written through their emotions, setting up terrains of mourning and contestation. In the process of grappling with the consequences of compound trauma, these artists examined emotions that they are aware, cannot be rendered digestible in one lifetime. These narratives thus become vehicles for making sense of the past while attempting to imagine and shape a future free from the fear of death *and* the fear of not belonging. Trauma is, we may add, something that is most difficult to grasp and communicate into words, as it is something that "digs itself in at the level of the everyday life, and in the incommensurability of large-scale event[s] and the ongoing material details of experience."[11] Through these difficult articulations, writers may formulate new ideas of self and identity.

Although they live in different countries and are of different generations, the novelists and poets in this chapter share a mutual understanding of what it means to be in between cultures, to survive, and to represent. They allude to both historical and domestic trauma they sense lies deep within themselves beyond the scope of language. Notions of resilience and detachment surface from theses explorations. From these fluid spaces, Ocean Vuong and Kim Thúy begin their conversation by speaking against common expectation of writing about the Vietnam War. Rather, they speak of beauty and suffering in relational terms outside the binaries of strength and weakness. They stand as experts of their senses and of the immaterial lessons of survival that have been psychically, bodily, and affectively passed down from parents, grandparents, and great-grandparents. Poets and writers Bao Phi, Dao Strom, Cathy Linh Che, and Diana Khoi Nguyen further address how intergenerational trauma compounded by racism impacts their relation to their identity and creativity. The notions of *hiding (flight)* behind the mask of "coolness" or of *resisting (fight)* by speaking against mainstream representation of the Vietnam War or by centering family trauma is, Phi and Strom allude, for instance, a response to the multiple layers of violence that have been both inherited and experienced.

DIALOGUE BETWEEN KIM THÚY (CANADA, EAST COAST) AND OCEAN VUONG (UNITED STATES, EAST COAST)

OCEAN: I read your work when I was in college, years ago. I think about Ru a lot.... I think it's one of the precursors to a lot of women of color writing in hybrid forms, including lê thị diễm thúy, *The Gangster We Are All Looking For*. The fragmentation, the vignette, it's also very French, right? Duras. Barthes. Wittgenstein. And I wanted to ask about that form for you because I think you were ahead of the curve. Now, that form is very trendy. My students whom I teach, every year out of thirty students, there're two or three students working in that form, and we have Maggie Nelson, Claudia Rankine, Bhanu Kapil, so many writers who're working in this form. Can you talk about how you arrived at the fragment vignette and what it means to you?

KIM: Oh my God. I didn't know that I was ahead of a curve or that it was a fragmentation even. When I wrote it, I wrote it in my car at red lights because I fell asleep a lot at red lights, and that was one of the ways for me to stay awake to take notes, and at first, no.

I ate watermelon seeds, because it's really difficult to crack those seeds, so they kept me awake, but over time you break your teeth. My brother, who is a dentist, he said, "Okay, you stop eating those seeds," and that's how I started taking notes. First, I didn't know that it was a book, so they were just notes that I put together and then put into paragraphs. And it became this book, and if I had studied literature, if I knew the rules, the writing and the forms and all of that, I would have followed the rules, and I thought I was following the rules.

OCEAN: I'm glad you did it. I tell my students this, and I say, "Sometimes the most helpful part of the rule is just knowing it, not really doing it. Just knowing the rule is like knowing where the guard rails are when you're driving, knowing where the sidewalk is. That's it. Just knowing that it's there allows you to move around it," and you don't even have to play by the rules. That's the part of your playfulness, and something a lot of readers never attribute to Asian American, particularly Vietnamese American, literature. They want us to be sad and serious and heartbroken, missing home, right? Always nostalgic for the homeland, but in fact we are very playful. The beauty was when I came to your text, it was like mischievous. It was a mischievous work.

They see Vietnamese stories as almost things to be harvested, ethnography to be harvested—give us more, give us all of it—as if we were supposed to be tour guides to the motherland or the suffering, but you trusted yourself to say, "This is enough. One page, sometimes two. One room at a time was enough." What gave you the confidence? When you were publishing, did editors tell you, "We want more from you"? Did they demand that?

KIM: I didn't have a publisher. I didn't even know that it was a book, and I didn't send it myself to the publisher. A friend of mine took it to the publisher. I would have loved to send it and lick on those stamps because I get high on the glue. Really, I cannot drink. I cannot hold alcohol. I cannot drink coffee. So the only thing that gets me high is the glue of the stamp.

But a friend of mine took it to the publisher, and I still remember that there was no title, and the pages were not numbered because I didn't know how to put it in the computer with the numbers. I remember my editor saying, "Oh my God. If we drop that pile of paper, what will happen to the text?"

Because I didn't know, I gave myself a lot of freedom, and freedom is everything, right? Freedom gives you the opportunity to follow your instinct in a way because I had no pressure about writing a book, and the difference between a writer in the US or France. . . .

When you write about Việt Nam in Canada, it's very different because we don't have the same history. We don't carry the weight. Even today many people would tell me, "Oh, yeah, we heard about this Vietnam War, but we didn't know much about it," that I was the one who basically talked to them about the Vietnam War whereas in the US, it's almost impossible for anyone to not know about this war. So I think that's the likeness almost of the text.

OCEAN: I see maybe that is why a book like yours existed in Canada. I don't know if a book like that would have existed here [in the United States]. Maybe today, yes, but at that time, a decade ago, I don't know if it would have existed in America because America wants Vietnamese

American writers, I found, to just do one thing. "Tell us what it is on your side. We heard a lot about white writers writing about Việt Nam, Tim O'Brien, all of that, documentaries, but we want your side," and what happens for someone like myself, I go on tour, and older readers will say, "Why didn't you write about the war?" I said, "Việt Nam is much more than just the war. Vietnamese people are much more than about the war," and I point to your work.

I say, "I'm following the footsteps already laid out by my elders like Kim Thúy, and we are much more than a war. We're much more than the debris of geopolitical violence." The expectation is always there from an American viewer to get more out of the war as cultural tourists. I had to do a lot to keep saying no to that.

KIM: And when I read *you*, I couldn't believe that you were twenty-five years old. Your poetry. You just succeed on every page. I read you with a pen in hand. I couldn't have read you without a pen because I loved every single sentence that you wrote. I went looking for your interviews, because I didn't understand how you could have written what you did. You had arrived to the US quite young—at two years old. I said: "You cannot have any of those images in you." How were you able to extrapolate? And because of your book, I thought: "Maybe we have that memory in our DNA."

OCEAN: DNA, yes. That's why I use the butterfly motif because it is an example of epigenetic strength. Butterflies figured out how to move three thousand miles taking five generations to get to Mexico through trauma. Every time they lost their numbers, they learned a new way to go. To this day, butterflies remember that when they go up a mountain, they must curve around it, after so many of them had died; their deaths changed their DNA.

It's trauma, but it's also strength. One of my goals as a writer is to show the strength of Vietnamese people having a country the size of California with ninety million people who've been at war for nearly one hundred years straight. That creates a lot of strength and a lot of mental illness, and I wanted to show that.

KIM: But at the same time, it's very strange because I wonder how we could have survived all these traumas but we're still functional.

Coming out from all these obstacles and challenges and atrocities, how could that be? I asked a cousin of mine in Việt Nam, and he said, "Oh my God. We're all crazy. That's why you don't see it."

But at the same time, I think it's because of the Vietnamese language. We don't have tenses. We only have the infinitive. We don't have past tense or future and with the French language, you have conditional, you have subjunctives. Just for the past, you have different tenses, etc.

For Vietnamese, we only have one scenario, and it's only now. We do the best we can with what we have now, right? I think the language has affected us.

OCEAN: And our sense of futurity is flipped as well. *Kiếp trước* [literal translation, "the life in front"] is before, and *kiếp sau* [literal translation, "the life behind"] is later. The future is called the past, and the past is called the future. So I think it's almost like time is up to us. We can manipulate it.

KIM: I think our time is circular. It's not a line because of reincarnation in Buddhism, I think, right? Whatever you do today, you will come back.

OCEAN: You said earlier, "Oh, when I read you, I couldn't believe it's a twenty-five-year-old man," and in my head I thought, "Oh, maybe because I died very old in my past life."

I come from a line of rice farmers, and there are days where I believe that Vietnamese people are like the superheroes of our species because we've been through so much. We were a bunch of farmers who invented poetry, systems of thinking, and sometimes I don't know how we made it here.

I also think every time I step into a Vietnamese household, I hear laughter. No matter what's happening, I hear it. It must be because our traditions are so old; they've been carried on for so many generations.

I lost my mother last year. She passed away on November 2. So this will be her one-year anniversary. It's been a hard, hard year.

KIM: Oh, I'm going to cry. Because with your book, I think I cried at every second page. I'm sorry. When I started reading you, I cried not because of the pain only. I cried for your beauty.

OCEAN: Oh, you're going to make me cry.

KIM: No, but you agree with me that beauty also brings out so much emotion, right? It makes you cry when it's so beautiful.

OCEAN: It's a Vietnamese thing. My mother and I would go look at a sunset at a park, and most Americans and English-speaking people around us, would say, "Ah, so beautiful. So gorgeous." But my mother would say "buồn quá" ["so sad"]. But it was also beauty. The way she described *buồn quá* is not sadness. There's no real English translation. It's a beautiful sadness. It's this deep sadness and a deep beauty.

KIM: Because it touches you down here, right? It's not intellectual. Beauty is not intellectual. It's here. The beauty of your writing is. . . . It's a punch sometimes, but sometimes it's visceral because it's so beautiful. That's how I feel about your book.

OCEAN: I learned it from my mother—about learning how to see beauty in a deeper way, not just something we enjoy. In the West beauty is decorous. Beauty is what you decorate, and it's pleasant. Vietnamese beauty is tinged with pain and loss. Even in our folk songs, when I heard it as a child (singing), and it's like a calling across. Loss begins even before language for us, and I think it must do again with the violence that has passed through our tiny, tiny country for hundreds of years.

KIM: Yes. But at the same time, because you were talking about how Việt Nam has gone through so much and yet is so rich culturally. We are strong and creative because otherwise, you cannot eat. My uncle was a journalist, he wrote a book called *Người Việt giữa mặt nạn*, and that's us. Being between two lines of fire and surviving this. We had to be very creative, to feed our children even.

OCEAN: It's like a sonnet. Our history was like a deadly sonnet and the sonnet constricts and then people who work within that form find incredible creative ways to work within a constriction, and I think Việt Nam was a sonnet.

Roland Barthes once said: "When two languages fail, a third is back and forth," and I wonder if that happens and if it's even possible. I think of untranslatable words in Vietnamese like the word *ơi*, like *con ơi*. There's nothing. No language will ever translate *ơi*.

KIM: Impossible. I have two questions for you. You'll have to send it to me, but first question, did you give yourself the freedom just to write and not censor yourself?

OCEAN: I gave myself freedom to go at every subject because I was inventing around it. When I come close to something that's difficult, I would invent another way around it, and that's where . . . I think by the time the book was finished, it looked so far from my life. It's almost like a stranger's life, and I think in some ways, Little Dog, the character in *On Earth We Are Briefly Gorgeous*, is much better than me. I think he's much more patient. I'm a little hot tempered. I'm a little crazy, but Little Dog is much more patient. Every day, I strive to be more like him, I think.

KIM: I think writing or being an artist is already an act of interpretation, almost like a gift, a diamond that we have polished, and we present it to you. So it cannot be reality.

OCEAN: Yeah, and I think sometimes I live better in that world than the one I live in. You say you started writing when you were driving, and I must confess that I cannot drive. I don't know why my brain cannot move the things, and I think if I have a good line in my head, poetry or something, and I'm driving, people can die. I would just keep following the other world. Yeah, I say I spare the world. I'm very dangerous when I'm dreaming, so I don't drive. I can ride my bike, but that's about it.

KIM: I have a second question. What is your relationship with Việt Nam now? How do you see Việt Nam now?

OCEAN: Việt Nam has always been very difficult for me as an embodied experience. When I visit, I have family there, and they're still rice farmers, and they are still in a time capsule because so much of their family left them because of the war. Our families broke apart because of the war. When we visit, it's never tourism. When I go, I just give money and cry. That's it.

I think a lot about this theologist or philosopher, Ferdinand de Saussure, when he talks about symbols as arbitrary. But when you are displaced, one symbol is displayed, then you take the color red outside of the semiotic code of a stoplight, and you put it on a card and now it's not stop, it's Valentine's Day. Then if you take red and put it on an exit sign, it no longer means stop, but rather, "Get out."

This is how I feel about going to Việt Nam. I am out of place. My semiotic code has been transformed because of others, and I'm revisiting as a relic, as a refugee, and it's sad to me. When I look at the Coca-Cola signs, it should be happy because I go to the market and there's so much life bustling. But I feel loss, emptiness. My grandmother's grave is in the country. I travel and see so many faces that resemble my family and yet they are not my family.

But I'm hopeful because I see the younger generation of Vietnamese children and artists coming to America to study, and I meet them on the road, and they're so excited to create. Their families are more stable than mine was, and they have the luxury and the privilege to learn and to break away from their families' desires and really become individual artists, and they're hungry for that.

I have a lot of hope for Vietnamese in Việt Nam and Vietnamese Americans writing, and when I go to Germany, it's the same thing. I feel good about the diaspora. In Việt Nam I think people are thriving economically and culturally now, but for me it will always be very difficult going back.

KIM: I had a chance to go back to Việt Nam to live for a couple of years when I was a lawyer, and like you say, I'm always sad when I'm in Việt Nam, and I'm not someone who has the tendency for depression or for sadness, but for all the years that I was in Việt Nam, all I felt was sadness, and I could not name it, and I could not put my finger on it maybe because of my childhood, because I was a sad child.

At the same time, I love Vietnamese culture so much, but is it still home? I still have family and we're still close. There's so much happiness and joy and pleasures at the same time. I experience a sadness there that I don't have anywhere else in the world.

OCEAN: You're saying everything I feel and even in more articulate ways because you've been through it, I think longer than I have, but I almost feel like I'm the next generation after you, and I will just say I feel exactly the same. It's not better. I don't want it to be better either. I don't want to go to Việt Nam one day and be completely happy either because that would mean I would have lost something.

I remember just going to Việt Nam and getting the rush, coming back, coming to Tân Sơn Nhất Airport.[12] The humid air, the taxi drivers, coming through the city, and getting home to my aunt's apartment in Sài Gòn, and then just seeing a little girl eating noodles in the alleyway squatting and just lifting the bowl of *bún riêu* [a rice noodle soup with crab and tomatoes], and then just hearing the mother go, "con ơi, ăn xong chưa?" ["my child, have you eaten yet?"] I had to turn away. I don't know why it's so sad to me, and I think for me, that image, all of Vietnamese life is in that image. A little girl eating and a mother calling, but that *con ơi* [my child].

KIM: The first time I came back, I heard a waitress ask me, "sao cưng, ăn gì cưng" ["what would you like to eat, sweetness?"], and I melted. It's more beautiful than a *darling* or *cherie* or *mon coeur*. And she called everybody *cưng* [sweetness], of course, but I felt like it was personal. You feel sadness and happiness and closeness in all of this together and it's so complex.

OCEAN: Your body transforms. I think the cells in your body are called into another being. It's called to something that you rarely inhabit. It's called into a shell. When someone says *con ơi*, you're pulled into another shell that was always there but never filled, and then you're filled, and you're just completely alive, and everything fires at once.

That's where we write from, that place where we're in the middle of the transition. We're back and forth, and that liminal space, that borderless space is where we create. It's unstable, but we create entire worlds that we can feel from that, and it's a beautiful thing.

KIM: If I had not had the chance to go to Việt Nam and work there for two years, I certainly would not have been able to have seen the Vietnamese culture with a distance and at the same time sink into it as a Canadian. I think it helped me to find that the word *Ru* is so beautiful because of my French, right? Otherwise, in Việt Nam, who cares about the word *ru* [lullaby] and its banality.

OCEAN: And also in the French, *rue* means "road."

KIM: Yes, a road. In Vietnamese *ru* means really to love and lull your child until he or she falls asleep. It's a very long process. We don't have that in French. The one syllable carries a whole idea. My most recent book is called *Em* [little sister or brother]. With my brothers I don't call them *em*. I call them by their name, and somehow we refer to each other as *tôi* [I] and *mấy người* [us]. And I don't understand why I'm *mấy người*, since I'm one person. So I never used the word *em* almost because in my everyday's life, everybody is older, so I'm always *con* [child].

With the word *em*, this is where it's linked to you. When I wrote the foreword for you, I said, "I don't want to call you 'Ocean,' because in real life, I would call you *em*," and this *em* carries so much for me. To me, it was so enduring, so warm that I could finally use the word *em* for someone. For you.

OCEAN: It was so beautiful to be the recipient of that rare opportunity to be someone's *em*, especially across different families, different eras, and likewise, to call you *chị* [elder sister].

DIALOGUE BETWEEN DOAN BUI (FRANCE) AND BETH (BICH) MINH NGUYEN (UNITED STATES, MIDWEST)

DOAN: We have never met but strangely enough, having read your books, I have this feeling I do know you somehow. That's the way books work, creating bonds between strangers: I am always stunned by this magical trick, when writers manage to put words on my thoughts, peeping into my soul. Because my place in society, there is something troubling that comes with this as well. For my whole life, I have mostly read books written by white writers: I had to identify with heroes who were very different from me and my family. I wanted to be *les petites filles modèles* [model young girls] in the book series written by Sophie Rostopchine, also known as *La Comtesse de Ségur*, those adorable aristocratic demoiselles, playing with their dolls in a castle. I wandered in my dreams in *les salons des Guermantes* described by Proust.

I was very keen on *Les memoires de Saint Simon*, having a weird fascination for those long lineages of French noble blood.[13] Of course, there were exceptions. Pearl S. Buck's books, for example. I read them all when I was a little girl. For one reason: the heroes were Asian. Asian described by a white writer, but still. I found no books about Việt Nam while growing up, so I guess that's why I transferred my need to know about my homeland to its neighbor: China. What an irony: I hate it when people take for granted that I am Chinese and greet me with "ni hao" in the streets . . .

That's why discovering your books was so compelling. As a kid, I couldn't really understand my American cousins raised in California, surrounded by other Asians. I grew up in le Mans, a small town, where we were the first Asian family to settle. La Sarthe, the department where le Mans is located, is very French, very countryside, like your Michigan.

Your novels were the first I read, talking about how it felt being Vietnamese in a white American city. It is a defining experience, indeed, to grow as "the different one." To be remembered as *la chinoise*. I never had Asian friends, as I never met Asian people. Even when I moved to Paris to study and then to work, it was the same. I have been a journalist for the past twenty years. In my newspaper there are 2 nonwhite people out of 120 people. The book industry in France is also almost totally white. Each time I talk with publishers, they are white. My world is white.

You cannot imagine how wildly excited I was to read your novel, *Pioneer Girl*. I was not the only one to be obsessed with the Ingalls family! In France, *Pioneer Girl* is known as *La petite maison dans la prairie*. The book is not as famous as in the US, but the TV series (which is crap) is. As a kid, I loved Laura Ingalls. As there is comfort food, there are comfort books. Pioneer girl series were my favorite comfort books. I read them, again and again, with my little sister. I don't know why I was so in love with the Ingalls family, which represents the quintessential American family. Maybe because they were migrants, in their own way, always leaving a place for another? Or because I thought that we, my lonely Asian family in this French town, we were pioneers also? Why did you start writing?

BETH: Like a lot of writers, I started writing because I loved reading. When I was growing up, my family rarely traveled (could not afford it), but I could always travel in the books I read. I would study maps to understand where stories took place. You mentioned Laura Ingalls Wilder and *The Little House* books, which I read long before I could understand how problematic they were. You asked if Laura was a role model. This is a difficult question because in a way, yes, she was supposed to be a role model for all girls of my generation.

We were supposed to identify with her. It would be years before I figured out what that meant: that we were supposed to identify with whiteness. If all our role models are white, what does that mean for us? I think it means we take in and grow up with an enormous sense of distortion. And then spend the rest of our lives trying to see more clearly. The work is continuous because we are surrounded by mostly white industries like journalism, academia, and publishing, and dealing with mostly white cities, media, and perspectives. In my books I have tried to question and reconsider what I thought I knew about family and cultural representation and storytelling. I am still trying. Sometimes I feel like that's all writing is, for me: an ongoing effort to rethink, unsettle, remake.

On my end, I have been wondering how you have been dealing with pandemic life. What you're reading and what you're eating. What Paris is like, now. If Asians there are made to feel more self-conscious and scared, as they are here in the United States. If you have found new, beautiful sources of joy or comfort.

DOAN: During the lockdown I read one of your texts about comfort food in a delicious anthology named *Eat Joy*. You wrote about spaghetti at Denny's. Spaghetti with tomato sauce. It's my daughter's favorite! As a child, my only experience in restaurants was eating in Chinese restaurants. I always begged my parents to take us to French restaurants such as *Courtepaille*, a chain-restaurant you find on highways, or Buffalo Grill, with this cowboy hat, a Promised Land of juicy steaks and fries.

"It's bad food and expensive," they said. They were right, but I still wanted to taste it. During weekends we would drive to Paris, my parents would meet other Asian people (you know, all those people that we had to call aunt and uncle, with numbers, cô năm, chị hai, etc.). From Paris, I just knew the Thirteenth District, best known as Chinatown with a huge Asian superstore called Tang Frères. It was messy. It stank. I longed for the neat and aseptic French supermarket in le Mans, with cheese, mashed potatoes, macaroni, yogurt, Corn Flakes, instant soup. I wanted so badly to be a perfect little "French" girl, that I thought I had to "eat" France to become *La France*.

I am talking to you from Paris, where I live. My reusable masks are drying, I put them on my bamboos, it's my special touch for decoration. I guess it's an inheritance from my Vietnamese background. It's September but there is still a summer perfume in the air. My daughters have started school again, with masks on. Wearing a mask is mandatory in the streets or at work. I must be the only one who doesn't hate it. Wearing a mask is like being anonymous. With a mask no one stands out. It reminds me of the first time I went to Việt Nam, and I thought, *This is the first time everyone in the streets looks like me.*

You write a lot about food. When I became a mother, I started to cook for my children. Vietnamese food. I remember the first time I made *phở* about five years ago. Such a victory. And you, do you also cook *phở*?

BETH: For years now, I have been saying I am going to make phở, but I haven't. Partly it's because my *Bà Nội's* [paternal grandmother] *phở* was perfect, and I neglected to learn adequately from her before she died. And partly because all *phở* reminds me of this loss, which is a loss within losses. Writing to you made me realize that I need to snap myself out of this and just try it already! If for no other reason then so my children can see me making *phở*, and maybe they can learn too.

DOAN: Your words make me think about shame—about my bizarre relationship to whiteness, this word I can hardly use here in France, for fear of being targeted as a *communautariste*. There is currently a very nasty ideological fight in France about wokeism, like in the US, except that it's especially heated when it comes to race. Use those words—"white" or "nonwhite"—and you will be branded as a suspect. It sometimes feels like a witch hunt. Lately people were fighting about *réunions non-mixtes* [meetings for people of color]. *Réunions non-mixtes* are those meetings where people from a racial minority (or a sexual minority) decide to gather without white people, cis people if they are LGBT, men in case of a feminist meeting that would be "women only." A lot of people are angry about those meetings. They think they represent a danger for La République. Politicians, such as our former minister of education, wanted those *réunions non-mixtes* to be forbidden.

The first time I went to a Vietnamese meeting, I felt overwhelmed with embarrassment. It was not exactly a *réunions non-mixtes*, but it looked like one. I was like, "It's not for me, I am French!" I wanted to escape. But I stayed. I listened to the speakers. I met with other participants. And I learned a lot about myself. In 2017, I also attended a real *conférence non-mixtes*, organized by a "decolonial summer camp." There was a lot of press coverage about this event, almost presented like a terrorist meeting. I remember going to the youth hostel where it took place, going past the cameras (so that white journalists could not get inside) and being accepted because I was not white; it was a weird feeling. I expected something devilish. Instead, I met a bunch of interesting people. Activists who had never found a place in political organizations, unions, because they were silenced and surrounded by white people who would decide for them what should be the issues to fight for. We had intense and candid conversations. And some sensitive topics could be addressed—for example, racism between communities or even in your own family.

I didn't write about this experience in my newspaper. I must say, I was afraid of the backlash. Anyway, I know now from my experience that those *réunions non-mixtes* are precious. They are safe places where words can flourish and help you grow. It is easier to talk about racism with people who share the same experience. But I still struggle to explain this point of view. "Are you comfortable with excluding me from those *réunions non-mixtes*? What about your daughters? Are they white or non-white?" asked my husband.

I told him that he should not be part of those meetings, even as an "ally." He thought it was bullshit. We argued. I stuck to it. In 2020, I was looking forward to this perfect *réunions non-mixtes*, one week in the DVAN [Diasporic Vietnamese Artists Network] residency, in France, in spring 2020, with Vietnamese women writers. Unfortunately it was canceled because of COVID. But maybe it would have risen a big controversy, like France loves them, about *communautarism*, ha ha! And every one of us would have been put on a list of *ennemis de la République*.

BETH: You speak about shame, a feeling that is very familiar to me as well. I can't help thinking it must be familiar to every person of color in white-run spaces. We are told to be proud but not too loud. To be ourselves but only in the way they define it. When we defend ourselves, they say we are being offensive. Shame is meant to keep us quiet, and too often it works.

So, of course, we need our own spaces! How can we ever feel at ease if we don't get to have that? How can we pursue our art, our writing, if we don't feel safe and supported enough to do so? Even this brief exchange between us, Doan, has felt like a space for me. A sense and source of support. To know that we are not alone. When I was a little girl, I spent a lot of time by myself. I read books and wrote stories that I threw away, and sometimes I just stared into space. My sisters would tease me about this and ask what I was thinking about. Of course, I never told them. I never told anyone. Except you, right now: sometimes I imagined that whatever I was looking at—a traffic light, a storm cloud, all the characters I admired on TV shows I watched, and yes, the moon and constellations—was also being looked at, in the same moment, by other kids who maybe were feeling the exact same things I was feeling. One day, I figured, I would meet them.

I am so thankful to say that I have. I've met so many, and I keep meeting more. Like you! I only hope we can meet in person one day soon. Until then, I look forward to more of your writing and work.

DOAN: When my memoir *Le silence de mon père* came out, journalists asked me about racism in interviews. At the beginning, I used to answer that I had never suffered from racism. But then, I would tell them about all those nicknames I had been given, all those words like *chinetoque* [a French curse word for "chink"] that people gave me. I thought about all the guys who catcall Asian women in the streets and say "ni hao," expecting you to answer them and smile, as you must be Chinese (in the eighties, they said "sayonara"). I remembered that each time I have been catcalled, it was not as a woman but always as an *Asian* woman. I realized then that I was in denial: of course, all of this was racism. I just didn't want to see it.

My memoir is an intimate recollection of my family but by no means a political statement. As a journalist, I rarely write op-eds; I rarely say "I." To be clear, I am not an activist, I just tell stories. Still, I remember this journalist calling me a few months ago: he was seeing me as an *indigéniste*, a left-wing activist who was importing dangerous race notions from the US in my newspapers. I remember also having been described as *un danger pour la République*, by a former colleague, in a magazine. I felt betrayed. Compared to the daily amount of hate messages any activist receives, especially when they are women, I know I should not complain. It's nothing. But I wonder, *Am I brave enough? Why am I so cautious? Why am I so afraid to speak out?*

You say: "We were supposed to identify with whiteness. If all our role models are white, what does that mean for us?" I am still asking myself those questions. I am grateful that you wrote that beautiful essay in *The New Yorker* about changing your first names, from Bich Minh to Beth (Bich) Minh Nguyen. I am very nostalgic of my full name, Bùi Đoan Thùy. But I had no choice. I had to shorten it and I became Doan Bui, as it was so much easier for white people to say it. I still wonder what it feels to be a Marie or a Laura. Thanks to you, to Viet Thanh Nguyen, to all the wonderful writers in this book, I know now that we deserve to tell our stories. Our voices deserve to be heard. I have a complicated relationship with being a writer. I feel like a fraud. The label of "writer": it was not something meant for people like us.

BETH: I am grateful for your candor, openness, and thoughtfulness. Racism and white supremacy are global problems, that is for certain, and it's both startling and not startling to see how similar the tensions are where you live. Here in the US there's a right-wing campaign to ban the teaching of race and racism, and actual legislation has already happened in various states. I know; it makes no sense. It's deeply horrifying and depressing. And it's part of the backlash that always happens whenever progressive and civil rights are advanced. It shows how intense white supremacy is too, how far it will go to preserve itself.

We are always being asked to think about white people—their presence, their *feelings*—and frankly this gets tiresome. Every time I leave the house, I must consider how I might be looked at, and what might happen as a result. For one thing, reported anti-Asian hate crimes have increased over 160 percent in the past year. And then there's the general worrying. The fear and carefulness. I think, *I'm fully vaccinated, yes, but do I really need to go anywhere today?*

Next there's the pondering and second-guessing of our reactions and assessments. We have been trained to gaslight ourselves because that's what we've heard from others: "Are you sure that's what they said? Are you sure that's what they meant? Maybe you misunderstood. Maybe it was a joke. It was probably a joke. Don't you think you're being oversensitive?"

DOAN: I am right now finishing *La Tour*, a novel that I started five years ago. A work of fiction. One of the characters is a guy who hates Asian people, especially Asian women. He's rambling on the internet about his hate toward Asian women, his disgust against Chinese prostitutes he has seen in Belleville, his sex obsession, etc. My publisher didn't like this character. Too dark. Too racist. Too much. I rewrote it. To make him less racist. But then the 2021 Atlanta shootings occurred.

I was, like everyone, horrified. I thought about my character, and I wondered. All the publishers and editors who read my manuscript are white: would they have reacted differently, if they were nonwhite? Maybe this character was not "too much." Maybe he was, on the contrary, "not enough." Reality is darker than fiction. Fetishization of Asian women is a reality. Woman-hate, Asian hate is a reality. And it can lead to this horrific reality: the murders in Atlanta. This second murder is the media that makes assumptions about the victims because they worked in a spa.

I remember having lunch with my daughters a year ago in a Chinese restaurant. There was a woman besides us, making jokes: "On va manger à la chinetoque" ["We are going to eat in a chinks way"], she said. I didn't say anything. But when I came out of the restaurant, I felt the sting of shame. Again. Because I let her go with that stupid joke, in front of my daughters. I told my daughters I didn't say anything because I didn't want to embarrass them. They told me: "You should have. She is the one who would have been ashamed." They were right.

DIALOGUE BETWEEN BAO PHI (UNITED STATES, MIDWEST) AND DAO STROM (UNITED STATES, WEST COAST)

DAO: Shall we begin with some contemplation of where we each come from? We are both Vietnamese refugees, of course, but our American cultural experiences have evolved in quite different types of settings. And yet, I think there are still some commonalities, on a fundamental level, that we've each wrestled with, as writers, as people, as Asian minorities in this society, and maybe too as parents (I've been a single parent too). But I want to start with poetry and, to put it simply, identity. I am looking at your first collection, *Sông I Sing*, at the poem "Called (An Open Letter to Myself)," which I dog-eared (years ago probably, when I first read the book), and I find myself caught by these lines in particular:

> It was tough for us those times it seemed
> our arms braced between not being seen and
> the American dream———

and

> They called us gook, chink, blanket ass, spic, nigger, coon———
> (and what was really sad is, we called each other that, too)

BAO: I grew up the youngest in a family of refugees fleeing directly from war. I was a baby when they were shelling Tân Sơn Nhất, my family tells me I didn't cry as the bomb shelters shook for hours from the explosions. I was physically present for that, but I have no memory of it. What I do remember, however, is growing up in Phillips, South Minneapolis—a known epicenter of urban Native American life, where the American Indian Movement started. It was Minneapolis's largest, poorest, and most racially diverse neighborhood.

I both experienced and witnessed a lot of racism and cross-racial hostility toward me, my family, other Southeast Asians. Many people blamed us for the war, even though my dad fought on the same side as the Americans. There was also police harassment and institutional racism—everything from name calling to being chased by racist bullies to institutional racism. It was so common that I just thought this was what life was like. Unlike my siblings and my parents, I wasn't tough. I hid in books, in the library. I came of age, I'm guessing like you did, during Reagan and the first Bush. I had a lot of internalized racism, toward other BIPOC but especially against other Asians. Asians were not cool—the ones that stuck together seemed like they had their own thing going, but they seemed so removed from what life in America was like. I wanted to be white, and then, as I got older, I wanted to be a cool man of color. Not Asian, though. Funny, it wasn't until I was much older that I would discover I wouldn't be accepted as any of those things no matter how hard I tried.

What about you? You grew up in a rural, white environment, right?

DAO: Yes, a lot of what you are recalling resonates for me, though in a quite different context. I grew up in a small, rural hick town in the mountains of northern California, on the—so aptly named—American River. My stepfather, a Danish American immigrant, had decided to move us out to the country, build a house, raise chickens, all this mythic western Americana, pioneer, do-it-yourself spirit. I grew up with dogs and ponies, living in a trailer, surrounded by lower-income, rural, working-class, white families mostly, some ultra-religious. There was quite literally no other family like ours in that area. In this setting I was always an outsider, awkward, shy, physically smaller, etc.

Like you, at times I also wished I were white, but maybe unconsciously so. I didn't even see my own race. I erased it myself, in effect, by denying it, by believing myself exempt from it. It was only in my post-college and -graduate years that I really started to look at my Vietnamese roots and embrace them, along with the particular traumas and complications that came with them.

You talk about going from wanting to be white to wanting to be a cool man of color—these projections of ideal American selves we've inhabited over the years.

BAO: I often think that if Asians are allowed to be "American" at all or to any degree, it necessitates an erasure, or a cosigning of our racial invisibility. That's part of the price. I went through something similar, where I felt like I was more legible and more visible as this vague idea of being a person of color than if I was viewed as Asian. You know, the "good" Asian, whether that means the "good" Asian to white people, the model minority, or the "woke" Asian to activist people, the ally—we're only seen through someone else's lens, through someone else's rubric, on their terms. And we must be okay with this, or we are erased or scorned. Even in progressive, multiracial environments, this is true. Asians can be seen as individual participants across the political spectrum or in different spheres. But we as a people, a community, remain inscrutable, illegible, backward.

This was especially pronounced in the Midwest. There were Asians here before, but Southeast Asian refugees were the first large, visible populations to come and create a sort of culture clash or crisis. We were (and continue to be) racialized through the lens of war. This is gendered too. Asian men are seen as smart but sexless, or dangerous and sexist. Asian women are seen as objects or victims needing to be saved. We have no control over this narrative or its permutations. I'm not sure if this answers your question, but I keep going back to this idea that Asians aren't cool in American culture. And when you're young, so much of your identity is formed in that potent and toxic push-pull of wanting to be cool or wanting to be different. Asians don't even register on that scale. We're not even a possibility, you know?

Do you feel similar? What was it about college and post-college life that made you want to explore your culture?

DAO: Right after graduating from college, I moved to New York City, leaving California for the first time. This was the farthest I'd been away from my parents, geographically, and maybe this distance also allowed for perspective. During that time my mother wrote me a couple long letters and for the first time told me the detailed story (which I'd known in broad strokes) about her past relationship with my birth father. They were both writers and journalists in Saigon, pre-1975, and together ran an independent activist newspaper, *Sóng Thần*. This was when I began to learn more about the circumstances—political, personal—I was born into as a person of South Vietnamese descent. I was about the age (or coming into) that my mother was during her writer years in Saigon.

Then I went to graduate school and I had a travel stipend that made it possible for me to return to Việt Nam, in 1996, for the first time since 1975. I met my birth father on that trip. This was a very emotional and essentially life-changing moment for me. In effect, I'd done something my family narrative thus far had told me would be impossible to do—return, reconnect. I began to feel the weight of our history, and some sense of what I might call "responsibility" toward the legacy of my parents but also in general toward artists and writers behind me.

But, as you've noted, growing up Asian in American popular culture was definitely not "cool" in the imagery most readily available. But I think the concept of coolness can also be suspect? And maybe it is to our benefit, and part of the path, to have to redefine what determines—what feeds into—our images of possible ways of being in this culture. In my experience my personal family history was something I eventually discovered could not be contained by the conventional American containers—and I am speaking aesthetically now too. Socially, artistically, and in many other ways, I've had to contend with the truth of myself—my history, all the influences that make up my desires of self and expression—as being too unwieldy, atypical, messy, dark, complicated, etc. to "fit." Then the question becomes: Do we want or need to fit in? What is the cost, if any, of choosing *not* to? Can we build a new context, a new structure, for articulating on our own terms?

Are there ways in which your poetry has evolved over the years to represent your most important truths more effectively? Or did you come at it always from a clearly rooted sense of being? Did you have any turning points or revelations along the way, in regards either to form or content?

BAO: Well, I came up through slam and spoken word, and in many ways it was a marginalized art form that eventually became commodified. I say that because I don't want to insinuate some type of artistic purity. I wrote and performed my poetry because it felt natural to me; it felt like something I could do. It was an art form I intuitively resonated with and wanted to grow stronger in. I felt more at ease with the poets who did slam and spoken word, as many of them also came from historically silenced communities and identities. I internalized a lot of the ideas of spoken word: that people would not be interested in my work on the page, that publishers would not be interested in me, etc. Connected to what you said about defining and redefining cool, I had the notion I would never experience any mainstream success, but in so doing, found a way to redefine what success looked and felt like.

But the most recent big artistic change in my life had nothing to do with the industry. It occurred when I became a father. Long story short, that was around the same time I was thinking more about my family, what we went through, and what effects it would have on my daughter.[14] The work became more internal, more personal. I embraced and attempted to deal with my contradictions, my cognitive dissonance.

I want to loop back to your trips to Việt Nam. I remember one of your poems was about a negative experience with a native Vietnamese man, involving dynamics of your gender and your mixed-race identity. I think sometimes there is a narrative that those of us who are refugees or immigrants are expected to have a very romantic "return" to whatever our homeland is, when our homelands are just as flawed and human as anywhere else. Did you find this to be true, and did it influence your writing? Did you feel any apprehension writing about your experiences?

DAO: Writing about Việt Nam is tricky, no doubt, as it's full of tensions. In writing, I'm committed to looking at everything as honestly as possible, and I try to root the work in compassion, ultimately, even when I am writing (and I often am) about imperfect dynamics.

About the expected romance of return . . . On my first trip back, I felt a sense of return, not romantic but still cathartic, in the sense that it woke up the skeptical, Americanized me to the fact that, yes indeed, there is such a thing as collective consciousness, and collective trauma, and that I am a part of it. I felt sorrow emerge in me, bodily, to things I had no personal memories of. But my experiences of returning to Việt Nam (especially with the most recent trip in 2014) have also brought into sharper relief the fact of my disconnection: I miss this place, this piece of me, that I also never truly knew. Because you can long toward a past place or future hope, for years telling yourself that recovering either will amend something within yourself. But then when you go and do it, at least for me, I began to realize the disconnection lay within my very self, that the consequences of displacement may be, for me, a little irreparable. Or maybe this is so because I've believed it for so long? It's hard to say. But these quandaries are very much connected to the fact of being Vietnamese and from Việt Nam.

The other truth, though, is I really don't belong in Việt Nam either. I am so obviously not "of there." When I was traveling there, locals looked critically at me (especially after discovering I don't speak the language), men hit on me in unpleasant ways, and I felt othered, even amid bodies that otherwise looked like mine. So I might say that everywhere I go, to some degree, I am made aware of myself as at odds with whatever the dominant culture, be it white American, or "traditional" Vietnamese American, or Vietnamese. Have you felt this too, to any degree?

Even in terms of being South Vietnamese, I am atypical, having grown up in a Vietnamese-Danish-American family, and then also because my mother was an atypical Vietnamese mother. She was a writer, she had her children out of wedlock, she was very modern and rebellious in her youth, and those markers of culture and custom that many Vietnamese easily gravitate toward—namely, food and language—she did not effectively pass on to her children. In short, I have to say that return is never simple, and maybe sometimes it is impossible, or maybe it is a continual process.

If I may, I want to ask you about your daughter, and in tandem how parenthood connects to writing and to lineage in terms both of family and poetry. We're each in our ways dealing with lineage, inheritance, the family line, and the role art has played or can play in all of this. Would you be willing to elaborate a little more on how parenthood has affected your poetry? There is the lineage of our families' personal experiences, and then there is the lineage you are creating as a poet. How do these lineages connect or intersect for you, for your daughter? And do you ever think about what the future of diasporic writing will be? For instance, what do you imagine it evolving into, in its best forms, for our children and next generations?

BAO: I can relate. When I went back to Việt Nam, my language skills in terms of listening and tone were okay, but my vocabulary and grammar were severely limited. I was told a lot of horror stories—about how Vietnamese in Việt Nam hated Việt Kiều like me and would try to extort money or abuse me.[15] I went when it was still very much a third world Communist country, in the late 1990s. On top of that, there was the personal alienation: I was often assumed to be Korean, Japanese, or Hong Kong Chinese. I had braces and glasses, bad acne, and I didn't dress like a typical Vietnamese male—local or Việt Kiều.

While I didn't encounter the sexism you had to endure, people did comment on how they felt I wasn't "male" or "masculine" enough, and I noticed a lot of internalized colonialism and colorism when straight white males in my cohort were treated differently than I, from local Việt men and women. One thing I had going for me was that I was pessimistic. I didn't expect to have a good homecoming because I've always felt insecure and odd in America, because I was most often seen and treated as an oddball. I assumed it would be the same if not more so in Việt Nam. I was able to decenter myself a bit and take the experience in—the good and the bad. Overall, it was a good experience. But the bad . . . whew! Maybe it hurts so much when it comes from people who look like you.

Becoming a parent affected my relationship to parenthood in many ways. For one, since I was physically present for the horror of our exodus but don't have a conscious memory of it, I just assumed I had no claim to examining or talking about it. It wasn't until we went to the nurse at the beginning of the pregnancy who asked if any of us had a history of cancer, diabetes, or war in our family that I began to learn that such trauma could be passed on genetically.

And even then, the first years of her life were incredibly difficult. I was exhausted, depressed, and lost. Long story short, it wasn't until the breakup, and when she moved far away from me with her mother, that I realized how much I wanted to be her father, how much I needed her as much as she needed me. It wasn't malicious—her mother had gotten an amazing job in another city, and we were still committed to co-parenting together—but emotionally, for me, it was a breaking point. Luckily, one year later her mother got a job back in the city, and honestly it felt like I had won the lottery. Being so far away from her broke me down, and I had to figure out which parts of me were worth keeping when I put myself back together. I write about it as a way of working through it. And as a way to remember.

In the current climate of kids being separated at the [US–Mexico] border—it's so heartbreaking. Viet families have been and still are separated by war and empire. And of course, this country has a long history of separating nonwhite families from each other as a means of control, power, genocide, and border managing. That's the big picture. But then after what I went through, being far away from my kid—I mean, we were not separated by government mandate, and I saw her at least once a month, not even including frequent Skyping—it was almost more than I could bear. I can't imagine what these families are going through right now.

Have you felt anything similar regarding this climate? Has it affected your writing at all?

DAO: No doubt, it is heartbreaking what has been happening to families on the US–Mexico border with the current [Trump] administration; I can't even imagine how I would endure being separated from my child in such circumstances, especially when he was younger (he is twenty-two now). I still have many anxieties as a parent—as we all do, of course—but I am also aware that some of my moods and tendencies extend beyond what is "normal" and are related to my being a refugee and to inherited trauma. That your nurse was astute enough to ask about if there was any history of "war" in your family, alongside other illnesses, is incredibly salient.

We have acknowledged PTSD as a real illness that inflicts veterans and their families, and I think the same validation should be given to the emotional and mental health issues of refugees and people who've grown up with refugee or displaced parents. By now I've had enough conversations with other Vietnamese of our generation to know that many of us grew up affected by absorbing our parents' (often unacknowledged) traumas from the war, as well struggling with our own (even unconscious) experiences. These "echoes" reverberate in all sorts of ways, from minor to major dysfunctions. Separation is at the heart of so much pain, to put it very simplistically.

The crucial things I felt were missing in my childhood, I have tried to give to my son: (1) a sense of connection to the past and access to it (that is, the ability to return, the possibility of both holding *and* moving on from the trauma of the past); (2) my emotional presence and support. I will say very simply that I understand and see clearly that the cause of the difficulties in my own family life had everything to do with both of my parents' pasts of war and displacement.

For myself I want to ask: What if we were instead to simply drop our desires for belonging and embrace our not-belonging, or mutable sense of belonging/not-belonging? To instead find strength and acceptance of ourselves through that. I want to put the power and responsibility back into our own hands, in short. I want to believe this can apply in terms of both our art/professional and personal lives.

BAO: Absolutely. As my journey has gotten longer and I've tried to grow and learn, one of the most painful things to acknowledge is how we are complicit in many of these systems of harm that we are critical of, whether it hurts people who look like us or people who don't look like us at all. And as you say, rather than trying to fit in or "win" the competition, perhaps we have the potential to empower ourselves by actually not participating. Refusing to participate. Or, as a more positive spin, imagining ways to grow and to be, to create outside of the narrow parameters of success and expectation that all of us are taught is the way to be in this world. I don't know if I am smart or strong enough to carry through, but I know I want to.

What about you?

DAO: I wholly agree with you, especially on the realization that there is a path of empowerment that involves "not participating" and "imagining ways to grow and to be, to create outside of the narrow parameters." I think you say it wonderfully there.

My deeper wish is to live in a world where those "portraits" of power lose their power over us, in effect. What if instead we start to perceive of nonaction, gentleness, the small, the quiet, the nonphysical, the slow, the undetermined, and the willingness to doubt and change, as empowered ways of being? I think this would yield a very different manner of interaction and ambitions amid people.

These are easy things to say but harder to enact, of course. I think some of the work does lie within ourselves—in our perceptions and our ability to go out on a limb or stand out in the cold and do the "not participating" that you speak of. Or the *differently* participating, we might say, and inviting others to do that with us. I don't profess to know the solution or presume my own capacities either. But I think maybe something starts with us endeavoring to stand up in these spaces and valuing ourselves and others in terms of our own inner lives foremost.

DIALOGUE BETWEEN CATHY LINH CHE (UNITED STATES, EAST COAST) AND DIANA KHOI NGUYEN (UNITED STATES, EAST COAST)

DIANA: In your work *Fade In*, I was struck by the radical empathy of entering into the point of view of your family members, of your mother, your father, from times before you were born.

CATHY: Thank you. I wonder about this sometimes. It feels both necessary (because I've been collecting interviews over the years) and perhaps a problem. I have never written in persona before, and I wonder about the creative license one should be taking when representing others. I think of Saidiya Hartman's concept of critical fabulation, but this happens for her when the voices are long in the past, and not people who have their own voices and who can tell their own stories.[16] In some ways I wonder if preserving their voices wholly and offering a translation would not be truer.

DIANA: I worry all the time about persona poems (and for me, that lyric entry feels like appropriation, even if it is someone I know so well)—I haven't yet found a way to give myself permission to write the eye/"I" of my mother, my father, my brother.

In your persona poems I saw the crafting of voices, as in the audio commentary over [Francis Ford] Coppola's *Apocalypse Now*, and am now struck by this idea of layering home videos and personal archives on top of *Apocalypse Now* as a kind of bold redaction of that awful film. But then it's also complicated: your mother as extra in the film, but then also in these private home videos, all of these pieces (like a video lasagna) curated and crafted by an estranged daughter.

I too have media from interviews I did with my parents and grandmother (*bà ngoại*) but didn't know how to step into their masks and suits. Instead, I write a play where I lifted dialogue from transcripts for characters who represented them . . . with a character like myself weaving in between.

CATHY: Thank you. I'd love to read it. I felt a clear feeling of kinship between the type of work that we are thinking through and engaging with.

DIANA: Yes, me too—so many similar threads.

CATHY: I was also interested in your thinking through ideas about time in your video work. I was specifically drawn to the idea of palimpsest, layering, a recapturing of memory into a present. I've always felt allied with history, both personal, familial, and political, and I felt a sense of your wading through source material to make new meaning, through many different intersecting forms: video, sound, fashion, language, physical building structures, nature.

DIANA: Yes, a lot of the video work was my hoping to coexist with those past memories—a body that contains the past but can run alongside it as well. In many ways my brother is still alive on home video.

CATHY: The body does contain the past, but there is a contemporary body as well. And it's amazing to watch videos of your brother that show so many aspects of your lives as children. It brings me joy to be in conversation with your book *Ghost Of* in this way.

DIANA: In trying to do this "next book" or project that zooms out to move through the Vietnamese diaspora, I just could only zoom out to my family, or to look at my family from another standing point or point of view. I can't stop thinking about our familial past—what haunts me—but also those moments of joy where my siblings and I were children (that I've forgotten, as I only remember the traumas, abuse, and violence at the hands of our mother). I've given up trying to move toward the diaspora, and just trying to give space and bear witness to what my mind wants to investigate and noodle in.

CATHY: That resonates with me. I found myself struggling when I had to think about my "next book." There was a distinct desire not to replicate the last project, but memory, pain, loss, and obsession doesn't really work that way.

And I had to face this feeling that I didn't have what it took to do "research" properly. *Apocalypse Now* is such an iconic film. When talking about the project, I was continually approached by folks who have seen the movie many times over, who declared it a masterpiece and their favorite film. They asked me if I had seen the making of and if I knew about the folklore surrounding it. I felt underread, and the film is so storied already and takes up so much of everyone's imagination, that it made me nervous and afraid to even contemplate beginning it. There was also the question of form. The source materials were almost too rich; it was dizzying to even know where to begin.

DIANA: I think that the film takes up so much cultural and imaginative real estate in many Americans that it is precisely why you should assert yourself as boldly as you are—in between, on top, underneath.

To the question of form: There is something that Douglas Kearney does sometimes at readings and presentations, what he calls "Critical Karaoke" where he plays a music video with problematic moments (like Michael Jackson's iconic "Thriller," for example), then sings along to the music video, but will suddenly pause the video and interject a lyrical, critical commentary on what's happening in the visuals and lyrics of the song and video. I'm already seeing your own anti- and ante-*Apocalypse Now* project as something similar in thrust, but what moves me, grounds me to the experience is the deeply personal nature of your work and the high stakes of its various forms of resilience and vulnerability.

CATHY: Resilience and vulnerability... I see this a little bit in the concept that you're exploring with Đổi Mới, which is a larger historical Vietnamese and diasporic question. I love that the poems return, insistently to family, and to the natural violence of the insect and arachnid world. I love the many valences: butterflies are so often figured as symbols of beauty, but they are also in your poems, the name for genitals, which are figured as secret and portending the possibility of both love and violence.

DIANA: Oh yes, portents and portals for love and violence. Your generous observation of the "Đổi Mới Series" helps me to see my own obsession and reality. First, I wanted to look outside at the larger Vietnamese history and diaspora, yes, but kept turning back to my family, as if there was something I had missed, something preventing me from going outside. Second, in the first book, I noticed a trend in looking at fables and animal behavior as a way to understand human and my own family's actions, and yes, this figures into the violence and ecosystems of trauma of the war and its legacy. I'm now realizing that perhaps this new sequence is looking in a macro sense in seeing the insect and arachnid realm, but also, as if I'm getting as close as possible to the pores of my family, the pores of memory. What exists in this semipermeable membrane/layer (skin) that keeps the "us" of us in and the rest of the world outside?

CATHY: I am listening.

DIANA: For your work on *Apocalypse*, I found the manuscript to be a reclamation/retelling of it from the perspective of those who are from the country. There are so many lenses: that of the mother, the writer/curator of the manuscript, as well as what the reader "knows" from having seen the film. At times the poems felt part of a larger screenplay, and that form emerges most definitely by the end, intersecting with the current apocalypse: the COVID-19 pandemic. I see a kind of auto-ethnographic tracing/dialogue occurring between archive (photographs, e-mails, home videos) in your memoir and revisiting of the personal/familial/American film past.

CATHY: I am actually talking to a filmmaker who wants to compose a short documentary of this narrative. We have no idea what that means though: What is the audience? What is the register? Within the film world, how "experimental" are we talking versus how much are we aiming at a more "general" audience. Still, all the pieces and projects: *Apocalypse Now* as a film, the poetry, the creative nonfiction, the home videos and e-mails, the possible future performance of these works feel as though they are part of the same project.

DIANA: The interested documentary filmmaker sounds very exciting! But at the same time, I immediately thought: *Oh no, I'm only interested in Cathy assembling and curating these experiences and pieces*. But it would be fascinating to see your personal material handled by another artist. I wonder what would open in your own understanding/viewing/knowing/reading of the work when a nonfamily member enters into it by way of making art with it.

Speaking of multivectored works in a project with distinct topics: I am reminded of experimental artist/writer Caroline Bergvall, whose work *Drift* is a book of poetry but also an installation, video piece, and so forth—which is to say: seeing her work and its changing forms liberated my thinking that work needed to have discrete containers, beginnings and ends. All aspects of *Drift* are like new facets to the same organic living thing. That it's still alive, living, aging.

CATHY: It's a question, I think, of technical expertise and access. This filmmaker who I am collaborating with has access to a different world than I do, the one of film festivals, for instance, that would move me. He also knows how to edit film in a way that I don't. But there are other aspects that feel unsettling. For example, he suggested that we could hire voice actors to read out the parts of my parents, and that seemed like a replication of the violence that Coppola committed when using Vietnamese refugees to authenticate his film.

DIANA: Very unsettling to think of voice actors reading the parts of the parents. Have you seen Sarah Polley's documentary about her mother and family, *Stories We Tell*? She has her (spoiler alert) father who we, along with Sarah and everyone else, realize that it's not her biological father, read a nonfiction narrative of their mother's/his wife's life. I love the idea of employing our own family members to read their parts, kind of like what Abbas Kiarostami does in his faux-documentary *Close-Up*)—except I don't think I would ever be able to get my parents to do this. Currently my parents and I are estranged from each other (hopefully for the last time and hopefully not)—which is not unlike your own estrangement with your parents.

CATHY: I am drawn to notions of documentary but am not sure why. I think part of this is the idea of seeing personal effects as precious archival material. Also, there is a desire to go in and reconstruct something: story, meaning, throughline. It feels like an insistent urge for me, to make connections, to walk in and walk out with a new discovery and new clarity.

DIANA: Reading your "Essay on Beauty" opened so many emotions—the sympathy and empathy I feel for you now, you as a younger Cathy—but also, I saw a kind of mirror: these events, facts, histories I recognized as versions of my own history and story as well.

CATHY: For me, I was struck by seeing your parents' wedding video with your mother and the little tiara, with the incense sticks at the altar. I was transported to my own parents' wedding photographs (which feel miraculous to have as documents at all! I'm not sure how these images managed to survive all these years). There was something decidedly traditional and modern being provided in the same rendition. I was also moved by hearing your father's voice when he was narrating the house. It reminded me so much of my own father.

DIANA: I got chills when you mentioned that hearing my father's voice reminded you of your own—there's an uncanniness to this experience I have when I hear my parents in the accented English of other (Southern) Vietnamese strangers speaking to me—at a restaurant, grocery store, university campus, hospital, or anywhere I might encounter strangers and be able to eavesdrop.

Yes, I am shocked and grateful that the privilege of technology was (1) available in the eighties to my parents and their families, and (2) that these archives survive to this present moment, where I think I am the only one to have watched or worked with them—my parents do not revisit the video-past at all.

CATHY: I'm wondering how you see your video work, performance work, and poetry/creative nonfiction intersecting? Are they a whole and conversant project? How do you understand media and genre, and why do you suppose we have been utilizing so many formats to engage with these narratives? What do different "genres" or "formats" offer you?

DIANA: Right now, I'm at an impasse with the various pieces intersecting. I do think the pieces constitute a whole and overlap both literally and textually, and are in conversation with each other, but not in an intentional way, only in the sense of a record skipping sometimes, because my mind is stuck on certain details or major or minor facts.

I think of media and genre as various approaches, containers, ways of encountering a moment, experience, or "thing." Of course, one can get advanced academic training in any of the media and genres, but there isn't enough time in one lifetime to become fully-trained in all of them. After I gave myself permission to stray from poetry and enter into a play-mode in other fields (of media, writing, etc.), I think I needed to engage with these other formats because they offered up possibilities of capturing silences, tensions, and memory in ways that writing a poem couldn't open up for me. That is to say, nonpoetry media afford another way of looking, listening, and immersing oneself.

And it helps me navigate my ethical self-questions as well—for example, my fears about appropriation in writing persona poems of my family members.

CATHY: I do think of my mucking around as a form of play. I feel freer. After my first book I became bored with my own poems. And I didn't know a way out. It took a long time to get to a point where I felt able to engage in something that felt exciting again. I'm not sure when that happened exactly, or why, but prose offered something new that allowed me to be funny, for instance—my poems tend to be dead serious!

DIANA: I was struck by how you've approached the details of your childhood sexual traumas in *Split*, this new manuscript *Fade In*, and full-on in "Essay on Beauty." Each time I recognized the event(s), but it was always different. As if I were entering into the memory via Cathy from a different access point: door, window, garage, chimney, etc.

CATHY: I think it was the media that brought new experiences of these events: so watching a home video or revisiting photographs with my cousin and neighbors. I will say, after *Split* my relationship to my memories of sexual violation and nonconsent were forever altered. I no longer had dreams or cinematic images playing in my mind. The poetry book served as a container for those reels. And the act of public and familial disclosure altered my relationship to the internal, secret, private world that had been for so long contained within my body and within my imagination.

I guess new access points offer themselves up all the time. The *Apocalypse Now* project research overlapped with the birth of a niece and a nephew and therefore my father's stability as the patriarch shifting. In the aftermath he disowned me, and we still have not come to a true peace as a family.

TWO

Authorship and Authority

THE AMERICAS AND VIỆT NAM

Where does the authorial voice come from? According to Henry Louis Gates Jr., it is undeniable that a writer's "histories, individual or collective, do affect what [they] wish to write or what [they] are able to write. But that relation is never one of fixed determinism. No human culture is inaccessible to someone who makes the effort to understand, to learn, to inhabit another world."[1] What seems to be an obvious statement is in fact complicated within an American context, for Gates's query keeps returning in different forms to this problematic: "Is it alright for any writer to write from the perspective of any person, regardless of race?"

The question of authenticity has its roots in the vexed American history of conquest, exclusion, and exploitation of minorities along racial lines. This history has produced a culture whereby Asian Americans have been represented for more than a century through predominantly white lenses.[2] The academic field of Asian American literature, for instance, did not emerge until the Civil Rights Movement in the late 1960s, when a few Asian American activists and scholars excavated books by Asian American authors in the back of bookstores to create curricula and fight, at the risk of going to prison, alongside other people of color for the creation of classes that teach the humanities and the social sciences through the perspective of people of color. This was in response to undeniable invisibility and gross misrepresentation in academic knowledge production. Through organized scholarship and political action, these scholar-activists institutionalized what is now called Asian American literature so that they would be taught, read, written about, and valued.[3] The initial function of these texts was for Asian American students to become aware of the human costs of racism and to become empowered as Americans. This in turn encouraged Asian Americans to claim America in their writing and prompted critics and reviewers to write about Asian American texts as a distinct category. In tandem with this development is the emergence of theories that insisted that race is not a biological factor but rather a social construction.[4]

As racial awareness increased, Asian American writers started to have a platform of their own. In the process they inadvertently became "the voice" of their community. This platform fueled a heightened sense of racial awareness for Asian Americans as a group, leading to more empowerment, more organizing, and more allocation of resources. The formation of such identity politics is an American phenomenon. In France, for example, writers have to identify as French writers, first and foremost. French Asian writers do not have an institutional platform along racial and ethnic lines to write from, and racism toward the Asian French diaspora is barely recognized and addressed. In this context we see that a platform (as in the United States) is better than no platform at all (as in France). Yet identity politics is far from perfect and resulted in unexpected consequences. White writers have at times tried to pass as people of color in the United States to have access to a "special" platform (which has understandably angered people of color). Writers of color, although they have benefited from this category, have also felt boxed in within a category such as "Asian American," because they may only be valued as representative of their community by the majority or as the only ones responsible to fight against racism by members of the community—possibly to the detriment of their creativity or desire to write about other topics.[5]

Further complicating the notion of authenticity are writers who are mixed race and those who do not have full ethnic/Vietnamese names and have been adopted. Such writers denounce the diaspora for what they regard as its literary domestication of their work, referring to the ways in which the diasporic communities and dominant readerships are determining what Vietnamese people can or cannot write. Yet, on the other hand, to not be perceived as authentic can offer a kind of freedom. These communities and readerships define the literary conventions by which mixed-race writers are expected to abide. They spatially metaphorize the diaspora as a "hierarchy" that organizes Vietnamese people based on their appearance, age, immigration history, Vietnamese language skills, and class status in Việt Nam in the past and the diaspora in the present.

In this chapter writers contemplate if Vietnamese artists forge their own authority or have it thrust upon them. Through this process of dialoguing, authority emerges as a gendered and racialized process. Writerly authority is something that they in large part deplore because it tends to pigeonhole writers of color into racial, cultural, and aesthetic borders. In reaction, they write and express themselves against stereotypes while simultaneously taking on the task to rectify how Vietnamese have been represented in history because of the outcome of the Vietnam War—which has also been called the Second Indochinese War or the American War by those in Việt Nam.[6] They ultimately argue that to be Vietnamese is not a racial condition but rather an affect. In response to the weighty burden of representing the Vietnamese diaspora and trying to effect a sense of belonging to it, they fight like early Asian Americans writers, for the right and freedom to write on their own terms.

DIALOGUE BETWEEN MONIQUE TRUONG (UNITED
STATES, EAST COAST) AND VIET THANH NGUYEN
(UNITED STATES, WEST COAST)

VIET: You wanted to talk about the authority of the author as a writer.

MONIQUE: I was thinking about how an author is placed in the position of being an authority, and it could be subjects that you write about or subjects that you've never even touched upon. Basically, depending on who you are, your gender, your ethnicity, your sexual orientation, you are placed in that position of authority. Clearly, for you, it happened like that. [snaps fingers to emphasize how instantly the authorial positioning is accrued.]

In the sense that you're a scholar of Asian American literature and American studies, you were in probably the best position of any Vietnamese American author writing and publishing today, to be placed in the role of, or to assume the role of an authority, right? On Vietnamese Americans, on immigration, on the refugee crisis; but at the same time, I could imagine if you were a different person, you might have resisted it. I'm interested in hearing how you were able to assume the authority that's been placed in front of you?

VIET: Sometimes writers seek authority, and sometimes writers just have authority thrust on them. I think you're speaking partly about the latter, because if you are a so-called minority writer of whatever background and you write something that's related to that minority background, you oftentimes simply have authority thrust on you, and people ask you all kinds of questions about your minority's history or politics or whatever, and you're expected to be the spokesperson. That is something that a lot of writers don't want to have thrust on them. It's something that many writers who are not minorities of whatever kind don't have put upon them, right?

MONIQUE: That's right.

VIET: But it is true that I think writers often have a type of authority put on them regardless of anything else. Let's say you write a book about cooking of some kind, and you become an authority on cooking, whether or not you wanted to be. I can understand that. It happens to all writers, but it's obviously an unfair or unequal burden put upon those of us who are writers of color. In my case, I think because of the minority background you just talked about, I wanted to have that authority because I knew that there were a lot of people speaking about Việt Nam, or about refugees, or about war, whose opinions I did not completely agree with, or whose answers were not completely satisfactory to me, and if they can be authorities, why can't I be the authority in that case?

Now I'm being asked to speak about immigration issues and refugee issues. Yes, I have a background in that, but it's not something that I would say I'm an expert on, it's just something I have a strong opinion on with some knowledge of. So that puts me in an interesting situation, again, where I feel like I am not as expert as some people are on these topics, but if I'm being asked my opinion, it still feels like it's an opportunity that I shouldn't avoid because these issues are so urgent, and sometimes perhaps expertise is not all that is needed but moral conviction.

Now I think of you, when your first novel came out, *The Book of Salt*, this was 2003. I remember that moment very clearly because I was in Paris when I read it and it's set in Paris. As an outcome of that, did you find yourself turned into an authority on all the various things that the book touches on?

MONIQUE: No, not necessarily. I was given more of an opportunity to write about food in food magazines and newspapers, but the borders of what they thought I could be an expert on or have conviction in, that land mass was actually very small. Sure, Paris, but the rest of France? No. Vietnamese food? Yes. I remember [that] the very first food article I wrote was about my favorite Italian restaurant in New York City, and that was a huge struggle. This was not an article where I was going to presume to talk about my knowledge of Italian food, it was my knowledge of a particular place that has a history in my life, and even that was a struggle.

VIET: That was a struggle for you personally, or was it a struggle for the people who were accepting the article and editing it, and so on?

MONIQUE: Exactly, for the magazine.

VIET: They didn't see you as a legitimate voice on this restaurant?

MONIQUE: Yes. Later, when I was doing more travel articles and I was pitching things, it was very clear. There were certain parts of the world I would never be assigned. I didn't write the novel so I could go and write travel articles, so it wasn't like a big disappointment to me, but it just made it clear to me what sort of readership I have and about what the gatekeepers thought of me.

VIET: I think this is one reason why I find it very hard to say no to things. I feel like I need to pursue what someone has proposed to me, because I can demonstrate then that I'm like any other writer who can write about anything. That's why in my role now as writing for occasional op-ed essays for the *New York Times* or the *Washington Post* or *L.A. Times*, I'm always trying to push things so that I don't always get restricted to the beat about Viet Nguyen. My ideal is, just let me write about something so far off that would be fun to do, and food is something that you should have been an authority on because the novel, that first novel, was all about cooking. It wasn't just about Vietnamese food. It was about [Gertrude] Stein and [Alice] Toklas and their cookbook, so you should have at that moment become the authority on traveling and food.

MONIQUE: I want to share with you a story about the *New York Times*. The op-ed page for whom I had written a previous piece about summer, Paris, being young. . . . They contacted me a couple of years later and asked if I would write an op-ed in defense of eating dogs.

What was the impetus for this? There was apparently a law that was being proposed in Hawaii, the State of Hawaii, that would punish anyone who raised dogs and cats specifically for the purpose of consumption. They wanted me to write a defense based on my cultural background and history about why we should be able to eat dogs. I adore dogs, not as an entrée but as a companion.

When I first got that request, I thought, *This must be a joke, right? This is a joke. This is like a setup.* I wrote back to them essentially saying that, but in a more professional tone and they wrote back saying, "Well, I mean you could be playful with it, if you'd like." I thought, *My God, somewhere at the* New York Times, *in a room full of people, someone sat down and asked, 'Who's a dog eater?'*

VIET: Or who comes from a culture of dog eaters, in your case.

MONIQUE: Maybe I should have just shrugged it off, or wrote some sort of caustic, biting piece. I'll be honest with you—what I did was: I actually cried. I sat there and I cried. I called my husband and I said, "This is what they think of me," you know? It was also shameful. I felt a lot of shame. I see that you're in a position to go on CNN and talk shows and present a self that you're really comfortable with. It is not a self that someone else has imposed upon you. You also seem to be very comfortable having an opinion. That's why others ask for your opinion.

VIET: That's one reason why I can't back down when the opportunity presents itself, because I got a great opportunity by winning the Pulitzer Prize. Not everybody gets this opportunity. There has been enough of a cultural shift so that there are enough people, maybe not too many, but enough people in positions of power that have more cultural awareness now, so that so far, I haven't been asked that dog-eating equivalent question.

That, to me, seems to be so much of our struggle—it's not that we want to have the opportunities to be excellent, I think we should have the opportunities to be mediocre. That's the equal opportunity playing field, instead of us having to demonstrate that we are super-qualified for everything, we need just to have the same opportunities as all the mediocre people of the majority. That's the long-term struggle for me.

MONIQUE: The other thing I was thinking about is that this is a very critical moment in US life, in our political life, in terms of just questioning who we are as citizens of this country. Perhaps this is also a strong consideration for you, that in this moment you cannot afford to not speak. I'm wondering if you could talk a bit more about that.

VIET: I do think that we're going through a major crisis in our country's history, our nation's history. That would probably be true for Việt Nam if we consider ourselves to be a part of that country too. That's a different discussion that we should probably have in just a moment. I feel like I have been preparing my entire life for this moment, because I'm not doing anything different now than what I did when I was twenty.

Then and now, the perspective was always: you don't have to wait to be famous before you have an opinion. You should be doing what you believe in and taking every opportunity that you have to express it. Then when the big opportunities come up, you're ready to go. That's what happened to me. When *The Book of Salt* came out in 2003, when we were going to war at that point, did you feel like this was a crisis for you?

MONIQUE: It did, but now Trump feels like an anomaly: a terrible presence that was dropped upon us. Of course, that's not true. He's absolutely a product of the society we have constructed and are living in today. I think about how as authors we all have our short bios that we send out. I used to say I'm a Vietnamese American author. That's always been a part of my short bio. Then beginning with the [2016] election, I started to insert "refugee" because it felt incredibly important to remind everyone that comes across my name and my work that I come from this experience, this same experience that we're debating about as a country and that it's a relevant and a formative experience.

VIET: Maybe it's just my imagination, but it seems to me that Vietnamese American writers are getting angrier. I always felt like I was the angry one, and I'm still the angry one, I'm still out there making forceful opinions, but like you were saying, I think the political climate has changed. Many other Vietnamese American writers who may not have been too political in the past seem to be getting more political now, more vocal on social media, and maybe getting ready to do something else with their art.

MONIQUE: I've always seen myself as a political writer. Even when you look at *The Book of Salt*, it's about the critique of labor and whose labor is compensated, remembered, celebrated. Toklas is Bình's double in that book. She is remembered as being a wonderful hostess, and if you read *The Alice B. Toklas Cook Book*, you know that she had maids and live-in cooks. But was she in the kitchen cooking? No. She was perhaps saying, "I would like to have an omelet."

I consider myself a political writer, but that's not how I'm received. I think that academics recognize that my work is not a gauzy piece of food writing, because that's not how I approach it. But perhaps to a mainstream readership, this is why they come to the book. It's about Paris, food, and there's a Vietnamese-ness to it. That was part of the reason why the book received the success it did and was translated into multiple languages. That same reception was not there for *Bitter in the Mouth*, which is a very American novel. It's regional, Southern, and a clear example of where I did not have perceived authority, and that really affected how the publishing house approached the book. If I were African American, or a white woman, I don't think they would have had any problems allowing me to claim my Southern-ness.

VIET: With *Bitter in the Mouth*, and we're going to have to give away a little bit about it, but halfway through, there is a turning point: the narrator is a Vietnamese adoptee in a Southern white family. At that moment the book changes. Predominantly I think that before, the first half of the book was about the neurological disorder, synesthesia, where she tastes things when she hears words. That's still there in the second half. But in the second half the book gets a lot angrier, I think, especially when we start to talk about the question of her ancestry and how she came to be in this family. Of course, as an angry writer myself, I'm wondering if that threw readers off because of the question of authority that we talked about earlier—when you're talking about Southerners and basically identifying these underlying Trumpisms, several years in advance of the actual manifestation.

MONIQUE: I hate to bring it back to the *New York Times* yet again, but they did me a huge disfavor when they reviewed that novel. They allowed their reviewer to identify the narrator as an Asian American in the first sentence of the review. They defanged and declawed the narrative and the structure that I set up. I believe that it was done simply to say, "Oh, don't worry readers, she's not writing about white folks, she's actually writing about something or someone that she knows." I feel like that novel was never allowed to have a certain kind of punch.

VIET: I didn't read the review, and it can certainly be an outcome of a racist culture to begin with. But what you're saying is, someone with the name of Monique Truong can't be just writing about white people or Southern America without having a Vietnamese component to it.

MONIQUE: Yes, and I think this goes back to what we began talking about: author versus authority, right? This goes back to the question of the author. How we are seen as human beings who have a rather limited function for the society at large. You're Vietnamese American? Okay, you can write about perhaps your refugee experience, someone else's refugee experience, immigration, but if you write, if you claim a regionality, an American regional-ness, that's too complicated.

For me, I've lived in the American South, in North Carolina for the first three years of my life; I learned my English there, and I claim it again and again: I was reborn there in the sense that I was no longer the same little girl after living there. The process of publishing *Bitter in the Mouth* really, pun intended, left an acrid, bitter taste in my mouth about what it meant to be a published writer, you know? Perhaps this was one of the reasons why it took me so long to really reengage again with another novel, because I knew now what it would mean. When I wrote *The Book of Salt*, I honestly had no idea what the publishing process was going to be like. It's brutal, I think.

VIET: If I remember right, with your first book, you had a problem with your agent, with your initial agent who didn't understand *The Book of Salt*, and then you had to get a different agent.

MONIQUE: No, it was the editor who acquired it, based on the first one hundred pages, who ended up despising it. I had to leave that publishing house because the manuscript was rejected. That happened to me with *Bitter in the Mouth* as well. When an author sells a work before it's completed or as an idea, the house can turn around and say, "This is unpublishable." That's actually a legal term in the contract. That means you give back the advance.

VIET: It makes me think, what makes a book "unpublishable"? Basically they mean "unmarketable" in their point of view. That's what happened with *Bitter in the Mouth*?

MONIQUE: Yes, but "unmarketable" has to be couched within assertions that the work lacks quality and merit. The same thing happened to both novels. In each instance, though, my agent was able to find another publishing house that was interested in the manuscript.

VIET: The worst part of writing *The Sympathizer* was when marketing or money issues came up and my agent would tell me, basically, "I don't know if we can sell this book." I didn't want to think about that, because I was having such a great time writing the novel, but then of course we're stuck in that as writers we are also part of this world of labor that you had mentioned earlier and that kind of labor is invisible to the consumers of these books, the readers. I think most readers don't know how these books are made, marketed, and published, and the politics of advances and all that kind of thing.

It's interesting that you are very comfortable with the academic side of reading and writing, and that's a different kind of authority. A lot of writers don't feel comfortable with academic authority. They don't like the way critics treat their work. They don't like the way the critics talk in general. They may find it puzzling to be in a college curriculum, but you find that very amenable. Do you like the ways academics have talked about your work?

MONIQUE: When the essays were starting to appear, it was fascinating to me. I was a literary studies person; this was what I majored in in college. The language was familiar to me, the constructs were familiar to me. It was so exciting and so exhilarating to see my work feeding this kind of academic dialogue. When I first began to publish, in literary journals back in college, I was thinking about my younger sister. I wanted her not to feel so lonely. Then with my novels I thought about my colleagues and the younger folks who are doing this kind of academic work. I wanted them to have something interesting to deal with, something really meaty that they can get into. Same goes for the undergrads reading Asian American literature. The works out there when I was in college seemed a bit one-dimensional to me; they didn't resonate with me. Do you know the scholar David Eng?

VIET: Yes, we were students together at Berkeley.

MONIQUE: I write for David Eng. He's been among the first readers of *The Book of Salt*, *Bitter in the Mouth*, and now *The Sweetest Fruits*. I send the final drafts to him. I just know that if he writes back and identifies the themes that I've been playing with, then my job is done. Then I'll fight and I'll fight with the editors to keep the things that will seem obscure and irrelevant to them about the narrative. Yeah. I'll fight.

VIET: I think you might be one of the first writers I've heard who would acknowledge that one of their primary readers is an academic. Other academics might say that of course about academic work, but rarely have I heard that from a writer. Maybe somebody like Claudia Rankine would be someone very forthright about saying she's been influenced by various kinds of literary and cultural critics and philosophers like Judith Butler, but that that kind of creative writer, fiction writer or poet who acknowledges the importance of theory and criticism and the role of critics is extremely rare in American literature. I find it refreshing, maybe a little shocking as well.

I could see where David would be an authority figure because he's always been an authority figure in Asian American and queer studies.

MONIQUE: Yes, I know. You know how you always get that question at readings: "Who do you write for?" and you kind of answer: "No, I don't write for anyone, I write for myself." But to be truly honest, it's for David Eng.

VIET: He's going to love it when he reads this.

DIALOGUE BETWEEN LAN CAO (UNITED STATES, WEST COAST) AND VINCENT LAM (CANADA, WEST COAST)

LAN: I was born in Việt Nam and thus was immersed in its being from birth. It's the background, the foreground, the surround sound of my life. Việt Nam the country is seamlessly a part of me, even years after I left it. I feel a love for it the way a child remembers mother's milk, childhood lullabies, thumb sucking, sour mangoes with salt. But I was also born into a country that was already at war, and so the war was also ever-present, but in a different way. It's like a beast, a Vietnamese sea monster that you know is there under the water, sometimes unseen. But because it's so big and powerful, even when it's far away from you, you can feel its movement, its thrashing, that churns up the water and makes it turbulent. Once you've seen it, felt it, been affected by its movement, you can never forget it. It stalks you. Its dark energy is inside your deepest core of your deepest being. Even after the monster is dead.

When I was in Việt Nam, the war monster was always orbiting around us even when it's not in Chợ Lớn, Saigon's twin city, where I lived.[7] My first memory was of my father in an airman's uniform. He was off doing battle somewhere far away. When he returned, his boots were muddied. My uncle was a Việt Cộng and he too wrestled with the war monster. When he visited us at our house, it was a secret. Sometimes the war was closer to the capital, and we could feel the windows shake from explosions. Whether nearby or distant, this war just seemed like it was going to be a forever thing. And no one in our family thought it would end or would end in the defeat of the South. People thought America would never let that happen, let the war end with a loss.

VINCENT: I was born in Canada, not long before the fall of Saigon. My mother and father had both left Việt Nam separately as students. My father went to Australia. My mother came to Canada. My father later emigrated to Canada. My parents had known one another as children, and met again in Canada, fell in love and were married. Canada is my home and my country, and yet Việt Nam, its echo, and the repercussions of the Vietnam War framed and shaped not only my understanding of myself in the world but my relationship with the country of my birth, Canada.

I am so envious of your visceral connection to Việt Nam because my connection was always one of longing, absence, and misunderstanding. Meanwhile, I grew up in a place that was comparatively sterile, interpersonally cool. I was further distanced from Canada—the country of my birth—by the sense that others had, and which I could not help but take upon myself, that I was from "somewhere else." As a child growing up in North America, the word "Việt Nam" was inevitably followed by the word "war." In the public sphere this was the only meaning to the place, a country of violence, death, and for the white combatants with whom I felt the most familiarity as a North American child, shame. Shame for having "lost." Shame for having disgraced some imagined mantle of nobility. Yet without the Vietnam War, I would not be a Canadian.

LAN: I think refugee identity is a formative identity to me, and it came upon me as a shock. It is accurate to say Việt Nam is part of my identity, but that would be the case also of a student or tourist from Việt Nam who goes abroad to study or visit, respectively. Việt Nam is part of my identity in that seamless way I mentioned earlier. One is born into it, absorbs it, feels its history and culture in one's bloodstream. But being a refugee is an extra electrical current that comes from a wire being ripped open and the charge that you feel is sizzling and numbing at the same time. This experience has been totally encompassing and defining to me, making me see, for example, the rules of law, the narrative, the perspective from the point of view of the smaller things in life, the smaller countries, the poorer countries, the smaller people within a country, within a family.

Professionally, it made me interested in international human rights, particularly women's rights globally, international law, especially international law from a third world perspective, international trade and how international trade rules affect the economic development of poor countries not fully integrated into the Bretton Woods system. So basically, being a refugee has affected even the topics I write about in my legal scholarship, not just my nonlaw writing.

I identify as a feminist writer. Being a refugee made it easy for me to expand my core perspective to explore the outsider status of others. In my first novel, *Monkey Bridge*, I wrote about the shock of leaving home. It was primal, like being ejected and banished from the Garden of Eden and becoming psychologically a perpetual itinerant in search of a feeling of home. That's the refugee condition. But I also wanted to start from the refugee frame and go on and make parallels with the female condition. Most societies subscribe to a patrilocal, patrilineal, and hence patriarchal system. It's considered a tradition for wives to leave their villages, their homes, to join the husband's.

In *Monkey Bridge*, I showed the everyday disappointment that the mother endured in her marriage, ironically to a politically enlightened Vietnamese man who was a philosopher well-versed in French philosophy. His universe was no longer about just Vietnamese village tradition but encompassed equality, liberty, and fraternity, except, as is very often the case, this new philosophy was extended to the outside world only, the world of politics "out there." At home, he remained traditional. And in many ways this mix is worse for his wife. If he had stayed traditional, he would have understood the meaning of duty and community. Now he became an autonomous man with individual rights but no corresponding duties, leaving the wife worse off.

Because being a refugee is formative for me, it's also affected how I see myself in the new country. Who am I in America? Do I assimilate in a way that makes me more acceptable and palatable to the mainstream? Do I dare squat the Vietnamese way? At the beginning, no. Squatting was what pajama-clad peasants did. Now I'm very comfortable squatting everywhere. In long lines waiting for theater doors to open. I don't care what I look like. Maybe that comes from age. But maybe I imagine passersby being envious I am so flexible I can squat, now that everyone is doing yoga and appreciates weird positions.

VINCENT: Being "other" has always been a strong part of my identity. Born in Canada, I understood how the world looked through the eyes of white-majority Canadians. I could see myself through those eyes and knew that I was "other." Part of this was painful. It was also liberating. I am glad that I never decided to follow the crowd with the fashions of childhood—such as wearing popular clothing and shoes or tried to be part of the in crowd. I intuited that this would not likely work out. I also had enough confidence in the sense of self that my family gave me, that I did not feel this was necessary. So, as a child and teenager, I took a kind of perverse pride in dressing unfashionably, in going through phases of wearing multiple sets of identical outfits day after day, in reading books, in having similarly uncool friends, as if to say to my white-majority classmates: "That's fine! I'm glad to do my own thing!"

I remember when I was about nine or ten years old, riding my bicycle down a street near my home in suburban Ottawa. A car pulled up alongside me, and teenagers in the car began to yell "Hey gook, go home!" over and over again. The driver honked the car horn, and the passengers kept on yelling, and I continued riding my bicycle along the road—staring ahead—until the driver pressed the accelerator and they roared away. I was terrified, angry, indignant. I remember my heart pounding, the fear of knowing that they could have run me down if they had chosen to do so. I also remember that I was already analyzing the episode. They were ignorant, I immediately concluded. They had called me a gook, which was the term that referred to Việt Cộng combatants.[8] They did not even know that my family had come from South Việt Nam, the part of the country that was (nominally) against the "gooks." They did not know that I was ethnic Chinese, part of a group that had often positioned itself as being distinct from the Vietnamese, and whom many ethnic Vietnamese did not regard as being "truly" Vietnamese.

All of this intellectualization allowed me a space, a buffer, in which I could imagine that I was above such racist abuse. I could tell myself that I was smarter than the white kids in the car. I understood both my own history and the history surrounding their choice of slur better than they did, and therefore I could claim not only the moral but the intellectual high ground—I stood above their crass taunts. This was part of an overall pattern that I developed, of coping with racism, racial stereotypes, and microaggressions—by taking the stance of being "smarter than that jerk" or "better informed than that racist." To the extent that relying on intellect for social capital, and for insulation from the barbs of such incidents, I may also have been conforming to another set of equally problematic stereotypes: "Asian people are smart."

LAN: Việt Nam and the geopolitical considerations that dictated in many ways the way the war was fought, the policies that were imposed upon Việt Nam by a superpower like the US have made me very conscious of and curious about the international order. I am intensely interested in global politics and international affairs. As a law professor, I teach international trade and international business transactions, and my scholarship centers on international issues and how they are affected by power, politics, and economics.

Both my legal writing and creative writing, as I mentioned, are rooted in my identity as a refugee. This means that I want to write about things that have preoccupied me emotionally and politically and legally. I am very clear about how I approach this. I am not saying that I am allowed, or I have allowed myself only the right to write about this "small" sliver of the world, where Việt Nam, Vietnamese, and refugee stories touch. I feel I am still confounded by this knot and I'm still looking at it, and slowly untangling it. I'm not the sort of writer who can just pick any issue to write about. My interest just isn't there. It's not that I've disempowered myself or divested myself from the authority to write about something other than war. At the same time, I just don't know what the reception would be if I were to "trespass" into other areas.

VINCENT: The Chinese in Việt Nam are the subject of my novel *The Headmaster's Wager*, and much of the book deals with the politics of being an outsider. Like you, I am very interested in international politics, and these forces also resonate through that book. Being a racialized person has certainly affected the kind of writing that I do. I write alone. Literary fiction is a solitary project, and I realize that this gives me a complete domain within which to work. This allows a great deal of integrity and independence.

An episode in my writing career solidified this direction, which helped me understand why writing in a solitary mode suits me as a person of color. After winning the Scotiabank Giller Prize, Canada's most prestigious literary prize, and after my first book, *Bloodletting and Miraculous Cures*, was adapted for television, where I worked on the show as a consultant, I was invited to be part of the writing room for another television show. The writing room was composed entirely of white Canadians. One day, when I was away from the writing room, an e-mail was circulated by one of the other writers that contained an anti-Asian racist joke. I could not sleep. I was flooded with memories of all the anti-Asian incidents that had occurred to me as a child. I contemplated saying nothing but of course could not do that.

When I spoke to the showrunners about this racist email they explained—with great embarrassment—that there had been some humor mocking Asian people in the writing room during my absence. They recognized this was inappropriate and offensive, and said that they never imagined it would become the subject of an e-mail. The management of the show did everything they should do. They apologized profusely. They had the writer who had sent this e-mail call me and apologize. They promised me that nothing of the sort would happen again. Nonetheless, I decided to leave the show.

This incident, although incredibly hurtful to me, is a minor incident in the horrific range of acts that are committed out of racism. I am recounting it mostly to explain why I think that being "other" has influenced the kind of writer that I am. I left that show, despite the incident being handled properly, because I just did not have the energy to deal with that kind of hurtful dynamic in my life as a writer.

My other area of work is that I am a practicing physician. In that work I routinely handle racialized aggression. I summon the energy to do it because I feel this is part of my contribution to a vital, multiethnic society. A physician's work is inherently in the public eye, and the way in which a physician interacts with every other human being is part of that work. If racism makes my work more difficult, then I should incorporate my responses into my professionalism, I tell myself. I believe that being the best and most humane doctor that I can be slowly begins to challenge racist stereotypes among those who hold them. Despite these fine-sounding words, it is tiring, tiresome, and I wish I did not have to do it.

In contrast, I have decided that in my life as a writer, I do not wish to carry the burden of helping other people reconsider their racism. At least not interpersonally. Readers can take what they will from my books. So I choose not to work on things like television shows that require collaboration. I write my books. I wish for my life as a writer to be deeply true, and so it seems best for it to be solitary. Perhaps this would also be true if I were white, but I think this sense is amplified because I am a person of color.

Who is *your* audience?

LAN: Originally I thought of my audience as the vast empty space that is the non-Vietnamese space. I wandered through the central and branch libraries in Arlington County and Fairfax County, where we lived in Virginia. I saw that there were so many books about Việt Nam but not one had a Vietnamese name as author. So I noticed what was *not* there. And I wanted to fill in that space. That was a very abstract objective. When I actually started writing, I was on the subway in New York City, going to midtown Manhattan, where my law firm was. All around me were faces of strangers, and suddenly I thought these are the strangers who could be my audience if I were to write, and I started writing on the yellow legal pad I had with me in my briefcase. I had no real plan to write, but I just started writing. My mother was sick so somehow a character emerged that fit that story.

I thought a lot about audience and whether one's form and writing style would change depending on that audience. I also thought about my relationship with that audience and that would be a two-way street, between who I am, my natural inclination and propensity, and the audience itself. Because I am a minority writer interested in Việt Nam and war, I knew that many of the readers might have a different perspective than mine. What is my stance? Because I was immersed in political philosophy in college and law school, ranging from [Jürgen] Habermas to [Herbert] Marcuse, the issue of knowledge (and its production, propagation, and interpretation) isn't a peripheral issue to me. How do I write about Việt Nam and the war? And the Vietnamese diaspora community?

I wanted to be understood and seen, and I wanted to write in a way that would facilitate that. I wrote in a way that created a "translation" of what's Vietnamese tradition, food, culture, for the readers, which could include Americans knowing nothing about Việt Nam, Americans knowing the wrong stuff about Việt Nam, and Vietnamese born in America who were seeing Việt Nam through American Hollywood eyes. I've always been fascinated by translation and the issues embedded in that act. How can you study or write about Việt Nam and not know cultural imperialism and all the issues explored in Edward Said's *Orientalism?* These are the issues that helped me determine who my audience is when I write. My novel *Monkey Bridge* is metaphorically also about bridges. From one side to the other. Hopefully it's a reciprocal, two-way crossing. I embrace translation as a way of creating steppingstones and bridges.

VINCENT: Does the Vietnamese diasporic community impact how you write?

LAN: Not in a way that causes me to alter how I write or what I write. But it is part of my audience. I have never lived in or become deeply a part of this community. I left the hometown I lived during my high school years in Virginia where there is a thriving Vietnamese community. And after college I never returned. My professional life and identity are in the wider mainstream, so I am functional in that world. But I have a lot of feelings for my parents' generation, their trauma, their quiet suffering, even if I can be mystified by their old world ways of being. I try to understand where they come from, what their loss was, and not look down on them as being dinosaurs or reactionary.

I do see a communication gap between the younger and older generation. I write about Việt Nam the country, its culture not just the war. I sometimes think it would please them to see that I still remember my past. But in many ways it's probably irrelevant because most of that generation aren't going to read an English-language novel.

DIALOGUE BETWEEN AMY QUAN BARRY (UNITED STATES, MIDWEST) AND THANHHÀ LẠI (UNITED STATES, EAST COAST)

AMY: I won't speak for you, but we may be outliers in the Vietnamese American community. Can you tell me more about your background? I find it really interesting—your family immigrated to the South and lived there, correct? How did you form your identity in that context?

THANHHÀ: My mother is purebred Vietnamese, according to her. She says that we come from some amazing lineage. I don't know who any of these people are, so I just nod yes to her when she tells me about the family, but this has no meaning to me. There's supposedly a cemetery in North Việt Nam where our last name lies. It's there, and it's four thousand years old and it's as old as the country itself—you've got to be somebody to be in that cemetery. I'm probably not going to be in that cemetery when I die, and I'm okay with it. So then when we landed in Alabama, we were seen so much as others because . . .

AMY: And that was in the 1970s?

THANHHÀ: This was in 1975, at the end of the war. Desegregation basically just happened in Alabama. George Wallace was the governor; everything was just upside down then. So we found ourselves in this place and everyone kept looking at us as the Vietnamese version that they saw in a war on TV. So, starting from the age of ten, I was already having to answer other people's projection of my Vietnamese-ness. Of course, by now, at fifty-four, I don't care. Whatever you see is what you see. I know what I am.

AMY: You also have an interesting story about growing up in 1970s Alabama, about feeling like you had to choose a community. It was either a white community or a Black community, and you had to choose, no?

THANHHÀ: I didn't choose. I'd walked into the lunchroom, fourth grade, not speaking English, looking so foreign, looking like one of the war kids they'd seen on TV. Remember, no one knew anything about anything about the Vietnamese then.

AMY: Were there army bases nearby in Alabama where you grew up?

THANHHÀ: No, we were in Montgomery because they were starting to accept refugees there, and a man came and sponsored us, and this man lived in Alabama. So when I walked into that lunchroom without knowing English, I knew I was supposed to choose because it was so visually apparent. White kids on one side, Black kids on the other, I was like "I don't know." Of course, I knew I was supposed to choose the right one, but I didn't know what it was. Both sides were making fun of me. It wasn't like one side said, "Hey, come over here, you're so cool, stay with us." None of them did this; both sides rejected me; both sides made fun of my name.

I just went and ate in the bathroom and called it a day, and this went on for a while before a teacher felt sorry for me and intervened. A teacher found me and asked me to come eat with all the teachers.... At the time, I really wanted to fit in. By now I now longer try to please others and respond to expectations of me. It is too exhausting. For example, going back to writing, I now write about what interests me. For my next novel I am writing about a Texas cowboy inspired by my old classmate. You do this too, right? You wrote about a Mongolian monk, didn't you?

AMY: Yeah, I have. I wrote a novel about Tibetan Buddhist monks who go in search of a reincarnation in Mongolia. It was inspired by a story I heard about the Dalai Lama, maybe ten years ago. He'd said at the time that because He was afraid China was going to name His reincarnation after He dies, He was maybe going to take the incredible step of reincarnating while He's still alive. He doesn't talk about that anymore. But when He said it ten years ago, I was like, *Wow, what would that mean, how does one even go about finding a reincarnation?*

So I have two books coming out in the next couple of years. The book I ended up writing is not about the Dalai Lama's reincarnation per se but about a different reincarnation and the various monks who go looking for it. Like you, I wrote this novel because I was really interested in that story, and I felt I wanted to know and learn more about the subject. I've been to Mongolia and traveled a lot around Asia. I went to Dharamshala, the Dalai Lama's residence-in-exile. I went to Bhutan. I did a lot of research for the book. And I'll say that one of the reasons why I feel free to be able to write this book is because I also don't necessarily feel like I'm a member of any specific diaspora, or a member of any particular community.

I was born in Việt Nam in 1973. Presumably from what I've been told, my mother was Vietnamese and my biological father was an African American soldier, but I was adopted in 1974 and I left Việt Nam at the age of six months. I was raised by a white family primarily on the North Shore of Boston. My parents had three children biologically, and then they adopted my brother, who's half-white, half-Black; and then me—I'm half-Black, half-Vietnamese. In the 1970s and 1980s it was a time when parents, who adopted children transracially, didn't really raise them in the cultures from which they came. In many ways I know more things about being German and Irish, which my parents are, than I know necessarily about being Vietnamese. I suppose some things are lost and some things gained in being raised this way.

One gain has been that I feel free to investigate all different kinds of cultures. I feel like I don't necessarily have a particular label that I necessarily identify with, which allows me to just follow the kinds of things that interest me, wherever that leads. For example, in my first novel, which came out in 2015, I wrote about a Vietnamese psychic in Việt Nam who has the power to hear the voices of the dead. I went to Việt Nam to research that. I'd like to think that because someone like me could write that book, anybody, if they had the interest, could do the same kind of research that I did and could write that book without necessarily being "Vietnamese," whatever that means.

THANHHÀ: And who's to say that a so-called authentic Vietnamese person would be able to do the job that you did. It all has to do with commitment. What are you willing to do? How much blood are you willing to give to this project? And once you've decided that, anything is open to you. I commend you for going out there and just doing what you want. . . . You do not speak Vietnamese, and you went out, and you did that project. Just because you speak Vietnamese does not mean you can do a good job with a novel about Việt Nam.

AMY: Yeah. Again, I feel like my story in some ways should be liberating for all kinds of writers. But I can see that although I'd like to live in this la-la land where anybody should be able to do these kinds of things, I can also appreciate that within the publishing world, there are other kinds of pressures. Look at Chinese American writer Bill Cheng, who wrote *Southern Cross the Dog*—people gave him a hard time for being a Chinese American writer who wrote about Black blues men in the South.

THANHHÀ: Right.

AMY: And again, the question is: Would people have had the same kind of issues if he himself were African American? I do feel like in certain ways my novel might have been given more scrutiny, or at least a certain kind of scrutiny, if I did not have the middle name Quan.

THANHHÀ: Doesn't it have to do with how your characters and how your story represents characters in the novel itself? For example, it doesn't matter what background you're on, if you're going to do a disastrous job developing your characters and make them all look like idiots, you're going to have a problem. So shouldn't it go back to the writing of the text itself?

AMY: Exactly. For starters, I mostly choose not to use any kind of author photos. I'm not on Twitter, I'm not on Facebook. And part of the reason why I've chosen not to do those things is because it's not who I am. I'm just a very private person in certain kind of ways.

THANHHÀ: Bravo, we need more of that.

AMY: There's that, but then there's other stuff too. I publish under the name Quan Barry—I don't use my first name, which is Amy. Part of the reason for that was that I liked the idea that Quan sounds unisex. I like the idea that it's not clear if the author is a man or a woman. There are various ways in which I've tried to erase myself as an author, and I can see the pros and cons of that because I understand that it's important for younger authors to be able to see writers who look like me and have my kind of story. I get the importance of that. And yet for me personally, I just felt like I didn't want to have to play that game. I feel like by erasing myself in certain kinds of ways, it may have allowed me to be not quite as pigeonholed as I might have been. So, like I said, I can see both sides, the pros and the cons of that.

THANHHÀ: Where did Quan come from?

AMY: According to my parents, Quan was my last name. It's been interesting to think about that again in terms of, when you do erase yourself, what do you gain, and what do you lose . . . those kinds of things. Because I'm half-Black, and I look half-Black, when people see me they tend to assume that I'm Black, and they don't assume that I'm Asian. As a child, when I would be called racial slurs, it would be the n-word, that's what people see. It's interesting now that I have this "career."

I think it would have been interesting if the name I published under, instead of being Quan Barry, if the name was Amy Barry, because Amy Barry is such a generic name, it could be anybody. You don't necessarily hear anything ethnic in the name. I've done online searches for Amy Barry and they're all mostly white, you know what I mean to say? Now I think it's too late for me to change that, but I sometimes wonder, if I had just published under Amy Barry, would readers' heads explode? But yes, going back to something that you'd said earlier. I'm interested by this idea of hierarchy within the diaspora.

THANHHÀ: It is also about who gets to decide what story is published, and which story is good.

AMY: In all kinds of diasporas, you hear people talking about this.

THANHHÀ: For a woman writer who is seen as Vietnamese, you also must deal with the pressure from the community. This has been hard for me. There are always certain self-appointed readers in the community who are going to take one of the roles of watchdogs— people who will tell you whether you are good enough for this or that. For Vietnamese women writers it is hard to disentangle the public persona from the personal. I feel scrutinized. There's a universal idea of what a Vietnamese perfect woman is like: to be a virgin when she gets married, be financially successful, manage the house and raise five perfect children, and a husband who never has to change a diaper. These myths put a lot of pressure on people like me, and I know people who aspire to that myth and have been able to do it, at a high cost. Thirty years later, they're exhausted, they feel they're about to die, but they did it. They tried very, very hard.

I knew right away this wasn't for me. But the pressure to be perfect is very strong. For whatever reason, I never had it.

AMY: I hear what you're saying. This must make things difficult to become a writer. In terms of publishing. I just came back from a book festival in India with all different authors from Southeast Asia and South India and South Asia. And the question of authenticity always comes up, like, you can't write about Việt Nam unless you include a water buffalo somewhere. I met an Indonesian author who said that nobody in the States wants to publish stories in translation about contemporary Indonesia; they only want stories that take place under the dictatorship. It's more about America's need for certain kinds of familiar stories than the writing itself, it seems.

THANHHÀ: Right.

AMY: Do you feel that if you branched out and were writing about subjects that didn't necessarily have anything to do with Việt Nam, the response to your book and to you would be different?

THANHHÀ: It has already happened. My first book was about a refugee girl, the dire war girl who does not know English and must pull herself up. That story is very popular, it's being taught in eighth grade. My second novel is about a rich girl growing up with parents from Việt Nam. She's American, she doesn't even want to speak Vietnamese, she doesn't want to have anything to do with Việt Nam, she's a surfer girl, she drinks mango smoothies, she eats fish tacos. That story didn't go very far because she's rich, and she's annoying and not authentically Vietnamese in the way that one may expect it to be.

AMY: What do you mean by "it didn't go very far"?

THANHHÀ: People aren't reading it; people aren't buying it in the same way as the other book. And as an author, if I let this affect me, it would be hard. I just had to say, once I finish a story, that I'm done. Whoever buys it, whatever happens to it, is none of my business. I don't even read my reviews. My editor sends the ones she wants me to read, and I only read those ones, that's it; I don't look myself up on Goodreads.

AMY: Yeah, I know. It's hard.

THANHHÀ: Who's reading my story and how they interpret my story may be very different from what I intend. Maybe teachers use my first book to send the message to refugee kids and immigrant kids: "You can do it, because Thanhha did it." You cannot say this about my second book, which is more about traveling to Việt Nam and privileges. Teachers may think that it may make the kids feel bad about their own situation, remind them of inequality and disparity. I get it. So it's fine with me. Do I regret writing it although it is not as well received? No, I don't.

AMY: I've always had that attitude too. It's my job to write the book, and it's the publisher's job to sell it. They either do it or they don't. I had this interesting conversation with my agent. Basically she was telling me that Americans don't read novels that aren't set in the United States and don't have white characters in them. My first novel was set in Việt Nam and there were no white characters; the second book is set in Mongolia, and there are no white characters either. I was surprised to hear my agent hint that it may be hard to sell this book because of this; it's not about the writing.

THANHHÀ: For a certain kind of reader, there's now a huge movement to go beyond what you know and read outside of that. But the writing is still very important; the book still has to be interesting and has to be good. And who's to say what's good or not; it's like food in a way. We cannot get upset about reviews.

AMY: It seems there's an implicit understanding of what people are interested in reading, and that writers sometimes give into that demand to be read widely. You mentioned that your first book was the pluckier immigrant story in a certain way.

THANHHÀ: Right. In general, I do not think about the audience. To just write a novel is already so taxing, by the time I get the voice, the pacing, the characters, the surprises, and the magical moments.... Once I get all that done, I don't have time to consider anything else. Instead of thinking about Vietnamese-ness, I am more concerned about gender. I will never write about a sappy woman character that I would not want to hang out with. I expect her to have some spunk, I expect her to be able to do things on her own, and I expect her to be active. To me that's the benchmark. I have to be able to look at my character and think she is interesting, whatever that means to me.

This may have to do with my own experience. Mainstream reviewers and readership are one thing. I also feel much pressure from family and community. Although I was more carefree as the youngest child, I was still supposed to grow up, marry a doctor and be a virgin until I got married, and then have two kids, live in a big house, have a new car every two years, the whole nine yards that makes refugeehood shine. I had to rebel against these pressures to be a writer. Maybe this is a bigger fight and issue for me. It is very selfish of me in a way to write what I want and create female characters that I find cool. But that's what I do and that's as far as I've gone.

Do you feel like you must make Vietnamese look good when you write?

AMY: I don't have this family pressure. Similarly to you when I write, I don't consider that. I consider what the character needs, what the story needs. But I now realize in my novel, in hindsight, there's one moment that made me pause. There's a scene where a dog is served up as food in a restaurant. I needed this to happen, but the way the dog is prepared is just brutal. And again, the story needed it, the moment needed it. After the book came out, I chose this section to read at public events because the section is self-contained; it's an easy piece to read to an audience. After a while it became problematic for me though, to read it. One day, somebody asked me if it was true, if this happened? And then I realized that people are thinking that it does. I responded that people maybe do still eat dogs, but there's a more humane way of preparing it. Basically, in the story the dog is beaten to death to make the meat more tender. The questions about "is this true" made me uneasy and had me thinking about my responsibility.

THANHHÀ: Did you feel that you were perpetuating stereotypes?

AMY: Yes, which I hadn't thought about at the time I wrote it. Nobody's ever come up to me and said, "You shouldn't have had that scene in there, it sets us back." But it's complicated.

THREE

―――――

Writing Feminism and Disobedience

In their literary and poetic work, diasporic Vietnamese women writers are conscious about not depicting their diasporic female characters as stereotypical prostitutes nor as passive, exotic victims ready to sacrifice their lives for white men, such as in the Broadway musical *Miss Saigon*. They do not represent Asian women as Dragon Ladies as heartless and hypersexualized characters perpetuated and disseminated by Hollywood movies, ranging from Fu Man Chu's daughter to movies starring Lucy Liu.[1] Furthermore, none of these writers represent Vietnamese women as strictly sacrificial mothers, treasonous prostitutes, or waiting wives as in films produced in Việt Nam by Vietnamese men.[2] On the contrary, these women live and write *against* heterosexist and racist stereotypes of Vietnamese and diasporic Vietnamese women so prevalent in society.

Since the unprecedented success of Maxine Hong Kingston's *The Woman Warrior* (1975), autobiographies and creative nonfiction by Asian American women writers have flourished in Asian American literature. According to Asian American literary critics Elaine Kim and Lisa Lowe, it has indeed been relatively easier for Asian American women writers to publish a memoir about their relationship with their mother than a novel or a collection of short stories with more threatening themes.[3] Less understood, however, are the pressures Asian American women writers experience so as not to embarrass or shame their family by revealing secrets and personal matters. For Vietnamese American women writers and others in the diaspora, this pressure is particularly complicated because refugee families have been strained to make extremely difficult choices when forced out of their country and during resettlement, leading at times to domestic violence.[4]

Community pressures on cultural productions have been less acknowledged in academia due to people of color's collective drive and need to unite in the face of racism.[5] For Vietnamese Americans there is the additional need to defend the community from cultural amnesia in relation to a war lost.[6] In addition, as daughter of Asian parents, they may feel the weight of being the recipient of parents' sacrifices. erin Khuê Ninh explains that parents from Asia who have internalized the belief that Asian Americans are inherently destined to be successful model minorities can discipline their daughters by speaking of their sacrifices in excess and severely restricting their daily lives. Experiencing parental love as conditional, daughters can be forced, through guilt and shame, to become diligent, docile, and chaste, and not express the hurt and psychological wounds this process may cause. It is no coincidence, Ninh highlights in her scholarship that anger and bitterness, leading to self-destructive thoughts and behaviors, pervade literary narratives written by second-generation Asian American women writers.[7]

Vietnamese American women writers of the second generation such as lê thị diễm thúy, author of *The Gangster We Are All Looking For* (2003), can be subject to the *triple pressures* of being the "good silent" model minority, the "good silent" Asian American daughter, and the "good silent" daughter of refugees responsible for protecting the family's honor. Such a writer rebels against such pressures at a cost. They furthermore cannot easily trust mainstream readers because of their insistent voyeuristic gaze that has been shaped by a US history of racism and (hetero)sexism against Asian American women, a gaze exacerbated and shaped by wars in Asia where women were commonly treated as sexual objects of conquest.

The act of writing against white mainstream expectations *and* community pressures is shared in the following dialogues. Whether they create graphic novels, music and songs, memoirs, novels, or poems, these artists live and write against mainstream audiences' gendered and racialized stereotypes, and to not succumb to community pressures of filial piety. It is because their works and their voices put forth incisive critiques of identity politics that still prioritize race over gender, we regard them as feminist.

DIALOGUE BETWEEN HOAI HUONG AUBERT-NGUYEN (FRANCE) AND VAAN NGUYEN (ISRAEL)

HOAI HUONG: What are your main inspirations in the poetry of Israel, Việt Nam, or other countries?

VAAN: I started writing poems and short stories at the age of ten, but I was growing up free of style because I was just reading literature until the age of sixteen. Then I discovered British poetry via a secondhand book I found in a market stall. They were Wordsworth, Villon, Byron, Lawrence, etc., who gave me a glimpse into the magic you can do with words. I didn't understand the poetry fully because English is not my first language, but I enjoyed it overall—both their poems and biographies. I understood their way of life, mainly because I didn't plan to live longer than the age of thirty, and I just wanted to be something great until the end.

On my twentieth [birthday] a lover gave me a book of Yehuda Amichai's love poems, and my elder sister gave me a book by Zelda, both of whom are Hebrew poets. I was amazed by their works. It was a new chapter in my writing inspirations. I tried to write with Zelda and Amichai aesthetics and found a mix of voices were inside of me, since their poetry is completely different from one another. Zelda is more religious and humbler; her poetry is like a string of smart little pearls, so private and full of beliefs. And Amichai gave a delicate and immediate map of different realities. I then went on a search of all the greatest Hebrew writers that I haven't still been able to read, but it was a journey to learn more about this literature and also my Israeli cultural identity.

On a trip to Paris in my early twenties I bought a Beat anthology and found out about the American modernists Ginsberg, Ferlinghetti, Di Prima, and so on; it really blew my mind. For once, I finally had music in my head while reading, but I'm not music-oriented and have no talent for it. But it felt different, and I realized it was my notion of an urban kind of rhythm. I wanted to adopt it and really got into writing poems. Around this age I wrote most of my poems. It came out naturally, without much hardship, and it felt spiritual. I didn't come across Vietnamese poetry until recently, when I got involved with the

Vietnamese American scene, and through these connections I have been exposed to contemporary Vietnamese American poetry. I wish to be acquainted with more, this is a lack on my part, since there aren't many Viet-Israeli writers in Israel except for me, but that's because there are only about three hundred Viet-Israelis here, so what are the chances? Also, I don't read Vietnamese, so the only solution is to search for English translations. I believe this will be a new and significant part of my research. I wish to know more about my fellow Vietnamese in diaspora.

What are your main inspirations in the French, Vietnamese, or other country's poetry?

HOAI HUONG: I was a rather lonely child, so I found friends and refuge in books that made me travel through stories and imagination. I first discovered French poets as different as Marie de France, Victor Hugo, or Arthur Rimbaud, and surrealist poets as Apollinaire or Paul Éluard, whose texts seemed very enigmatic to me. Nevertheless, in their work I found an inspiring feeling of freedom and passion, and the belief that poetry was a way to seek out beauty and mystery in the world.

When I was fifteen or sixteen years old, I traveled to Ireland, where I discovered the Celtic culture and the work of poets like W. B. Yeats or Seamus Heaney, who mix myths, magic, and reality. I also traveled to England and to the United States, and love the poems of Shakespeare, Lewis Carroll, Edgar Allan Poe, or Emily Dickinson. I was fascinated by their powerful expressions of desire, love, and madness, and also by the wit and the humor that appear in a lot of their texts.

When I began my literary studies, I discovered Asian poetry. I admire ancient Chinese and Japanese literature: the Tang's dynasty poems or the haiku poems in the spirit of Bashô, which are so humble and delicate. Naturally, I am also very attached to the Vietnamese literature, even if I have to learn more about it, like the work of Nguyễn Du, or modern ones as the poets of Thơ Mới [New Poetry].[8] In their works I discovered a great way to express the fragile beauty of nature and the human tragedy, especially in the poetry of Hàn Mặc Tử, a young Vietnamese poet who had contracted leprosy and died at twenty-eight.[9]

All these poets and their works are inspiring to me, inciting me to search for the connections between cultures and the music of words and images. I started by writing poetry in a haiku style in French and imagined a dialogue between a French and a Vietnamese voice in my collected poems, *Perfumes* (2005), for example. After this I wrote novels where I tried to intertwine a narrative with a poetic voice; I also wanted to talk to my Vietnamese and French mixed cultures through the evocation of the Indochina War, as with my first novel *The Soft Shadow* (2013). I have never been to Israel, but the Bible and the biblical tradition in art and literature are also an inspiration for me.

What about you?

VAAN: Yes, the Hebrew Bible is being taught here in Israel from elementary school to all pupils from secular and orthodox systems in various depths. It has an influence on the soul and artistic life of Jewish Israelis. There are also different studying systems for Christian Arabs and Muslim Arabs, but I'm not sure they study the Hebrew Bible. The language in the Hebrew Bible is amazingly beautiful but archaic, we don't use this kind of Hebrew in our daily lives. When one mentions poetry in the Bible, people are referring to the book Song of Songs, which is believed to be written by King Solomon and contains love poems for a lover or for God, depending on one's interpretation.

The only book from the Hebrew Bible that I found myself reading over and over again is the Scroll of Ecclesiastes, a mesmerizing piece. It was said that three people wrote it, maybe King Solomon in his old days, maybe King David or his son etc. Anyway, the narrator is Kohelet, and he writes in third person. The book contains a poetic search for and wise notes on the existence of a man and the meaning of life. The message revealed is that everything is meaningless, all is vanity and doomed; a man dies in the end, but really he should enjoy his life in moderation because there is no real advantage in what he gains or does in life, and in fact we should focus only on working with God.

What kind of inspiration do you find in the Bible? Do you mean the Hebrew Bible or the New Testimony?

HOAI HUONG: The Hebrew Bible and the New Testament are both very inspiring for me. The Song of Songs is a masterpiece: the fine writing, the symbolic theme of the garden, the search and the expression of love are truly poetic ideals. I am fascinated by the stories and myths of both the Hebrew Bible and of the New Testament. There are so many patterns that it is impossible to mention them all. But if I have to talk about one element that touches me particularly, it may be the role of women in these books. In the Hebrew Bible there are so many wonderful female figures: Eve at first or Ruth, who faithfully stays with her mother-in-law; or Judith, who beheads Holofernes; or Bathsheba, who seduces King David and becomes King Solomon's mother. In the New Testament there are also many extraordinary female figures: the Virgin Mary but also her cousin the old Elisabeth who comes to prophesy, or the cruel Herodias and her beautiful daughter Salome, or the wise Martha, or the mysterious woman who pours perfume on Jesus's body before his crucifixion . . .

These heroines are inspiring: they are wives, widows, mothers, sisters, lovers, warriors. . . . They are both darkness and light and have moments of joy and sorrow. They can be sinners and murderers, but they also give life and contribute to salvation. This complexity is a fascinating point of these stories. Are figures of women an inspiration for your work?

VAAN: It's good you mention Ruth, she was a Gentile, that's how Jewish call non-Jewish people. I grew up hearing about her from friends, parents, and educators since I was a kid. They told me I should convert and be like Ruth the "Proselyte" because of how she left her country and her parents, to follow her mother-in-law to a new nation. They wanted me to leave my "Vietnamese" heritage, they couldn't grasp the idea that I'm not fully Vietnamese and should really consider myself more Israeli culturally. But that's not right either, and I'm torn and refuse to declare either way.

When I became a young woman, Jewish mothers were afraid I'd date their boys, like Ruth did, seducing Boaz in the field. One mother told me that I am "the nightmare of every Jewish mother." Of course, it offended me a lot. Until this day I'm not sure if she said it because I was a non-Jewish or because I was a seducer in her eyes. Anyway, during some years I converted and became a Reformed Jew. I wanted to belong, and this was the closest to my beliefs. But I do ceremonies, like lighting candles and welcoming Sabbath with a prayer. Sometimes I celebrate the holidays with my secular Jewish friends. It's formless and I prefer these flexibilities in my rituals. Eventually I want to write spiritual poetry. I think living a wondrous life in wonder is a start.

Do gender issues matter in your work? How do you relate to the MeToo movement as a female writer?

HOAI HUONG: #MeToo is a powerful movement for women's rights and equality between men and women. It is important to me as a woman and a citizen, and it is also an important theme of my books. In my first novel, *The Soft Shadow*, the heroine is Mai, a young Vietnamese girl who falls in love with a French soldier in the 1950s. The book is about the wish for life and happiness in a time of war. In my second novel, *Under the Burning Sky* (2017), there are different female characters: a mother with her two little girls, or a teenager whose father wants to take her and her whole family to fight in the Việt Nam social revolution. All of them will die because of the madness of war.

In these stories the female question is related to issues of education, of motherhood, of belonging to a group, or of individual freedom. It leads to a reflection about what is respectively expected of girls and boys. For example, in the first novel Mai's family wants her to marry a rich man that her father had chosen for her. In the second novel the main character Tuân doesn't want to become a soldier, so he is accused of treason and cowardice. But the reason is that Tuân doesn't want to kill other people, he doesn't want to take part in a terrible and senseless struggle. The best way for him to fight is to become a writer—to share his desire for life and peace. And the best way for Mai to free herself is to refuse an arranged marriage, even if it exposes her to shame and ostracism.

I am moved about how you talk about your experiences. How does the fact of being a woman between two different cultures influence your life and work?

VAAN: As a woman, I'm in the middle of a long conflict, it starts with a domestic life as a future wife, where my dad tells me to get married with whomever and have kids, abandon cigarettes and writing, be "a woman," move back to Việt Nam maybe and be modest. I am a "leftover" woman, because to be single at my age is unacceptable. But on the other hand, there is an existential wish to fulfill my soul and to choose for myself, not to compromise my life and art. Anyway, I'm not sure I chose this life, because I didn't find myself being a rebel to tradition, it just happened. So, with my foray into poetry, people had expected me to write about late femininity—about motherhood—but it turns out I'm writing about sex.

As a poet between two cultures, I get the chance to portray local and exotic themes in an authentic way, like in my poem "Mekong River," there is the Mekong River and the Tigris-Euphrates River, but it doesn't seem disconnected. I can use banal motifs from two cultures, and it seems to work for me. Here is the whole poem (translated from Hebrew by Adriana X. Jacobs, taken from *The Truffle Eye*) for context :

Mekong River

Tonight I moved between three beds
like I was sailing on the Mekong
and whispered the beauty of the Tigris and the Euphrates
under an endless moment
looking
below the left tit
I have a hole
and you fill it
with other men.
Notes of Tiger beer
on your body.
Alone,
crickets drone south of Laos.
Showers of cold air from Hanoi
the back gasps
the tight ass, an ink stain on the belly.
Sketch me a monochrome
flow chart
on fresh
potted flowers.
I'll release roots at your feet,
I want to come to puke
specks of dust
in my crotch. Rest your hand
in my pants. Make it personal
Who dares abandon an illness mid-sea?

What about you? How does the fact of being a woman between two different cultures influence your life and work?

HOAI HUONG: Your poem is amazing! I like the music of your words and the strong images connecting the Mekong River and the Tigris and Euphrates Rivers. Thank you for sharing. I am sorry, my books are not translated in English. I hope they will be someday, so that I could share them with you.

I was born in France, so I was not supposed to be a traditional Vietnamese girl, and I was not expected to be a typical French girl either. Growing up between two cultures gave me a kind of freedom— to become someone else, someone who was not determined only by her native culture, someone who could choose her own way of thinking in a very different country that welcomed my parents at a key moment. France was a great chance for my family and for me. As a writer, I am inspired by my Vietnamese culture as well as my French culture, and moreover, by my relationship between them.

My two first novels take place between France and Việt Nam: the first one in Belle-Ile, Bretagne, and Hà Nội; and the second one in Chantilly, near Paris, Huế, and Sài Gòn. The stories talk about the Indochina and the Vietnam War, but they also talk about French and Vietnamese intertwined histories. The two countries struggled against the other in the colonial war, but they also intertwine in terms of my characters' lives or in the arts in general. For example, the Citadel of Huế is a treasure of Vietnamese traditional culture, but it was also built with the help of French architects: the pagodas, the dragons, and the phoenix are strangely surrounded by walls and ramparts constructed in Vauban's style.[10] Some of my Vietnamese characters fall in love with the French culture, in spite of the war and, in the mind of one of them, the trails of Chantilly's forest lead to the banks of the Perfume River through memory and imagination.

My third novel, *The Cry of Dawn* (2019), is a bit different. I tried to imagine a place that doesn't exist. This place is called An Linh and looks like Việt Nam in the nineteenth century, but it is not Việt Nam. It is an island that resembles some islands in France, but it isn't France either. In this place you can find names, landscapes, trees, and flowers of both countries. It is an imaginary world that mixes the two countries and traditions.

I understand that you were born in Israel. How did you feel when you first went to Việt Nam?

VAAN: I was ten years old when I first came to Việt Nam. I remember a lot of bicycles on the streets and the smell of food and incense everywhere. I went to sleep early on the eve of Tết, but I couldn't because of the fireworks that were going on the whole night.[11] I remember going to the village, for my father's side of the family, and there were no modern toilets. I remember being scared to go out at night, to look for a hole in the ground where everyone in the village used as a toilet. I remember smiling people.

Since then, I have come to Việt Nam seven times. Each time, I feel like everyone is my family (because I used to hear Vietnamese only from my parents, so it made me feel close and comfortable like it was home). As I grew up, the notion of belonging was strong in my adolescence, because I had a hard time during middle school because I looked so different from my classmates. But in Việt Nam everyone looks like me.

My Vietnamese is very thin, I use only a few basic words, daily words. I can't have meaningful and deep conversations, and I can't hold more than ten minutes of talking. So that alighted me and I began to look for "my people" in Israel, where I found friends and a sort of community of artists, a milieu. These days [in 2020] I'm in quarantine in Việt Nam, it's been a boring and hard two weeks, but tomorrow I'll be out. My dad wants me to meet men for the purposes of marriage. He says he'll arrange it somehow. I told him I don't mind and *que será*.

Were you born in Việt Nam? If so, how was your first time going back there after it opened up to Việt Kiều? If not, were you born in France? How was your first trip to Việt Nam? How did you feel?

HOAI HUONG: I first went to Việt Nam when I was around twenty years old. I traveled with my husband, Thomas. We were students then and *tây ba lô*, as people say.[12] I should say that Thomas is French, he doesn't speak Vietnamese, even if he understands some words and knows a lot about Việt Nam's culture. It was a great discovery. Our first impression was the beauty of the country: the rice fields, the rivers, the East See, the pagodas, the people. . . . We walked around the Sword Lake, or Hồ Hoàn Kiếm, in Hà Nội, we admired the *hoa phượng* on blazing-red trees and the city's life all around.[13] Everything was new and amazing for us. But I also remember the difficult relationships we had with some people because we were of mixed origins and unmarried at that time. But we didn't mind.

During this trip I discovered the country of my parents, and so many things I had heard about as a child: the hot and humid climate, the monsoon rains, the lush landscapes, the noisy streets, the different Vietnamese accents, the markets, the food, the fruits, the flowers, the smells.... It was like going back home but to an unknown place. My parents moved to France on the April 30, 1975, just as Saigon fell.[14] Then, when I was born, they chose for me the first name Hoai Huong, where Hoài means "to remember" and Hương is "the country." It was essential for me to discover Việt Nam, even if I am from two countries.

I wish you the best for your travel. What are your plans or ideas for your third poetry book?

VAAN: I have already written a couple of poems during my quarantine here. I hope to write about village life, when I go to my father's family in Bồng Sơn in northern Việt Nam. I wish to write poems about my mental journey in Việt Nam, maybe around family and identity issues. I believe this is my most important trip to Việt Nam because this is my last chance to have a long trip before I settle down. I believe spirituality is a continuation of the head and body, and I want to do more research on spirituality before I write. This journey will be documented in my third book in an Ars poetic manner.[15] It will be a reflective, a capsule of feeling, and of living a life after the age of thirty-eight. It won't be wild; it will be my private, domesticated poetry. My poetry provides a place for me to distance myself from everyday existence and create my own private mythology. The stories I tell in my poems map my relationships with other people, with my community, with art, nature, and the world.

What are your plans or ideas for your next fiction book?

HOAI HUONG: I am working on *Tender Darkness*, a new novel that takes place in the north of France in the 1950s. It is the story of a young woman whose mother is Vietnamese and whose father is English. She is a pianist and lives in a strange house by the sea, where people say there are ghosts. It will be a kind of tragedy because of a destructive love relationship with a madman. This book talks about mixed cultures, about passion and music, and addresses the subject of women and the difficult transition from childhood to adulthood. The writing will mix fiction and poetry by the insertion of short poems in the narration. I am also working on a poetry book titled *Leaves in the Wind*. I wrote the poems and a friend of mine, Valérie Linder, who is a wonderful French artist, has made the illustrations. This book is about nature, the landscapes, the beauty of spring, rivers, trees and leaves, and a reflection about the need to protect nature. . . . It will be a dialogue between texts and images, between simple words, drawing, and colors.

Thank you very much for this friendly and stimulating dialogue.

DIALOGUE BETWEEN ABBIGAIL NGUYEN ROSEWOOD (UNITED STATES, EAST COAST) AND VIOLET KUPERSMITH (UNITED STATES, EAST COAST)

ABBIGAIL: How does being a disobedient woman play into your work?

VIOLET: That's one of my most favorite topics. Do you see yourself as a disobedient Vietnamese woman?

ABBIGAIL: Being disobedient, I feel, implies a framework, an expectation you're working against. Growing up in Việt Nam, I was often praised for being demure and quiet—qualities valued in a traditional culture and in a traditional Vietnamese woman. For a long time I took pride in revealing my presence through means other than my voice. Being an Asian woman living in the United States and possessing feminine-representing attributes like my long hair, a high-pitched voice, I sometimes feel the pressure to subvert stereotypes because people tend to assume introverted individuals don't have much to offer. If I were to react against the Western assumptions of Asian women and force myself to be more outspoken and abrasive, then I would still just be reacting. The shadows of the frameworks are still there, both the Vietnamese one and the American one.

Rather, I focus on being loud in my work, as truthful as I can be, and with as much courage as I can muster. When I was still in my MFA program, I repeatedly received the message that my writing needed to signal the Vietnam War in some ways. During the semester students would get the chance to meet with their professor one-on-one a few times to discuss their progress. Once, in class, my professor gave me the advice that my short story needed to mention the Vietnam War. I decided to never go to the one-on-one meetings. I was angry. Perhaps it was arrogant of me, but I thought to myself, *If they really have that perspective, there is nothing I want to learn from them.* The world had already told me over and over again that my perspective didn't belong, and I didn't need to willingly submit myself to more brainwashing. Professors can be deeply wrong. Being disobedient can just mean questioning, especially questioning authorities, whether it be the niche world of fiction or the White House. Artmaking is disobedient as society is constantly shouting at us that it neither values nor has room for art.

VIOLET: I think that my decision to make a living through artmaking is the root of my own Vietnamese disobedience. From a young age I was very aware of the traditional Asian American doctor-lawyer-engineer acceptable career trifecta. As a child of immigrants, you have the responsibility to transmute your parents' sacrifice into success, and this is what success looks like to them. It certainly doesn't look like me—I write ghost stories for a living.

ABBIGAIL: Which is awesome.

VIOLET: It's awesome to me, but it's not something that my very large, very Catholic Houston Vietnamese family has ever really understood. To be a twenty-nine-year-old unmarried and childless woman with an unstable income from writing books is something aberrant. All of my other first-generation cousins have chosen "appropriate" careers and lives for themselves in the eyes of our diaspora's ecosystem. Their "Vietnamese-ness" is acceptable and mine is not, per their rubric. And I think that there's something kind of twisted about the fact that one of my greatest acts of unacceptable "Vietnamese-ness" was going back to live in Việt Nam.

ABBIGAIL: Why did you go back?

VIOLET: I went because I thought it was the best way to the stories I wanted to tell. On some level I knew that to write effectively about misbehaving women, I would have to follow their lead.

ABBIGAIL: Against what your family expected of you.

VIOLET: Yes! My writing is heavily inspired by fairy tales, and my favorite ones are the kind where everything gets set off by an act of disobedience. Someone eats something they're told not to or goes into the forbidden woods or through the forbidden doorway or steals something they shouldn't. Because nothing interesting can happen if everyone follows the rules. Do you relate to this?

ABBIGAIL: I love fairy tales for the reasons you mentioned. The protagonist tends to get into trouble by breaking the rules, and not listening to the advice of an old sage. Then something spills, cracks, and catapults them onto a physical or psychic journey, often one inducing the other. Good stories tend to burst forth from this open wound, this defiance of tradition. If I were to think of my mother as a character in a fairy tale, I believe she would be described as a disobedient woman.

VIOLET: How so?

ABBIGAIL: I don't think she was ever happy as a stay-at-home mother. In the context of a fairy tale, my father's death might be drawn as the prince who was trying to climb up Rapunzel's tower but ended up falling into the abyss. Once the worst had happened, my mother the princess had nothing left to fear. So she cut off her own hair and wove it into a rope to help her climb down the tower, then went on her own solitary adventure. It's funny, my mother has always had short hair, but coarse and strong. In my imagined fairy tale of her, I can visualize this rope of hair linking her to her past self. Somewhere, that rope is still there, untethered. People say that love gives strength, but so does losing love—after such loss the princess knew there was nothing in the world she couldn't overcome. It's ironic because it requires the death of my father to crack open my mother's false shell of a princess waiting for a prince. I believe she was always meant to be what she has become.

How about your mother?

VIOLET: I think in our fairy tale context my mother is equal parts princess and equal parts dragon. When I think of her, what always comes to mind first are her dragony parts—her bravery, her fierceness, and her protectiveness—but she spent a lot of her early life in the convent, which feels very close to the trapped damsel archetype.

ABBIGAIL: That's the ultimate obedience. As a nun, I imagine she had many rules imposed on her, but she found her way beyond them.

VIOLET: The very fact that I'm here right now is proof that she did. If she was a trapped princess, she torched her own tower, and I hope that I inherited at least some of that rebel DNA.

ABBIGAIL: A seed planted from one generation and passed down to the next.

VIOLET: It feels very matrilineal to me. I think the seed came from her mother, who inherited it from her mother.

ABBIGAIL: Việt Nam is quite matriarchal compared to other Asian cultures. Like the story of Hai Bà Trưng, which I believe shapes the national consciousness.[16]

VIOLET: Yes! It is the greatest story. Warrior sisters on elephants, right?

ABBIGAIL: They rode elephants into battles while pregnant. So fierce.

VIOLET: I love that. Maternal warriorhood is brilliantly subversive.

ABBIGAIL: Even though Vietnamese women may feel pressured to be obedient, those stories hint at a different reality, where women can gain strength from their very femininity, like Hai Bà Trưng from their pregnancies. These tales are a part of my DNA.

VIOLET: How does this DNA appear in your books, if it does.

ABBIGAIL: In my novel *If I Had Two Lives*, the protagonist doesn't follow the heterosexual and monogamous relationship orientation. Love guides her to challenging places. She falls in love with a woman and in a way with the woman's husband as well. She gave birth to this couple's child but ended up raising the child with her neighbor. The story organically evolves into what it is today, but I was working with the consciousness that there are countless relationship orientations, familial structures, infinite ways to love.

Does this DNA appear in your work?

VIOLET: In my new novel, *Build Your House Around My Body*, there are a few central queer relationships, two of them very clear, and a couple that can be read a little more ambiguously, which was intentional. I like working in these spaces that resist easy classification. And in my earlier work I think that this DNA was most present in a story from *The Frangipani Hotel* about a nineteen-year-old Vietnamese American girl in Houston. It doesn't explicitly discuss her feelings about her gender identity, but she cuts her hair short, dresses androgynously, and tries to pass as a boy whenever possible. This is both a source of protection and a source of freedom for her, and one of many ways she tries to defy the expectations of Asian American womanhood that she feels suffocated by. Society tells women that they should be invisible, so she turns this on its head by refusing to be "seen" as a woman at all. The supernatural elements of the story are more literal explorations of shapeshifting to escape the limits placed on us.

ABBIGAIL: Part of our work is about taking up space, fiercely owning the space that we claim. The act of obedience starts in the imagination. With social media, which bombards us with information to manipulate our real-life actions, it becomes even more crucial to zealously protect the imagination. I think that's why I love writing from a child's point-of-view. Their exposure to the world is still limited, so they are reliant on their imagination to make sense of things. In the first part of my novel, the protagonist and her friend would play "what if" games. They have no props, no expensive toys, only their imagination. It allows them to metamorphose into anything and anyone. The friend becomes a ghost, the protagonist's father. Boundaries are blurred.

VIOLET: Is it why you did not name your main characters?

ABBIGAIL: Partly, unnamed characters are more fluid, interchangeable. They can move between worlds, languages, memories. Part of making art is resisting definition, and when something is named, it has already been defined. Sometimes I wish I could get away with not having a name and still being able to function in the world.

VIOLET: Do you think there is power in the name of the author?

ABBIGAIL: A name impacts how people read, interpret, and receive the author's work. I'm fascinated by authors who use multiple heteronyms like Fernando Pessoa, who had seventy-five. It's a good way to resist the reader's expectation of what you will write next, which in contemporary publishing is a kind of suicide. Though it's one I'll most likely commit.

VIOLET: We both have Vietnamese and English names, and you especially are very conscious about choosing your English one to be your writing name.

ABBIGAIL: I've had several English names as well. I have considered using a different name for my next novel.

VIOLET: And I considered using my mother's family name in my author's name because I was afraid that I would never be seen as a Vietnamese author without a Vietnamese name. But then I was afraid that this would be the equivalent of binding myself to a single identity when my life and my writing are built around dual selves. I wanted to still be able to slip in and out of identities.

ABBIGAIL: I love that: identities as something we can slip in and out of.

VIOLET: And I'm fascinated by the idea that we wear our different languages in the same way we wear our different selves. How there is more power in some Vietnamese words versus English words in certain scenarios, and how by juggling this in our writing, we can sometimes wring out extra meaning or darker subtext.

ABBIGAIL: Like saying "I love you" in Vietnamese is much harder than in English. Vietnamese people don't say "I love you" very often, except maybe once on their deathbed. I wonder why the phrase even exists in our language. I appreciate this unspoken way of loving—subtle, nuanced, articulated in the space between words. It's a quality more practiced and appreciated in Asian cultures. American culture calls for direct communication, and sometimes bluntness is mistaken for truthfulness. I question if the truth can be bluntly expressed. Poets tell the truth.

VIOLET: Do you have names in your book?

ABBIGAIL: Yes, I believe three of my supporting characters have names.

VIOLET: That sounds like such a tricky feat that you've pulled off beautifully in the book—balancing your slippery, fluid characters against named ones, and I think that what you choose not to define also creates a kind of space where a lot of interpretive work can be accomplished. When I choose names for my characters, I like to play with the way that Vietnamese names look and sound and the images they conjure up to an English-speaker's ear, and vice versa.

ABBIGAIL: Let's talk how Việt Nam is not a single story. Karl Ove Knausgaard can write thousands of pages about being human—

changing diapers, giving birth, being afraid, failing in one's marriage. Minority authors constantly bear the weight of representation, so being disobedient could mean simply writing whatever we want to. Our sorrows are multidimensional and not limited to identity struggles.

VIOLET: That's beautifully put. Something I get asked all the time is when I plan to write my family's coming-to-America story. Even from my own family. There's a kind of undercurrent of "If you have to write instead of being a doctor, you can at least do something useful by chronicling our history." Like it would at least add a small crumb to my minuscule pile of Vietnamese American respectability. But I bristle at that, and I honestly don't know if I'm capable of writing about the war. Books about horrifying refugee boat journeys exist already, and other authors have done it well. It's not a story that I feel needs me to tell it, or that I could tell in a way that was particularly new or moving. So I write about ghosts and monsters instead.

ABBIGAIL: I'm not capable of writing about the war either, nor do I want to.

VIOLET: I can only address it indirectly. I write about imaginary horrors to write about the real one. The monster acts as a proxy because in a way it's closer to how I understand the war.

ABBIGAIL: Truer to how you feel. Do you feel like you must prove how Vietnamese you are to the community?

VIOLET: I've always struggled with that. I think that because my face can't say or prove that I am Vietnamese on its own, even if I had perfect language skills, and even if I spent the rest of my career writing about Việt Nam and Vietnamese Americans, it would never be quite enough.

ABBIGAIL: Wanting to prove that must have come from a place of love.

VIOLET: The funny thing is that I've spent more time in Việt Nam than all my full-blooded cousins, living there on my own, and far-removed from expat communities. But that isn't the kind of cultural currency that seems to matter to them. My insecurities about not being *really* Vietnamese to them don't keep me up at night, but I know they'll always be there.

ABBIGAIL: What caused that insecurity?

VIOLET: I don't know if all mixes feel it on the same level as I do, or if mine was magnified by the family I happened to be born into. My mom was the first person in her family to marry a non-Vietnamese person, and it was a very shocking, very unacceptable thing. It's weird to think about how upsetting it was to everyone when mixes are everywhere now.

ABBIGAIL: Interracial marriages only became legal in the sixties. Not that long ago.

VIOLET: Yeah. So their marriage was seen as very unnatural and so by default I was too, as the product of it. I would jokingly get called "The Mutt" and things like that.

ABBIGAIL: I'm sorry to hear that.

VIOLET: I mean, it comes from a sort of place of love. I suppose. But not being accepted by Asians was always more painful than not being accepted by white people for how I look.

ABBIGAIL: Ambiguous.

VIOLET: Yeah. When I get called slurs, they're never Asian slurs. I feel like my looks land right in the middle of white and Asian, but instead of getting to be both, I'm just neither.

ABBIGAIL: If we look far back enough in the history of humanity, there is no such thing as pure blood. My great-grandmother on my mom's side is half-Chinese, and my grandmother on my dad's side is half-Cambodian. If you feel Vietnamese, then that's who you are.

VIOLET: I don't know if I feel Vietnamese. Or maybe I felt more Vietnamese after living in Việt Nam, but I still didn't feel any more Vietnamese American.

ABBIGAIL: It comes and goes for me. I feel more Vietnamese lately. I think it has to do with my going back, reconnecting with my relatives, people who still remember me as a child, and consuming more culture. I'm proud of what young artists in Việt Nam have done. They inspire me. I've been watching these Vietnamese rap battles recently. Am I assimilating Vietnamese-ness? I'm not sure.

VIOLET: I want readers to be unsettled. People in online reviews have said that the book isn't scary enough, but I can't write by trying to anticipate the fears of internet strangers. I only know my own fears, and the book spooked me!

ABBIGAIL: It's eerie, which isn't a cheap scare. It's more psychological than *boo!*

VIOLET: Yeah. *Boo!* doesn't stick with you; eerie does.

ABBIGAIL: More haunting.

VIOLET: Yes, that's the idea. My mom sometimes reads my work and is concerned by it.

ABBIGAIL: How so?

VIOLET: Well, I think she gets alarmed by seeing what lives in my head, which I can understand. Fiction isn't a one-way mirror. How about your family?

ABBIGAIL: I gave my book to my mom for my birthday. After reading about thirty pages, she admitted to my sisters and me for the first time that she has regrets—how she treated us and how she wishes she could have shown us love. We didn't know we were loved. That's the power of fiction. Had I told a story directly and factually, it wouldn't have communicated what I needed it to.

VIOLET: It's such a powerful tool if it allows you to have those difficult dialogues. The story is the intermediary. It's coding your truth to be able to say it. What is the sentence of your book, like its heart? If your book's soul were a single sentence, what would it be?

ABBIGAIL: "My mother had no daughter. It was her gift to me." How about you?

VIOLET: It's in the first story—something about papayas and diarrhea. No, that's not true. I would have to think some more. We didn't talk about refugee stuff at all, did we? That's not really in your fiction.

ABBIGAIL: What about yours?

VIOLET: Maybe it's just refugees that are my book's heart if it can't be a sentence. It's about their dislocated trauma—how the condition of un-belonging is inherited by the next generation, and how the pain of displacement gets transmuted into different forms. Ghosts and monsters are convenient metaphors for trauma, haunting memories, and PTSD.

ABBIGAIL: So it does influence your work.

VIOLET: Definitely, but like I said earlier, indirectly. I can't describe this hand gesture I'm making right now—I'm squirreling. I'm doing squiggly lines. That's what I'm trying to do in my writing. I'm trying to evade and subvert. I'm trying to tell the overstory in the negative space.

ABBIGAIL: What is your writing routine? Do you have one?

VIOLET: I'm terrible. I'm a night writer. I think I just got into the habit in college and can't break it. I just do my writing from 9:00 p.m. to 3:00 a.m. On a good night. And . . . it's not always a good night. It's rarely a good night. It's also partially because I'm trying to write about spooks.

ABBIGAIL: You want to spook yourself out?

VIOLET: Yes, and the spooks come at night. So when I'm writing well, I'm not being a good adult who exercises and eats vegetables and responds to e-mails and sweeps.

ABBIGAIL: At 3:00 a.m. you eat whatever is available and within reach.

VIOLET: And doing that, living in that weird midnight writing zone and freaking myself out and then just talking to . . . I mean, it's such a weird career. I feel like all I do is just talk to myself. What is your process?

ABBIGAIL: I envy your unique process. I write at coffee shops. I'm not exaggerating when I say that my writing is dependent on coffee. Caffeine makes me hyper focus. And I listen to soundscapes, instrumentals, music without lyrics. I can't write without music.

DIALOGUE BETWEEN THI BUI (UNITED STATES, SOUTH) AND THẢO NGUYỄN (UNITED STATES, WEST COAST)

THI: Thảo, I've been a huge fan of yours for years. The first time I saw you perform live was on your tour for your 2013 album, *We the Common*. I read that the album was inspired by the volunteer work you did with the California Coalition for Women Prisoners (CCWP), during a break from constant touring and recording. How did you begin working with the CCWP?

THẢO: I joined a weekly women's empowerment group with the SF County Jail, so with the CCWP, we have visiting groups that go to state prisons. Valerie Bolden was the first person I met doing those visits. She was the first person in the morning that walked in on my first day visiting. I remember that we had just a very nice rapport. You're sitting down and talking to a stranger, and she had this amazing sense of humor and remarkable candor. But the things that struck me were so many people inside, there are so many women and people in the women's prison who were survivors of violence and assaults and domestic violence and domestic assault, that were defending themselves and then were charged with whatever happened in their self-defense, against their attackers.

THI: Did Bolden or any of the women you talked to in prison ever hear your album?

THẢO: They heard the song ["We the Common"]. Valerie heard it too. She transferred down south years ago, which was part of what she had wanted. I haven't been in touch with her directly in a long time. I fell out of touch with her. But it was hard, we couldn't get the album into, you know, you can't send stuff into the prison. When the album first came out, it was a real acrobatic feat trying to get it entered into a prison catalog of acceptable things. I never did that. But I think she was able to hear the song over the phone.

I've written her a little bit over the years. But that's one of the things that I wanted to ask you about. How much of this do you do, being a part of advocacy work, or activist work, when it's not your job? How to find that balance? And how painful is it to know that you can't devote yourself the way you wish you could?

THI: When I was nineteen, I wanted to be a civil rights lawyer. I was really inspired by advocates who tried to make a difference through the law. I was a legal studies major, and I was excited about applying to law school. But my sister who was in law school at the time talked me out of it. She said, "You're not going to be happy; you should apply to art school instead." So I did, and I entered this real asshole world of the New York art scene, where I didn't really belong. I was left out because I didn't have the right mind-set. I think I was too earnest, too political. I was told I was too narrative too because I was in MFA for sculpture, where I didn't belong. But I just didn't know it at the time.

Eventually I found my way to comics, to tell stories through a visual medium. But I think I always wanted to connect with people through my work and try to make changes. But I also had to confront my own capacity, and my own strengths, right? I went from wanting to be a lawyer to now, I'm sort of a groupie for lawyers who fight for peoples' rights. You're totally ahead of me on the issues that I work on. My next book is called *NOWHERELAND*, and it's about prisons and immigrant detention centers, and it's called this because these spaces are where people get moved into from the outside, so those outside no longer have to think about them.

I got pulled into it because somebody asked me to help signal boost a campaign to draw attention to the roundups that were happening of Southeast Asians in the fall of 2017 under Trump. I had no idea about deportation. I didn't know how to stop deportation. I had read about tons of deportations happening after Obama, but this was the closest to home it had come for me. Knowing people who were fighting it, and hearing about Vietnamese families being upended by it. Then just reading more about it and trying to understand how do these people with these very, very old sentences get deported back to a country that maybe they weren't even born in, or they left as babies.

The madder I got, and the more I wanted to do. I'd start out with something feasible and simple because that's what I've learned how to do. It's like, *Okay, what can I do in an hour? I can draw a picture in an hour. If you send me some facts, I can tell a story that's compelling, and I can share it on my platforms.* You get diminishing returns if you keep using the same tactics, though. After a couple of portraits with some personal stories, I thought, *I need to do something deeper.* Then I pitched a story to the *Nib*, where I could do a more researched comic to try and explain the situation.

Then after that, I just convinced my publisher to let me switch my book topic from climate change in the Mekong Delta to Southeast Asians and immigrant detention and deportation. I started interviewing people in earnest, and they got me into San Quentin to talk to people through this program called Roots, which is an Asian American studies or an ethnic studies program that started there. It's amazing. Like you, I didn't really know what to expect coming in, but the candor and the humor and the resilience, as you're saying, of the people there, is surprising, because it's such a depressing situation, right? But people are amazing in the ways that they manage to survive and keep their spirits alive. The way that they support each other, when they have a space to do that, is beautiful to watch the transformation that happens. Just how welcoming they were to me was amazing. All of them. It was mostly men that I worked with. They were all the most enlightened men that I've met. They felt like my brothers, or boys that I went to high school with. Because they were very familiar. Their identity was very familiar to me.

We were not that different. The fact that my life had followed this model minority trajectory, and theirs had not. I thought a lot about what kind of shadow you cast on other people when you get the spotlight. But I think because I was introduced into this world by lawyers and people in policy, they were always very encouraging of the role I could play. They were candid about the limits of the law. They felt like art had a way of pushing the culture and changing peoples' hearts and minds in a way that helps their work too. So even if I couldn't go before a judge and argue about changing laws, I could bring attention to the issues in a different way and talk about things in a different way.

That's been helpful for me, as a guideline for how I tell the stories. When I look back at the comic that I did for the *Nib*, I would write it completely differently now and just try to simplify the language so that it's more direct. At the time, I had to get it copy edited by a lawyer to make sure that I had everything factually correct. But the result is that it has too many words.

But another way that you were ahead of me in the issues that I cared about and worked on was, a couple years ago, when you came to one of my talks; I wasn't yet working on electoral politics [in 2018]. I think I had invited you to a DVAN party first, and you had said, "I'd love to, but I can't, because I'm going canvassing this weekend."

THẢO: I should've gone to that party! We were canvassing, which is so funny because nobody opens the door.

THI: Maybe you need to go canvassing in the South. I hear people are friendly.

THẢO: I think I'm so shy and I don't think I can do that again. I'm sure you were phone banking a ton, right?

THI: I'm really shy about phone banking, too. I got burned in 2018 because I phone banked for John Ossoff the first time he ran for the Senate [in Georgia]. I did it in Vietnamese, which was really hard. I got my mom to do it.

THẢO: Awesome.

THI: I'm still kind of scarred from that experience. But mostly I worked on political ads for this election [in 2020].

THẢO: That's huge. I would love to hear how you got started with PiVOT [the Progressive Vietnamese American Organization], because it's a remarkable organization and you've done so much with them. I can't believe how much of yourself you gave to this past election.

THI: Part of it is: there's issues and then there's people, right? When the issues you care about are being worked on by people you really admire and want to work with, that's doubly motivating. I think that kind of relational organizing is what I want to do from now on. Although it has its limits too. I always looked forward to my Friday meetings with you and the team that worked on your *Go Vote* music video. The video was so beautiful and creative and weird and wonderful. The political organizing can be kind of yucky, I've heard. Some of the meetings can be just not pleasant. I remember being a social studies teacher, and I always hated the meetings with all the social studies teachers, because they're just a bunch of contentious people.

THẢO: Yes. And nothing gets done.

THI: Yes, so it was nice to have that balance of being creative, thinking out of the box, and have a bit of a slowness to our approach to balance out the work with the politics and get the results you want.

THẢO: Did you get started through your sister?

THI: My sister pulled me to a meeting in January 2017. I hadn't been involved with Vietnamese people in that way before. I generally avoided them before. Mostly PiVOT has a lot of members who are professionals. It was interesting to sit in a room with professional Vietnamese people who were progressive in their colleges. I was like, "Whoa, I don't think I've ever met this many all at once before." And we talked mostly in English, but it was Vietnamese-inserted, just enough to make you laugh and feel comfortable and appreciate the sense of humor. It's very particular, right?

But it wasn't really until 2020 that things really heated up and I jumped in in a different way, and I guess I used my organizing skillsets that I have from grassroots organizing back in college and being in student government throughout my childhood. I guess sometimes it was surprising to some of the volunteers, who knew me as author of *The Best We Could Do*. But I didn't really wear that hat when we were in meetings and doing work together.

THẢO: Right. Did you decide in 2020 that you would just leave it all out on the field?

THI: Well, fear is a great motivator.

THẢO: I grew up with all white friends. The kids that I did know, who were Vietnamese, were the kids when I was very young, just friends with my parents' friends. We all grew together to a certain point. But when I was probably around nine or ten, when stuff with my dad was kind of consuming my family, and those were his friends, whose kids I had grown up with, I never saw them again. Then from that point, aside from my mom's side of the family, of the aunts and uncles, I didn't belong to a broader Vietnamese community.

What was it like for you to grow up in that regard?

THI: Probably in California it was a little easier. Because there's just more Asians and more Vietnamese. I grew up like two hours outside of Westminster. I always had access to Little Saigon, and all the Vietnamese I could want. The food was great. There were things that I liked. But some of the other stuff I thought was hella cheesy. I didn't want to do any ribbon dancing or follow the templates for what a proper Vietnamese girl should act like or be like. I was resistant to the patriarchy. It wasn't until I grew up and moved around a lot and met younger Vietnamese people that I thought, *Vietnamese doesn't have to be just what these self-appointed elders say it is*. It's a lot of things.

THẢO: Yeah. I know. Honestly, it wasn't until that night at CAAM [Center for Asian American Media], the night of the documentary's premiere where I met you and some of your friends from DVAN that I just had eliminated the possibility of knowing Vietnamese people, because of my associations with it. All I knew were my aunts and uncles and the elders. I never felt comfortable. But I assigned that to everyone. I think there's those elements of internalized shame, internalized racism a bit. It's taken me quite a while to grapple with that, and acknowledge it, as being present for me growing up, and as I become an adult, I'm nearing forty, thinking about it.

You can't do anything until you acknowledge it. And it's so wild, even all the work of me wanting to get more into Get Out The Vote efforts in Asian American communities, in Vietnamese communities, I can't go do that until I acknowledge that I am Vietnamese, and I am Asian American. But I have such love for the culture, that's the thing. I've been raised to have a lot of respect for and reverence for it. But be so separate from it for myself. It's nice to be different now compared to what I was then.

THI: That's white supremacy for you. What now? Are you just going to Vietnamese it up?

THẢO: Yes, in my own way. I'm more open about celebrating Vietnamese things, and it feels so natural to do it. It's easier to talk about it now. But there are aspects of my career, the arc of my career, what has happened, what has not happened, that I've always internalized. I didn't know that I wasn't white. Things have happened and not happened because I am not.

THI: Really? You've never had a moment in your life where you were like, "That is racist as fuck"? Or "That was sexist as fuck"?

THẢO: Now I look back and think a ton of things were. There was only the one thing. Even when it was blatantly racist, I couldn't feel anger, I just shut down. I couldn't confront it. The music writer, with my first album, said I had written it in a foxhole.

THI: Man, that makes me retroactively mad for you.

THẢO: Padma Lakshmi has an interview in the *New York Times* magazine where she's just talking about her career and she's like, "There's this Italian saying that it's like being slapped in the dark." Like, being a woman of color in the industry, it's like being slapped in the dark. You know it's happening, you don't know where it's coming from, and so when I read this, I thought, *yes*.

THI: I too have been slapped in the dark. Let me turn on the lights and bust a kneecap. I think that maybe you and I are similar in that we need a kinder world in which to thrive. Well, maybe I'm not. But I'm sure that you are a very compassionate person who gives a lot of benefit of doubt. I think that what's strong about that is that you're able to get outside this narrow notion that a lot of Vietnamese refugees have, that our suffering is somehow special. I don't see that sentiment from you. You are very attuned to the suffering of lots of people. I see that in your understanding of women prisoners and the injustices that they have faced, and the way that you've embraced the Movement for Black Lives, and are very open, and just not withholding about your advocacy.

It's a strength. But it sucks for you because who advocates for you? I think this is how this world should work: you defend everybody else, then we can come defend you.

THẢO: Was the story about anger and white supremacy inside you for a long time? Did you know that you would put it in prose form?

THI: Since my late twenties, I wanted to tell it. It took ten years to make it happen. I think I was angry about white supremacy and the way that it had affected stories about us, like Vietnamese Americans. Because I had this legal studies background, and a history background, I felt like I had the tools to tell a corrective history. I know young folks today, sometimes they groan when another book comes out that's about the Vietnam War. I feel like that's valid, but we haven't had a whole lot written by us. Most of it is written by old white men.

THẢO: I was so struck by your book *The Best We Could Do* because I learned so much that I never would've heard otherwise. I would only ever hear about it in my family, but I would never hear anything but just a kind of distant reference of the French presence in Việt Nam. I don't even question, it's funny because I want to get the history from other Vietnamese people, but I don't want to get it from my family, because I don't believe that they will tell me the whole thing.

THI: About politicizing art, I think a lot of artists are wary of making political art because they have this notion that it's a sacrifice of aesthetics. I'm pretty sure you and I disagree with that. I feel like I see it in just something as simple as your social media posts about getting out the vote. You don't use the same language that everybody else uses. You find a way to surprise people with language that's disarming.

THẢO: Well, that's part of being a songwriter. The things you're exploring are not necessarily. . . . The reason I write songs is to communicate. Nothing I'm communicating is new. But part of the challenge is, How do you convey and elicit real connections around a subject matter that has already been traversed? That's the challenge, but it's also the joy of the craft. Yes, sometimes that extends to my Twitter messaging.

THI: Yes. Then the way that you've written about political things too, there's always some surprising lens. It's very rare when I hear you say a word that is in the popular usage in politic.

THẢO: Thanks. I really appreciate that. That means a lot coming from you.

DIALOGUE BETWEEN NGUYỄN PHAN QUẾ MAI (KYRGYZSTAN) AND HOA NGUYEN (CANADA)

QUẾ MAI: So you were born in Việt Nam. How old were you when you went to the States, and how?

HOA: I was just younger than two. I'm Eurasian. My mother is Vietnamese, and my father is a white American man who worked for the US government; they met there, had me, married, and left Việt Nam in 1968.

QUẾ MAI: Do you consider yourself a refugee?

HOA: Growing up, I did not feel that my experience had much in common with people who arrived in North America after "the Fall." My exit, my family's leaving, was informed by war—even as it was my parents making a life together and seeking a more certain, less violent future. I've since asked my mother this very question: Do you consider yourself a refugee? And she said, no, she does not consider herself a refugee. Maybe because our story doesn't fit the typical refugee narrative. Ours is a different narrative even as it is also affected by colonialism and war. It could never be considered historically neutral. We "voluntarily" left—it wasn't under the same pressure as other Vietnamese families who were leaving. I would say that the refugee experience *inflected* my experience. I think that might be another way of putting it. Our leaving was absolutely part of a larger context, a significant historical moment in the Vietnamese diaspora. It utterly marks my experience growing up in the United States in the 1970s as a mixed Vietnamese American person.

How about you? Did you have to move your home as a child, and how did the experiences shape you?

QUẾ MAI: I was born in 1973 in a small village in Ninh Bình, in the northern region of Việt Nam. I grew up witnessing the war's devastation. Since life was extremely difficult, my family had to leave our village and move south in 1979. Our new home was in Bạc Liêu, a small town on the southern tip of the Mekong Delta. The North and the South had been two different countries just a few years before that, so it felt like we were moving to another country. I remember the move very vividly. At six years old, I had never traveled outside of my village. And then my father came home and said we had to uproot ourselves. He told me that in the South, girls wore their hair short. I loved my long hair and I sat there in the yard, crying when my father used a big pair of scissors, cutting my hair so it hung above my neck. I think he had my interest at heart, and he wanted to help me fit into the South. I believed him and thought I was prepared, but I wasn't.

The evening that we arrived, we were eating dinner when a big rock hit the tin roof of our new house, exploding like a bomb above our heads. The rocks exploded often at night, for years to come. There were no streetlights. We rarely had electricity and we never knew who threw those rocks. Worse than the rocks was the taunting I received on the street or at school. Southern kids were singing "Bắc Kỳ nó ăn rau muống nó lỳ như trâu" [Northerners eat so much water spinach, they are as stubborn as buffaloes]. I was called all types of names. I didn't understand why I was hated. My parents were secondary school teachers, and their salaries were so little that we had to do all types of jobs to survive. We worked almost every day on our field to plant rice, beans, and sesame; we grew and sold vegetables in the market. After school hours, I walked the many streets of Bạc Liêu, selling cigarettes. Life was difficult and my parents didn't want to talk about the resentment we faced. I think they were trying to convince themselves, my two brothers, and me that the move was good for us.

I missed my village, and I was sure that my parents had made a huge mistake. But now, looking back over the years, I know that without growing up in Bạc Liêu, I wouldn't be the person I am today. Without growing up in the South, I wouldn't have understood the division among our people, the division that still runs deep. When I was growing up, many Southerners considered Northerners as those who invaded their land, taking away jobs. They were angry because many important positions at schools or factories were occupied by Northerners who had been appointed by the new government. In my neighborhood there were Southern women who were alone with their kids, because their husbands were at reeducation camps. I was told that these men had volunteered to go to these camps, and it was good for them. But later, I learned that it wasn't the truth.

In Bạc Liêu sometimes my classmates would just disappear. Whispers said that they had escaped in secret with their families. Bạc Liêu is near the coast, where many Chinese Vietnamese lived. As the border war between China and Việt Nam broke out in 1979, Chinese Vietnamese were "encouraged" to leave. They had to pay large sums of money or gold to be able to get on small boats, entrusting their lives to the vast ocean. Southern Vietnamese whose properties had been nationalized by the government or who had faced persecution started to become boat people too. Until today, I still don't know what happened to my classmates who disappeared. I grew up in the middle of that turmoil but had to pretend that everything was normal, because it was forbidden to talk about such sensitive issues such as reeducation camps, boat people, the nationalization of assets, resentment between the North and the South, etc.

HOA: How did your early and ongoing experiences influence your sense of history and narrativity?

QUẾ MAI: My childhood experiences taught me that our history is much more complex than what's available in textbooks and made me curious to hear the oral accounts from people I met throughout my life. Via my research and writing, I want to discover the truth and honor people's memories. I grew up with too many secrets around me. Secrets that people still hold inside their hearts. There's too much pain for many people to let go of their secrets, and there's danger too. I face that danger, but I feel the need to write about the experiences of my countrymen, otherwise certain aspects of our history are lost or forgotten.

I'd like to write about the experiences of Vietnamese people, from both North and South Việt Nam. When someone asks whether I am Northern or Southern Vietnamese, it's hard for me to answer. With my writing, I want to claim my identity as a Vietnamese who is not divided into either North or South. I especially want to write, with empathy and understanding, about the lives of those who might have thrown rocks onto my house's roof and of those who had taunted me. I feel that there are still too many unresolved issues among the Vietnamese community, inside and outside Việt Nam. These issues need to be written and talked about so that we can start to break down the invisible walls among us. Somehow I feel that that wall is getting higher and thicker as time goes on. In that aspect, I think the work of DVAN is critical. With DVAN's facilitation, we can come together, exchange our honest views and work together to foster understanding and reconciliation.

How about you, Hoa? How have your childhood experiences and your mixed identity affected your writing so far?

HOA: I grew up during a time of intense protest regarding the American war in Việt Nam—and there was, as now, prejudice against racialized difference, white supremacy, and xenophobia. As a mixed-race Vietnamese person in a mostly white context, I felt this, and it troubled my childhood. My family experienced racism. My mother remembers being shunned and snickered at in public. And worse. As a child, I felt it, heard it, was subjected to it. It influenced my mother's desire to assimilate. And because we arrived early in the formation of Vietnamese diasporic communities in the United States, I experienced the rupture or the separation inside of this assimilation as complete: I lost a whole language and sense of place, everything I knew, even memories. It happened and wasn't spoken of. It was an inchoate rupture.

My mother was not interested in transferring language or culture to me—she focused on her life, her white American husband, and being "American." She shed her skin like a snake: she was born in the Year of the Snake, a Silver Snake, and so when we settled in the Washington, DC, area in 1969, we became an English-only household. She left the old behind and transformed into the new. I have long since felt that I write poems to bridge or address that rupture, to language it.

QUẾ MAI: I'm sorry to hear about the racism you faced and the loss you endured. Do you consider that your writing helps you heal?

HOA: Yes, I suppose it has; I believe that finding and bringing language to experiences helps us heal and offers ways to create meaningful narratives. It allows for new perspectives and possibilities. I tend to avoid thinking of creative writing as a therapeutic method, but of course it also can be therapeutic. For me, the act of writing is connected to a kind of shamanic practice that I have come to locate in a deep sense of kinship and lineage. Like the elevated Buddhist state of oneness and absorption in contemplation. The word for this in Sanskrit, *samadhi*, translates into "to collect" or "bring together."

QUẾ MAI: Yes, to heal and to "bring together" is what we all need. I think that as part of your healing journey, you returned to Việt Nam?

HOA: I finally returned in 2018, fifty years later—visiting Hà Nội. I came back with a clearer and deeper version of myself. I went to or rather returned to Việt Nam as a mature artist practicing my art, an art of language that is part of the language-loss of my original language. To share poems within a diasporic context with a group of literary people interested in poem-making within that multinational context was powerful.

QUẾ MAI: That's great because you didn't go to Việt Nam as an orphan searching for a home that she had lost.

HOA: Exactly. I think that was the big emotional barrier that prevented me from returning previously. My mother refused to return to Việt Nam, her home for twenty-seven years. So the idea of facing my return was a proposal of aloneness, or I thought so. But it wasn't that; instead, it was a return not as the Forever Exiled Orphan but as the mature Seeker on a journey that also leads inward.

QUẾ MAI: I am so sorry your mother couldn't return. I read the poems you wrote during your return trip and saw her in those poems. You honor her so beautifully with your writing, Hoa. When my order of your poetry collection *A Thousand Times You Lose Your Treasure* arrived, I was delighted to see a picture of your mother on her stunt motorcycle, and she looked impressive. In those poems Việt Nam appears so vividly, so achingly. I remember that you wrote about tree shrines and I love that. A lot of Vietnamese believe that ghosts inhabit certain types of trees. That's why we have altars there. The tree you described is called *bồ đề*. And I love how you honor those ghosts by poetry—one of the finest forms of the art. I think that the poet's task is to grow words so that they become roots of trees.

HOA: Yes, and trees have deep wisdom and knowledge. They are sacred and offered us a panorama of time; their messages were about the nature of time and how our modern understanding of time is too simple, based on a colonial structure. They remind us that we are part of a vast web partially visible, that if you were to draw it into space, it would be interrelated spirals.

I've been thinking a lot about what that would mean to write with language that mimics the actual structure of time. Related to this, I think shrine-making in trees is a way to appeal or speak to unsettled ghosts and ancestors. This is a reminder to me: that of the dead in literal and figurative terms and how poems can address and include a multiplicity of voices including the voice of the dead. I'm interested in talking with the dead in poems to connect across time and generations, across lineages of kinship. I want writing that exposes its own troubles, that self-problematizes and risks uncertainties to sculpt language with an ear to that including how language might slide and slip as a ghost might: between sound, sense, meaning, and contexts.

How does the idea of the dead inform *your* writing?

QUẾ MAI: A lot actually. One of my poems is about my grandma who died in the Great Hunger of 1945, which killed around two million Vietnamese. When I was born, both of my grandmothers had died. I always felt like I wanted to talk to them. So I talked to one of them via this poem:

The Poem I Can't Yet Name

My hands lift high a bowl of rice, the seeds harvested
in the field where my grandmother was laid to rest.
Each rice seed tastes sweet as the sound of lullaby
from the grandmother I never knew.
I imagine her soft face as they laid her down into the earth,
her clothes battered; her skin stuck to her bones;
in the Great Hunger of 1945, my village
was starved for graves to bury all the dead.
Nobody could find my grandmother's grave,
so my father tasted bitter rice for sixty-five years.

My two feet cling to the mud.
I listen to the burning incense of my grandmother's soul spread,
joining the earth, taking root in the field,
where she quietly sings lullabies, calling the rice plants to blossom.
Lifting the bowl of rice in my hands, I count every seed,
each one glistening with the sweat of my ancestors,
their backs bent in the rice fields,
the fragrance of my grandmother's lullaby alive on each one.

I wrote this poem originally in Vietnamese, then translated it into English with the help of the poet and Vietnam War veteran Bruce Weigl.

HOA: That was gorgeous. I see that voice is important for your writing. How does feminism inform your writing or practice? What other issues are important for you?

QUẾ MAI: Feminism is a pillar on which I build my work, actually. I aim to write back to colonialism and the male gaze. Many novels written by white male writers and many Hollywood films have presented Vietnamese women as naive, shallow, opportunist, and stupid. We are much more complex than that. In my second novel, *Dust Child*, I have my Vietnamese female characters oppose the male gaze on them. I also write back to the white gaze by including the viewpoint of Dan, a traumatized helicopter pilot. *Dust Child* also writes back to the gender discrimination that is deeply imbedded in the Vietnamese culture too. In the book my female characters challenge such sexist proverbs as "đàn bà đái không qua ngọn cỏ" [women can't pee higher than the top of grass blades], or "đàn ông nông nổi giếng khơi, đàn bà sâu sắc như cơi đựng trầu" [when naïve, men still seem as profound as a deep well; when thoughtful, women are no deeper than a flat-bottomed betel leaf container]. Just a few days ago, I was reading a social media post where a woman commented about the ongoing Men's World Cup and a man told her off by saying "đàn bà đái không qua ngọn cỏ" [women can't pee higher than the top of grass blades]. This still happens in 2022 and I am enraged!

How about you, Hoa? How have you transferred feminist practices into your work? How about trauma? I'm interested to know the pathway for you to present trauma in your work.

HOA: Putting together my early collection of poetry (*Red Juice: Poems 1998—2008*), I was amused to see how many poems have feminist themes. I've long called myself a proud feminist, and my work and teaching are an extension of that. And in my engagement with the diasporic materials—in my sense of connecting or yoking together experience, I continue to be interested in how writing connects to my sense of speaking with the dead—with the world that is alive itself. Looking at the animistic practice in Việt Nam aligned with speaking with the dead—shamanic practices—led me to understand how my interest in poetry and making poems is bound up in something essential for me: the numinous, time, and transfiguration. I consider the ways that my work attempts to language a retrieval of lost energy (or soul) from traumatic events.

QUế MAI: When we write about Việt Nam, it's almost impossible to avoid the issue of trauma, isn't it? The trauma of our war is inherited and passed on from one generation to the next.

HOA: Yes, epigenetics confirm what we have known—collective and individual trauma is carried in the body. To write as a poet is to see that the songs of the living and the dead resonate inside of everything. They are there already, and we can sing with them, even when we don't know the name for the song.

QUế MAI: The concept of the same songs being sung together by the living and the dead is breathtaking. I am amazed to hear that you talked to your ancestors. I did the same thing. When I was growing up, my parents were strict, and I couldn't tell them about certain things. So I would go to the altar, burn incense, and talk to my grandmothers. My novel *The Mountains Sing* is told in the voices of a grandmother and her granddaughter. They take turns telling stories about their family. The novel opens with this line: "My grandmother used to tell me that when our ancestors die, they don't just disappear, they continue to watch over us."

HOA: So that we call "time" is more complicated than how we imagine it and experience it in its assigned linear concept of past, present, and future. I know that it is vaster and more complex in its dimensionality and structure. This might be a good time for me to read you the poem that I wrote in Hanoi. It's called "Ficus Carica Sonnet," named after the large classification of trees, the fig family of which the banyan is part.

Ficus Carica Sonnet

Cinched belt tugged tight around the heart
5 or 6 aerial roots dangling A strangler fig
Do homeless ancestors live inside the tree?
Child of noise Hold the loosened ends You

may miss the moon or fall in love with it Embrace
ashes I too am far removed A thirst that wanders
thirsting And I could never ask the name of the boy
who died A baby boy who died but what could you do

and maybe words hang in sinew and care Writer
of dead words or living words and life's hammer
Encase the host tree and erase it I don't know
the folk songs on farms far from here The dead buried

and gone To dig the grave Who dug the graves
Darling The sea widens for you tonight and deepens

QUẾ MAI: What a stunning poem. While listening to it, I could feel the pain of loss, of separation, of wandering that has been experienced by so many Vietnamese people.

HOA: I want to return to lullabies, especially in reference to your poem and your grandmother's lullabies. Something I want to do for my next project is to encounter and record them in the southern delta region, to make field recordings of lullabies.

QUẾ MAI: This project sounds so important as not many Vietnamese people sing lullabies anymore. I feel the need to hold on to lullabies and that's why I always feature lullaby singing in my novels. The first novel in English that I attempted to write is called *Rice Lullaby*, actually. In the novel my main character saves a boy's life with her singing. It's fate that we have met, Hoa. We have so many things in common!

HOA: It does feel like fate: lullabies and all.

FOUR

Representation, Writing, Reception

The Vietnamese American community is the largest population outside of Việt Nam, followed by other Vietnamese diasporic communities in Australia, Canada, and France. With a population of nearly 2.3 million and a third generation who is coming of age in the United States, Vietnamese Americans represent the largest ethnic group that has emigrated to the United States since the immigration of displaced Jews during and after World War II and is the fourth-largest Asian American ethnic group.[1] The vast majority came as refugees as a direct result of the end of the Vietnam War in 1975. In that war, rarely mentioned is the fact that more bombs were dropped on Việt Nam—a country two-thirds the size of California—than in all of World War II. Also elided in mainstream narratives in the United States and Việt Nam is that the body count in Việt Nam for all sides was closer to one-tenth of the population (ranging between three million and four million), while the American dead amounted to about 0.035 percent of the population.[2]

Unlike immigrants, refugees are forced out of their countries and tend to have a strong attachment to the country of their origins; they constitute a highly diverse group. Vietnamese refugees, who arrived in Australia, Canada, and the United States from 1975 to the early or late 1980s, were diverse in terms of class, education level, religion, ethnicity, and experience. Vietnamese started to immigrate to France (unlike the United States and Australia) *before* the Vietnam War. They came as part of the France colonial project, many as students in the early 1900s and then as soldiers on the onset of World War I and World War II. When Việt Nam became independent in 1954 and during the Vietnam War, more Vietnamese loyalist and students immigrated to France. Both Anna Möi and Marcellino Trương Lực were pre-1975 immigrants. The largest influx of Vietnamese arrived in France, however, as refugees after the end of the war in Vietnam in 1975. Although the last waves came from all social standings, the average level of education was higher than those settled in the United States and Australia. France received the third-highest number of refugees from Vietnam after the United States and Australia.[3]

The first group of adult post-1975 refugees often had familial ties with the American military complex, spoke some English, were mostly Buddhist, and more educated than those who left four years later by boat. Unlike the formal departure process by plane, refugees who escaped by boat had to do so in secrecy. Should they be caught, they would be put in jail. They were known as "boat people" because they risked their lives crossing an ocean, doing so aboard haphazard vessels unsuitable for the journey. Among them were ethnic Chinese persecuted by the government. Their destinations were refugee camps across Hong Kong, Indonesia, Malaysia, the Philippines, Singapore, and Thailand, from where most would then apply for asylum to the Australia, Canada, France, or the United States. It has been estimated that only one out of seven boats made it to shore. Poet Vaan Nguyen, presented in chapter 3, was born in Israel. Her parents were part of the 366 Vietnamese refugees who escaped Vietnam by boat between 1977 and 1979 who were granted asylum there.[4]

For diasporic Vietnamese refugees the end of the war signified the loss of a country and the beginning of a life in exile. The Vietnam War was not only one between the United States and Việt Nam in which several other countries were directly involved, it was also a civil war between a country politically divided between the South and the North.[5] While the media focused on stories of people in small boats grateful to be rescued, a sense of betrayal ran through the collective cord of the community. When American troops left Việt Nam, many of those who sided with Americans were sent to reeducation and labor camps for years—where they were malnourished, tortured, labored, and feared for their lives. It took a decade and more before Vietnamese military personnel who were allies with the United States and who were incarcerated in reeducation/labor camps in Việt Nam, and the children of American soldiers, to be eligible to immigrate legally to the United States through international policies such as the Orderly Departure Program and the Amerasian Homecoming Act, respectively.

These histories and policies surrounding Vietnamese refugee migration are tied to questions of cultural representation, which continue to be sore issues for diasporic Vietnamese. Decades during and after refugee migration the Vietnamese have been poorly represented in Hollywood movies more preoccupied with retrieving the manhood of American soldiers who had lost the war than understanding the lived experiences of the Vietnamese. As a result of World War II, most Americans saw themselves as belonging to a heroic nation fighting for freedom that could not be defeated, and especially not by a small third world country. In Vietnam War movies the Vietnamese have been depicted as a mass of killable (and thus "ungrievable") people, corrupt officials, childlike creatures, and prostitutes.[6] In conjunction with expressing feelings of gratitude, diasporic Vietnamese writers index a nagging feeling that reminds them that they have a responsibility to uphold and fix problematic Vietnamese representations in the industry, an imperative that flickers in and out to their consciousnesses as artists. The representation of the past is indeed most significant to one's identity.

Their memories differ from accounts present in history books. History books are important as they answer the question, Who are we as a people?[7]

History weaves together selected events to construct an incomplete yet authoritative narrative about the past. It is written by intellectuals, themselves shaped by political events and ideas. Most French and American historians of the Vietnam War were born during the Cold War and have been influenced by Marxist ideology and the antiwar movement that set many parts of the globe aflame during the 1960s and 1970s. It is then perhaps not a coincidence that more history books cover the plight of the North Vietnamese than that of the South Vietnamese. The writing of history has furthermore been reinforced by television, which started to populate households in the West in the middle of the twentieth century.

The Vietnam War was the most widely covered war in television history.[8] During the war images of a North Vietnamese person killed at point blank by a Southern Vietnamese officer and of a naked little girl running away from a village bombed by Americans were mass-produced in support of the antiwar movement. After the war clips of Vietnamese bodies desperately climbing into a small helicopter and that of wretched bodies in boats floating without food and water were repeatedly shown on television. Across media, representations of the Vietnamese—whether they were allies or enemies—have been deeply imprinted in America, rendering them as either "Orientally" inscrutable villains or as passive victims.[9]

That the United States and France lost their respective war with Việt Nam further fueled a national fascination in these countries toward those who defeated them. During the war Vietnamese were depicted in the media, the military, and by GI writers as inferior both militarily and racially. Historical amnesia is not the same as ignorance but rather the result of selective choice of events by people on one side of a conflict obscuring the human losses of another.[10] In the case of Việt Nam in the United States, it is the side of refugees that has been put aside and willed to obscurity driven by national guilt for having abandoned them and a desire to forget a humiliating war lost to a small third world country. In France, because of a century of colonization in Việt Nam, Vietnamese are seen as "good, colonized subjects" as opposed to those from Algeria or Morocco. The general public in that country maintains a paternalistic and romanticized view toward anything that has to do with Việt Nam, mired with nostalgia for a power lost. While the word "Vietnam" no longer has the same hold in the United States and France as it once did, writers from two generations in this chapter continue to live with either the terrible memory and weight of having lost their country, and/or are burdened by the task of humanizing the Vietnamese people and/or that of representing authentic personal stories.[11] They write about what they care most with ambivalence because they have been either erased or stereotyped from normative narratives of the First Indochinese War with the French or the Second Indochinese War with the Americans, while also being pigeonholed by the publication industry.[12]

DIALOGUE BETWEEN LE LY HAYSLIP (UNITED STATES, WEST COAST) AND DƯƠNG VÂN MAI ELLIOTT (UNITED STATES, WEST COAST)

MAI: I completed my manuscript of *The Sacred Willow* in 1998. At that time, as you remember, it was very difficult for Asian authors to get published in the US. And then for us Vietnamese Americans who wanted to write about our lives, our stories, and our experiences during the Vietnam War, we also ran into the problem that in general Americans were very tired of the war, and they wanted to forget about it. And if they were still interested in the war, it was mainly centered around what Americans had done in Việt Nam. On top of that, before you published, publishers didn't have confidence that a Vietnamese American author could sell books.

But when your book *When Heaven and Earth Changed Places* came out in 1989, you opened a path because you proved that Vietnamese American authors could sell books. What were some of the problems you met when you wanted to write and publish your book?

LE LY: For about three to five years, I tried hard to do without an agent, and I sent out the story outline and some chapters to many publishing houses, I'd say about twenty of them. Only Paladin Press in Boulder, Colorado, had an interest in it, but they were too small, so I did not go with them. But there were many, many rejections. Like you said, they did not accept the idea of a Vietnamese writer, or the story of the enemy on the other side. They didn't want to hear about it. And especially by a woman, who was not one of them. They want to hear about the American GI trauma, the politician, or somebody who can tell their side of the story. And every time I saw that, I wondered, *What do you know about us? What do you know about the Vietnamese? That is our country, our culture, our story. And you're there for one or two tours of duty, come home, and you write about us.*

It wasn't fair and that motivated me to write to tell our side of the story. We had to write from the inside out what we know about our war. The more they rejected me, the harder I tried. The more they talked about the enemy, I tried to write about the enemy from my perspective. As you said, I think it took the right time, place, and story to open the path.

MAI: The key at that time, and now, is to find an agent. I was lucky to find an agent who believed in my book, and she opened the doors to the publishing world for me. Someone who believes in your book and your writing, and who will take you on. Otherwise, you have to forget about trying to publish. In your case it took you twenty tries to find somebody who believed in you.

LE LY: And I was lucky. I went to a writers conference in La Jolla [California] in 1985. At the time, it cost $375 to attend, but I went. There I was: Vietnamese woman, five-foot-one inches tall, about one hundred pounds, among five hundred people. They had their story, like how to quit smoking, how to lose weight, how to go through a divorce. They had all kinds of stories to tell, and here I come from out of nowhere and I said, "Here is my story." My English was very poor at that time, but it made everybody cry. And after I shared the story about me at ten years old involved in the war, and how I had been raped, tortured, and went to a refugee camp. It was just too much for an average American to take in. But little by little, they withdrew their proposals because it's just too overwhelming for them.

And so, I'd say that finally publishing the book was a gift, because I prayed. I prayed very hard the night before. I got down my knees, and I prayed. And I made a vow, I promised if the book succeeded, all that money would go back to Việt Nam. And if the book was made into a movie, everything would go back to Việt Nam. And for thirty-five years I had no pay, because everything went back to Việt Nam with the work of the foundation [the Global Village Foundation].

MAI: It's still difficult to get published because of the economics of publishing. I think that agents and publishers don't take on a book unless they think it can sell, and they can make money out of it. On the one hand, it's gotten easier for Vietnamese American authors to publish, because there's a resurgence of interest in Việt Nam and the war. And by Việt Nam, I mean the war not really the country. Also, I think that now there's a lot of interest in the stories of refugees and immigrants. Even though it's easier for Vietnamese American authors to get published, they become pigeonholed because there's a view that they can only write with authenticity about Việt Nam, and the war, and its aftermath. I wonder if they write about something else, whether they could get published as easily as if they were writing about themselves, their families, their life stories, the war. Being a refugee, being an immigrant, facing problems in America as a minority, and so on. While I think it's easier, it's also become more of a niche for Vietnamese American authors.

LE LY: Talking about "niche," I've always wanted to talk about ghosts in my writing. It used to be that a lot of psychics and spiritual mediums were in the village. Everything had to do with spirits, between the living and dead, heaven and earth, father and mother, and graves and not-graves. Talking to ghosts or spirits or our ancestors is like how we're talking right now. It's just the older I get, the more I think it needs to be written.

MAI: How has your book been received in Việt Nam? My book is not welcomed in Việt Nam—but it's not banned either—because I'm critical of the policies of the Communist Party in certain periods of time. So, for example, if I want to send a copy of my book to someone in Việt Nam, that person will have to get permission from the Ministry of Culture to get it out. But people in Việt Nam, some people do have copies. A friend of mine went to Hội An and found an unauthorized copy of my book, a reproduction of my book.

LE LY: My book is still banned there. Anyone can copy and sell it on the street. I saw your book just like mine being sold everywhere and it's cheap, one to five dollars. My books have been translated into about seventeen different languages but not in Vietnamese. When tourists come to Việt Nam, they have copies of our books, but after their travels they just give them to the tour guide.

MAI: Yes, I've been asked to have my book translated into French and Chinese, but in China it's just too difficult and I haven't agreed to the project. And it's just too much of a headache to have it translated and deal with another country.

So anyway, back in the US. . . . At that time when my book came out, the wounds of the war were still raw, and the refugee community did not think that my book was anti-Communist enough. So they didn't say anything about it, basically it was ignored. So my book didn't get much notice, though I did get interviewed in a Vietnamese newspaper in Westminster (known as *Little Saigon*) in Orange County in California. But now, from what I've heard, the younger generation is more interested in learning about the war. They're also interested in learning about Vietnamese traditions, society, culture, history—topics that I covered in my book through the history of my family. So I think that the younger generation is more receptive to what I have to say in my book. How about you?

LE LY: Same, yes. Because of the movie, the older Vietnamese in the US know of my books. But because they can't read English, they have a minimal understanding of what I wrote. Because I have been involved with the Việt Cộng, they assume that I write for the Communists and promote Communist propaganda. They question me about the book; I give them answers clearly and directly. They protested and boycotted me when I gave talks. I sang songs and told them stories from both sides; little by little, they accepted, but only a few people, not the whole community. That's the way it was then and still is today, I think.

MAI: Yes, I guess I didn't encounter as many difficulties as you did. I remember you encountered a lot of difficulties within the community. My book was on sale at a bookstore in Little Saigon. People were buying my book in dribs and drabs, but now I think it's become a lot more interesting for younger Vietnamese Americans who are reading my book.

LE LY: But a lot of people have learned from our books—about why we fought the war, why we wanted to become independent, and why my family went to the North and the South. I think if more Vietnamese people were writing books, we can educate others about who we are and our culture.

MAI: What are your major challenges or benefits as a minority writer? I think that if I write as a Vietnamese American, if I write about Việt Nam and especially the Vietnam War, then I benefit as an author. Because publishers, agents, and readers view me as somebody who can write knowledgeably about these topics. And they believe that my voice is authentic because of who I am and my background. I think that this is true for other Vietnamese American writers as well, and I think we've talked about this before. I wish the day would come when Vietnamese American authors could write about anything and be taken as credible voices. And that they can go beyond the wall, of being refugees, being an immigrant, and get published, and get noticed.

And for me, since my two books are nonfiction like yours, your book was nonfiction, I've been pigeonholed as a nonfiction writer, so it's hard for me to break out of that perception. I've written a novel, but I haven't gotten any interest in it because I'm viewed as a nonfiction writer, not as a novelist. How about you? Your book has been classified as nonfiction, right?

LE LY: Right, it's a memoir. Both books are memoirs, but see you're much luckier than I am. You are educated; your English is better; and you have a better chance to do research. Your family come from upper class in the North. You were a refugee from the North to the South in 1954. In those days the United States funded the new Sài Gòn government to bring the refugees who were Catholic in the North to the South. That is part of the history most people don't know about.

MAI: Yes, we flew. Most of the refugees were Catholic. But my family was Buddhist, we were not Catholic, and my father arranged a flight for us. But you're right, most of the refugees from North Việt Nam were Catholic, and they were evacuated by American ships.

LE LY: Whereas in my time as a refugee, we had nothing. Not even a government behind us. But after 1975, I learned from many Vietnamese who came to the US. And through these conversations with them as friends, I learned that many young village girls became refugees in the city and were raped by their bosses. Now we have #MeToo. I can tell a lot of these stories to MeToo, for so many Vietnamese women. We don't talk about these things, but they need to be brought up because it is still happening today.

MAI: Another question I thought we'd talk about is, When we write our books, who are we writing for, who is our audience? When I wrote my book, I thought of writing for the general American audience who didn't know much about Việt Nam and then for the younger generations of Vietnamese Americans who I thought would not have firsthand knowledge of Việt Nam. I think we touched on this earlier, there was a big lack of understanding in the United States about Việt Nam and the Vietnamese. To use a cliché at the time, Việt Nam was a war not a country, so there was a big lack of understanding. Americans, if they talked about Việt Nam or if there were TV shows or movies about Việt Nam, Vietnamese were always in the background. They were secondary figures, shadowy figures, but in your movie *Heaven and Earth*, for the first time a Vietnamese American (Hiep Thi Le) played a central role.[13]

When my book came out, six thousand books had already been written about Việt Nam and the war, but none of them really dealt with Việt Nam and the experiences of Vietnamese. I wanted to show the Vietnamese in a different light. As people from a country with a culture, and tradition, and as major players in their own history, not just as supporting actors in an American drama. I wanted to show Việt Nam and the Vietnamese in all their complexities—good, bad, at peace, and at war. Like I said, my other major audience was Vietnamese Americans who had come to the US as children, or who were born here and didn't have a firsthand knowledge of Việt Nam.

LE LY: Yes, I agree. When Americans came to Việt Nam, all they knew was what they had created: To them, Việt Nam is a prostitute, Hamburger Hill is a battlefield. And I said, "Let me share with you who we are. We're not Communists, we're not POWs, we're not MIAs, and not all of us are boat people. We're not all refugees, bar girls, or hookers, and not go-go girls or Saigon tea girls. We are Vietnamese. We have five thousand years of culture and tradition that we follow. We have our ancestors' graveyard. We had parents before and children after us. We are the farmers, not well educated but we're not uneducated."

This is the kind of remark that gets me boiling every time I hear "Go back where you come from." I am proud and happy that Việt Nam can teach American individuals how to live in this world together and about forgiveness.

MAI: Americans wrote about the Vietnamese that they had met: the peasants, villagers, government officials, Vietnamese soldiers, bar girls, and the maids who worked in their houses, or the people who worked in American offices. Their view of Vietnamese society was very limited, because of their personal context. I wrote about my family because I thought that there had not been any focus on the Vietnamese middle class. The assumption at the time was that the Vietnamese middle class were anti-Communist, and they were pro Saigon government, but that wasn't really the case.

There were a lot of middle-class Vietnamese who didn't support the Americans, or they didn't support the Communists either. A lot of them were in the middle. I wanted to show that the Vietnam War was also a war between the Vietnamese. During the colonial period there were people like my father, they didn't like the French, but they didn't like the Communists either; they sided with the French because they were more afraid of the Communists. But there were also middle-class Vietnamese who joined the Việt Minh at the time, like many of my relatives including my older sister. This perspective was lacking in the understanding of the Americans about the middle-class Vietnamese, and the division within Vietnamese society between those who supported one side or the other.

I have to admit I haven't followed the literature closely, but from what I've read or have heard, there seems to be a refugee aesthetic in the sense that Vietnamese American writers or overseas Vietnamese writers tend to focus on their own experiences. Which in their case is as refugees, as immigrants. But also, because it's a topic that we feel is most compelling, because it affects us and our families so deeply. We tend to write about things that are compelling, we tend to gravitate toward these topics, and in that way we also feel that our voices are most authentic. But it may be that some of us also write what we're expected to write, because we have more credibility when we write about ourselves, our families, our experiences. So maybe it's a self-selection that we write about things that make us more credible.

What is your view?

LE LY: Yes, I think it's the second generation who is developing the idea of a refugee aesthetic. There are two factors here. One is the younger generation, those who have gone back to Việt Nam and want to understand what their family, parents, and grandparents went through and write about their experiences. Another is that they found our motherland to be very beautiful. I'm glad they're writing about these issues, but with our generation we are committed to telling the truth about what happened in our generation.

The truth is that in 1975, the Communists took everything away from people. I came here in 1970, so I wasn't there and didn't see all the bad things. However, I was not knowledgeable about politics, but I saw enough about the war. Therefore I have a different point of view and was happy to see the war end. I saw things in Việt Nam before 1970, which still bothers me today. I am Vietnamese, and yet my countrymen over here called me a "whore," an "American madam," and all kinds of names because I help the poor Vietnamese back home. I don't understand that. It all comes back to what you said, what we carry. This is what I want to share with the younger generations. I would like to see more Vietnamese writing about what they know best. Again, we need to try to get the record straight so that our culture and our traditions will carry on for the future generation.

MAI: Yeah, I don't think there's anything wrong with writing about our life stories and our family's experiences. I think it's important because we're not going to be here forever.

LE LY: That's right.

MAI: And what we write about serves as a record of our generation, and the generation of our parents and grandparents. And I'm so glad I wrote my book and interviewed the people I did for it, because I captured their stories, their memories, their recollections, and of course a lot of them are gone now. I think that if Vietnamese Americans, or overseas Vietnamese, would capture the stories of their families that will be great, because it's something that's ephemeral. People get older, they forget, they die, so I think it's very important to capture the experiences of our generation, and the generation after us or before us before we all pass from the scene. I don't think there's anything wrong with the refugee aesthetic, I think it should be encouraged.

DIALOGUE BETWEEN ANNA MÖI (FRANCE) AND AIMEE PHAN (UNITED STATES, WEST COAST)

ANNA: I started reading your book *The Reeducation of Cherry Truong* and, well, first I really liked the title, the fact that you play with the word "reeducation."[14] Obviously she's not going to a camp: she's a Vietnamese American going back to find her brother there. My experience was similar in 1992 when my husband, who is French, was posted in Việt Nam. It wasn't a choice. It was a random opportunity that he was able to go there.

AIMEE: Have you ever been there before?

ANNA: We went there briefly. We were living in Thailand at that point, and we went to visit like tourists in the 1990s. We thought we were going for just one year, because the contract was for one year, then it became two, and then three, and then my husband switched jobs. The French government wanted him to run a business management school, a French-Vietnamese cooperation project, and that lasted for a while. Our kids were three and four, and the third one wasn't yet born. When we decided to go, Louis was just born, so my two older boys grew up in Việt Nam.

AIMEE: What was that like for you?

ANNA: You know, Việt Nam in the 1990s was such a great experience, because the country was just opening up.[15] People were in their own bubbles but then they caught on very quickly with the internet, mobile phones, and Facebook and now Viper. Everyone is very connected. Yes, and so I was interested in asking you, Why did you send your characters to Việt Nam? Is it a wish that you yourself have or had, or a fantasy?

AIMEE: I think it ended up becoming this: I was certainly working through how the possibility of returning to Việt Nam was going to play out for people like me, people my age who, when I was growing up with the 1980s in America, Việt Nam was a tragedy that we could never return to. . . . The way my parents spoke about it, my grandparents, they were like, you can never go back. It is our lifelong sorrow. I had an aunt who had been trying to escape for years, and she and her son kept getting caught and punished, so it never occurred to me as a child to return. It just seemed like Việt Nam was forever lost.

Also, when I was in high school in the 1990s, I was friends with these three Vietnamese girls who were sisters. One of them was the girl who always wore makeup and had boyfriends, and even though all three girls were very smart, she was considered the "rebel." She was considered the bad daughter, and she did not come back for her senior year of high school. We found out that her parents had sent her back to Việt Nam to live with relatives, and it was like a punishment for being too rebellious in America. For me, it turned into a symbol of what happens when you get corrupted by America. Your Vietnamese parents can send you back there, and I used that as a threat in the book. Also, the parents couldn't handle Lum, who always felt like he was never good enough in America, but he suddenly experiences incredible success in a country that is reborn and has new success.

I wanted to explore that. I was seeing it happening with my own friends. I have friends who live in Việt Nam now who I went to college with. They are pursuing art and filmmaking, all these opportunities that they say they have much more access to in Việt Nam than they ever would in America. And so it was, again, playing with this idea of where do we feel most comfortable or most welcome? And it's interesting that you don't necessarily feel most welcome in the country that's supposed to be yours. What does it mean to have a country? I wanted to play that out with the character. I wrote the novel over a period of eight years. I took a long time with it. It's about the main character coming to terms with the fact that some things cannot be repaired, cannot be reunited, as I think her young self would have wanted.

But it's interesting to me, this question of, What would happen if I went back to Việt Nam? Would I feel at home there? I'm not sure I would. There's so much uncertainty right now in America as it is, so many disappointments and so many concerns that I have, even though I also know that we're incredibly fortunate for all the things that we do have.

ANNA: We have this openness in our society, despite everything?

AIMEE: Yes, but it's also hard to see on a day-to-day basis how people continue to struggle no matter what country they live in, and how many assumptions are placed, and how much class plays into it. When I read your writing, I feel more opportunities are happening in Vietnamese literature. How do you explore the very personal experience of a girl's adolescence and burgeoning sexuality with the incredibly chaotic politics that were happening in Việt Nam? How does the body become political, become radicalized? How do we come to terms with a changing body and adolescence, and how we deal with changes that are outside of our control with the changes happening in the world?

ANNA: One of my points and my main point in *Butterfly's Venom* is that chaos is not only war. Chaos defined Saigon society at that point, and it was the sexual violence that sometimes has nothing to do with the war or Saigon that I wanted to talk about in the context of Communist Việt Nam. I was thinking of this because I left before the war ended in 1973, but my parents and I never talked about the war, you know? They were not landowners, so I don't have the feeling that there was a strong resentment in my family toward the Communists who displaced Southerners after the war.

AIMEE: So they don't feel the loss of a country like other diasporic Vietnamese feel?

ANNA: Yes, they did not. They tried not to be radical. I remember this incident when I was living in Saigon, and we went to a pho restaurant in Orange County with my parents. I met a friend of my father's, and I was asked: "Oh, where are you from?" And I said, "I live in Việt Nam," but my father started kicking me under the table, trying to let me know that he didn't want anyone to know that I returned to Việt Nam.

AIMEE: Speaking of Việt Nam: Have you gotten any reactions from Vietnamese readers about that, challenging you about the ways that you address politics?

ANNA: You know, my Vietnamese readers are those Vietnamese who can read French, because my books have not been translated into Vietnamese yet, and I'm sure it's because of political reasons. I had written about the Côn Đảo prisons where political activists and Communists were jailed.[16] My first book *Riz Noir* is the story of two sisters. But the real story is that they switched their lives and politics and stayed in Việt Nam. I think that the government doesn't feel that I am entitled to write that kind of stuff. Strangely enough, some people do know me, because the books in French are sold in bookstores in Việt Nam.

AIMEE: How would you feel if your work was translated into Vietnamese?

ANNA: Oh, I'd love that. Once, my short stories were translated into Vietnamese and were read at a literary festival in Berlin, and it was a great experience. I read my work in Vietnamese, and I thought, *Wow! Did I write this?* Because as you know the matter of pronunciation is very complicated in France. And the short story was especially hard to translate in the sense that the narrator uses "you" instead of "I"; it can be very ambiguous, the "you" and "I," and they managed to translate it.

AIMEE: Did you feel like it had the same meaning, or did it change for you, hearing it in Vietnamese?

ANNA: I felt like it changed a little bit, but I liked it. I liked the fact that it doesn't resonate quite the same way that it does in French or in English.

AIMEE: About a year ago, *The New Yorker* featured a Chinese writer named Lillian Li who wrote about how she grew up in Beijing, and how she could not write in her native language, because she couldn't write about the pain and the trauma that she had experienced in that country. She could only write in English. It's a great article. I teach it to my students. They love it, but it made me wonder about what it means to articulate different words in a different language. Writing in English allowed Li to touch on very painful subjects.

And you, you wrote your last book originally in English [*The Butterfly's Venom*] and then you translated it yourself? Did you talk about why you decided to start writing it in English first? What was your motivation?

ANNA: Well, the first thing I ever wrote that was published was a poem in English. There's something about the language that rhymes with my inner self, and I think the fact that it's an accentuated language that is more like Vietnamese than French. So it was very natural for me. English was a third language that I learned in school, but I identify with the language.

In *Butterfly's Venom* the first sentence in the book is about a young girl's tits. I couldn't find the right word in French that would work. Instead of trying to find the word, I decided to switch to another language. It's not easy to write "tit," you know? It's a very common word now, but I had a problem when I retranslated the book into French. My editor said that I used the slang word *nichon* for breast; but why not just write the word "breast," which is *sein* in French? But that was not the language for that character. So I struggled with that until the very end.

AIMEE: What did you select?

ANNA: I selected *nichon*. But there were other passages regarding sexual words and innuendos that would have been hard for me to write it in French as a first draft. Once it was written in English, it was easier for me to translate in French. It's different than inventing the whole thing in French.

AIMEE: Do you feel like if you put a Vietnamese translation of French in English of your work, do you feel like there's one where it's most at home with your intent? What's the truest artistic version of your writing, and is it owned by a certain language?

ANNA: With *The Butterfly's Venom* I felt that it was English that reflected my true intention, and I managed to translate it into French. People liked the book enough to give it a try. But when I reread the English version, I feel that some of it was still a little lost in translation in the French version. I even skipped some lines because I couldn't translate them.

AIMEE: But I feel like you really are at home in a way with both France and Việt Nam.

ANNA: Yes. I feel the same about some of your characters who are French or are living in France, so perhaps we do not so much have a doubled identity but rather we have a tripling of identities.

AIMEE: That's very reflective of the diaspora. We see so many people who have been displaced who feel like they're running away from so many countries. What must it feel like to be more at home? It was good news to know that the fears that my parents had and that so many people had in the 1980's about what would happen to Việt Nam didn't come true. They really thought they had lost their country, but they didn't. It is a different country, but it's still . . . that is still where their ancestors are from, and it hasn't collapsed, and it's still there.

ANNA: The traditions are still there.

AIMEE: Exactly.

ANNA: I think that for me, going back to live in Việt Nam for twenty years, lifted the veil of nostalgia that the diaspora sometimes has of their homeland.

AIMEE: So you're not nostalgic anymore, because you know it. It's a reality.

ANNA: And I know now if I want to go back, it's very easy.

AIMEE: Do you find there's a lot of differences between those people who've been away from the country, and people who stayed behind? My next book, one of my next writing projects, is about Vietnamese people who stayed behind. And what it means to be a young artist or a young scientist living in Việt Nam.

ANNA: What I found was that the people who stayed behind would be people at least my age or older, like sixty-three. But the younger generation do not feel that they are left behind. They just grew up.

AIMEE: Yes, then they became part of an economy that was actually very young, and they got to take part in it. Well, at least with certain classes, the wealthy or middle class, for example. Class defines how you are as a Vietnamese diasporan. I saw my parents go through that struggle wanting to make sure that their families in Việt Nam were taken care of. It is the idea that if you are in America, you must be rich. And you're asked invariably: "Why aren't you sending more money back home?"

ANNA: Does that still happen?

AIMEE: I hear about it from a lot of friends who have family back home and obligations. That became a very strong part of the narrative in terms of how they saw going back to Việt Nam. I didn't depict it in my book. I think my current book was doing something very different, but it's something that I hear a lot about. From the Việt Nam you're describing, there's a lot of success today in the country. For writers in Việt Nam too, I wonder about the difficulties they have. Did you ever have any concerns about speaking up and being able to speak politically about issues that you feel are important? Do you think writers face that challenge in Việt Nam?

ANNA: Oh, yes. There's no freedom of speech. Some of the writers have been silenced. In Việt Nam they don't care what you write as long as you write it in a foreign language. The weirdest thing is that they sell my book there, but they won't translate it. In most cases it's indignation about one specific topic. And that specific topic is usually trauma. I write about trauma. Not only the trauma of war but also of sexual abuse.

AIMEE: In terms of trauma, I had experienced something where I saw loss in my family and my parents, and I wanted to explore it, and through my writing it allowed me to remain close with characters who were trying to solve those problems, trying to solve issues that were happening within themselves, within their new communities, with each other, and so I find that kind of always coming back in my writing. How do we solve this? I wondered why did you start writing? What was the impetus for you? Was there a question you wanted to solve? Was there something that you witnessed that you really wanted to explore?

As writers we have to find ways to make sure that we keep the reader, we don't alienate the reader . . . but there's also something to be said for feeling uncomfortable in reading about trauma and imagining the experience of it, especially in the wake of the MeToo movement, the question about how much we can show.[17] How brutally honest we can be about this trauma?

ANNA: I think we can on an artistic level, but do you have to be graphic?

AIMEE: I think that's a choice, there are parts in my first book [*We Should Never Meet*] that are violent . . . but at the same time, I am very sensitive to violence as a reader. In my first book, I was describing a home invasion in Orange County. I can't read it even though I wrote it, and I'll have students who have studied the book say, How could you do that to this absolutely lovable character? When I was writing this scene, I thought about this actually happening to my grandfather in real life. I couldn't shut the memory off. I had to write about it.

Writers have choices. It can be the very same writer making the choice to push out a scene or decide it's actually more effective to leave that scene and allow the reader's imagination to take over. It's a really thin line, and I think we explore it as humans, and we do explore as writers how much can we handle. But the truth is, people do experience these traumas.

ANNA: Yes. But you know, in my writing I wouldn't want it to be too far from poetry. So when it becomes graphic, it leaves poetry aside. So if it doesn't relate, I don't do it.

AIMEE: I think that the lovely thing about writing is that you have these choices. The language can reinvent itself. The words can be used in so many different combinations and have different effects on readers. You don't have to be graphic to be haunting. But sometimes I think I understand a writer's decision and realize, you know, as a writer we make so many choices about where to stop and where to keep going. I think that's the beauty in its diversity in terms of how far and how much we tell.

DIALOGUE BETWEEN ANDREW X. PHAM (UNITED STATES AND THAILAND) AND MARCELINO TRƯƠNG LỰC (FRANCE)

ANDREW: Hi Marcelino. I see that you've studied law. Did you practice law? Are you practicing still, in addition to your work as an artist and graphic novelist?

MARCELINO: Yes, I studied French constitutional and administrative law as part of my studies at a Parisian school called the Institut dÉtudes Politiques, commonly known as Sciences Po. This was a long time ago. My father was hoping I would later enter the École Nationale d'Administration [ENA]. I graduated from Sciences Po in 1977 when I was twenty. To my parents' dismay, I chose to take a year off and travel. Those were still the counterculture years. I had this complex of being too square. When I took up university again, it was to study English literature at the Sorbonne. The ENA seemed too stuffy for me, and I suppose the artist in me was calling. I really could not imagine myself assuming a position of authority over French people as a public servant.

ANDREW: You had more curiosity than I did at that age. As a child, I wanted to be an astronaut. When I realized, halfway through high school, that this fanciful notion wasn't going to happen, I thought that if I couldn't be on the rocket ship, then maybe the next best thing was to be a part of the engineering team. While the education was interesting, the actual work—the 8-to-5 routine, the cubicle, the petty office politics—was soul killing. I thought I might become a painter but somehow got caught up with words and stories, so I became a writer.

If you don't mind my asking, did your parents have mild or serious misgivings about your choice to pursue arts over the safe path? Were you the "black sheep" in the family? What repercussions did your choices have on your relationship with your parents? Who was more accepting of your choices, your father or your mother?

MARCELINO: An astronaut! You must be scientifically minded, which I'm not, unfortunately. I used to think myself as very literary. I envy scientific minds. As a child, I do remember having fancied myself as a racing car driver, just because I had seen a film called *Grand Prix*.

My interest in public and constitutional law stemmed from my childhood experience and from the troubled history of the Republic of Việt Nam [RVN]. Military coups were a constant menace in the early years of the short-lived First Republic of Việt Nam. As a five-year-old, I witnessed the bombing of the Presidential Independence Palace in February 1962. President Ngô Đình Diệm was brought down by a military takeover in November 1963. The leaders of this military putsch later issued a postage stamp depicting the coup as a people's uprising against a tyrannical presidential clique, adorning themselves with an aura of legitimacy.

As a teenager in London, I would follow the TV news about Việt Nam. I was surprised by the use of military force to suppress riots in Sài Gòn during President Thiệu's Second Republic of Việt Nam. The military—armed with wickerwork shields and truncheons—were sometimes ordered to put down protesters. This was shocking to Western eyes and contributed to the negative image of the South Vietnamese regime in Western medias. In democracies a special antiriot police force must be created in order not to involve the military in such internal affairs of public order. But the RVN knew no such distinctions. This inappropriate use of the army in civil affairs made us look like fascists. Western observers were often more lenient with our Communist counterparts in Hà Nội. They seemed to assume that it was all sunshine and roses between Uncle Hồ and his people, up North. But riots were simply not tolerated up there, as a matter of principle.

Before I answer your second question about my parents' reaction to my choice to pursue art over the safe path, could you tell me how you decided to become a writer, Andrew?

ANDREW: Sure. I actually wanted to become an artist and graphic designer. As a boy, I really enjoyed sketching and was encouraged by an art teacher at an impoverished public school in one of the rough neighborhoods of Shreveport, Louisiana. He spent his meager salary to buy me a pen set! Imagine that. I was like "legitimate" instantly. One of my early ink drawings won an honorary prize at the district competition in middle school. Proud little-boy me showed it to my father and he, with love and good intentions, crushed all my artistic aspirations in the bud. I never took art seriously again but continued to draw and doodle well into my teenage years—until I discovered girls and tennis.

As a boy, I was a lonely, bookish kid and read mountains of books. When I was bored out of my skull in engineering school, I gravitated to the bookstore and read whole novels standing in the aisle among the shelves for years on end until my graduation. One day, while sitting in class, a marketing course in an MBA program, I was so numbed with boredom that I started writing a fantasy novel while the professors lectured. I realized that I had little literary talent—truly, writing isn't easy for me—but I had passion and was gifted with stubbornness. So began my literary career.

Marcelino, I've never read a graphic novel. Your graphic memoir was an eye-opening first for me. What a beautiful accomplishment! The creative multifaceted approach delved seamlessly into complex subjects with emotional delicacy. I'm officially a fan of your work and of the graphic novel! When did your interest in art begin? And how did you settle on this medium? By chance or through trial and error?

MARCELINO: I have not ordered your books yet, which is a shame. Apart from work, this is such a busy period for me. I am in the middle of coloring thirty-five pages of comic art.... This is for a commission. This job requires so much toil and patience! So does writing, I imagine. Please tell me more about you and your family.

ANDREW: Well, my older sister ran away about two years after our family immigrated to the US. She was around seventeen at the time. She wanted to be a boy and she eventually had gender reassignment surgery to become a man. He married, divorced, became unemployed and depressed, and eventually committed suicide. It took me a long time to deal with it, and I made some big decisions at a pivotal point of my life because of it. I haven't been back since 1999, before my first book came out and was banned in Việt Nam. It's a bit of a mixed bag of feelings for me. It's one of the reasons I spend most of my time in Thailand. This way, I'm in Southeast Asia without being in Việt Nam and without all the historical and personal emotional baggage.

MARCELINO: The story of your older sister is important. I have a similar experience. I had an elder brother, Dominique Aí Mỹ. He was roughly five years older than I. Of us four siblings, Dominique was the most European-looking. A very handsome guy. Very artistic. I can't help thinking he could have become a fine painter. Unluckily for him, school didn't seem to be his thing. My father and mother were both expecting good school reports from us. I remember the dread of the end of each term period in London when we would receive our school reports from the French Lycée through the mail. Dominique's report was dismally bad and damning, except in art and sport. So it was a weekend of gloom and tears and terror when our parents would discover the bad news. Our father was a true Vietnamese scholar and he valued education. Our French *maman* Yvette was more of the artist kind. It is a pity that she was harassed by manic depression all her life. I describe our family life in fairly great detail in both my graphic novels: *Such a Lovely Little War—Saigon 1961–63* and *Saigon Calling—London 1963–75*.

Dominique struggled at school and gradually dropped out. These were the late sixties and seventies in England. Dominique became a hippie, and traveled to India, where he became enamored with the Puna sect of guru Bagwan Shree Rajneesh. In 1979, Dominique jumped off a six-story building in the city of Orange in the south of France, probably because Orange was the color of the Puna community and the color that they associated with rebirth. As it has been for you with your older sister, Dominique's death weighed heavily on all the lives of our family.

It is partly the reason for which I drifted toward an artistic career too. I suppose I wanted to do what Dominique had left unachieved. There was also an element of rebellion in my decision, which seems a little silly to me in retrospect: I wanted to show our learned and industrious father that one could also succeed in life without having a university degree. Looking back, I'm glad I received a good university education. It opened my mind.

ANDREW: Thank you for sharing your brother's story. Your father was a brilliant scholar. It must have been hard to live up to his standards, to grow up in the shadow of such intellect. My father is quite good in software engineering, and he is gifted with a near photographic memory. I received neither in my genetic package. I am good at math with a weird talent for dynamics and orbital dynamics, but I am fascinated by art and literature. I also like design and tinkering.

Here is something that came up over dinner with some poets last night. They asked for my opinion of Việt Nam, a general assessment of the country as a travel destination as well as a possible retirement place for expats. I prattled a while and later considered it some more. As they say, no voyager can ever return to the home he left. The same is true for emigrants. For me, Việt Nam diverged into two entities the moment I became a child refugee. One Việt Nam lives on within me. The other Việt Nam exists in the real world as a country I never knew. I prefer to explore and write about the country I knew and, by extension, the motherland of my ancestors. I don't have a connection to the real-world Việt Nam of today. How could I? I left the country as an eight-year-old boy. In my twenties I returned and bicycle-toured the country. A few years later, I went again, this second time as a tourist with a girlfriend, traveling right before my Việt Nam bicycle-memoir was published in the US. I took the trip because I suspected that my book would be banned in Việt Nam, which it was. A good friend who was a high-ranking Party member strongly advised me not to return. Consequently, I have traveled and lived all over Asia, but I have not returned to Việt Nam in twenty years.

People still ask me to comment on Việt Nam, but I can only say that I know little of this modernizing country, powered by a youthful population, thriving with a special blend of capitalism and communism, and that its leadership aggressively imprisons dissidents and critics with blatant disregard for human rights. So, while I yearn to visit my country of birth as a tourist and as a foodie, conscience and common sense have kept me away. After all, the world is a big place with many wonders to explore. I'm done with Việt Nam as a country. Am I done with it as a topic? Almost. My current project—a biographical novel based on my grandmother's life—is nearing completion. When it's finished, I will be done writing about Việt Nam. As an artist, I owe it to myself to explore other topics, other mediums too. As an author, I owe it to my readers to know when to shut up.

When I first began, twenty-five years ago, there were few Vietnamese American voices. The yoke fell on me. If I did not tell "our" stories, no one will. All our sufferings and struggles would certainly be forgotten. Not even my own brothers and cousins remember what happened. How could I expect the world to know when there is no record of it? In *Catfish and Mandala* I wrote about a self-immolation I witnessed as a child in downtown Sài Gòn, one night not long before the South fell. It could have been a monk or a man or a woman. It could have been intentional or accidental. I could not tell as I came upon the scene after the flames had engulfed the person. I was seven years old with a seven-year-old's eyes. The memory was recalled in the voice of a young boy.

Many readers accused me of falsehood and said that the Buddhist monk immolation was years before. Of course, the world knew about that event because international reporters were there and they took photographs of the monk before, during, and after the immolation—consequently making it an iconic event. A shocking piece of news that captivated the attention of the world. Does this mean that what I had witnessed as a child that night never happened? Does it mean that the only self-immolation that ever happened in Việt Nam was the one the international news reported? Without reportage and publication, things don't really exist? Stupidity? Myopia? A little of both?

I did feel the responsibility to write about certain things and still do, to some extent. I even felt the responsibility to translate Đặng Thùy Trâm's wartime diaries, *Last Night I Dreamed of Peace*, simply because I was a witness; I had the capacity and endurance to do it; and as far as I was aware, there was no one else doing it. But now, there are many fantastic writers with beautiful voices and clear visions. I gladly yield the floor. It's their turn.

MARCELINO: Your work is important. Earlier on, you asked me if my parents had been supportive when I chose to pursue an artistic career, instead of becoming a university professor of English literature or the like. My French mother Yvette was the most supportive when I started out. She understood my strange about-turn when I quit being a *professeur agrégé d'anglais* and chose the artist's brush instead of the academic's fountain pen. For instance, Maman helped me buy some of the more expensive equipment, such as a light table. My father, at first secretly dismayed, I'm sure, refrained from opposing any kind of veto. He must have been disappointed. But later, when I held on and learned my artistic trade at the job, he followed my work enthusiastically and was especially excited when I illustrated articles in the press, especially when published in the French daily *Libération* or other periodicals. He himself had been a journalist.

As I said, my elder brother Dominique's suicide in 1979 weighed heavily both on my own decision to quit a safe academic job and to go for art, especially comic art (*bande dessinée*) is a big thing in France, and on my parents' quiet acceptance of my radical change of course. Dominique hadn't fit in the school world, in spite of family expectations, but he might have found his way in the art world. He showed early talent in art. We all had a guilty conscience of having missed offering him that opportunity. But then, I must add that when you choose an artistic career, you sometimes must do it against the advice and opinion of others. Don't expect too much help or encouragement, I would say.

I am so interested about what you said about Việt Nam. I can really relate. The country and its history have fascinated me and have provided me with a subject, a topic, and right now, I am up to my neck in a new graphic novel project. It is about the fictional story of Minh, a young artist painter living in Hà Nội, toward the end of the First Indochina war. The reader follows him from 1953 to 1955. Minh, the young painter, dreams of traveling to France and Europe, to see the Louvre, Florence, and the world. He is a sort of hedonist, as far as that sort of stance is possible in a country at war, and in a traditional, superficially Westernized but still Confucian middle-class Vietnamese family. He is by no means a revolutionary, but the man has a heart and has empathy for his people. He is attracted by Western culture and loves jazz and French novels.

But the war is raging. To avoid conscription in Bảo Đài's French-trained nationalist army, he hops on a rural bus to travel to the family's home village lying in the eastern part of the delta. When he arrives, he is arrested by a local Việt Minh militia. The village is totally under Communist control, and the local cadres are actively implementing the land reform program, to motivate the peasantry to join the People's Army for the final general counteroffensive against the warmongering French colonialists. To avoid certain death as a member of the landed gentry, Minh has to volunteer into the People's Army. He is immediately dispatched on foot to China for a three-months intensive Maoist infantry training course. After the boot camp we follow the young artist when he is assigned to an armed propaganda unit, making its way, like thousands of Vietnamese youths, to enter the final fray, in the valley of Điện Biên Phủ.

This will be a 260-page story. I have completed 160 pages and 100 more to go. Then all that will need to be colored. A huge, backbreaking job. Hugely underpaid too. But I suppose that this is a self-inflicted mission, after which I promise myself there will be no more graphic novels. No more comic art. No more politics. Only pictures of the beach, the sea, of swimmers and fishes. Why all this exertion? All these hours of work? I have undertaken the Sisyphean task of altering the romantic vision many Europeans had and sometimes still have of the Vietnamese Communist revolution and nation-building effort. I can't forget how biased so many intellectuals, journalists, writers, artists in the West all too often were during the Việt Nam wars. They had a very romantic image of Mao and of his protégé Hồ Chí Minh. They were blind to the totalitarian traits and streaks of these Asiatic regimes. They were deaf to their violent calls to arms, or rather excused them, as these were "just, rightful, people's wars," weren't they?

But this is an uphill task, in Europe and especially in France. You will be lauded, over here, if you condemn—as one should—the Nazis, and the fascists of yesterday and today, as I have done many times, as an illustrator. However, over here, if you criticize, question, or offer a more realistic depiction of Stalin's criminal empire, of Mao's bloody reign, or of Uncle Hồ's sometimes violent path to and in power, you will soon be suspected of being an awful reactionary, a lackey of Western imperialism, an unpleasant and uncool right-wing conservative, and so on.

Traveling in Việt Nam also becomes a bit risky for me. My last trip there was in 2013. I went to Hà Nội and Điện Biên Phủ to meet former French-speaking Việt Minh cadres who had fought in the First Great

Patriotic Resistance, as they call it. I am less and less attracted to Việt Nam, as I observe all the changes taking place over there. The cars, the skyscrapers, the plastics, the pollution, the ridiculously pompous architectural nouveau-riche projects being carried out at full speed. And of course, also unattractive is the unending reign of an omnipotent, single party, nowadays busily conducting corrupt red capitalism.

DIALOGUE BETWEEN TRACEY LIEN (AUSTRALIA AND UNITED STATES) AND ANDRÉ DAO (AUSTRALIA)

TRACEY: Shortly before my debut novel was published, I did media training to help prepare for interviews. I practiced answering questions on craft, inspiration, research, etc. But one of the questions I wasn't prepared for (that, to my surprise, came up *a lot* in the US and UK) was a statement *posing* as a question: "I didn't even know that there was a Vietnamese/Asian community in Australia!"

What usually followed was an empty space I was expected to fill, and I never really knew what I was meant to say. *Uh, yeah? We're here?* I think the reason this statement-question kept catching me off-guard was because it was a blunt reminder that we're not really part of the image or narrative that Australia exports. I don't think we're even part of the narrative that Australia tells itself. I remember how discouraging this was to me as a kid, how it led me to believe that so many things— books and creative pursuits, even reading!—were simply not for me.

You and I are both Aussies who have spent considerable time abroad. Our debut novels came out within a year of each other. We've shared the stage more than once on the Australian writers' festival circuit. You've even met my mum! And yet, I know so little about you. I'm curious about your experience of growing up and becoming a writer in Australia, whether the feeling described above resonates with you.

ANDRÉ: For me, going overseas has always produced an ambivalent response to my identity. On the one hand, being overseas, I feel more Australian than ever before. And on the other hand, I'm never less Australian. More Australian because when I'm in Edinburgh or Paris, I get the sense—and what could be more Australian—that I've traveled from some far-off backwater to the center of the world. And less because I'm confronted by the fact, as you say, that we don't figure in the image of itself that Australia exports.

Actually, that ambivalence was particularly acute in Asia. In Indonesia I met plenty of writers who posed versions of your statement/question. For them, Australia was undoubtedly a white nation. But at the same time—often in the same breath—they'd tell me that they had never read an Australian writer. The idea that there exists an *Asian* Australia was a revelation—and also something that drew their interest, perhaps for the first time.

    I think that reflects, in a way, my experience of growing up in Melbourne. When I was still very young, my family moved away from the heavily Viet suburb where they and everyone they knew had first settled. The new suburb was a mix of Anglos, Greeks, and Italians. So I didn't really grow up around other Vietnamese kids. Too late, when I was eight or nine, my parents tried to put me in Saturday Viet school, but I didn't much like being in class with the four year olds. Looking back, it feels like that distance from the Vietnamese community was decisive: I internalized the image of Australia as a white nation and, without any other community to fall back on, I tried to make myself in that image—especially by what I chose to read and how I chose to write. It was only much later that I had the revelation that Australia has always had an Asian history, and that there is a rich tradition of Asian Australian writing—which was the beginning of me starting to feel that, despite everything, this is in the end, "home."

    I've been wondering about where home is for you—you've been in the US for a while now. But when we did an event together in Cabramatta (maybe the most Vietnamese suburb in Australia, and also the setting for your novel), that seemed to me—perhaps in a complicated kind of way—almost like a homecoming for you.

TRACEY: It's funny you use the term "homecoming" because when my publisher told me about the event—a panel of Vietnamese authors! To be held in my (very Vietnamese) hometown! The setting of my novel!—they also called it a "homecoming" and my internal monologue went, "Oh god, oh god, oh god." You see, I moved to the United States eleven years ago (Oakland, California, for a bit, then Lawrence, Kansas, for grad school, and now Brooklyn, New York), and I have by now spent a third of my life away from Australia. Despite growing up in a predominantly Vietnamese area, I'd also internalized the image of Australia as a white nation, saw the types of stories that achieved prominence, the kinds of people who got to count. It gave me little reason to feel Viet pride.

    And so, many years later, when I started working on *All That's Left Unsaid*—a murder mystery set in Cabramatta about a real-life heroin epidemic—a kernel of fear emerged. Did I have a right to tell this story? Did setting a novel in Cabramatta equate to laying claim to the community, and, if so, was I allowed to do that? I was cognizant of the narrative scarcity surrounding Cabramatta. I understood that even if it wasn't my intention to speak *for* Cabramatta, the mere act of speaking *about* Cabramatta meant that I was representing the suburb and its people. I did *so much* research, not just on Cabramatta but on the ethics of representation. I had all these debates in my head with imaginary people—*You don't even live here!* But I used to! *You're not really Vietnamese!* I'm ethnically Teochew but my family is from Vietnam! *How could you depict us all in a bad light?* I didn't! I'm being truthful! No community is perfect and lying about it does a disservice to everyone! *We didn't ask for you!* I didn't ask for me either! I'm not claiming to be an authority on anything! Aahhh!

All of that weighed on me at the Cabramatta event. I went in fully armored. And, of course, everyone was lovely, the audience asked generous and smart questions, and nobody had any kind of bone to pick. It was such a relief. Afterward, without the antagonism of my imagination, Cabramatta felt, if not like home then at least homelike. My neighborhood in Brooklyn feels homelike. Someday I hope to figure out this "home" thing for real.

What imaginary people did you argue with when you worked on *Anam?*

ANDRÉ: That's a constant question for me—who has the right to tell this story? In some ways the answer, when it came to *Anam*, was obvious: it's a novel heavily based on my family history, especially the lives of my grandfather (who was a political prisoner for ten years) and my grandmother (who raised their children on her own as a refugee in France). In one sense the answer to the question is obvious: of course I have the right to tell the story of my own family.

But I think the more difficult—and perhaps more interesting—question is whether that right is conditional. Sure, I can tell my grandparents' stories, but do I have to tell it in a particular way? For a long time I definitely felt that pressure, to honor my grandparents as saints and heroes. That was how they'd been seen by the rest of the family. And that was what, I suspected, my family was waiting for, ever since I first said I was writing a book about them. So for a long time I was having an imagined conversation with my whole family—conversations in which I tried to make the case for telling that which was dark, perhaps even shameful. There was also a political element to it, in that I was also arguing with what I presumed to be my family's—and the wider diaspora's—memories of South Vietnam and the American War. I went as far as giving these imagined opponents a name—Anamites—the kinds of aunts and uncles who would say: How dare you imagine the perspective of the Communists? After everything we've been through? Those imagined conversations left me in deep dread—an anxiety that lasted all the way up to and beyond publication.

Those fears turned out to be more or less unfounded. Like you, I expected a fight—but what I got instead was mostly pride and love and joy. Some bafflement too, for sure—I think it would take more than a book for my family and I to come to really understand each other. But as good a marker of success as any is that after *Anam* came out, my parents started sharing new stories about Vietnam with me—stories that were more ambiguous, more vulnerable, than any I'd heard before.

But one set of phantom interlocutors I haven't mentioned—and with whom I've been having conversation of one kind or another my whole writing life—is the white literary world. How to put this: I've long been worried about being read as *only* a migrant writer, a Vietnamese writer, a child-of-refugees writer. Does that resonate with you? How have you found the reception to *All That's Left Unsaid* beyond the Viet community? Has anyone read it as an Australian novel, no hyphen required? Does that matter?

TRACEY: At least a few (white) people have read *All That's Left Unsaid* as an unhyphenated Australian novel. I know this because they have told me so (literally: "This is such an Australian novel"). And quite a few have read it as something else. I know this because they have told me so, either via the labels they've slapped onto the novel, onto me, or the revealing questions they've asked. My feelings about it are complicated. On the one hand, its reception as an Australian novel matters to me because it makes me feel like I've succeeded in what I've set out to do. If I have told the story well enough, if I have rendered the characters and the social situations in a nuanced enough way, then a reader should understand that my characters have been shaped by Australia, that the problems they face are a product of Australia, and that thematically, what I have depicted is cyclical in Australia. In contrast, when a reader calls *All That's Left Unsaid* an immigrant tale, a novel *about* refugees, a Vietnamese story, I feel like I've come up short on a craft level.

On the other hand, whether the novel is viewed as Australian doesn't matter because it's up against forces much bigger than itself. Coming back to the idea that Australia has told a very selective story about itself over the past two-hundred-plus years—key to that narrative is that Australia is a white country. Even the most progressive of Australians have internalized that to some degree. During the Australian book festival circuit in 2023, for instance, I had white readers approach me to thank me for "telling the Vietnamese story." I had a reader of Mediterranean heritage gush about the book, then tell me they were thankful for "the Asians" because, once we came along, we bore the brunt of Australia's racism.

Several people asked me about life in Vietnam. And, look, I'm not here to give anyone a hard time—everyone I met at those festivals was generous and kind, and I do think they genuinely wanted to find connection. But is it any surprise then that I'm considered a Vietnamese Australian author who has written an *immigrant* novel about *the* Vietnamese community, even though I'd never previously called myself Vietnamese Australian (if anyone asked, I said I was ethnically Chinese, born in Australia, although my parents and their ancestors are from Vietnam—a mouthful, I know), my characters aren't immigrants, and there is no monolithic Vietnamese community?

I want to unpack those phantom conversations you've had with the white literary world. When you imagined being boxed in, how did you talk yourself out of the box? And now that *Anam* has been published, how have those worries or conversations changed?

ANDRÉ: Writers festivals do seem to be full of well-intentioned but slightly off-the-mark comments! I think it's interesting that you mentioned not wanting to give anyone a hard time—I have a similar tendency, once I'm on stage, or at a signing table, to be the good guest, to avoid being the killjoy. Like you—like anyone, really—my identity is complicated, unfixed, and certainly not captured by clumsy labels like Vietnamese or Australian. But in the interests of avoiding conflict, I tend, at public events, not to push back too hard on the reductive premise (of the Vietnamese face means Vietnamese novel kind).

It's something I'm still working on, to be a little more disruptive in those conversations. After all, my writing life has in a way been about writing my way out of the boxes I've been put in. It's one of the reasons it took me so long to finish writing *Anam*. And here we get to some very real, rather than imagined, conversations with people in the white literary world: around ten years ago, when I first started talking to editors about this book, I was advised to shape the story into a worthy memoir—something that would elicit (white) tears. That wouldn't take a whole lot of care or craft—as one editor put it, I should be able to write a book like that in about six months.

What happened instead was that it took me years to shake those expectations loose from my writing. Sometimes I went too far in the other direction, making my writing so dense, so knotted, that at least no one could say that I was pandering to white sympathy. In the end, the thing that saved me was failure: it took me too long to send a manuscript to those publishers, they lost interest, and then I was left to write on my own, for myself. For a while I even gave up on the idea that the book would be published at all, which meant I had the freedom—and burden—of grappling alone with problems of craft and voice and meaning. What did I want to write? Why? And how was I going to do it?

I think *Anam* is the book it is thanks to that period, when I taught myself how to write outside any of those reductive boxes (Vietnamese, immigrant, refugee—but also literary, novel, best-selling) because all the boxes had disappeared. So in some ways my acquiescence to questions about identity at writers festivals felt a little like I had, after all that effort, walked straight back into the boxes those editors had wanted to put me in a decade ago. But to come back to craft: I was struck by your feeling of coming up short, in craft terms, if *All That's Left Unsaid* is read as an immigrant tale.

Does your sense of craft transcend a writer's background and history?

TRACEY: I would like it to and, broadly speaking, I believe it can. But there are times when it seems like the answer lies in a decision tree.

Title: Will Your Craft Transcend Your Background?

>>Are you an author who belongs to a minority group? If yes, shuffle left.

>>Does your audience have, as Percival Everett puts it, a "colonialist reader's eye"? If yes, shuffle left again.

>>YOU HAVE LANDED ON: "NO, READERS WILL THINK THIS NOVEL IS ABOUT YOU. SORRY!!!"

I'm obviously being facetious, but sometimes it feels like that's what we're up against. There are no shortage of anecdotes from authors of color about how their fiction is often received as autobiography, how they're underestimated in their abilities to make things up, as though the only thing they're good for is regurgitating personal traumas. I cannot even count the number of times white interviewers have asked me how my own life inspired the plot of *All That's Left Unsaid* and whether I modeled the protagonist after myself, *even after* I've told them that it's fiction, it's fiction, it's fiction. Frankly, it's kind of rude.

But in the spirit of optimism, let's keep going with the decision tree and answer "No" to the last question. Shuffle up.

>>YOU HAVE LANDED ON: "CONGRATULATIONS! With an audience that isn't intent on boxing you in, your craft *might* be able to transcend your background. Success or failure is all on you. Good luck!!!"

And that's the future I'd like for us all—for audiences to read without a colonialist's eye, for our work to be received based on what's written, and judged on the quality of our craft.

ANDRÉ: I like to think that that future already exists in pockets. Of course, I had a slightly different experience to you, in that *Anam* was very much playing with that line between fiction and autobiography—so I could hardly blame people for conflating my narrator with me. But readers could still come to that with a colonialist's eye—they could, for instance, treat the correspondences between the narrator's life and my own as evidence that the book was "just" a refugee story; "thinly disguised," etc. Or they could, as many readers did, engage with the decisions made about voice and narrative and sentence and structure and image and so on—that is to say, to treat it as literature rather than as some anthropological artifact.

Interestingly, it was often people who were themselves from minority backgrounds who were the most astute readers of craft in my book, which suggests to me that there's more to be said about the relationship between life experience and what we're willing to understand as literary technique. In a way I feel as if we've only just started to scratch the surface: if we'd had more time, I'd want to talk about *why* we write—not, or not *only*, because we want to do something as programmatic as addressing *representation* (or whatever else is assumed about why minorities write), but because there is something—the word that comes to mind is *joy*—in the act of creation. Yet another thing that gets boxed out by the colonialist's eye: the joy—and frustrations—of craft.

TRACEY: Joy is a wonderful note for us to end on. The truth is, despite the frustrations, anxieties, and complicated feelings that come with doing what we do, it's all worth it to me because I derive so much joy from the work. Writing a novel is one of the most fun things I have ever done. On the outside I might look like a beleaguered lady hunched over a laptop, but on the inside I'm swinging from monkey bars and going down a water slide. It's what keeps me writing, and reading, and prevents me from becoming discouraged—the satisfaction and joy and fun of it all.

FIVE

Form and Future

> these pages have described aesthetic and political practices that need to be seen as necessary modes of stepping out of this place and time to something fuller, vaster, more sensual and brighter. From shared critical dissatisfaction we arrive at a collective potentiality.
>
> —JOSÉ ESTEBAN MUÑOZ

We've come to the final chapter of *The Cleaving*, a book that has pored through the detritus of the past and the destruction that colonialism and imperialism has wrought (and continues to) for the formerly colonized, the malingering effects of which live on in our everyday lives. Especially for those in the United States, the past and ongoing acts of genocide, slavery, and warmongering bring us to this moment. At the time of this writing, we endure the machinations of a white supremacist heteropatriarchy, empowered by the Supreme Court and other enablers of a fundamentalist far right, in their acts to overturn abortion rights, to perpetuate the onslaught of anti-Blackness and racism in the form of police brutality, and to preserve the "slow violence" of climate catastrophe onto the earth.[1]

This edited volume attests to the deep knowledge that the United States is a death-dealing country and culture, and that we, as refugees and diasporans, have emerged from such a violent environment, embedded in settler colonial histories as "settler refugees" ourselves.[2] And yet we insist that there must be paths forward, so we arrive here—to this critical text by Muñoz, a monumental cultural studies and queer theorist who died in 2013 and has offered us a "resource for the political imagination ... a flight plan for a collective political becoming."[3] It is to this "collective political becoming" that we explore here with mostly second-generation poets, visual artists, activists, and scholars the question of what our "political imagination" can look like in the *futur proche*. It is to these conversations that we move from questions regarding the past—of "what happened" and "why"—to questions about our collective futures—of "why not this" and "what if that?"[4]

As scholars and writers who think about better and just futures for all, we have been inspired by queer and BIPOC theorists who discuss futurity as a thematic, an aesthetic, a tactic to heal ourselves, and by extension according to some Indigenous artists, to heal the land. In a sci-fi installation titled "Future Ancestral Technologies," Indigenous artist Cannupa Hanska Luger collaborates with partner Ginger Dunnill to engage us in an "imaginary post-consumption future, in which white technocrats, having bled the earth of its resources, depart for colonies on Mars, leaving Indigenous people to live in the tailings of their progress."[5] In so doing, they display futuristic Indigenous fashions and show the technologies of battle and resistance, all which are embroidered with a profound sense of "survivance." At one point in the work the voice of a robot asks: "How to heal a wound that is still being cut? By traveling into the future, we survive you."[6] Coined by Native scholar Gerald Vizenor, the term "survivance" refers to an "active resistance and a repudiation of dominance [and] obtrusive themes of tragedy, nihilism, and victimry."[7] Against such "obtrusive themes," we return to Muñoz's metaphor of (time) travel to explore a collective being whose bonds are grounded in survival, possibility, and "relationality."[8]

What does survivability and futurity look like for Vietnamese Americans? Ly Thuy Nguyen eloquently describes "refugee futures" as aesthetic, politicized enactments of refusal.[9] More specifically, Nguyen posits a "queer dis/inheritance" that "marks a critical shift in how we understand refugee lineage and the possibilities of remembering outside of heteronormative, possessive individualist formations of familial structure. Centering refugee maternal relationships, [Nguyen] points out the paradox between inheritance and dispossession beyond masculinist discourses of gains and losses, forwarding an intricate understanding of queer(ing) legacy."[10] Of this legacy, Nguyen asks, how does one "radically, queerly 'inherit' a *difficult* life."[11]

The dialogues contained in this final chapter deal with queerness as well as the difficult lives and afterlives of imperial wars. These conversations bring to the fore the things the artists have inherited, which include notions about gender (hetero)norms and whiteness, the form and craft of established poetry, as well as the need for estrangement from family and pervasive images of "Vietnam." The need to embrace this estrangement animates the dialogues among a younger generation of Vietnamese diasporans. Refusing the white gaze, for example, poets Duy Đoàn and T.K. Lê look to film images to deconstruct image of "Vietnam," as in the "sniper girl," a reference to Stanley Kubrick's 1987 *Full Metal Jacket*. Images in film, as the two poets argue, syncopate with the ways they play with words, form, and tone. For Đoàn, the films by Wong Kar-wai are especially evocative and affords him words and cinematic worlds to play with questions of time and language (hence the title of his poetry book, *We Play Games*). Both writers thematize playfulness within the space of the poem, using both English and Vietnamese languages to accent this play.

Between visual artist Matt Huynh and poet Hieu Minh Nguyen, one of the foci of their dialogues is the estrangement from family, albeit for different reasons. The interlocuters begin as such, interrogating in the process what other forms of masculinities within the Vietnamese diasporic family could have been. Their dialogue is rife with the want and desires of their child and adult selves, which they argue become expressed within the planes of their art and writing. Huynh and Nguyen discuss the concept of chosen families and the ways that choosing to be estranged within one's family affords them an opening (and not a closing) of creative possibilities. As crucial and painful as it was for the artists to take leave of familial spaces and relations, it was also a choice for them to cultivate a network of artists and audiences. Creating new forms of family and communities is what is at stake for these artists, who want to claim an expansive place of their own to remake their pasts and presents in the form of art and poetry.

And finally, there is talk here, in the shape of a roundtable discussion between Paul Tran, Minh Huynh Vu, and Philip Nguyễn on community building and engagement. This conversation explores the coordinates of "something fuller, vaster, more sensual and brighter," to use Muñoz's words, for the purposes of building communities of care and political consciousness.[12] This last and final dialogue investigates what robust forms of scholarship, activism, and poetry might look like in our near futures.

DIALOGUE BETWEEN T.K. LÊ (UNITED
STATES, WEST COAST) AND DUY ĐOÀN
(UNITED STATES, EAST COAST)

DUY: I see the freedom of joy in your poetry and the instinct I sense in them to preserve that joy, it leaves so much to be admired. When I think about the joy of writing, I think about the way I read poems or watch movies: I read and watch primarily for formal pleasure—content often plays a subordinate role. I'm thinking of your poem "sniper girl." It's a poem that's set up by a striking context, yes—the title is immediately intriguing and violent, and the epigraph is evocative: the photo by An-My Lê and the sniper scene with Ngoc Lê from *Full Metal Jacket*. But this poem would have been striking to me even without the epigraph.

Can you talk about the epigraph, the draw of the photo and the movie scene to you? And then can you talk about some of your formal decisions in writing the poem? I'm particularly curious about the order of the sections and the strange and various subheadings or categories (for instance, *rabbit hole, looking glass, rabbit run, hide & seek, knickknacks, these boots*).

T.K.: Thank you for finding joy and curiosity in your reading of "sniper girl," because it is about that, and it is also about despair and rage. I felt all these things as I wrote the poem. It came out of me almost as a stream of consciousness, but it has also been living in my body for a long time. At first, I hated myself for defaulting to yet another war poem, but something felt new to me. It felt like I was breathing life into the sniper girl image, not just writing against it. I was doing what An-My Lê and Ngoc Lê had done. I could revel in the chaos and make sense of it after. I mashed up the two poetic forms, broke the lines into couplets, and gave each line categories. I like that the American cultural references are in brackets, almost subordinate and background—but they ultimately guide the reading of the lines that follow. For better or worse, that is true to my experience living in the US.

Many of the poems in your debut collection, *We Play a Game*, feature Vietnamese puns, which remind me of the word games I used to play with my parents.

DUY: A lot of the poems in *We Play a Game* are bilingual (Vietnamese and English). Some of them are grieving poems about the Vietnamese language dying across generations in the diaspora, some are whimsical tongue twisters, others are reflections about diacritics and the tonal nature of the language, others are about how my siblings and I bonded over language and the loss of the language. Many of the poems in the book are also about moments from my childhood—about my parents, brother, sisters, grandmothers, grandfathers, aunts, uncles, cousins (everyone).

So in one aspect the book has bilingual Viet poems and then in another it has childhood poems from someone who happens to be Vietnamese. After the book came out (and somewhat before), the subject people asked me most about was my Vietnamese identity, which at first was exciting to have the opportunity to talk about, in a bit of spotlight. I really enjoy reminiscing and chatting about the culture, the language, and our idiosyncrasies. But that excitement quickly wore out. It was a weird gaze to be under suddenly. People's—especially white people's—insistence or attention to details regarding anything Vietnamese dulled the enthusiasm I had for talking about how cool it is to be Vietnamese. I'd say too, though, that that enthusiasm was also expended through the act of writing the Viet poems. Maybe that need was exorcised over time? In my current manuscript there's only one Viet word, *Đức Mẹ* (Mother Mary), which I think is kind of funny.

T.K.: This brings me to your poem "2046 is on the 24th floor," a tribute to Leslie Cheung and a rereading of the characters he portrays in Wong Kar-wai films. You skillfully use space to breathe life into the image, almost as if the lines are taking flight—which is a central image of your poem. To me, you write to the ways in which private tragedies can be fit into neat, touching, and incomplete narratives that maybe we don't have a right to know. If the metaphor for Leslie Cheung's character in *Days of Being Wild* had been different, as you say, the film's world would crumble: "it wouldn't be fitting for Lulu to play the leading lady anymore. And that's not what the audience wants / and needs. . . ." Can you talk more about what compelled you to write this poem?

DUY: Leslie Cheung has been a fundamental influence on me. My favorite movies starring him—*Happy Together*, *Days of Being Wild*,

Farewell My Concubine—were all transformative for me. "2046 is on the 24th floor" mentions some of my favorite Wong Kar-wai films, films that no doubt have influenced me. The technique I see in his films, the skillful restraint—or the sensibility of restraint—is intoxicating. Many of the works of art that I love operate this way. Starting out, it was Ernest Hemingway's *In Our Time* and "Hills Like White Elephants," James Joyce's *Dubliners*, Rita Dove's *Thomas and Beulah*, and then later, Louise Glück's *The Seven Ages* and Carl Phillips' *Silverchest*.

I have some poems about family violence. With some of these the way I write about certain events comes out of a resistance, a realization that I'm not obligated to tell readers all the details of a story. I can just create the negative spaces and I can avoid lingering on certain images. The technique, the moments of restraint and understatement I sought in movies and writing, including my own writing, served two purposes: they gave me a chance to emulate my favorite artists while also protecting certain truths. The artists I discussed and their technical moves provided the tools I needed to try to frustrate any confidence readers might have in narrowing down conclusive information about family violence. Writing these poems had less to do with telling stories about violence than it did with formal concerns, in this case: How do I sketch out the negative spaces to imply the drama? Poems and movies that do this successfully have always drawn me into their worlds. They set you on edge. And it's what they *don't* tell you that sets you on edge.

T.K.: You've said that as storytellers it's easy to get caught up in details. I totally agree with that. For a long time before this, I'd been trying to tell the authentic story of my family's history, thinking that I would understand my family better, and if I could understand my family better, that I would understand myself better. And once I understood these things, I could have some peace and heal us all. I kept trying to find details about my family's stories, to name and make sense of the pain they have both experienced and inflicted. At several points in time, I wondered if I was telling my parents' stories, or [if] I was telling on my parents. So how could I write something honest without getting lost in the search for truth?

Because at the same time, the Vietnam War is one of the most photographed and filmed wars in US history. There is an immense archive, and even with all these primary documents, the war has somehow been enfolded in US empire in a way that justifies continued violence here and abroad. In terms of poetry, I turned to my lived experience to guide me. I knew that my parents had certain precious objects and small stories they felt comfortable sharing. I learned that their tight grip on physical things was in large part due to immense loss, grief, and abuse. I realized that contextualizing their trauma did not recuse them from the abandonment and abuse I experienced growing up. And so I did what I had done as a kid. I spent time with these objects, to talk to them, to listen to them. In that way I could discover something new about the people who held them closely. I could perhaps feel close to them too.

You turn to form to "free" yourself from the trap of historical accuracy and detail. It can seem counterintuitive to turn from one fussy thing to focus on to another, but you make it work in *We Play a Game*.

DUY: Yes, received forms or fixed forms free me up in a lot of ways. I still think I'm driven by accuracy and details when writing, but I don't want to become fixated all the time on telling the details of my life. I remember hearing Robert Pinsky say that with a first collection, maybe a poet feels the need to say a lot about their own life—they feel those stories are important to tell. But a second collection brings with it the opportunity for the poet to have the courage to look around at the world more. I feel this way too. At least I'm not writing about childhood or Viet identity or queer identity now. But then of course there's the pleasure, over time, of gaining fluency in hitting the ball, having a fluid stroke, a variety of shots, etc. When you've developed fluency, then you can mix it up and see if you can try a new creative shot here and there. This is where working within fixed forms becomes even more fun.

I wonder if we can talk about your poem "The Fisherwomen and the Fisherman." There's the beautiful (and fun) moment that starts halfway through the poem when the fisherman is asleep, and the women sneak off and have *sầu riêng* by themselves. He has forbidden them to eat it because "the stench reminded them of past, of death." But while he sleeps, they're quietly laughing and eating *sầu riêng*. Before they playfully share the *sầu riêng,* however, they pass through a spell of weeping: "Our closed mouths became ovens, thawing out relics from lives we were told to leave." But then one of them bursts out laughing. I love that moment; they're all instantly transformed by someone's spontaneous laughter. I can feel what she's tickled by.

Makes me think of how, in a significant way, it was really my aunts who raised me. When I was young, at family gatherings, the men would be at the dining table eating, drinking, being boisterous, while the women continued to work in the kitchen. Passing by the dining table made me nervous; that energy always made me anxious (not as an adult, though—I admit to liking this energy now). But all the boisterous talk and posturing is just a pissing contest. It's competition. When the men at those dining tables during my childhood were laughing, they were mostly just laughing at their own jokes. Meanwhile in the kitchen, as with the women in your poem, my aunts seemed to be having the real fun. Their exchanges felt more truthful and intimate. And if I passed through the kitchen, they'd be very sweet and say things like "Cố gắng học, nhá, con" (telling me to work hard and persevere in my schoolwork) or "Đi tu đi, con" ("become a monk, enter the priesthood, my child").

My aunts were directly teaching me real life lessons. Makes me think of your line about the women: "Laughed at all the things the fisherman did not know." What was your favorite part of the women's *sầu riêng* story, or what was the most important thing you wanted to communicate or capture?

T.K.: Yes! I love that this piece brought up memories of your aunts in the kitchen, Duy. It was important for me to write about a collective of fisherwomen and a singular fisherman. Men in my life have pushed a message of individual struggle and success, a sense of patriarchy celebrated and magnified by the conditions in which they were allowed to come here. Meanwhile, everyone else is a background prop, there to make the scene beautiful, or profitable. This is how the story is cast from a position of power. But as you know from your own experience, "behind-the-scenes" is full of life, and action, and laughter, and small gestures toward the possibility where your own future could be different.

DUY: I'm happy to say that I find the formal qualities of your poems to be pleasurably intriguing, the formal elements that you create as moving, working parts in the machine of each poem. And you always supply the magic or spark that eventually lights up all the parts. I was wondering if we could talk about your poems "Afterlives" and "Afterlives II." In these two poems I sense that maybe something magical (not necessarily good) happens to the refugees fleeing by boat, or rather, magical things happen to them. Or maybe the magic is happening to you? I'm referring to what's happening with color in the poems:

> what follows is color running off the page
> your bright fabric signal waving surrender to grayscale

and:

> i can hold the technicolor of your trauma in my unwashed hands.

T.K.: Writing those poems, I returned to the vast archive of Vietnam War media, to those gritty black-and-white photographs and videos. "Afterlives" and "Afterlives II" used to be one poem, a long string of words. But that's not how trauma exists, right? It's not one neat line, and it's not isolated in its own little world. We learn to creep around it. We accidentally set it on fire, and then find better ways to cache it away. And what do the traumatizers do? They frame our suffering in such a way that excuses them from the violence they cause. They omit facts. They reword history books. The gymnastics of logic, the twists and stretches, that the US government has made to justify its presence in Việt Nam is so absurd, and yet it works.

"Afterlives II" is from my own foolhardy optimism that I could reclaim it, disrupt it, fix it, and somehow I could save all of us from this cycle. At this point I don't know if there will be an "Afterlives III," because that would make it feel complete. The way I live now, it is in constant suspension, anticipation that something will topple, or maybe sometime later things will get better, maybe through magic. It seems like the arc of your first collection, *We Play a Game*, follows the arc of the opening poem, "We Play a Game Using Tomatoes." You use Vietnamese to guide the piece from fun, to curious, and finally to a darker place. (It almost reads like a Grimms' fairy tale.) I love how it ends on the word *chua* (sour) and the act of taking in someone whole.

It speaks to the experience of wanting to know the entirety of something but not being completely prepared for the answers.

In this poem a small change in diacritics shifts the tone from playful to inquisitive to a little serious. There's also "First-person Plural," which highlights the ways in which pronouns change in one person's particular relationship to another. One diacritic can change an entire sentence. In your poems they can transform an experience of a memory. It's not as if the change from *tu* to *tử* in "History Lesson from Anh Hai" negates one sentence, but rather both sentences take on even more significance. Spelling out your name in US military code also renders you strange, both to the reader and, it seems, to yourself.

DUY: Regarding bilingualism and diacritics, I enjoyed the formal challenges. Those poems were fun to play with, but I think there was probably more at stake with the bilingual poems than with the book's other formal questions. Mainly because I wanted to showcase to non-Vietnamese readers that Vietnamese is an awesome, complex language that can be extremely perplexing and intricate. It was very important to me that the first poem of the collection be "We Play a Game Using Tomatoes" because I wanted to make it explicit that the book was going to have Vietnamese in it (the poem also is about queerness and that was important for me to communicate as well, right at the start of the book).

The small changes in diacritics you mentioned were vital to the fun. And, as you said, the shifts can lead to the kinds of discoveries that we might not want to encounter, something dark or unfortunate. Or we might learn that discovery isn't always a monumental event or a eureka moment. It might instead be a hushed insight.

T.K.: In "sniper girl" I liked that Hà is a name with weight on it, the diacritic forces the voice to drop. I wanted to end on that kind of a note. In your work I find that from the diacritics and lessons from your aunts and the poets you speak through and about, and from the arc of your first poetry collection, they all serendipitously reflect the sequencing of the opening poem, and how the last line ends with *chua* is almost literally a chef's kiss. I'd like to think in this way that our poems speak to each other too. Imagine the conversations they'd have.

DIALOGUE BETWEEN HIEU MINH NGUYEN (UNITED STATES, MIDWEST) AND MATT HUYNH (AUSTRALIA AND NEW YORK, UNITED STATES)

HIEU: We're going to begin the conversation by discussing what it means to be estranged from our family, being like distant sons and how our proximity to our family affects our proximity to our culture. I grew up in a family of basically all women. All the men in my family left their wives and their families and I was the only son. This is the kind of family I grew up in and we all lived together at one point. They were like siblings. And then they moved away when I was nine. I discovered that distance between us was possible then. We were not able to close the gap after that.

MATT: I think something like that happened with me and my brothers too. Maybe this has to do with age difference. My brothers are seven and nine years older, so it always felt like they did not understand me. Did you fall into an older brother role in the dynamic with your cousins?

HIEU: Yes, I would say so. We were born and lived in Minnesota, and when they moved to Michigan, I felt left behind. I realized then that this was the only attachment I could ever have.

MATT: I have the same sensation in my own relationships with friends and my siblings. Do you think these strong ties came from proximity?

HIEU: I think so. We all grew up in the same house. For example, with my aunt, my grandmother adopted her at a refugee camp and took her in. My aunt is half-white and because of that, she was able to come to America and then sponsor my grandmother and my mother to come to America. And this is how I got here.

MATT: I am curious about the dynamic between you and your cousins and your extended family. I think I was in the opposite situation, where I belong to a nuclear family and am the youngest. I never felt I had to be responsible for anything and to anyone. I didn't really have any contact with my extended cousins or with my grandparents or any other family members.

HIEU: We always believed in the concept of a chosen family. My family has always been this collection of other lonely children. My mom has talked about how people find each other because they need each other. My family is a collective of people who found each other. All my mother's sisters, for example—all the people I consider aunts—aren't blood-related.

MATT: I think about family a lot now since I moved across the world and left everyone behind. They moved to Australia, and I don't blame them for their choice. We're all seeking to establish a life from instability. But I chose to move away and to pursue quite a difficult profession. I chose to build my own idea of what family is. This journey made me ask a lot of these questions: What is home? What makes a home? What makes a family? Why do I need to have that feeling again of being among family?

HIEU: I understand. Have you found people here in New York, that you would consider family?

MATT: Yes, my partner; she's my rock. But I had to mature quickly, and you quickly learn, especially in a place like New York, who your real friends are. How is it for you?

HIEU: I felt very close to my Vietnamese heritage and culture growing up until I was fourteen, when I came out. My mother just rejected me then and there. She believed that I was diseased and that I needed to find a specialist, that I was demonic and needed help. And then I also had uncles on my dad's side; there were masculine figures around me, telling me that I wasn't masculine enough. They were abusive to anyone who allowed any kind of tenderness or vulnerability in the house. They saw tenderness as a weakness. And for the longest time the people who hurt me the most were all Vietnamese. This caused a caesura in our relationship, and this ended by creating a caesura between me and my access to the Vietnamese culture because it was through my family that I knew the culture.

    I first started writing poetry around that time. I was writing to escape. I used it, believing that poetry was like a performance. I used to use poetry to imagine the person I wanted to be, somebody who was in love with girls and was charismatic and funny. I made fun of myself for being Asian or overweight before other people could. In my poems I can't be hurt by racism, by the people I love, or the rejection by my family. Poetry is my shield from the world. Along with that I found assimilation as a kind of safety, where English became a barrier to protect me from a culture that I felt hated me.

MATT: I've used drawing and comics in a similar way, especially when as a kid. It was a way to escape and have power fantasies in reaction to being misunderstood or underestimated. Looking back, I've used comics as something my family didn't understand to create a safe space for myself. I show things, and I do not use words as much. When I'm attempting to grasp ideas and experiences that I don't have a complete hold on, I can recognize my intended expression in the expansiveness of visual art rather than running up against the limits of language and prose.

HIEU: Yes, there's safety in poetry and you don't have to explain everything. There's always the desire to be understood, but also a freedom in forfeiting the idea of being understood. In poetry you can give yourself permission to say what you want to say and not have everything be understood by people who will understand you. Like you, my mother doesn't read and neither does she speak English; it felt safe to write in that form and to hide from having to say the truth or hide it.

MATT: I described comics as visual poetry and an economy of sorts. It's an economy of line, like two dots and lines of faces you are stripping, stripping, and stripping. It's about how many characters and words you can fit in a bubble, and it becomes as much about the moments you leave out as the ones you leave in. It's about the gutters and the closure between the panels on a page. In comics you're letting people actively inhabit that emptiness, that absence to create meaning. I love the ambiguity. A cartoon is a house of cards with the lines precariously holding up your message. The cartoonist needs to know every dimension of what they want to leave on the page to allow just enough to reach the reader. At the same time, you can be a complete coward. You can hide in the absence.

HIEU: To feel safe is not the same thing as to be a coward. It is okay to keep things for yourself. While I believe that to tell the truth is brave, I don't think hiding is cowardice. It is not the same thing.

MATT: I agree with you. My work is about understanding myself and working toward creating that image of myself that I can recognize. There is also the question of the audience. My position to my audience varies. Sometimes I tell them in my head: *I am going to lie to you; I'm going to seduce you; I am going to romance you; I am going to come through you; I am going to be very vulnerable and rigorous for you.* At other times I tell them: *I'm going to shake you up; I'm going to knock your socks off.* It could be any and all of these things. Whatever it is, I ask myself: *How am I taking care of my audience's time? How am I not wasting their time?*

HIEU: What do you want your audience to see?

MATT: That's a hard question. I always hesitate at answering this question directly. What I want changes over time. I don't want to hold myself to one answer. Do you have a sense of clear mission or vision when you write or read to an audience?

HIEU: I don't know if there is a singular thing that I'm striving toward. What I know is that poetry has helped me. I use poetry to discover and understand the violence of my family and their history. Poetry has also helped me discover tenderness and beauty. It's perhaps not empathy but a discovery in forgiveness, of intention. Poetry gave the space to not place myself at the center of every moment of my life.

MATT: I think that definitely helped me with my stories too. I wonder if you've experienced this in transforming the work, in transforming the history, the characters in a poetic form. I've had this kind of unexpected consequence when I've made an animation, a comic and illustrations. I didn't think I was interpreting anything, I'm not a journalist. But my work is very stark and deliberately so. I think it is both ugly and graceful; regardless of any technical or aesthetic choices in executing the painting, an audience must be aware that I've had to pay a subject a lot of time and attention if I've decided to paint it, even if that subject is undesirable or possibly offensive. Just by turning my attention to the subject and pointing the audience to it, it is transformed. This in turn transforms my relationship to the characters and communities I draw.

HIEU: When you say "transformation," what do you mean?

MATT: I mean, sitting and ingesting the source materials, whether that's researching for generating the writing itself.

HIEU: That translation between the idea and the product.

MATT: It could be like after researching the protest movement in New York, or after researching the refugee camps in Malaysia. Obviously that process is quite wrenching and exhausting.

HIEU: And then what comes out of it, people describe it as beautiful. Is that what you're saying? That the pieces of art are inspired by these kinds of traumatic moments, but then they get simplified by beauty.

MATT: The thing is, I'm not trying to do that, I'm trying to selfishly fill a gap in my knowledge and experience. But yes, the reception of my art shifts and pivots my own relationship to it. I am troubled by this because I'm honestly not trying to convince anyone that what I do is beautiful.

HIEU: Sometimes there's something similar that happens in poetry; when readers come up with their own interpretation and it is not what you've intended. I think those interpretations must exist; I like the misreadings of my work, when people read my work in a way that I didn't expect or didn't see. It doesn't mean that they're wrong; it means that they found something in it that spoke to them about their own lives.

But there will also be people who read it exactly the way I intended it to be read. Those are the people that I feel "seen by." When someone sees you through all the barriers of art and all the barriers of their own personal experiences and sees you for you, it is powerful. These are rewarding moments—when you are seen through all these possible translations.

MATT: Yeah, I fully understand what you are saying, especially in the context where, obviously, there's a lack of representation of our experiences and our stories in this society. When this happens, it's piercing.

HIEU: Yes, there are those moments when you find your people; poetry is a way to remedy loneliness in a way. We're trying to communicate something and if someone understands it, it makes us feel less lonely for a moment. I do not take these moments for granted. Sometimes readers impose a fixed identity on your work. Sometimes someone will come up to me and say: "Oh my God, this poem is about the Vietnam War," and I'm like, "No, that poem is about a flower." They would impose these interpretations onto it. For me, poetry is like a filter to find your people.

MATT: I think that is important because they become your core.

HIEU: What about a writer's responsibility—of trying to navigate responsibility by documenting, or archiving our family stories? I think every family has a storyteller in the family. Sometimes you do it through visual art. Sometimes you do it through photographs. I've chosen the role as the storyteller in my family but also tried to understand the many responsibilities that come with it. It's not a pressure on me because it's the life I've chosen. But I want to also be responsible to the truth, whatever that means. And then I think: *What am I allowed to talk about and not talk about? What is mine to share? Which experiences are mine, or are they secondhand experiences that come with distance?* I'm writing the story from a place of distance, not from a place of actual experience. Sometimes these responsibilities and questions keep me from writing though; and I don't know if it's good or bad.

MATT: One of the ways I navigated this is by differentiating my responsibility from other people's stories and their sense of "truth." I've done a lot of work with media and journalist outlets and archivists. Obviously these people are interested in the truth, but a lot of marginal people have been left out of records and artistic records. Truth is linked to perspective. But people like us don't have a record, and the best way we can do this is from memory and storytelling. I think what you need to do is to aspire to what feels true. And that often involves having to go to fiction because there's nothing else that can capture it.

HIEU: Yes, it's not only about representing one thing. Representation allows a widening; we can widen what is our stories or what we are capable of. Sometimes if my audience hears Vietnamese, they want me to speak about the Vietnam War, even though I didn't experience it. They want me to speak of my family's experience with the war, stories of suffering and fleeing—the refugee narrative. But I want to represent the story of other things that happened in my life and family: my aunt, mom, dad, and uncles; they were all shitty teenagers during the war and did shitty teenage things. My mother actually loved the refugee camp. She said she had a great time there.

MATT: I made this comic very quickly about my parents' experiences in the refugee camp, and I did it fast; it is something I avoided for a long time. It's kind of a poetic telling of it, and it's very sparse, but it's about their experience there and how they were in their early twenties, two kids trying to learn how to be parents in a refugee camp. I drew them on a beach, having a romantic time and chasing clouds. My dad got a blazer made there, which I now own, and in the piece he has saved up enough money to buy cans of Coke for my mom. There are certain things no matter what is happening, people will find a way to find joy or continue with their life.

HIEU: Their lives go on. I think forgiving is a privilege, but sometimes our bodies allow us to forgive or forget something that's happening to survive. I remember that my mom talked about how she and my aunt would just run wild and have so much fun. And I think one of my uncles was talking about how he and his brothers were playing near a stream. They saw planes drop bombs on this village, and they were cheering on the bombs and the explosions. They were so happy about it, and they were cheering it on. And then they realized it was their village, and then they ran back to it. There was, in that moment, a short time when they were allowed to be children.

MATT: Moments like these are missing in our narratives. In my family's stories they're in the camps where they talk about being in between places on an island; they run away from home; they're waiting to hear from the UN where the next home is going to be, where they're going to be designated. In another moment they are talking about their baby son who has to learn his first words, to eat and to walk. I think we need to add weight to those experiences and impressions.

HIEU: Yes. When I speak of wanting for many, many years to articulate the experience of myself and my friends, it's similar to what you're describing with your family; they're all impressions of war. It's like the impression of war generations later, a permanent song for an entire life. It is not like in the movies; it is inescapable.

MATT: Absolutely.

DIALOGUE BETWEEN PHILIP NGUYỄN (WEST
COAST, UNITED STATES) AND PAUL TRAN (EAST COAST,
UNITED STATES), AS PREPARED BY MINH HUYNH VU
(EAST COAST, UNITED STATES)

This dialogue was forged out of a need for connection—between each other and across generations—two years into the pandemic and counting. A series of letters between unfamiliar yet still familial strangers, this braided epistolary essay is simply a shared attempt of trying and tying, together, some temporary threads of meaning that are bound to come apart. The intimacies and itineraries tracked here are fugitive—both fertile and futile—attempts of navigating between the various crises of the present: an always tentative blueprint of cultivating emergent relations amid constant emergency. Here, the interlocutors shuffle and share their strategies as simultaneous artists, academics, and activists—a shapeshifting that is vitally necessary to move through and against the "creative destruction" of neoliberalism and its demands of individualism.[13] —Minh Huynh Vu

PAUL: This letter of terrible crystals is written *to* you, Philip, as much as it's written *for* you from thousands of miles away, though as our words embark the distance toward each other, I too feel like I'm with you, a sibling from another lifetime, about to congress with the past, the present, and the future all at once.

I just stepped inside from an Oakland summer night. A cool wind had cut through the hot air, and the bright tip of my Newport recalled the cigarettes my uncles snuck off to smoke during holiday dinners decades ago, before I first ran away from California and swore never to return. Although they'd enter the house smelling of menthol, my cousins and I pretended they didn't. As children of refugees, pretending was our first job. Nobody's marriage fell apart. Nobody's father abused them in a garage across from Our Lady of the Sacred Heart. Nobody's sister-in-law schemed out of greed or shame masquerading as spite to prevent their family from being sponsored to the United States from Vietnam. We pretended not to even know these secrets, setting another steaming *banh bot loc* onto our plates as the aunties traded murmurs designed precisely for us to hear, and we pretended not to use this information against each other. Circumstance, or fate, was never fixed.

Who knew when someone's misfortune would pale beside ours? Pretending nothing happened as we ran down to the end of the street, where we flew kites made from string tied to the handle of Lucky Seafood bags and watched light disappear behind the burning hills, was how we intended to persist.

PHILIP: Paul, I write to you as a part of this unique opportunity to be a time traveler alongside you—to *vượt thời gian* (cross space)—miles and worlds away in conversation with you, as a part of this project for diasporic Vietnamese literary arts and culture. It is indeed somewhat strange though, even as we have not yet been able to meet each other in person due to the ongoing pandemic, I feel a deep sense of almost inarticulable familiarity and comfortability with you as we embark on our own journeys across spaciotemporalities of children of refugees.

If silence, sacrifice, and secrets are the fuel for the time machine that teleports and transports us sequentially and simultaneously to a shared futurity and history, then this contemporary moment must be fated serendipitous circumstance, *duyên phận* (fate). I light three sticks of incense to gently place in my home's *bàn thờ* (altar) and kneel to recite prayers passed on from the past, beholden to the invoked presence of our ancestors, to help guide us through these difficult times, ironically spent safely with my refugee parents whose language of survival fills in the gaps that my Vietglish may not be able to reach.

PAUL: Back where the song of waves tumbling ashore was indistinguishable from wildfire, my fidelity to pretending has lifted like the fog covering the coastal highways at dawn. I pull a can of jasmine tea from the cabinet. I turn on the kettle. I'm no longer that eighteen-year-old with two heavy suitcases at the San Diego airport, arrogantly sure I could escape my family or peddle distortions of our history to get ahead. I'm thirty and washing dishes alone in my apartment, my hands wrinkling the way my mother's hands must've while she scrubbed the hours spent bent at the sewing machine from her good gray skirt in the kitchen sink by candlelight. When she was my age, the song of tanks trampling gates rang through her village, and Saigon got a new name. My grandfather was in the hospital, or gone, and my grandmothers sold even their mattress of banana leaves so my mother and her four siblings could eat. Although I understand them—that world where no matter how horrible people treated each other, the lies told and truth withheld to serve selfish versions of the truth, everyone bowed and smiled and pretended love was mindless obedience exchanged for security—I can't play that game. I miss them too much, and I love them too much, to go on like nothing happened.

The tea, now steeped too long, tastes bitter as it was when I was little and asked my mother if I could have the cup that she prepared each morning for Ngai Quan The Am. The color is that amber trimming the bodhisattva's shroud, the joss sticks my mother lit and held while she prayed. I wondered then what she asked for and what she bartered for her wishes to come true. My wish, these days, is to not merely transcribe but transform through language the people, places, and things I witnessed and imagined. I wish not only to help those I love envision and appreciate our triumphs and tragedies anew but to position us as a provenance where knowledge can be produced about race, class, gender, sexuality, ability, war, imperialism, displacement, migration, decolonization, abolition, agency, freedom, and the genius required to start over and blaze unprecedented paths through unknown territories and territories of the unknown. I intend to document what we inherit as well as what we invent.

PHILIP: My latent inheritance of trauma was realized through the discovery of diasporic Vietnamese narratives in contrast to militarized dominant-narrative representations and massacres—literally and epistemologically—of our people. My survivability sensibility, what Thi Bui refers to as her "refugee reflex," had been suppressed by the sounds of fighter jet and import car engines in my birthplace of Lancaster, California, the desolate exurban city known for its contributions to aeronautics in the form of warplanes and the backdrop of the second *Fast and Furious* movie. When asked where I was from, my reference point was Garden Grove's Little Saigon, the mecca of Vietnamese America, two-and-a-half hours away via the 14, the 405, and the 5 freeways while traveling by my dad's pride and joy, his Honda Odyssey minivan, my mom in the passenger seat massaging her worn hands, while my younger sister and I tried to make sense of the Vietnamese radio static. Though we didn't talk much on these grocery trips, I became more inquisitive of how fate had led our family to be one of the only Vietnamese families in the Mojave desert, away from the epicenter of the *cộng đồng* (community) while still tethered to it by way of sustenance.

    I began to make sense of silence upon reading the memoir *I Love Yous Are for White People* by Lac Su, which had been simultaneously recommended to me as inspiration to write my college personal statements by my Vietnamese American friends in Key Club, also known as the Asian Club at any high school in California, and my mother, who had seen an interview with the author Lac Su on the Vietnamese-language television channels. As a child of refugees struggling to articulate what the word *thương* (love) conveyed in English, searching for similarity and familiarity in narrative representation then, *I Love Yous* became the critical entry point in my longue durée to demystify and debunk US imperial and colonial hegemony while (re)connecting to my diasporic Vietnamese heritage and experience. When I left home and tasted independence from my parents for the first time in my life upon entering college, my reflections on love, the Vietnamese kind that is shown through actions rather than spoken through words, became inflection points for building community with other children of displaced people in search of pride and purpose whose families had also ingrained in them a reverence for attaining a formal education.

PAUL: To achieve half-knowledge and self-annulment and discovery, I invented in *All the Flowers Kneeling* a new poetic form called "the Hydra." The form contains thirteen sections. Each section contains thirteen lines. The last line of each section contains thirteen words. The first word of the last line in section X becomes the first word of the first line in section Y. The second word of the last line in section X becomes the first word of the second line in section Y. This continues for the third through thirteenth words of the last line in section X and for the first words of the third through thirteenth lines in section Y.

The Hydra modifies the imperatives that drive received forms like the sonnet, the sonnet crown, and the sestina to more accurately enact the interiority, or the emotional and psychological life, of a survivor of trauma or extremity. Whereas a sonnet has fourteen lines, typically concluding on a conclusive couplet, the Hydra has only thirteen lines to resist as much as possible the psychological impulse to reach for closure and certitude. Whereas a sonnet crown repeats, typically verbatim, the final line of sonnet X as the first line of sonnet Y, the Hydra repeats in order and verbatim the thirteen words in the final line of section X as the first words of the thirteen lines in section Y to resist as much as possible the psychological impulse to import, cleanly and clearly, lessons learned from one experience to another.

Instead, by dividing and deploying the thirteen words in the final line of section X as the respective first words of the thirteen lines in section Y, the Hydra submits that lessons learned from one experience are hardly ever cleanly and clearly imported to another, though they nevertheless remain present, informing—and haunting—each new experience. And whereas the sestina deploys word repetition at the end of the line, the Hydra deploys word repetition at the beginning of the line to resist the psychological impulse to move from an unknown beginning to a known end. Instead, by moving from a known beginning to an unknown end, the Hydra enacts the experience of survivors embarking from the immediate aftermath of trauma or extremity toward an imagined future.

The rules of this invented form emerge, of course, from my belief that poetry isn't expression but enactment and also from my belief that every formal imperative must be driven by an emotional or psychological impulse. Informed by Audre Lorde's essay "The Master's Tools Will Never Dismantle the Master's House" and by Jose Muñoz's monograph *Disidentifications: Queers of Color and the Performance of Politics*, I sought with the Hydra to create new tools for poets like myself to investigate and discover new knowledge about our human experience. The performance of invention alone is my queer and diasporic critique of received forms that have been coins to realm in poetry and American letters. Those forms and their principles, when depended upon as embellishment or indication of occidental mastery, are imaginatively bankrupt and serve as inadequate vessels for marginalized and misrepresented experiences. By inventing new poetic forms, I thus hope to encourage poets like myself to continue pushing the art forward and innovating the tools by which we transform through language our lives.

PHILIP: Second-generation, children of refugee, and immigrant origin stories have laid the bedrock foundation for my pedagogy informed by art and activism. My decision to take a leap of faith and pursue ethnic studies and Asian American studies allowed me to build bridges between my, and my family's, experiential knowledge to the broader community through scholarship in ways that become embedded in my students' experiences, identities, and relationships. Whereas once it had been difficult for me to scour my public library seeking out Vietnamese authors not simply writing about the geography of Vietnam the country, ethnic studies' spirit of self-determination and community empowerment became enlightening, as the diasporic Vietnamese, Southeast Asian, and Asian scholars, writers, artists, and cultural producers informed my work while becoming my mentors, shaping my own mentorship.

PAUL: My current project is a second collection of poems that investigates even more intensely these inquiries about survival. Whether as my mother coming to California as a refugee in 1989, or me coming out to her as a queer and transgender woman, this book is curious about the nature of starting over, of what it means and what it's like to be given a second chance. In fact, as a poet and teacher of poetry, I find both my practice and pedagogy rooted in this commitment to investigation and therefore discovery. I tell my undergraduate and graduate students each semester that a poem has to be DEEP—the discovery and enactment of an emotional and psychological investigation into the vexed interiority of a speaker who has, through great agony and conviction, returned from silence with something to say.

Discovery opposes dominant modes of announcement or transcription, simply of what a speaker already observes about their experience. Discovery instead, to borrow a phrase from my mentor, the poet Carl Phillips, is achieved by restless transformation of experience.

This transformation occurs both at the level of content and form—a term I use to mean the patterning of language—to not express but enact experience. The experience enacted is hardly ever, for me, outside the self. That's why, in my poem "Scheherazade/Scheherazade," I say that "poetry is a mirror I use to look not at but into myself." The experience I explore is always an inward one, and it remains my belief that poems get there, to that emotional and psychological arena, or the unknown and its territories, by way of investigation and discovery.

Lately, one of the questions that's animated my poems, rather embarrassingly, is whether I'm wrong to believe that I can love or still be loved after all that's happened to me. I've thought, as a rape survivor, that being marked by such violence made me unlovable or incapable of loving others in a manner I might consider "well." It's been challenging enough to participate in the world, especially when considering how I hurt myself to reflect the ugliness I feel within, how I hurt others to displace, even momentarily, my own ugliness, and how the idea of my ugliness, pushing toward or against it, remains an influence on my worldview, behavior, and choices. It's been all the more challenging to stay open to the possibility that love, from another or myself or my life, can be built and is in fact deserved. As a poet, I can't help but see the word "lie" inside the word "believe." I also can't help but see, anagrammatically, the word "love" inside the word "violence." It's as though there can't be violence without love, but there can be love without violence. That act, just now, of lyric acrobatics, of inquiry and investigation, is what I mean by "discovery."

Discovery, to be clear, isn't synonymous with conclusion. It's not certitude. It's not closure. In my poems discovery leads to more questions about human experience, more poems, and it's therefore the cultivation of stamina for relentless investigation, poem after poem, that defines the charge and future of being, for me, a poet. There's a difference, however, between poetic investigation where things don't turn up immediately because the discovery indeed is an ambivalence to outcome and poetic investigation where things don't turn up because the poet themself, for whatever reasons, failed.

I've failed, many times, over and over again, to write what I feel, in my heart and in my spirit, is a real poem because I couldn't get myself or my ego, my investments in my doubts and beliefs, out of the way to reach for what John Keats calls "half-knowledge" or what Louise Glück, also my mentor, calls "self-annulment." I merely, to borrow the psychological definition of confirmation bias, rendered in the poem, lyric line by lyric line, what I wanted myself, my speaker and reader, to know. I controlled, as I do when I feel powerless, the entire process in order to feel, paradoxically, powerful. And even when I've been in complete denial, when I've sworn what I wrote was a poem, an act of enactment and all, the text, which I won't call a poem, betrayed me. No matter how skillfully I may have used the fundaments of poetry (rhyme, meter, syntax, grammatical mood, versification) or the easily decorative poetic devices (description, detail, imagery, figuration, objective correlative), ultimately the text revealed what I tried to conceal from myself and the world.

PHILIP: Undoubtedly, diasporic connections and disconnects are primary motivators for my involvement in, teaching of, and work across the diasporic Vietnamese community. In more recent days, and for what I expect will be reflective of my near future, I have found myself scattered virtually across the Vietnamese diaspora. I have been able to find some solace, that I share with you both here, in meeting driven and inspired individuals across the virtual diaspora-verse, if I may refer to it as such, through DVAN. These individuals have demonstrated the reflexivity of resiliency for me, through the act of *làm gương* (being a role model)—mentoring by example, mirroring those that have come before them while allowing themselves to be seen as a mirror for those that come after. By way of knowing how to navigate Zoom controls and utilizing pedagogical tools that I employ in my classroom, I have been fortunate to explore and deepen my relationship with the virtual Vietnamese diaspora-verse in the realm of public humanities with interlocuters through the pandemic. For me, particularly with respect to my role as a moderator and emcee for DVAN's virtual talk series "ÁCCENTED: Dialogues in Diaspora" that has brought together a plenitude of artists, poets, authors, filmmakers, chefs, and other cultural producers in intimate conversations, DVAN has made tangible the ways we can take action through organizing as we speak directly to silence and the silencing of our narratives.

PAUL: For my current project I'm developing a new poetic form I'm calling "the Twin," to explore the ways I have, essentially and inevitably, become my mother, adopting even her American name as my own. Inspired by my mother being a twin, and the legend of her twin dying so she could be born in 1954, this new form also honors my ghost aunt, my second mother, who I think has always known and accepted me for who I am, the difficult choices I've had to make, the compounding regrets I can't change and the possibilities for purpose, meaning, and fulfillment still ahead, in the future, waiting patiently as the dishes I washed earlier and left drying on the rack, ready now to be used again. As I open the cabinets to put them away until tomorrow, the future of Vietnamese writing throughout the diaspora seems to me a future of invention and imagination, reimagination and reinvention, dreaming and dreaming again. In addition to the narratives and commonplace ideologies we must repudiate and correct, we must fashion utterly new stories, ways of thinking, and thought itself. Isn't that what being alive means, or requires of us, anyway? Like the waves I can almost hear tumbling ashore and retreating, or the flames the winds bring down on the hills and the valleys each autumn across California, which allow the land to regenerate, the future is that echoing act of trying and trying once more, of simultaneous destruction and creation.

Once upon a time, pretending nothing happened was how I knew to love. Going forward, readying myself for that tomorrow, I love and am prepared for it, as I write in my poem "Orchard of Unknowing," with the knowledge that "things have happened. Are happening. Are about to." Too curious am I about our lives to proceed otherwise. I want to know, and then I want to know more, about who we are and who we can be. How might we live? What might we make, not unlike those before us, time after time, given the possibility of everything being possible, just a small step or bold leap away? Perhaps in the future we'll discover that all survival amounts to, all along, is that initiating decision to go, to go and keep going. Let's find out.

The moon is full tonight. There are no clouds outside my window, just sky as far and wide as the eye can see, like a vast and blank page to be filled with the light and shadows from our thrilling and terrible crystals. Thank you, from my heart of hearts, for being in this future, and for being this future, with me.

PHILIP: I hope for a future, beyond this presence plagued by pandemic and pandemonium, where we can "return home" together. Though I have never made the "return home" to Vietnam, the scattered nature of my Vietnamese mindbodyspirit, or *tâm*, has configured innovative ways to mend these ruptured connections to the place, and idea, of a homeland or *quê hương*. I will continue, alongside you both, to imagine and work toward a diaspora free from the throes of generational suffering and systemic oppression. However, to simply speak to our futurity is not enough, and we must act as historical agents with agency, as our refugee and immigrant ancestors did in their sacrifice for our existence, to create, imagine, and manifest ways to show compassion and care for one another in the face of transgenerational trauma and violence. If collective community healing is possible, then the onus of responsibility is on our generation, the barely-bilingual-mostly-monolingual, interpreter-translators, children and inheritors of refugee and immigrant histories, who have only ever known and thrived in liminality to begin to write as if our lives and livelihoods depended on it.

A porous "genre of suspension and impossibility," the letter always risks being lost/loss: rerouted, returned to sender, or unrequited altogether.[14] *Yet it is in this reality of getting lost, of feeling loss, amid the present entanglements of mass communication and misinformation, that the letter facilitates the joyous possibilities of deliberately desired connection. And so we have collected these dialogue fragments to send to you, the reader, as modest gestures to keep going. —Minh Huynh Vu*

Conclusion

ON BEING A WRITER AT THE BORDER

Isabelle Thuy Pelaud

I stood at the border, stood at the edge, and claimed it as central. I claimed it as central and let the rest of the world move over to where I was.

—TONI MORRISON

Following her 1993 win for the nobel prize in Literature, Toni Morrison explained her refusal of marginality and her resolve to bring the rest of the world to where *her* writing stood. Resonating across this book is a similar insistence to move readers to where *we* stand—at the border and at the edge—of literature and the arts. The collection of writers' and artists' voices found within *The Cleaving* asserts that in 2025 it is still necessary to insist that diasporic Vietnamese writers are full human beings with complex, diverse immigration histories and views. Like other artists, these writers are preoccupied with form and the arduous task of crafting art. That they come from a country that was colonized for a century by the French and at war for more than two decades with the United States produces a unique challenge to create freely on one's own terms.[1]

Through writing and art, the participants have forged new identities and viewpoints, as they have been racialized and at times pigeonholed in

Australia, Canada, and the United States, as people of war and in France as colonized subjects. As a group, these writers have developed critical strategies to create, distribute their work, and form community. When asked to share what matters most to them among themselves for the purpose of this book, our interlocutors offer important insights of what it means to be a writer and a writer of color from Việt Nam.[2] Whether they are a novelist, poet, young adult fiction writer, visual artist, or musician/song writer, many of these participants express ambivalence vis-à-vis assumptions emanating from the society in which they live about their identity and the publishing industry. Women and queer writers have also expressed ambivalence toward family and community expectations. Most wish to be more free to create. As diverse as their perspectives are, so are the large themes that they speak of—violence, authorship, feminism, representation, language, and form.

As editors listening, editing, assembling, and framing these dialogues, our initial hunger was for community and collective voices. What we found in this process are layers of external and internal pressures evident in the very act of writing, imagining, and representing.[3] *The Cleaving* offers a glimpse into these unspoken labors, articulated in some of the following questions: How do writers process and manage the invisible and tangible barriers that stand between their imaginative and actual lives? Are they aware of, and wary of, the predetermined images that flash in readers' minds when they see their name printed on the cover of their book? How do they find the inner strength needed to write for years in isolation, if one has internalized stories in which people like them are deemed not worthy of being heard or represented, or only so in ways that do not coincide with the views they have of themselves? And not the least important, how do they cope with what is perceived or/and internalized as being a selfish person who wants to create art at the expense of family's welfare, expectations, and well-being?

In light of these questions, we've gathered what these writers have chosen to respond to and reflect upon. What we also found is that language can be both a tool of acceptance and a weapon, and that to hesitate or to plunge headfirst into the unknown that comes from digging into one's psyche and imagination are issues underscored by different axes of power. These include one's sense of agency and empowerment entangled with class, immigration status, gender, and sexuality as well as one's history of immigration, where one waits to be "processed" and migrates to, and where one eventually settles and resettles, only to sometimes have to resettle again. This is why we continue to place value on infinite stories and of infinite voices in the making of cultural productions. Identities develop from the stories we tell ourselves and share with others. And yet it is important to remember that not all stories have the chance to be told and be heard equally. Although the United States is 60 percent white as of 2020, 89 percent of all books published are by white writers.[4] Who gets to write and who gets to be published are not matters of talent or merit alone. Those who are deemed as a voice for the voiceless are described as such because of the ways in which a select few writers are anointed to speak in elite literary spaces. This is what Viet Thanh Nguyen means when he says that to be called a voice for the voiceless speaks more about institutional structures of power than it does about the works authored by people of color themselves.[5] To counter this colonial-like mind-set and the common cultural practices of dividing communities of color, this edited collection of dialogues aims at providing an empowering perspective into Vietnamese diasporic creative and political lives, in ways that reflect the activist work of foregrounding perspectives that are too often invisible or seen as irrelevant. The book's commitment thus stands firmly in solidarity with Asian American activists and cultural producers of yesteryear to today—those who have worked tirelessly on a range of projects from inclusion and citizenship to abolition and decolonization.

Building upon their legacies, we've learned (and strongly believe) that in the United States especially, nothing is given to people of color; rather, all our gains have been earned through resistance and collective organizing, especially in response to racism, which is still very much alive today. A case in point: the association of COVID-19 with the "China virus" and the "kung flu" is but one part of the United States' long history of xenophobia in its treatment of Asian laborers, migrants, and immigrants and its labeling of Asians and Asian Americans as other, foreign, and diseased.[6] While the violence against Asian Americans is *not* considered an important racial problem by many, the 150 percent rise in anti-Asian attacks in the United States during the pandemic declares otherwise.[7] Verbal and physical assaults against Asians have accelerated in the United States over the two years of the pandemic with 11,500 documented hate incidents, the majority of the victims being women.[8]

Racism is not only a US problem. Việt Nam's association with war has spread to countries like Canada, most remembered in the United States for providing sanctuary to American GI soldiers during the Vietnam War. Less known is the fact that thirty thousand Canadians volunteered to fight in Việt Nam and that the Canadian war industry sold $2.47 billion worth of war materials (including ammunition, napalm, and Agent Orange) to the United States during the Vietnam War.[9] And that in 1981, Canada was 95 percent white, which certainly ties to immigration policies that are invested in notions of white purity, specifically negating Indigenous communities and their historical roots in the land.[10] These policies were changed only recently, because of Canada's need for a younger work force for the country to adapt to the modalities of globalization.[11] By 2016 minorities of color in Canada constituted over 20 percent of the country's population. However, racial discrimination reshapes itself and persists, as minorities and Indigenous communities have difficulties finding jobs, receiving equitable pay, and obtaining adequate housing. It is no coincidence that reports of racist incidents in Canada increased by 47 percent in 2020, the first year of the COVID-19 pandemic alone.[12]

Australia, likewise, has had a long history of racism toward both the Indigenous population and non-Anglo immigrants, being the only ex-British colony without a treaty with the original Indigenous owners of the land.[13] Unlike Canada, however, its relationship to Việt Nam is predicated more so on military intervention. The Australian government sent sixty thousand military personnel to fight in the Vietnam War, resulting in intense debates leading in part to a change of government in 1972. While Australia began to accept refugees starting in 1975, the response by the population was lukewarm.[14] The Vietnamese received exceptionally high media and public discourse attention due to the large number of Australians who did not believe the refugees could integrate into Australian culture. At the time, much of Australian conservative political discourse positioned the Indochinese as "imposters," and not bona fide refugees, understood as having left Việt Nam by choice for economic reasons.[15] During the COVID-19 pandemic more than eight in ten Asian Australians have experienced discrimination.[16]

Migration patterns and racial politics have also shaped the diverse politics of the Vietnamese French community (or the Việt Pháp), whose numbers are estimated to be about three hundred thousand today. Pre-1975 expatriate generations differ from those who are post-1975 refugees, as the latter group often takes a more militant stance against the current government of Việt Nam. The fractiousness of Vietnamese French identity politics plays out against a divisive cultural and national context in which this community has been perceived as other, despite generations of Vietnamese French citizens having been born there. French Vietnamese are seen as a submissive and silent model minority. By law, France does not count "race" in any kind of census polling. When ethnicity *is* considered, those who identify as French Vietnamese are often exoticized and associated with the French colonizing project in Southeast Asia.[17] A French Asian identity that counters a colonial style of racism and xenophobia is beginning to garner widespread concern and attention and has been building momentum only in the past few years.[18]

It is ironic that during these dire times, diasporic Vietnamese literature is enjoying recognitions across all genres and moving "hearts and minds." *The Cleaving* reminds readers that the writers in this edited volume speak of the pressures to represent "Vietnam" to a non-Vietnamese readership that only associates them with war; to rectify the wrongs done to communities forced to flee; to fight negative stereotypes associated with the Vietnam War; to protect the image of one's own families and not air dirty laundry; to convey a sonority in language that cannot be fully translated to readers through translation; to explain a culture seen as foreign; and so forth. As a consequence, Vietnamese diasporic artists continue to (re)visit old and new wounds, imagining different futures, and breaking creative ground anew. It is thus worth repeating that their creative works are universal and particular, tragic and satirical, and playful and complex in terms of form and language. They engage with the longue durée that is colonialism and imperialism and its aftereffects, as much as they wrestle with grief, longing, and the ghosts of the present.

In closing, we take this moment to reflect on the organization that made this book possible. *The Cleaving* has been a long-term project designed through the Diasporic Vietnamese Artists Network (DVAN), cofounded by Viet Thanh Nguyen and me to fight systemic and cultural barriers that prevent diasporic Vietnamese writers to express themselves freely and keep them largely invisible. To do this, in 2007, DVAN began as a series of large public Vietnamese American festivals in San Francisco, where an average of four hundred people would attend. We sought to bring together established writers to read alongside emerging writers across the diaspora; these gatherings were places of mutual support and joy that allowed participants to commune with one another. When possible, we included writers from other countries outside of Việt Nam to join as readers and guests. The events collectively became a global call to writers all over the world to gather at a salon we thought of originally in terms of a D(i)VAN.

Contacts between writers of different immigration histories, we maintained, were pivotal to honing each writer's craft while addressing our larger community, which has been divided along political lines due to decades of civil war in Việt Nam and the wrenching apart of actual and allegorical families. Since its inception, DVAN has exponentially expanded, as we've organized public events elsewhere—from nearby San José, Seattle and Los Angeles, to New York, Paris, and Melbourne. We have done special projects to support diasporic Southeast Asian Women and non-binary writers and artists by editing *Troubling Borders: An Anthology of Art and Literature by Southeast Asian Women in the Diaspora* and starting and nurturing the collective *She Who Has No Master(s)* for seven years. Viet Thanh Nguyen initiated an online magazine called *diaCRITICS* to a global readership in which we publish emerging and established Vietnamese and other diasporic Southeast Asian writers, profiles, reviews, essays, and book reviews.[19] To empower writers and encourage dialogues, we organized international writers residencies in Northern California, which eventually led to short- and long-term either solo or group residencies in upstate New York, Palo Alto, rural France, and central Vietnam. With the onslaught of the pandemic, we produced an online show called *ÁCCENTED* cohosted by Viet Thanh Nguyen and Philip Nguyen that featured conversations with Vietnamese diasporic artists, now made into a podcast.

To open opportunities for emerging writers, we started to work with Kaya Press, a leading publisher of transpacific Asian and Asian American literature, and Texas Tech University Press to create imprints. We did not expect established writers to send us their manuscripts—they trust us to advocate for them, they tell us, and they are frustrated with a publication industry dominated by a white workforce. Within three years DVAN, with very limited resources and a lot of hustling, contributed to the publication of seven books through Kaya Press's Ink and Blood series and Texas Tech University Press's Diasporic Vietnamese Artists Network series. By 2025, with the publication of *The Cleaving*, we expect to have published and translated eight additional books. DVAN is now effectively changing the landscape of diasporic Vietnamese literature with our calls for manuscripts, special projects, and translations; and by enlisting academics and other intellectuals to review, select, and disseminate the books. They say yes because they know how marginality is constructed and maintained. Moving forward, DVAN seeks to do more for other Southeast Asians with a shared history of colonialism, war, and racism. This is where we stand and claim as central in our work. This book is a vivid reminder that what we do is needed and that it will be so for a very long time.

Coda

Viet Thanh Nguyen, Lan P. Duong, and Isabelle Thuy Pelaud

Our diasporic cultures would not be possible without the wars that fractured and then unified Việt Nam. If the diaspora was cleaved from the homeland by war, the diaspora itself has been cleaved in different ways, including through competing and conflicting politics and beliefs. One of the challenges in conceiving and editing this collection has therefore been to address the tension between promoting a diasporic Vietnamese collectivity based on cultural and historical traits and articulating a logic beyond identity that justifies this book's project.

Two of the editors of *The Cleaving* are refugees and the son and daughter of refugees, raised in the United States, while one of us is an immigrant and daughter of an immigrant, raised in France. All three of us became academics and writers, with part of our education coming through Asian American studies. At the heart of Asian American studies and the Asian American movement is a belief in solidarity, the idea that the subordinated shall find strength in standing together rather than apart. This is a powerful if contradictory blend of identity and ideology, realized most acutely through the Asian American claim of radical solidarity, where those who may not seem alike can actually find shared kinship. So it is that Bangladeshis, Cambodians, Chinese, Filipinos, Hmong, Indians, Japanese, Koreans, Laotians, Pakistanis, Vietnamese, and more, who might have little reason to bond in Asia, have found themselves unifying as Asian Americans in the United States. The origins of the Asian American movement and Asian American studies in 1968 were founded on this vision of radical solidarity, born out of the antiracist, antiwar, and anti-imperialist convictions of a generation of young activists.

More than five decades later, this radical solidarity has for some congealed into a more limited solidarity around the question and limitations of identity, where the growth of Asian American populations has both enabled more Asian American power and perhaps transformed it. The mainstream of Asian American culture is now arguably focused on representation and the demand for inclusion in American society. For diasporic Vietnamese, solidarity can also be limited, an expression of self-interest and the advancement of one's community, with little regard for the interests of others. So it was that in the Trump administration some Vietnamese refugees who had benefited from an American refugee policy that had welcomed them into the United States agreed with Trump closing the country's borders, drastically cutting refugee quotas, separating immigrant children from their parents, and putting them in cages. We were the *good* refugees, some Vietnamese said. These people are the *bad* refugees.

This is selective memory, as there were plenty of so-called bad refugees among the Vietnamese communities, as some of the diasporic literature has addressed. Beyond this, however, we, as the editors of this volume and as writers and scholars, cannot abide by a limited solidarity that only calls for recognition of our own community and our own otherness, which sometimes comes at the expense of seemingly more dangerous others. While we recognize the ideological diversity of the diasporic Vietnamese community, including the assembly of writers and artists in this book, we conclude *The Cleaving* by arguing that it is not purely a celebration or a recognition of the community but is also born from our political and theoretical convictions about why a diasporic Vietnamese community even exists as well as its relationship to other minority and diasporic, refugee and immigrant, marginalized and exploited, colonized and occupied peoples.

As editors, we do not necessarily speak on behalf of the writers in this book about what we perceive to be the logic for it. Some may agree, some may not. But we would never have embarked on this book without a commitment both to the identities and cultures of the Vietnamese diaspora and to the political urgency of recognizing our solidarity with others who have been displaced, erased, marginalized, and shattered by the same forces that produced us as refugees and immigrants. The violence of war, racism, and colonization that shaped our lives and compelled us to find our voices continues today in the United States, where we live and work, and in the countries that the United States supports in their wars or where the United States fights. The war in Việt Nam—and Laos and Cambodia—was not isolated but preceded by earlier American wars, beginning with the very origins of the country, waged against Indigenous peoples whose lands would provide chances for Vietnamese refugees to own homes and advance their claim to the country. America's wars would continue into the Pacific and Asia in the twentieth century, affecting the Philippines, Hawaii, Guam, Japan, and Korea before reaching Southeast Asia. The American wars in Southeast Asia would fail and interrupt American expansionist ambitions, but after Operation Desert Storm in Kuwait and the terror events of 9/11, those hegemonic dreams would be revived with the wars in Afghanistan and Iraq, from Central Asia to West Asia.

A perspective based on limited solidarity would isolate Việt Nam and its history of war, resistance, and liberation from these other countries. Radical solidarity would require us to see the connections between the twentieth-century wars in Việt Nam and the wars in these other countries, and to see why some in the Vietnamese diaspora, such as ourselves, see parallels and connections with the American war in Việt Nam, Laos, and Cambodia with American wars in Iraq and Afghanistan, and with the American support of Israel's war in Gaza. This is to say that we cannot cleave the Israeli war against Gazans and Palestinians from how US imperialist wars against Southeast Asians have played out time and time again—with Goliath-like impunity, hubris, and military force.

Radical solidarity requires radical refusal, and vice versa, which allows for an expansive and expanding range of alliances, across the borders of races, nations, and cultures as well as classes, genders, and sexualities. War, racism, and colonization have never been only about race, nation, and culture but have also required strict borders between (and hierarchies among) classes, genders, and sexualities. A truly liberatory politics and aesthetics, which could include diasporic Vietnamese culture and identity, requires a collective refusal of these borders and hierarchies, a refusal for any of us who have been othered to permit the domination of others, especially those others who do not seem to be like us.

For us, being a Vietnamese diasporic writer today is to ruminate on the ongoingness of war and the violently "uncivil times" we are living through but also to reflect on our intersectional identities and the decolonial, feminist, and queer futurities we imagine we will share with others in our lifetime.[1] This is especially critical as we approach the fifty-year anniversary of the end of the Vietnam War in 2025, in which the narratives will proliferate in both word and image—in the United States, Việt Nam, and elsewhere—about how the war was lost and won. Rarely will these same narratives ask about what these polite but bombastic commemorations truly stand for, for whom and to whom they speak, and what acts of war and amnesia they promote.

The organic premise of *The Cleaving*—and indeed, of DVAN's efforts in total—emerge from the hunger that we, as diasporic Vietnamese editors, writers, and academics, feel. Instead of competing in a marketplace of voices for the voiceless, which is where so-called minority writers and artists are usually consigned in individual isolation, DVAN's vision is to fight to abolish the conditions of voicelessness *in the first place* and to work in solidarity with those who share experiences of displacement in a *multitude of places*. We will continue to assert the capaciousness and beauty of our imagination, rooted in diasporic Vietnamese experiences and carried out in the context of a radical refusal to go along with the abuses of power, as well as a radical solidarity with others who are like us and not like us.

We dare you to do the same.

NOTES

FOREWORD

1. Toni Morrison, *Beloved* (1987; reprint, London: Vintage, 2007), 324.

INTRODUCTION

The epigraph is from Li-Young Lee, "The Cleaving," in *The City in Which I Love You*, 77–87 (Rochester, NY: BOA Editions Ltd, 1990).

1. Yến Lê Espiritu, Lan Duong, Ma Vang, Victor Bascara, Khatharya Um, Lila Sharif, and Nigel Hatton (Critical Refugee Studies Collective), *Departures: An Introduction to Critical Refugee Studies* (Berkeley: University of California Press, 2022), 32.

2. When "Vietnam" is put in quotes, we emphasize that the country, its vast history and populations, has been constructed by the United States during the First and Second Indochinese Wars. The two words were conjoined as a result of US journalism during the war and the need to economize the country's name. The closed "Vietnam" represents the country's containment as a country of war and trauma for many in the United States. When we write out the country in two words—Việt Nam—we underscore its diacritics and the space in between.

3. See Sau-ling Cynthia Wong, *Reading Asian American Literature* (Princeton, NJ: Princeton University Press, 1993).

CHAPTER 1

1. Ann Cvetkovich, *An Archive of Feelings: Trauma, Sexuality, and Lesbian Public Culture* (Durham, NC: Duke University Press, 2003), 45.
2. See "The World's Largest Armies," *World Atlas*, www.worldatlas.com/articles/29-largest-armies-in-the-world.html. Accessed May 1, 2022.
3. Viet Thanh Nguyen, personal communication with Yến Lê Espiritu, April 24, 2006. In Espiritu's *Body Counts: The Vietnam War and Militarized Refuge(es)* (Berkeley: University of California Press, 2014), the author adds that "the decoupling of Vietnamese Americans from the Vietnam War" further "risks assimilating Vietnamese into the apolitical and ahistorical category of 'cultural diversity'" (16).
4. Barbara Tran, "Việt Nam: Beyond the Frame," *Michigan Quarterly Review* 18, no. 4 (Fall): 482.
5. Asian American literature has been influential in fighting institutional racism. The field of Asian American literature itself, along with the term "Asian American"—as opposed to "Oriental"—did not become institutionalized until the end of the Vietnam War, thanks to the efforts of the Civil Rights Movement that led people of color to work in solidarity with one another to fight racism and institutional racism more effectively.
6. John Okada's *No-No Boy* (1957), Maxine Hong Kingston's *The Woman Warrior* (1975), and Cathy Park Hong's *Minor Feelings* (2020) reveal the toxic emotions borne out of having internalized the gaze of the racist majority and feelings of inferiority.
7. See Elaine Kim's *Asian American Literature: An Introduction to the Writings and Their Social Context* (Philadelphia: Temple University Press, 1982).
8. Vietnamese Americans were not initially welcome in America. At the end of the war in 1975, 54 percent of Americans opposed receiving Vietnamese refugees, while only 46 percent favored their immigration. See James Freeman, *Changing Identities: Vietnamese Americans, 1975–1995* (Boston: Allyn and Bacon, 1995).
9. Bao Phi says he grew up not wanting to be Vietnamese and instead wanted to be a general person of color, whereas Dao Strom was constantly mislabeled and misrecognized as Filipino, Hawaiian, or Indonesian. Such absence, both writers argue, is caused by the process of erasure—conducted by the self and also society—which is ultimately determined by the politics of "cool." In order to make themselves "cool" Asian Americans as a way to cope with the toxic emotion of self-hate, Phi and Strom had to self-efface in order to masquerade more legible selves. This politics of "coolness," both writers intuit, is

gendered, racialized, and classed—as evident in the construction of the model minority figure, the passive object of the Asian woman, and the emasculated Asian man. Both writers end on a contemplation of poetics and parenthood as well as the call for a resistance to "coolness."

10. See Renny Christopher, *The Vietnam War the American War: Images and Representations in Euro-American and Vietnamese Exile Narratives* (Amherst: University of Massachusetts Press, 1995).

11. Cvetkovich, *Archive of Feelings*, 20.

12. This is the name of the airport in South Việt Nam, which was bombed by the North Vietnamese upon the end of the war to prevent people from fleeing. The airport's name has not changed since.

13. Louis de Rouvroy Saint-Simon was an aristocrat living in Versailles at the time of Louis XIV.

14. In January 12, 2023, email correspondence, Bao Phi wrote: "When this talk was originally written, my child was identifying as female. They now prefer they/them pronouns and requested this note be added instead of changing the text."

15. A Vietnamese term to designate overseas Vietnamese who return to Việt Nam.

16. See Saidiya Hartman's *Wayward Lives, Beautiful Experiments* (New York: W.W. Norton & Company, 2019).

CHAPTER 2

1. Henry Louis Gates Jr. "'Authenticity' or the Lesson of Little Tree," *New York Times Book Review*, November 24, 1991, https://timesmachine.nytimes.com/timesmachine/1991/11/24/483591.html?pageNumber=101.

2. See Ruth Mayer, *Serial Fu Manchu: The Chinese Supervillain and the Spread of Yellow Peril Ideology* (Philadelphia: Temple University Press, 2014).

3. See Frank Chin et al., eds., *Aiiieeeee! An Anthology of Asian-American Writers* (New York: Anchor Books, 1975).

4. See Michael Omi and Howard Winant, *Racial Formation in the United States: From the 1060s to the 1980s* (New York: Routledge and Kegan Paul, 1986).

5. The First Indochinese War was between the Vietnamese Communists and the Việt Minh in the South and the French. Beginning in 1946, the war ended in 1954 with the Battle of Điện Biên Phủ. In accordance with the Geneva Accords that were signed in 1954, the country was divided at the 17th parallel, creating the Democratic Republic of Việt Nam in the North and the Republic of Việt Nam in the South.

6. For example, in 1976, Forrest Carter wrote *The Education of Little Tree* as an autobiography. The book became a best seller through the claim of revealing the unique vision of Native Americans. It was later discovered that the book was not written by a Cherokee writer but by a white segregationist. In 1983, Danny Santiago published *Famous All Over Town*. This book was hailed by critics for its vibrancy and authenticity and received many awards. But Danny Santiago was a pen name. The actual name of the writer was Daniel L. James, a septuagenarian WASP educated at Yale. In 2020, Jeanine Cummins wrote *American Dirt* and received an unprecedented seven-figure advance. The book received enormous praise until reviewers started to explain that the writer was white. Her book tour was canceled under the flood of accusations that she was an imposter who took resources and visibility away from Latinx writers. And from the other side, whereas Zora Neale Hurston's *Their Eyes Were Watching God* (1937) prospered, her novel *Seraph on the Suwanee* (1948), whose main characters are white, remained in limbo. For more, see Gates's "'Authenticity' or the Lesson of Little Tree."

It is not a coincidence that early Vietnamese American writers like Nguyen Qui Duc and Andrew X. Pham could not find a publisher until they wrote about the perspective of Vietnamese Americans and that an accomplished writer such as Monique Truong received the John Dos Passos Prize for Literature in honor of an underappreciated writer whose work offers an incisive, "original exploration on specifically American themes, an experimental approach to form, and in a wide range of human experiences." See www.longwood.edu/english/dos-passos-prize/. Similarly, it is not only for the craft of his writing that until then-unknown white writer Robert Olen Butler received the Pulitzer Prize for Fiction in 1993, when he wrote *A Good Scent from a Strange Mountain*. See "Monique Truong Named the 2021 Dos Passos Prize Winner," *Longwood University News*, November 15, 2021.

7. Chợ Lớn has been referenced in Marguerite Duras's *L'Amant* (or *The Lover*) as well as in other films and novels. It is known historically and culturally as a commercial city inhabited by a mostly ethnic Chinese Vietnamese community.

8. "Việt Cộng" was a pejorative term to describe those who fought on the Communist side but were from the South.

CHAPTER 3

1. For further examination of these tropes, see Elaine Kim's important documentaries *Slaying the Dragon* (1988) and *Slaying the Dragon: Reloaded* (2011).

2. See Lan Duong, *Treacherous Subjects: Gender, Culture, and Trans-Vietnamese Feminism* (Philadelphia, PA: Temple University Press, 2012).

3. Kim's *Asian American Literature*; and Lisa Lowe's *Immigrant Acts: On Asian American Cultural Politics* (Durham, NC: Duke University Press, 1996).

4. See Long T. Bui, *Returns of War: South Việt Nam and the Price of Refugee Memory* (New York: New York University Press, 2018); and Nazli Kibria's *Family Tightrope: The Changing Lives of Vietnamese Americans* (Princeton, NJ: Princeton University Press, 1993).

5. See Yến Lê Espiritu's *Asian American Panethnicity: Bridging Institutions and Identities* (Philadelphia: Temple University Press, 1992).

6. See Viet Thanh Nguyen's *Nothing Ever Dies: Vietnam and the Memory of War* (Cambridge, MA: Harvard University Press, 2016).

7. See Erin Khuê Ninh's *Ingratitude: The Debt-Bound Daughter in Asian American Literature* (New York: New York University Press, 2011).

8. We are referring to Nguyễn Du's famous poem *Truyện Kiều* or (The Tale of Kieu). Thơ Mới (New Poetry) was a literary movement in 1930s colonial Việt Nam that tried to do away with Chinese influences in the writing of poetry. Poets of this movement opted to write in *quốc ngữ* (Latin-based alphabet) rather than in *chữ nôm*, shaped by Chinese colonialism and the Chinese writing system.

9. Hàn Mặc Tử was a twentieth-century poet famous for his romantic poetry. He died of leprosy (Hansen's disease) in 1940.

10. Sébastien Le Prestre de Vauban (b. 1633–d. 1707) was an architect during Louis XIV's reign (1643–1715).

11. Tết is the Vietnamese word for Lunar New Year, a most joyous holiday that involves eating, granting gifts, and expressing other rituals for the Vietnamese and the Vietnamese diaspora.

12. A slang term for Western backpackers. *Tây* means "Western" and *ba lô* means "backpack."

13. A type of flower and tree known colloquially as the Phoenix Flower.

14. On April 30, 1975, the North Vietnamese Communist army claimed victory over the South, specifically in Sài Gòn. Since then, to commemorate this day, the Vietnamese diaspora also call this day and the events that commemorate the "fall" of Saigon, Black April or in Vietnamese, Ngày Quốc Hận, the National Day of Resentment. In Việt Nam, however, this day is referred to as the Liberation of Sài Gòn, or Ngày Giải Phóng Sài Gòn.

15. Ars poetica is an ancient form of poetry style made famous by Horace, who talks about the art of poetry in his work.

16. Hai Bà Trưng are two mythological Vietnamese sisters who fought against the Chinese in ancient times. These two sisters, Trưng Trắc (the older) and Trưng Nhị (the younger), are national wartime heroines in Việt Nam. To this day, there are monuments and countless books for children and adults on these figures.

CHAPTER 4

1. Abby Budiman, "Vietnamese in the U.S. Fact Sheet," Pew Research Center, April 2021; and Yen Le Espiritu, "Thirty Years AfterWards: The Endings That Are Not Over," *Amerasia Journal* 31, no. 2 (2005): xiii.

2. According to Viet Thanh Nguyen (*Nothing Ever Dies*, 7), if we count what happened during the Khmer Rouge regime from 1975 to 1979, the number of dead would be an additional two million. See also See Khatharya Um's *From the Land of Shadows: War, Revolution, and the Making of the Cambodian Diaspora* (Minneapolis: University of Minnesota Press, 2015).

3. See Gisele Bousquet's *Behind the Bamboo Hedge: The Impact of Homeland Politics in the Parisian Vietnamese Community* (Ann Arbor: University of Michigan Press, 1991); and Charles Keith's *Subjects and Sojourners: A History of Indochinese in France* (Berkeley: University of California Press, 2024).

4. See Evyn Lê Espiritu Gandhi's *Archipelago of Resettlement: Vietnamese Refugee Settlers and Decolonization across Guam and Israel-Palestine* (Berkeley: University of California Press, 2022).

5. France, China, the Soviet Union, Laos, Cambodia, South Korea, and other US allies (e.g., Canada, Australia, and the Philippines) were significantly involved and impacted by the Vietnam War.

6. See Judith Butler's *Frames of War: When Is Life Grievable?* (London: Verso Books, 2016), in which she writes about the difference between those deemed "grievable" and "ungrievable": "Without grievability, there is no life, or, rather, there is something living that is other than life. Instead, 'there is a life that will never have been lived,' sustained by no regard, no testimony, and ungrieved when lost. The apprehension of grievability precedes and makes possible the apprehension of precarious life. Grievability precedes and makes possible the apprehension of the living being as living, exposed to non-life from the start" (15).

7. See Hayden White's *Tropic of Discourse: Essays in Cultural Criticism* (Baltimore, MD: Johns Hopkins University Press, 1978).

8. See Marita Sturken's *Tangled Memories: The Việt Nam War, the Aids Epidemic, and the Politics of Remembering* (Berkeley: University of California Press, 1997).

9. See Christopher's *The Vietnam War the American War*.

10. "While that name [the Vietnam War] has come to represent American defeat and humiliation, there is also elements of American victory and denial, for the name limits the war's scale in space and time.... The body count in Việt Nam for all sides was closer to one-tenth of the population, while the American dead amounted to about 0.035 percent of the population" (Nguyen, *Nothing Ever Dies*, 7).

11. See Bui, *Returns of War*, 110.

12. See Monique Truong, "The Emergence of Voices: Vietnamese American Literature, 1975–1900," *Amerasia Journal* 19, no. 3 (1993): 27–50, 49.

13. Hiep Thi Le (1971–2017) was an actress who played the part of "Le Ly Hayslip" in the Oliver Stone movie *Heaven and Earth* (1993). Le was known in the Vietnamese American film community for having played other important roles such as in Timothy L. Bui's *Green Dragon* (2001).

14. In the South the government inaugurated other disastrous policies that profoundly changed the constitution of the region's economics and demographics. It set up reeducation camps that detained and tortured those who had worked for or collaborated with the US government during the war. Those incarcerated included a range of high-level and low-level military officers as well as translators, police officers, and sex workers. Also punished were middle-class urbanites, many of whom were ethnic Chinese, as they were sent to New Economic Zones (NEZs) in the rural areas to live and work the land.

15. In 1987 the 5th Party Congress voted to implement a series of economic reforms called Đổi Mới, or Renovation. Thereafter the country opened itself to a market economy and eventually to globalization, with Việt Nam entering into a series of trade deals and memberships with nation-states and organizations to become an economic force within the Southeast Asian region.

16. During the colonial era, infamous French colonial prisons, such as the one on the islands of Côn Đảo, were known to have housed the most dangerous political prisoners. Or if they were not dangerous, they were known to have been revolutionized in the prison (famous for its tiger cages) after being released.

17. As described on the movement's website (https://metoomvmt.org), #MeToo is an international movement that envisions a world free of sexual violence and "centers individual and community healing and transformation,

empowerment through empathy, shifting cultural narratives and practices and advancing a global survivor-led movement to end sexual violence." We note this movement's force while we also recognize Tarana Burke for having established it in 2006 before white women like Alyssa Milano started using this hashtag.

CHAPTER 5

The epigraph is from José Esteban Muñoz, *Cruising Utopia: The Then and There of Queer Futurity* (New York: New York University Press, 2009), 189.

1. In terms of environmental destruction, Rob Nixon describes "slow violence" as that which impacts the global poor and is "dispersed across time and space, an attritional violence that is typically not viewed as violence at all—the long dyings." See Rob Nixon, *Slow Violence and the Environmentalism of the Poor* (Boston: Harvard University Press, 2013), 2.

2. Evyn Lê Espiritu Gandhi makes this crucial point throughout her book *Archipelago of Resettlements* (3), but she defines it succinctly as the "refugee settler condition: the vexed positionality of refugee subjects whose citizenship in a settler colonial state is predicated upon the unjust dispossession of an Indigenous population."

3. Muñoz, *Cruising Utopia*, 189.

4. This last question is a riff on the collective poem titled "Would That" by the She Who Has No Masters Collective, www.poetryfoundation.org/poetry-magazine/poems/156555/would-that. Accessed November 21, 2021.

5. Interview with Joshua Hunt, "Cannupa Hanska Luger Is Turning the Tables on the Art World," *New York Times Magazine,* June 16, 2022.

6. Hunt, "Cannupa Hanska Luger Is Turning the Tables," 14.

7. Gerald Vizenor, *Survivance: Narratives of Native Presence* (Lincoln: University of Nebraska, 2008), 2.

8. Vinh Nguyen, "Refugeetude: When Does a Refugee Stop Being a Refugee?" *Social Text* 139 37, no. 2 (2019): 110.

9. Scholars such as Carole McGranahan and Audra Simpson have discussed acts of (ethnographic) refusal. Audra Simpson, "On Ethnographic Refusal: Indigeneity, 'Voice' and Colonial Citizenship," *Junctures* 9 (2007): 67–80; and Carole McGranahan, "Theorizing Refusal: An Introduction," *Cultural Anthropology* 31, no. 3 (2016): 319–325, in which McGranahan argues that to refuse is to enact willfulness and generate inquiry among and with communities—that is, a move to refuse is to buck the status quo and its normalized, institutionalized structures of power.

10. Ly Thuy Nguyen, "Queer Dis/Inheritances," *Women's Studies Quarterly* 48, no. 1 (2020): 218–235, 222.

11. Nguyen, "Queer Dis/Inheritances," 222.

12. Muñoz, *Cruising Utopia*, 189.

13. David Harvey, *A Brief History of Neoliberalism* (Oxford: Oxford University Press, 2007).

14. Amaris Brown, "Touch at Your Own Peril," in conjunction with Charisse Pearlina Weston's "Through: The Fold, The Shatter," *Recess Art*, March 2021, www.recessart.org/projects/108-touch-at-your-own-peril.

CONCLUSION

The epigraph is from Toni Morrison, *Uncensored: Toni Morrison*, interview by Jana Wendt, a Presentation of Films for the Humanities & Sciences, Beyond Productions, 1998.

1. Việt Nam also has a long history of Chinese occupations and influences.

2. Some writers chose to record their dialogues (which we transcribed), while others chose to write their dialogues themselves (via e-mail).

3. For example, the pressure to represent community, the pressure to protect the community, and the pressure to accommodate a readership whose gaze has been shaped by stories produced by national geopolitical history mitigated by a need for redemption or resolution.

4. Richard Jean So and Gus Wezerek, "Just How White Is the Book Industry?" *New York Times*, December 11 2020.

5. See Viet Thanh Nguyen's "On Narrative Scarcity," https://vimeo.com/1 70099979?embedded=true&source=vimeo_logo&owner=5152755. Accessed April 5, 2020.

6. The entwined axes of racism and sexism are observable since nineteenth-century US policy that simultaneously hypersexualized and pathologized the Asian laborer. In 1875 the Page Act was introduced to "end the danger of cheap Chinese labor and immoral Chinese women," who were stereotyped in US law and culture as tainted prostitutes. Likewise, these gender and racial politics extended to Chinese men too with the Chinese Exclusion Act of 1882, which prompted the harassment, assault, and expulsion of immigrants who were classified as feminine, filthy, and therefore unassimilable. The fetishistic extraction of Asian people, particularly women, became not only an issue of economic labor and social aberrance but also a weapon of US empire as the nation-state oversaw sex trades across hundreds of overseas military bases throughout Asia.

Across centuries the migrant Asian woman remains as the foundational figure of continued sexual exploitation and anti-immigration US law through a prolific sex industry driven by trafficking and the delivery of so-called "mail-order" brides.

7. See Viet Thanh Nguyen's "From Colonialism to COVID: Viet Thanh Nguyen on the Rise of Anti-Asian Violence," *The Guardian*, April 3, 2021. For more instances of anti-Asian violence, see Kimmy Yam, "There Were 3,800 Anti-Asian Racist Incidents Mostly Against Women, in Past Year," *NBC News*, March 16, 2021, www.nbcnews.com/news/asian-america/there-were-3-800-anti-asian-racist-incidents-mostly-against-n1261257; Cathy Park Hong, "The Slur I Never Expected to Hear in 2020," *New York Times Magazine*, April 16, 2020, www.nytimes.com/2020/04/12/magazine/asian-american-discrimination-coronavirus.html; and Kyung Lah and Jason Kravarik, "Family of Thai Immigrant, 84, Says Fatal Attack 'Was Driven by Hate,'" *CNN,* February 16, 2021, www.cnn.com/2021/02/16/us/san-francisco-vicha-ratanapakdee-asian-american-attacks/index.html.

8. Numbers recorded by Stop AAPI Hate from March 19, 2020 through March 31, 2022 (https://stopaapihate.org/year-2-report/): 69.8 percent of the 3,800 of anti-Asian racial incidents were reported by women. See "Statement: Report Shows Almost 11,000 Hate Acts, Most Reported by Women," March 4, 2022, https://stopaapihate.org/2022/03/04/statement-report-shows-almost-11000-hate-incidents-most-reported-by-women/.

9. See Anh Thang Dao-Shah and Isabelle Thuy Pelaud's "The American War in Việt Nam and Its Diasporas," in *The Cambridge History of Asian American Literature,* edited by Rajini Srikanth and Min Hyoung Song, 469–483 (Cambridge: Cambridge University Press, 2016).

10. Francis Wilkinson, "Anti-Asian Racism Is Also Rising in Canada," *Bloomberg,* April 2, 2021, www.bloomberg.com/opinion/articles/2021-04-02/anti-asian-hate-crimes-in-canada-show-racism-knows-no-borders.

11. Craig McCulloch, "Canada's Most Asian City Faces Surge in Hate Crimes," *VOA News,* April 17, 2021, www.voanews.com/a/americas_canadas-most-asian-city-faces-surge-hate-crimes/6204668.html.

12. See Vanessa Balintec's "2 Years into the Pandemic, Anti-Asian Hate Is Still on the Rise in Canada, Report Shows," *CBC News,* April 3, 2022, www.cbc.ca/news/canada/toronto/2-years-into-the-pandemic-anti-asian-hate-is-still-on-the-rise-in-canada-report-shows-1.6404034.

Germany conducted colonial projects in China and Pacific territories in the nineteenth century as well. The racist programs in Hoyerswerda in 1991 and in Rostock-Lichtenhagen in 1992, as well as the murders of Nguyễn Ngọc

Châu and Đỗ Anh Lân in Hamburg in 1980, Phan Văn Toàn in Fredersdorf in 1997, Duy-Doan Pham in Neuss in 2011, and Yangjie Li in Dessau in 2016, among others, demonstrate examples of historical continuity. See "Open Letter Atlanta—What Exactly Happened? Against Anti-Asian Racism and Silence! For Cross-Community Solidarity and Decolonized Remembrance, Berlin," April 16, 2021, www.korientation.de/atlanta-offener-brief/.

13. In the 1980s racism in Australia continued to be fueled by controversies over Asian immigration and even increased due to the economic recession. The Vietnamese community is one of the newest communities of color there and has grown rapidly to become one of the largest ethnic groups. Pauline Hanson said in a speech to Parliament in 1996 that "we are in danger of being swamped by Asians. Between 1984 and 1985, 40% of all immigrants were of Asia origin. They have their own culture and religion, form ghettos, and do not assimilate." Vietnamese Australians documented that they are subject to a glass ceiling in the workplace and are targets of hate crimes. In spite of the resurgence of anti-Asian violence, no federal funding for a countrywide antiracism strategy has been released since the "It Stops With Me" campaign of 2013. See Gerald Roche, "Telling the China Story in Australia: Why We Need Racial Literacy," *The China Story*, July 26, 2020, www.thechinastory.org/telling-the-china-story-in-australia-why-we-need-racial-literacy/. Australia is the only ex–British colony that does not have a treaty with the original Indigenous owners of the land.

14. See Dao-Shah and Pelaud's "American War in Việt Nam and Its Diasporas."

15. Tara Magner, "A Less than 'Pacific' Solution for Asylum Seekers in Australia," *International Journal of Refugee Law* 16, no. 1 (January 2004): 53–90.

16. Within a three-month frame, 480 racially-fueled attacks were reported (April–June 2020), 65 percent of which are from women. A nineteen-year-old Vietnamese Australian woman based in Sydney describes her attack: "They attempted to kick me; called me an Asian slut and an Asian dog; told me to go eat a bat; threatened me with a knife; spat in my face, got spit on in my left eye." See Gladys Lai, "Asian Hate Crimes Are an Australian Problem, Too. When Will It Stop?" *GQ* (Australia), March 17, 2021, www.gq.com.au/success/opinions/asian-hate-crimes-are-an-australian-problem-too-when-will-it-stop/news-story/cf6871220622d1e8d8d35049edb6e720.

17. The colonization of Việt Nam by the French was conducted based on a rationale that it would civilize the so-called "natives," erasing the specific circumstances and challenges of those who came as refugees.

18. The anti-Asian racism during the pandemic led up to five men going on trial in Paris after they called for violence against the "Chinese" in tweets in

response to the announcement of the second COVID-19 lockdown. Protesters stood outside the Paris tribunal with signs that said: "In Atlanta or in Paris, no to anti-Asian racism." See Philippe Theise, "France's Asian Community Fights Back against Racist Attacks during Pandemic," *France24*, April 4, 2021, www.france24.com/en/europe/20210404-france-s-asian-community-fights-back-against-racist-attacks-during-pandemic.

19. DVAN has received a grant from the Luce Foundation to organize a number of writers residencies on the East Coast, in France, and in Vietnam for the years 2024 and 2025.

CODA

1. We use Roxane Gay's wording here in a 2022 opinion piece on the massacre at an elementary school in Uvalde, Texas, after an eighteen-year-old gunman shot and killed nineteen children and two teachers. The use of the adjective "uncivil" is a rhetorical understatement that Gay characterizes as part of a conservative discourse to cancel serious discussions with issues that matter most to people of color in the United States. We share in Gay's sarcasm and rage. See Roxane Gay's article, "Don't Talk to Me About 'Civility': On Tuesday Morning Those Children Were Alive," *New York Times*, May 25, 2022, www.nytimes.com/2022/05/25/opinion/roxane-gay-uvalde-school-shooting.html.

WORKS CITED

Balintec, Vanessa. April 3, 2022. "2 Years into the Pandemic, Anti-Asian Hate Is Still on the Rise in Canada, Report Shows." *CBC News*.
Bousquet, Gisele. 1991. *Behind the Bamboo Hedge: The Impact of Homeland Politics in the Parisian Vietnamese Community*. Ann Arbor: University of Michigan Press.
Budiman, Abby. 2021. "Vietnamese in the U.S. Fact Sheet." April. Pew Research Center.
Bui, Long T. 2018. *Returns of War: South Việt Nam and the Price of Refugee Memory*. New York: New York University Press.
Butler, Judith. 2016. *Frames of War: When Is Life Grievable?* London: Verso Books.
Chin, Frank, et al., eds. 1975. *Aiiieeeee! An Anthology of Asian-American Writers*. New York: AW.
Christopher, Renny. 1995. *The Vietnam War the American War: Images and Representations in Euro-American and Vietnamese Exile Narratives*. Amherst: University of Massachusetts Press.
Cvetkovich, Ann. 2003. *An Archive of Feelings: Trauma, Sexuality, and Lesbian Public Culture*. Durham, NC: Duke University Press.
De Certeau, Michel. 1984. *The Practice of Everyday Life*. Translated by Steven Rendall. Berkeley: University of California Press.
Duong, Lan. 2012. *Treacherous Subjects: Gender, Culture, and Trans-Vietnamese Feminism*. Philadelphia, PA: Temple University Press, 2012.
Espiritu, Yến Lê. 2014. *Body Counts: The Vietnam War and Militarized Refugees*. Berkeley: University of California Press.
———. 2006. "Towards a Critical Refugee Study: The Vietnamese Refugee Subject in U.S. Scholarship." *Journal of Vietnamese Studies* 1: 410–433.
———. 2005. "Thirty Years AfterWards: The Endings That Are Not Over." *Amerasia Journal:* 30 Years AfterWard 31, no. 2: xiii–xxiii.

———. 1992. *Asian American Panethnicity: Bridging Institutions and Identities*. Philadelphia, PA: Temple University Press.

Espiritu, Yến Lê, Lan Duong, Ma Vang, Victor Bascara, Khatharya Um, Lila Sharif, and Nigel Hatton. 2022. *Departures: An Introduction to Critical Refugee Studies*. Berkeley: University of California Press.

Freeman, James M. 1995. *Changing Identities: Vietnamese Americans, 1975–1995*. Boston: Allyn and Bacon.

Gandhi, Evyn Lê Espiritu. 2022. *Archipelago of Resettlement: Vietnamese Refugee Settlers and Decolonization across Guam and Israel-Palestine*. Berkeley: University of California Press.

Gates, Henry Louis, Jr. 1991. "'Authenticity' or the Lesson of Little Tree." *New York Times Book Review*, November 24. https://timesmachine.nytimes.com/timesmachine/1991/11/24/483591.html?pageNumber=101.

Gay, Roxane. 2022. "Don't Talk to Me about 'Civility': On Tuesday Morning Those Children Were Alive." *New York Times*, May 25. www.nytimes.com/2022/05/25/opinion/roxane-gay-uvalde-school-shooting.html.

Gee, Deborah, dir. 1988. *Slaying the Dragon*. Produced by Asian Women United. Available at Women Make Movies.

Green, Jonathon. 1990. *Encyclopedia of Censorship*. New York: Facts on File, Inc.

Hartman, Saidiya. 2019. *Wayward Lives, Beautiful Experiments*. New York: W.W. Norton & Company.

Harvey, David. 2007. *A Brief History of Neoliberalism*. Oxford: Oxford University Press.

Hong, Cathy Park. 2020. *Minor Feelings: An Asian American Reckoning*. New York: One World.

Hunt, Joshua. 2022. "Cannupa Hanska Luger Is Turning the Tables on the Art World." *New York Times Magazine*, June 16. www.nytimes.com/2022/06/16/magazine/cannupa-hanska-luger-profile.html.

Keith, Charles. 2024. *Subjects and Sojourners: A History of Indochinese in France*. Berkeley: University of California Press.

Kibria, Nazli. 1993. *Family Tightrope: The Changing Lives of Vietnamese Americans*. Princeton, NJ: Princeton University Press.

Kim, Elaine. 1982. *Asian American Literature: An Introduction to the Writings and Their Social Context*. Philadelphia, PA: Temple University Press.

Kim, Elaine, dir. 2011. *Slaying the Dragon: Reloaded*. Women Make Movies.

Kingston, Maxine Hong. 1976. *The Woman Warrior: Memoirs of a Girlhood among Ghosts*. New York: Alfred A. Knopf.

Lah, Kyung, and Jason Kravarik. 2021. "Family of Thai Immigrant, 84, Says Fatal Attack 'Was Driven by Hate.'" *CNN*. February 16.

Lee, Li-Young. 1990. "The Cleaving." In *The City in Which I Love You*, 77–87. Rochester, NY: BOA Editions Ltd.

Lowe, Lisa. 1996. *Immigrant Acts: On Asian American Cultural Politics*. Durham, NC: Duke University Press.

Magner, Tara. "A Less than 'Pacific' Solution for Asylum Seekers in Australia." *International Journal of Refugee Law* 16, no. 1 (January 2004): 53–90.

Mayer, Ruth. 2014. *Serial Fu Manchu: The Chinese Supervillain and the Spread of Yellow Peril Ideology*. Philadelphia, PA: Temple University Press.

McCulloch, Craig. 2021. "Canada's Most Asian City Faces Surge in Hate Crimes." *VOA News*. April 17.

McGranahan, Carole. 2016. "Theorizing Refusal: An Introduction." *Cultural Anthropology* 31, no. 3: 319–325.

"Monique Truong Named the 2021 Dos Passos Prize Winner." 2021. *Longwood University News*, November 15.

Morris, Julia. 2023. "As Nauru Shows, Asylum Outsourcing Has Unexpected Impacts on Host Communities." In *Migration Information Source: The Online Journal of the Migration Policy Institute*. Washington, DC: Migration Policy Institute. www.migrationpolicy.org/article/nauru-outsoure-asylum. Accessed May 28, 2024.

Morrison, Toni. 1998. *Uncensored: Toni Morrison*. Interview by Jana Wendt. Beyond Productions, a Presentation of Films for the Humanities & Sciences.

———. 1987. *Beloved*. New York: Vintage Books.

Muñoz, José Esteban. 2009. *Cruising Utopia: The Then and There of Queer Futurity*. New York: New York University Press.

Nguyen, Ly Thuy. 2020. "Queer Dis/Inheritance and Refugee Futures." *Women's Studies Quarterly* 48, no. 1: 218–235. https://doi.org/10.1353/wsq.2020.0026.

Nguyen, Viet Thanh. 2021. "From Colonialism to COVID: Viet Thanh Nguyen on the Rise of Anti-Asian Violence." *The Guardian*. April 3.

———. 2016. *Nothing Ever Dies: Việt Nam and the Memory of War*. Cambridge, MA: Harvard University Press.

Nguyen, Vinh. 2019. "Refugeetude: When Does a Refugee Stop Being a Refugee?" *Social Text* 139 37, no. 2: 109–131.

Ninh, Erin Khuê. 2011. *Ingratitude: The Debt-Bound Daughter in Asian American Literature*. New York: New York University Press.

Nixon, Rob. 2013. *Slow Violence and the Environmentalism of the Poor*. Boston: Harvard University Press.

Nora, Pierre. 1989. "Between Memory and History: Les Lieus de Memoire." *Representations* 26 (Spring): 7–24.

Okada, John. 1957. *No-No Boy*. Rutland, VT: Charles Tuttle Company.

Omi, Michael, and Howard Winant. 1986. *Racial Formation in the United States: From the 1060s to the 1980s*. New York: Routledge and Kegan Paul.

Palumbo-Liu, David. 1999. *Asian/American: Historical Crossings of a Racial Frontier*. Stanford, CA: Stanford University Press.

Pelaud, Isabelle. 2015. "War, Gender, and Race in le thi diem thuy's *The Gangster We Are All Looking For*." In *Themes in Contemporary North American Fiction*. London: Bloomsbury Academic Press.

Roche, Gerald. 2020. "Telling the China Story in Australia: Why We Need Racial Literacy." *The China Story*. July 26.

Simpson, Audra. 2007. "On Ethnographic Refusal: Indigeneity, 'Voice' and Colonial Citizenship." *Junctures* 9: 67–80.

So, Richard Jean, and Gus Wezerek. 2020. "Just How White Is the Book Industry?" *New York Times*. December 11.

Song, Min Hyung. 2013. *The Children of 1965: On Writing, and Not Writing, as an Asian American*. Durham, NC: Duke University Press.

Sturken, Marita. 1997. *Tangled Memories: The Vietnam War, the Aids Epidemic, and the Politics of Remembrance*. Berkeley: University of California Press.

Theise, Philippe. 2021. "France's Asian Community Fights Back against Racist Attacks during Pandemic." *France24*. April 4.

Tran, Barbara. 2004. "Việt Nam: Beyond the Frame." *Michigan Quarterly Review* 18, no. 4 (Fall).

Truong, Monique. 1993. "The Emergence of Voices: Vietnamese American Literature, 1975–1900." *Amerasia Journal* 19, no. 3: 27–50.

Um, Khatharya. 2015. *From the Land of Shadows: War, Revolution, and the Making of the Cambodian Diaspora*. Minneapolis: University of Minnesota Press, 2015.

Vang, Ma. 2021. *History on the Run: Secrecy, Fugitivity, and Hmong Refugee Epistemologies*. Durham, NC: Duke University Press.

Vizenor, Gerald. 2009. *Native Liberty: Natural Reason and Cultural Survivance*. Lincoln: University of Nebraska Press.

———. 2008. *Survivance: Narratives of Native Presence*. Lincoln: University of Nebraska Press.

White, Hayden. 1978. *Tropic of Discourse: Essays in Cultural Criticism*. Baltimore, MD: Johns Hopkins University Press.

Wilkinson, Francis. 2021. "Anti-Asian Racism Is Also Rising in Canada." *Bloomberg*. April 2.

Wong, Sau-ling Cynthia. 1993. *Reading Asian American Literature*. Princeton, NJ: Princeton University Press.

ABOUT THE CONTRIBUTORS

Born in Saigon and raised on Boston's North Shore, AMY QUAN BARRY is the Lorraine Hansberry Professor of English at the University of Wisconsin–Madison. Barry is the author of eight books of fiction and poetry, including the recent novel *When I'm Gone, Look for Me in the East* (University of Notre Dame Press, 2022), which follows a group of Buddhist monks as they search for a reincarnation in the vast Mongolian landscape. *O: Oprah* magazine described Barry's second novel, *We Ride Upon Sticks* (Pantheon Books, 2020), as "spellbinding, wickedly fun." In the spring of 2022, Barry's first play, *The Mytilenean Debate*, was produced by Forward Theater. She is one of a select group of writers to receive NEA fellowships in both poetry and fiction.

ĐOÀN BUI is a writer and a French journalist. She received the Albert Londres award in 2013 for her work about refugees. She is the author of the memoir *Le Silence de Mon Père* (Editions de l'Iconoclaste, 2016), which received the Prix littéraire de la Porte Dorée and the Prix Amerigo Vespucci and has been translated in Italian, German, and Vietnamese. Her first novel *La Tour* (Grasset, 2022) was shortlisted for the Goncourt Premier Roman and the Orange Prize. She is also scenarist for two graphic novels, *C'est quoi un terroriste* (Éditions Le Lombard, 2017) and *Fake News* (Éditions Delcourt, 2021). She is currently writing a book with Ukrainian writers about wars, exile, and memory.

THI BUI was born in Vietnam and came to the United States in 1978 as part of the "boat people" wave of refugees fleeing Southeast Asia at the end of the Vietnam War. Her debut graphic memoir, *The Best We Could Do* (Abrams ComicArts, 2017), was selected for an American Book Award, a Common Book for UCLA and other colleges and universities, and an all-city read by Seattle and San Francisco public libraries. It was also a National Book Critics Circle and Eisner Award finalist. She is the illustrator of three children's books: *A Different Pond*, written by Bao Phi (Capstone, 2017), for which she won a

Caldecott Honor; *Chicken of the Sea* (McSweeney's, 2019), co-illustrated by her son, Hien, and written by Viet Thanh Nguyen and his son, Ellison; and *Finding Papa*, written by Angela Pham Krans (HarperKids, 2023). Her short comics can be found online at *Reveal News*, *The Nib*, *PEN America*, and *BOOM California*. She is currently researching and drawing a work of graphic nonfiction about immigrant detention and deportation, to be published by One World Random House.

LAN CAO was born in Sài Gòn, Vietnam. Her critically acclaimed novel *Monkey Bridge* was published by Viking (1997). She is also the author of *The Lotus and the Storm* (Viking, 2015) and the coauthor of *Family in Six Tones: A Refugee Mother, an American Daughter* (Viking, 2020). She has taught at Brooklyn Law School, Duke Law School, the University of Michigan Law School, and William & Mary Law School, and she is now the Betty Hutton Professor of International Economic Law at Chapman Law School in Orange, California. Lan is a graduate of Mount Holyoke College and Yale Law School. In 2023 she received an honorary doctorate of humane letters from Mount Holyoke.

CATHY LINH CHE is the author of *Split* (Alice James Books, 2014), winner of the Kundiman Poetry Prize, the Norma Farber First Book Award from the Poetry Society of America, and the Best Poetry Book Award from the Association of Asian American Studies. She is coauthor, with Kyle Lucia Wu, of the children's book *An Asian American A to Z: A Children's Guide to Our History* (Haymarket Books, 2022). Her work has been published in *The New Republic*, *The Nation*, *McSweeney's*, and *Best American Poetry*. She has received awards from MacDowell, Tin House, and Bread Loaf and has taught at New York University, Fordham University, and Sierra Nevada College.

ANDRÉ DAO is an author and researcher from Naarm/Melbourne, Australia. His debut novel, *Anam* (Giramondo Publishing, 2021), won the New South Wales Premier's Literary Award for New Writing and was longlisted for the Miles Franklin Literary Award. In 2024 he was named a *Sydney Morning Herald* Best Young Australian Novelist.

DUY ĐOÀN is the author of *Zombie Vomit Mad Libs* (Alice James Books, 2014) and *We Play a Game* (Yale University Press, 2023), winner of the Yale Series of Younger Poets Prize and a Lambda Literary Award. Duy's work has appeared in the Academy of American Poets' *Poem-a-Day*, *The Margins*, *Poetry*, *TriQuarterly*, and elsewhere. He has been featured in PBS's *Poetry in America* and *Poetry* magazine's *Editors' Blog*. He received an MFA in poetry from Boston University, where he later served as director of the Favorite Poem

Project. He has taught at Boston University and Fordham University. (Duy Đoàn, pronounced zwē dwän / zwee dwahn)

DƯƠNG VÂN MAI ELLIOTT was born in Vietnam and grew up in Hà Nội and Sài Gòn. She attended French schools in Vietnam and is a graduate of Georgetown University. She also writes under the name of Mai Elliott. She is the author of *The Sacred Willow: Four Generations in the Life of a Vietnamese Family* (Oxford University Press, 1999), a family memoir that was nominated for the Pulitzer Prize. Her second book is *RAND in Southeast Asia: A History of the Vietnam War Era* (Routledge, 2019). She served as an adviser to Ken Burns and Lynn Novick for their PBS documentary on *The Vietnam War* and was featured in seven of its ten episodes. She is a frequent speaker on issues relating to Vietnam. She contributed a chapter for the Cambridge University Press three-volume work on the Vietnam War and recently completed the translation of her personal and family memoir into Vietnamese.

LE LY HAYSLIP is the author of *When Heaven and Earth Changed Places* (Plume, 1990) and *Child of War, Woman of Peace* (Doubleday, 1989). Both books were the subject of Oliver Stone's film *Heaven & Earth* in 1993. Hayslip recounts in poignant detail the journey of a young peasant girl through the devastation of the US war in Vietnam and the new life she established in the United States after landing in San Diego in 1970. Le Ly returned to her motherland in 1986 after a sixteen-year absence and was stunned by the devastation, poverty, and illness left by the American war and the US embargo against Vietnam. Seeing an opportunity to make a difference, she founded the East Meets West and Global Village Foundations to help rebuild Vietnam and bring people together to help heal the wounds of war on all sides of Vietnam conflicts.

MATT HUYNH (www.matthuynh.com) is an Emmy Award–winning visual artist. His brush-and-ink paintings are informed by sumi-e ink painting and comic books. Huynh received a World Illustration Award for his interactive comic *The Boat* and was Eisner-nominated for *Cabramatta*. His animated VR documentary *Reeducated* was honored with a SXSW's Special Jury Award for Immersive Journalism and by the Venice Film Festival in its Best of VR program. Huynh's comics, animation, and illustrations have been exhibited by the Museum of Modern Art, the Smithsonian, and the Sydney Opera House.

VIOLET KUPERSMITH is a Vietnamese American author of mixed descent. She is the author of the short-story collection *The Frangipani Hotel* (Spiegel & Grau, 2014) and the novel *Build Your House Around My Body* (Random House, 2023), which won the Bard Fiction Prize and was a finalist for the Center for

Fiction First Novel Prize, longlisted for the Women's Prize for Fiction, and named one of the *New York Times*'s notable books of 2021. She has been the recipient of fellowships from the International Writers' Workshop, the National Endowment for the Arts, the University of East Anglia, the Fulbright Program, and MacDowell.

THANHHÀ LẠI is the #1 *New York Times* bestselling author of *Inside Out & Back Again* (Harper Collins, 2011), her debut novel in verse, which won both a National Book Award and a Newbery Honor. The sequel is *When Clouds Touch Us* (Harper Collins, 2023). She also wrote the acclaimed *Listen, Slowly* (Harper Collins, 2015), the award-winning YA debut *Butterfly Yellow* (Harper Collins, 2019), and the picture book *Hundred Years of Happiness* (Harper Collins, 2022). Thanhhà was born in Việt Nam and now lives in New York with her family.

VINCENT LAM is from the expatriate Chinese community of Vietnam and was born in Canada. He did his medical training in Toronto, where he worked for thirteen years as an emergency physician. He now works in addictions medicine. Lam has also worked in international air evacuation and expedition medicine on Arctic and Antarctic ships. His first book, *Bloodletting and Miraculous Cures* (Doubleday Canada, 2006), won the 2006 Scotiabank Giller Prize and was adapted for television and broadcast on HBO Canada. He coauthored *The Flu Pandemic and You* (Doubleday Canada, 2006), a nonfiction guide to influenza pandemics, which received a Special Recognition Award in 2007 by the American Medical Writers' Association. His biography of Tommy Douglas was published by Penguin Canada in 2011 as part of Extraordinary Canadians series.

TRACEY LIEN was born and raised in southwestern Sydney, Australia. She earned her MFA at the University of Kansas and was previously a reporter for the *Los Angeles Times*. She lives in Brooklyn, New York. *All That's Left Unsaid* (William Morrow, 2022) is her first novel.

T.K. LÊ is a multigenre writer who grew up in Westminster, California. She received her MA from UCLA in Asian American studies, is an alum of the VONA Voices summer writing workshop, and was a 2019 PEN America Emerging Voices fellow. Her writing has appeared in *Strange Horizons*, *Uncanny Magazine*, and in the 2021 W.W. Norton & Company anthology *Inheriting the War*.

ANNA MÖI was born in Saigon, where she was educated early on in French schools. She worked as a fashion designer in Paris and Bangkok and lived for some time in Tokyo. Anna speaks many languages, including Vietnamese,

French, English, Thai, Japanese, and some German. In 1992 she moved back to her home city, now called Ho Chi Minh City, where she began to write in French and published two volumes of short stories, *L'Echo des Rizières* (Editions de l'Aube, 1998) and *Parfum de Pagode* (Editions de l'Aube, 2000). She is an award-winning author, and her bestselling text, *Riz Noir* (Black Rice, 2004), has been translated into four different languages. In 2006 she was named a Chevalier des Arts et des Lettres by the Minister of Culture in France.

BETH (BICH) MINH NGUYEN is the author of the memoirs *Owner of a Lonely Heart* (Scribner, 2023) and *Stealing Buddha's Dinner* (Viking Penguin, 2007) and the novels *Short Girls* (Viking Penguin, 2009) and *Pioneer Girl* (Viking Penguin, 2014). She has received an American Book Award and a PEN/Jerard Award, and her work has appeared in publications including *The New Yorker, Paris Review, Time Magazine, New York Times*, and *Best American Essays*. Nguyen is a professor of creative writing at the University of Wisconsin–Madison.

HIEU MINH NGUYEN is the author of *This Way to the Sugar* (Write Bloody Publishing, 2014) and *Not Here* (Coffee House Press, 2018), winner of the Thom Gunn Award for Gay Poetry from the Publishing Triangle. Among his honors Hieu has received a Wallace Stegner Fellowship from Stanford University, a Ruth Lilly and Dorothy Sargent Rosenberg Fellow from the Poetry Foundation, a McKnight Writing Fellowship, a Kundiman Fellowship, and a National Endowment for the Arts Literature Fellowship. His work has also appeared in *Poetry Magazine, Hobart, New York Times, Best American Poetry, The Atlantic*, and elsewhere. Originally from the Twin Cities, he now lives in Oakland and is a graduate from the MFA Program for Writers at Warren Wilson College.

HOA NGUYEN is a poet, educator, and member of the collective She Who Has No Masters, a project of multivoiced collectivity, hybrid poetics, encounters, in-between spaces, and (dis)places of the Vietnamese diaspora. Her books include *Red Juice: Poems 1998—2008* (Wave Books, 2014), the Griffin Prize–nominated *Violet Energy Ingots* (Wave Books, 2016), and *A Thousand Times You Lose Your Treasure* (Wave Books, 2021), a finalist for a 2021 National Book Award, the General Governor's Literary Award, and the Kingsley Tufts Poetry Award. Born in the Mekong Delta and raised and educated in the United States, Hoa has lived in Canada since 2011. In 2019 her body of work was nominated for a Neustadt Prize for Literature, a prestigious international literary award often compared with the Nobel Prize in Literature. She teaches poetry and creative writing as an assistant professor at Toronto Metropolitan University.

HOAI HUONG AUBERT-NGUYEN is a French Vietnamese novelist and poet. She teaches communication at the University of Versailles. She has published four novels: *L'ombre douce/The soft shadow* (Viviane Hamy, 2013), for which she has received literary prizes in France (Prix Marguerite Audoux, Prix littéraire Asie de l'Adelf), Belgium (Prix Première-RTBF), and in Switzerland (Prix du salon du livre de Genève); *Sous le ciel qui brûle/Under the burning sky* (Viviane Hamy, 2017) (Prix de la Renaissance française); *Le cri de l'aurore/The cry of dawn* (Viviane Hamy, 2019) (Prix de la Ville aux livres); and *Tendres ténèbres/Tender darkness* (Viviane Hamy, 2023). She has also published three collections of poetry: *Parfums/Perfumes* (La Part Commune, 2005); *Déserts/Deserts* (La Part Commune, 2009); and *Feuilles sous le vent/Leaves under the wind* (La Part Commune, 2021). She has co-directed, with Michel Espagne, *Vietnam: A History of Cultural Transfers*, a collection of contributions presented at a colloquium held at the Ecole Normale Supérieure and the National Library of France in 2014.

A poet and multimedia artist, DIANA KHOI NGUYEN is the author of *Ghost Of* (Omnidawn Publishing, 2018), which was a finalist for the National Book Award, and *Root Fractures* (Omnidawn Publishing, 2024). Her video work has been exhibited at the Miller Institute for Contemporary Art. Nguyen is a Kundiman fellow and member of the Vietnamese artist collective She Who Has No Master(s). A recipient of a fellowship from the National Endowment for the Arts, and winner of the 92Y Discovery Poetry Contest and 2019 Kate Tufts Discovery Award, she currently teaches in the Randolph College Low-Residency MFA and is an assistant professor at the University of Pittsburgh.

Born and raised in Việt Nam, NGUYỄN PHAN QUẾ MAI is the author of two international bestsellers, *The Mountains Sing* (Algonquin Books, 2020) and *Dust Child* (Algonquin Books, 2023), the poetry collection *The Secret of Hoa Sen* (BOA Editions, 2010), as well as eight books in Vietnamese. She has won the Poetry of the Year 2010 Award from the Hà Nội Writers Association, the 2021 PEN Oakland/Josephine Miles Literary Award, the 2020 Lannan Literary Award Fellowship, the International Book Awards, the BookBrowse Best Debut Award, as well as runner-up for the Dayton Literary Peace Prize. Her writing has been translated into more than twenty-five languages. Quế Mai is the Peace Ambassador for PeaceTrees Vietnam and Author Ambassador for Room to Read. She has a PhD in creative writing and was named by *Forbes* Vietnam as one of twenty inspiring women of 2021.

PHILIP NGUYỄN is the executive director of the Vietnamese American Roundtable (VAR). After graduating from UC Berkeley with BA degrees in ethnic studies and Asian American and Asian Diaspora studies, he earned his MA degree in Asian American studies from the College of Ethnic Studies at San Francisco State University, where he teaches courses on Vietnamese American literature and the history of the Vietnamese in the United States. He has been involved with community-based organizations dedicated to amplifying and advocating for Asian American, Southeast Asian American, and Vietnamese American voices to the forefront through his involvement with the Diasporic Vietnamese Artists Network (DVAN), the Progressive Vietnamese American Organization, and the Union of North American Vietnamese Student Associations.

THẢO NGUYỄN (better known simply as "Thao") is a veteran artist, songwriter, touring musician and producer, originally from Northern Virginia. Throughout her impressive career, she has released music via legendary labels Kill Rock Stars and Domino Record Co. imprint Ribbon Music and been featured by the *New York Times*, *NPR*, *Austin City Limits*, *Pitchfork*, *Washington Post*, and many more. Thao is the subject of the 2017 PBS documentary film *Nobody Dies*, exploring her first trip to Vietnam and her mother's first trip back to Vietnam in forty-three years. She was the 2019 guest host of the acclaimed podcast *Song Exploder* and most recently hosted the PBS series *Southern Sounds*, released in the summer of 2023.

VAAN NGUYEN (THI HONG VAN NGUYEN) was born in 1982. Of Vietnamese descent, she is an Israeli poet. Her first poetry book is *The Truffle Eye* (in Hebrew by Maayan publishing, 2008; in English by Zephyr Press, 2021, translated by Adriana X. Jacobs). Her second poetry book is *Vain Ratio* (in Hebrew by Gnat Press, 2018). Vaan currently lives in Tel Aviv-Yaffo.

AIMEE PHAN was born and raised in Orange County, California. She received her BA in English from UCLA and her MFA from the Iowa Writers' Workshop, where she won a Maytag Fellowship. She is the author of two books, *We Should Never Meet: Stories* (Tin House Books, 2009) and the novel *The Reeducation of Cherry Truong* (St. Martin's Press, 2013). *We Should Never Meet* was named a Notable Book by the Kiriyama Prize in fiction and a finalist for the Asian American Literary Awards. Her writing has appeared in the *New York Times*, *TIME*, *USA Today*, and CNN.com, among other publications. She has received residencies from the MacDowell Colony, Djerassi, Hedgebrook, and the Rockefeller Foundation's Bellagio Center. She has received awards from the National Endowment of the Arts and the Money for Women/Barbara Deming

Memorial Fund. Phan teaches writing and literature at the California College of the Arts in San Francisco and resides in Berkeley with her family.

Born in Vietnam, raised in the Phillips neighborhood of South Minneapolis, BAO PHI is a Vietnamese American Minnesotan and a longtime spoken word artist. He has two poetry collections, *Sông I Sing* (2011) and *Thousand Star Hotel* (2017), both published by Coffeehouse Press. He has written four children's books: *A Different Pond* (2017), *My Footprints* (2021), *Hello Mandarin Duck* (2022), and *You Are Life* (2023), all published by Capstone. He is a community member, a refugee, and a father.

ABBIGAIL NGUYEN ROSEWOOD is a Vietnamese and American author. Her debut novel, *If I Had Two Lives* (Europa Editions, 2021), is out from Europa Editions. Her second novel, *Constellations of Eve* (DVAN/Texas Tech University Press, 2022), was the inaugural title of the publishing imprint founded by Isabelle Thuy Pelaud, a scholar of Asian American history and literature, and Pulitzer Prize–winner Viet Thanh Nguyen to promote Vietnamese American literature. Her work can be found in *TIME*, *Harper's Bazaar*, *Salon*, *Cosmopolitan*, *Lit Hub*, *Electric Lit*, *Catapult*, *Pen America*, and *BOMB*, among other publications. She lives in Vietnam and New York with her husband and their daughter.

ANDREW X. PHAM is an independent journalist and author. He is the author of *Catfish and Mandala: A Two-Wheeled Voyage Through the Landscape and Memory of Vietnam* (Farrar, Straus and Giroux, 1999) and of *The Eaves of Heaven: A Life in Three Wars* (HarperCollins, 2008), among other works. At various periods of his life, he has worked as an aircraft engineer, researcher, technical writer, startup founder, farmer, food critic, pizza chef, bungalow builder, small business owner, a literary panelist, teacher, and an MFA faculty. His books have been on eight "Top Ten Books of the Year" lists. He is a Whiting Writer and a Guggenheim Fellow. He is the winner of the Kiriyama Prize and a National Book Critics Circle Award finalist. He is an active cyclist, ultralight pilot, paraglider pilot, tennis player, and skier. An avid cook, amateur brewer, and winemaker, he is a fan of alcoholic beverages and almost every type of cuisine. He divides his time between California, Hawaii, and Southeast Asia. He enjoys hiking and traveling. He is stabilized by a loving wife, two rambunctious dogs, and two fat lazy cats.

DAO STROM is a poet, writer, musician, and interdisciplinary artist whose works include the poetry-art collection *Instrument* (Fonograf Editions, 2020), winner of the 2022 Oregon Book Award for Poetry, and its companion song cycle *Traveler's Ode* (Poetry Northwest, 2019). Other works include the bilingual poetry-art book *You Will Always Be Someone from Somewhere Else* (AJAR Press, 2018); the hybrid-forms memoir *We Were Meant To Be a Gentle People* (Press Otherwise [and Paperdoll Works], 2015); the song cycle *East/West* (Press Otherwise [and Paperdoll Works], 2015); and two books of fiction, *The Gentle Order of Girls and Boys* (Counterpoint Press, 2006) and *Grass Roof, Tin Roof* (Houghton Mifflin/Mariner Books, 2003). She has received awards from the Creative Capital Foundation, the National Endowment for the Arts, and other organizations. Born in Vietnam, Strom grew up in the Sierra Nevada foothills of California and lives in Portland, Oregon. She is cofounder of two collective art projects, She Who Has No Master(s) and De-Canon.

KIM THÚY was born in Vietnam in 1968. At the age of ten she left Vietnam along with a wave of refugees commonly referred to in the media as "the boat people" and settled with her family in Quebec, Canada. A graduate in translation and law, she has worked as a seamstress, interpreter, lawyer, and restaurant owner. She has received many awards, including the Governor General's Literary Award in 2010, and she was one of the top four finalists of the Alternative Nobel Prize in 2018. Her books have sold more than 850,000 copies around the world and have been translated into thirty-one languages and distributed across forty-three countries and territories. She lives in Montreal, where she devotes her time to writing.

PAUL TRAN is the author of the debut poetry collection *All the Flowers Kneeling* (Penguin Books, 2023). Their work appears in the *New York Times*, *The New Yorker*, *Best American Poetry*, and elsewhere. Winner of the Discovery/Boston Review Poetry Prize, as well as fellowships from the Poetry Foundation, Stanford University, and the National Endowment for the Arts, Paul is an assistant professor of English and Asian American studies at the University of Wisconsin–Madison.

MARCELINO TRƯƠNG LỰC was born in Manila in 1957, the son of a Vietnamese diplomat and a French artistic mother. Trương's latest opus is a two-volume autobiographical graphic novel retelling the story of the Vietnam War, as observed by Franco-Vietnamese child living in Saigon and London. *Such a Lovely Little War: Saigon 1961–63* attracted much acclaim, and its follow-up *Saigon Calling: London 1963–71* is counted by the British daily *The Guardian* as one of the best graphic novels of 2017 (Arsenal Pulp Press, Vancouver). Trương's graphic novel *Quarante hommes et douze fusils: Indochine 1945* (Forty personnel and twelve guns; Denoël Graphic, Paris; 2022) is set at the end of the Indochina war (1945–54), as witnessed by a young Vietnamese painter serving as a propaganda artist in Hồ Chí Minh's People's Army. Arsenal

Pulp Press (Vancouver) published the English translation by David Homel in 2023.

MONIQUE TRUONG is a novelist, essayist, children's book author, librettist, and intellectual property attorney. She came to the United States in 1975 as a refugee and is based now in Brooklyn, New York. Her novels are *The Book of Salt* (Houghton Mifflin, 2003), *Bitter in the Mouth* (Random House, 2010), and *The Sweetest Fruits* (Viking, 2019). She is a contributing coeditor of *Watermark: Vietnamese American Poetry & Prose* (AAWW, 1998) and its twenty-fifth anniversary edition (DVAN series/Texas Tech University Press, 2023) and the editor of *Vom Lasterleben am Kai: Große Reportagen* (C.H. Beck, 2017). A graduate of Yale College and Columbia Law School, she is the recipient of a Guggenheim Fellowship, U.S.–Japan Creative Artists Fellowship, Hodder Fellowship, PEN/Robert W. Bingham Fellowship, American Academy of Arts and Letters' Rosenthal Family Foundation Award, New York Public Library Young Lions Fiction Award, Bard Fiction Prize, Stonewall Book Award-Barbara Gittings Literature Award, John Gardner Fiction Prize, and the John Dos Passos Prize for Literature, among other honors. She has taught fiction workshops at Columbia School of the Arts, Baruch College (CUNY), and Princeton University.

MINH HUYNH VU is completing their doctoral studies at Yale University in American studies and women's, gender, and sexuality studies with a graduate certificate in ethnicity, race, and migration. Their research and writing practice work through the everyday afterlives of US empire. Previous writings have been featured by W. W. Norton & Company, *diaCRITICS*, and academic venues.

OCEAN VUONG is the author of the *New York Times* bestselling poetry collection *Time Is a Mother* (Penguin Press, 2022) and the *New York Times* bestselling novel *On Earth We're Briefly Gorgeous* (Penguin Press, 2019), which has been translated into thirty-seven languages. A recipient of a 2019 MacArthur "Genius" Grant, he is also the author of the critically acclaimed poetry collection *Night Sky with Exit Wounds* (Copper Canyon Press, 2016), a *New York Times* "Top 10 Book of 2016," winner of the T.S. Eliot Prize, the Whiting Award, the Thom Gunn Award, and the Forward Prize for Best First Collection. A Ruth Lilly fellow from the Poetry Foundation, his honors include fellowships from the Lannan Foundation, the Civitella Ranieri Foundation, the Elizabeth George Foundation, the Academy of American Poets, and the Pushcart Prize. Vuong's writings have been featured in *The Atlantic*, *Granta*, *Harpers*, *The Nation*, *New Republic*, *The New Yorker*, the *New York Times*, the *Paris Review*, the *Village Voice*, and *American Poetry Review*, which awarded him the Stanley Kunitz Prize for Younger Poets. Selected by *Foreign Policy* magazine as a "2016 100 Leading Global Thinker," Vuong was also named by BuzzFeed Books as one of "32 Essential Asian American Writers" and has been profiled on NPR's *All Things Considered*, *PBS NewsHour*, *Teen Vogue*, *Interview*, *Poets & Writers*, and *The New Yorker*. He currently lives in Northampton, Massachusetts, and serves as a tenured professor in the Creative Writing MFA Program at New York University.

ABOUT THE EDITORS

A professor in the College of Ethnic Studies at San Francisco State University, artist, writer, and scholar ISABELLE THUY PELAUD has spearheaded many collaborations, including the formation of DVAN: Diasporic Vietnamese Artists Network, which she cofounded with Viet Thanh Nguyen. Pelaud is cofounder of the all-women writing collective She Who Has No Master(s). The author of the ground-breaking monograph on Vietnamese American literature, *This Is All I Choose to Tell* (Temple University Press, 2010), she has coedited the anthology *Troubling Borders: Literature and Art by Southeast Asian Women in the Diaspora* (University of Washington Press, 2014).

LAN P. DUONG is a poet and scholar of Vietnamese and Vietnamese diasporic cinemas. She teaches at the University of Southern California in the Department of Cinema and Media Studies. She is the author of *Treacherous Subjects: Gender, Culture, and Trans-Vietnamese Feminism* (Temple University Press, 2012) and coeditor of the anthology *Troubling Borders* (University of Washington Press, 2014). One of the founders of the Critical Refugee Studies Collective, Duong serves as the coeditor of the website www.criticalrefugeestudies.com, and is a coeditor of the Critical Refugee Studies Book Series for the University of California Press. Her book of poems *Nothing Follows* (2023) is published by Texas Tech University Press.

VIET THANH NGUYEN's novel *The Sympathizer* (Grove Press, 2015) won the Pulitzer Prize for Fiction. His most recent publications are the sequel to *The Sympathizer*, *The Committed* (Grove Press, 2021), and *A Man of Two Faces: A Memoir, a History, a Memorial* (Grove Press, 2024). His other books are a short-story collection, *The Refugees* (Grove Press, 2017), and *Nothing Ever Dies: Vietnam and the Memory of War* (Harvard University Press, 2016), a finalist for the National Book Award in nonfiction and the National Book Critics Circle Award in General Nonfiction, and *Race and Resistance: Literature and Politics in Asian America* (Oxford University Press, 2002). He has also published *Chicken of the Sea* (McSweeney's, 2022), a children's book written in collaboration with his son, Ellison Nguyen, and *Simone* (Minerva, 2024), a children's book illustrated by Minnie Phan. He is a professor at the University of Southern California and the editor of *The Displaced: Refugee Writers on Refugee Lives* (Abrams Press, 2018).

INDEX

Note: Page numbers followed by *n* refer to notes, with note number.

"ÁCCENTED: Dialogues in Diaspora" series, 176, 185
Afghanistan War, and US expansionist ambitions, 188
The Alice B. Toklas Cook Book (Toklas), 53
Amerasian Homecoming Act, 116
American Dirt (Cummins), 194n6
Apocalypse Now (Coppola): Che's *Appocalips* multimedia project using, 39, 40–41, 42–43, 45; use of Vietnamese refugees as violence, 42
Asian American literature: and Asian American writers as representatives of their community, 47; establishment as genre in 1960s, 46; initial function of, 46–47
Asian Americans: history of representation through white lenses, 46; increased racial awareness and empowerment, 47
Asian American solidarity: fissures in, over time, 187; as key principle in Asian American movement, 186–87; as part of larger solidarity with minority, immigrant, marginalized, and colonized peoples, 188; support for closed US borders as unacceptable affront to, 187. *See also* radical solidarity
Asian American studies: program at San Quentin, 99; solidarity among Asians as key principle of, 186–87; as way to build ties to Asian community, 174
Asian American writers: identity politics as useful but constraining for, 47–48; and social justice work, 9, 192n5
Asians, stereotype of, Phi on, 31
Atlanta shootings of 2001, Bui on, 27–28
Aubert-Nguyen, Hoai Huong: on Bible as inspiration, 79–80; on Biblical women as inspiration, 80; *Under the Burning Sky,* 81; *The Cry of Dawn,* 83; dialogue with Vaan Nguyen, 77–86; on gender issues in her works, 81; influences on poetry of, 78–79; *Leaves in the Wind* (in progress), 86; on living between two different cultures, 83; on meaning of her given name, 85; on MeToo movement, 81; mixing of French and Vietnamese cultures in works by, 79, 83; on parents' migration to France, 85; *Perfumes,* 79; *The Soft Shadow,* 79, 81; *Tender Darkness* (in progress), 85–86; on Vietnamese literature, 78; Viet

Aubert-Nguyen *(continued)*
    Thanh Nguyen on, xiv; on visits to
    Việt Nam, 84–85
Australia: anti-Asian racism in, 182–83,
    201n13, 201n16; anti-Indigenous
    racism in, 182; Asian Australian
    writing tradition in, Dao on, 144;
    Cabramatta (Vietnamese Sydney
    suburb), Lien's ties to, 144–45; par-
    ticipation in Vietnam War, 182;
    public's lack of awareness about
    Vietnamese/Asian community in,
    143; as white nation, difficulty of
    overcoming public perception of, 147;
    as white nation, Vietnamese Austral-
    ians' internalization of, 143, 144
authenticity of authorial voice: complex-
    ity of, due to American racial exclu-
    sion and exploitation, 46; as issue for
    authors of mixed race or with non-
    Vietnamese names, 47–48; and
    pigeonholing of authors, 48, 117,
    119–22, 124, 146–50
authorial voice: Gates on, 46. *See also*
    authenticity of authorial voice;
    authority of authorial voice
authority of authorial voice: subject-
    matter expertise and, 49–50; Truong
    on, 49; Viet Thanh Nguyen on, 49–50
authority of authorial voice, as gendered
    and racialized, 48, 49, 194n6; and
    authors writing under assumed ethnic
    identity, 194n6; Barry's refusal to
    accept constraints of, 67–69, 72; Lại's
    refusal to accept constraints of, 67, 68,
    71–72; as reality in publishing world,
    69; and responsibility of representing
    one's ethnic group, 49; Truong on,
    50–52, 54–55; Viet Thanh Nguyen's
    effort to move beyond, 51, 52–53

Barry, Amy Quan: avoidance of per-
    sonal publicity to escape pigeonhol-
ing, 69; as Black in appearance, 70;
    dialogue with Lại, 66–73; ethnicity
    spanning several groups, 68; family
    background of, 68; first novel about
    Vietnamese psychic, 68; on her
    middle name, credibility as Asian
    writer derived from, 69–70; novel
    about Tibetan Buddhist monk,
    67–68; on origin of middle name,
    70; on publishers' view of authorial
    voice as gendered and racialized, 69,
    71; refusal to be constrained by
    gendered and racialized authorial
    voice, 67–69, 72; on responsibility in
    representing Vietnamese people, 73;
    Viet Thanh Nguyen on, xiii
beautiful sadness in Vietnamese culture,
    Vuong and Thúy on, 15–16
Beloved (Morrison), xiv
Bergvall, Caroline, 42–43
Blue Dragon White Tiger (Dinh), xi
Bolden, Valerie, 97
Buck, Pearl S., 21
Bui, Doan: absence of books about Việt
    Nam in childhood, 21; on books
    putting one's thoughts into words, 21;
    on childhood emulation of white
    girls from French books, 21, 23;
    childhood in small French town
    without other Asians, 21, 23; child-
    hood love of Laura Ingalls Wilder's
    novels, 22; childhood trips to Paris
    with parents to meet other Asian
    people, 23; on *communautarisme*,
    French opposition to, 24, 25; cooking
    of Vietnamese food for her children,
    23–24; and decolonial summer camp,
    24; dialogue with Beth Nguyen,
    21–28; on Diasporic Vietnamese
    Artists Network (DVAN), 25; early
    denial of racism, 26; on fetishism of
    Asian women, 28; on French aversion
    to *réunions non-mixtes*, 24; on French

aversion to wokeism and discussions of race and racism, 24–25; on identification with whiteness, 26; influence of Beth Nguyen's works on, 21, 22, 23; on knowing Beth Nguyen through her books, 21; as left-wing activist, in view of some, 26; on life in Paris during COVID-1pandemic, 23; life in Paris surrounded by white people, 21–22; on masks in COVID-19 pandemic, pleasant anonymity derived from, 23; nostalgia for Vietnamese form of name, 26–27; other Vietnamese writers' influence on, 27; on severity of racism, 28; on shame felt in white-run spaces, 24; *Le silence de mon père,* 26; on *La Tour,* white editors' dislike of white racist character in, 27–28; on Vietnamese-only meetings, comfort found in, 24–25; Viet Thanh Nguyen on, xiv; work of, as storytelling, not activism, 26

Bui, Thi: and anger about white supremacy, effect on career, 103–4; *The Best We Could Do,* 101, 104; dialogue with Thảo Nguyễn, 97–104; on Diasporic Vietnamese Artists Network (DVAN), 100; discovery of Vietnamese community beyond traditional one, 102; early art career leading to comics, 98; early interest in law career, 98; as fan of Thảo Nguyễn, 97; growing up near Vietnamese community in California, 102; *The Nib* comic on immigration, 99–100; *NOWHERELAND,* 98; and PiVOT, 100–101; on politicizing of art, 104; on power of art to change culture, 99; on "refugee reflex," 171; resistance to patriarchy, 102; on San Quentin inmates and Roots program, 99; on Thảo Nguyễn's empathy, 103; on Thảo Nguyễn's facility with language, 104; time as social studies teacher, 100–101; Viet Thanh Nguyen on, xiv; on white supremacy, 102; work focused on anti-deportation activism, 98–99; work on electoral politics, 100–101

Bulosan, Carlos, 9
Butler, Judith, 57, 196n6

CAAM (Center for Asian American Media), 102
California Coalition for Women Prisoners (CCWP), 97
Cambodia: US war in, 188; war with Việt Nam, 8
Canada: anti-Asian racism in, 182; limited knowledge about Vietnam War in, 13; as participant in Vietnam War, 182; racism in immigration policies, 182; social expectations, Vincent Lam's decision to act in opposition to, 59, 60–61
Cao, Lan: deeply felt connection to Việt Nam, 58; dialogue with Lam, 58–65; early life of, 58; effect of refugee experience on her experience of America, 60; effect of refugee experience on her legal interests, 59, 62; effect of refugee experience on her writing, 60, 62; effort to understand parents' generation, 65; embrace of Vietnamese identity, 60; on her audience, 64; identification as feminist writer, 60; *Monkey Bridge,* 60, 65; on refugee experience as defining, 59; on starting to write, 64; and Vietnamese diasporic community, limited contact with, 65; Viet Thanh Nguyen on, xiii; on war trauma, persistence of, 58; writing by, as "translation" of Vietnamese culture, 64–65
Carter, Forrest, 194n6

Center for Asian American Media (CAAM), 102
Che, Cathy Linh: *Appocalips* (multimedia project using Coppola's *Apocalypse Now*), 39, 40–41, 42–43, 45; on creative work as play, 45; dialogue with Diana Khoi Nguyen, 11, 39–45; on Diana Khoi Nguyen's "Đổi Mới Series," 41; on Diana Khoi Nguyen's *Ghost Of,* 40; "Essay on Beauty," 43; estrangement from father, 45; *Fade In,* 39; interest in documentary, 43; on similarities between her family and Diana Khoi Nguyen's, 43–44; *Split,* 45; Viet Thanh Nguyen on, xiv; on time in Diana Khoi Nguyen's video work, 40
Cheng, Bill, 69
Cheung, Leslie, 156–57
Chinese Exclusion Act of 1882, 199n6
Chinese laborers in United States, US racism and sexism and, 199–200n6
Civil Rights Movement: and establishment of Asian American literature as genre, 46; and solidarity of people of color, 9, 192n5
"The Cleaving" (Lee), 1–2, 7
The Cleaving (Pelaud, Duong and Nguyen): as empowering perspective into Vietnamese diasporic creativity and activism, 181; goals of, 186; as project of DVAN, 184; significance of title, 1–2, 7. *See also* dialogues in *The Cleaving*
Close-Up (Kiarostami), 43
collective consciousness and trauma: new ideas of identity through processing of, 10; Phi and Strom on, 33, 35, 36
colonialism and imperialism: past and ongoing destruction by, 151; and underrepresentation of Vietnamese diasporic voices, 181
Communist victory in Vietnam War: and "boat people," 107, 115, 117; Lực new graphic novel on, 141; refugees' flight following, 5, 107, 115, 117
coolness/expectations of conformity: and Asians as not cool, Phi and Strom on, 30, 31, 32; as gendered, racialized, and classed, 192–93n9; hiding behind mask of, 11; Lam's decision to act in opposition to, 59; and self-erasure, 30–31, 192–93n9; Vietnamese Americans' need to build alternative structure, Phi and Strom on, 32–33, 37–38
COVID-19 pandemic: and anti-Asian racism, 3, 181–82, 183; interruption of in-person meetings between interlocutors, 2–3; treatment of Vietnamese as Yellow Peril in, xi; and white supremacy, 3
creativity in Vietnamese diasporic writers, liminal space of, 19–20
critical fabulation, Hartman on, 39
Critical Refugee Studies Collective, 4
Cummins, Jeanine, 194n6

Đặng Thùy Trâm, 139
Dao, André: on ambivalence about Australian identity, 143; *Anam,* 148, 149; on Australia as home, 144; on author events, tendency to avoid conflict in, 147–48; on author events, types of questions and comments at, 143, 148, 149; on childhood efforts to model himself on white Australians, 143; concerns about his right to tell certain stories, 145; desire to avoid being pigeonholed as Asian/migrant writer, 146, 148, 149–50; dialogue with Lien, 143–50; discovery of Asian Australian writing tradition, 144; on internal debates with white literary world,

146; on joy of writing, 150; on life experience's influence on readers' perception, 150; on parents' reaction to his writing, 146; pressure to honor family in his writing, 145–46; Viet Thanh Nguyen on, xiv; on public's lack of awareness about Vietnamese/Asian community in Australia, 143

Departures: An Introduction to Critical Refugee Studies (Espiritu et al.), 4, 5

diaCRITICS magazine, 184

dialogues in *The Cleaving:* and complexity and nuance of intersubjectivity, 5–6; COVID-19's interruption of in-person meetings, 2–3; framing questions for, 7; multivoiced plurality of, 6; pairing of interlocutors, 7; range of interlocutors' locations, 2; recurring themes in, 3, 6; series of in-person meetings before COVID-19, 2; wide range of life experiences of interlocutors, 3

Diasporic Vietnamese Artists Network (DVAN). *See* DVAN

Dĩnh, Trần Văn, xi

Disidentifications (Muñoz), 173

Djerassi Resident Artists Program, 2

Đoàn, Duy: "2046 is on the 24th floor," 156–57; on aunts' role in raising him, 159; authors influencing, 157; on childhood family gatherings, 159; dialogue with Lê, 153, 155–61; on formal elements in Lê's poems, 159–60; on freedom provided by fixed form, 158; and frustration of readers' confidence, 157; on good and bad aspects of public identity as Vietnamese author, 156; influence of Leslie Cheung on, 156–57; influence of Wong Kar-wai films on, 156–57; on job in Lê's poetry, 155; on Lê's "Afterlives" and "Afterlives II," 160; on Lê's "Fisherwoman and the Fisherman," 158–59; poems about family violence, 157; on sensibility of restraint in art, 157; turn from focus on himself to larger world, 158; Viet Thanh Nguyen on, xiv; *We Play a Game,* 155, 156, 160–61; "We Play a Game Using Tomatoes," 160–61; on writing skill gained over time, 158

Drift (Bergvall), 42–43

Dunnill, Ginger, 152

DVAN (Diasporic Vietnamese Artists Network): abolishing conditions of voicelessness as goal of, 189; "ÁCCENTED: Dialogues in Diaspora" series, 176, 185; changing of landscape for Vietnamese diasporic writers, 185; *The Cleaving* as project of, 184; cofounders of, 184; Doan Bui on, 25; exponential expansion of, 184; and global writers salon D(i)VAN, 184; initial set of Vietnamese American festivals in San Francisco, 184; international writers residencies, 184–85; Nguyễn Phan Quế Mai on importance of work, 108; Philip Nguyễn's connection to diaspora-verse through, 176; Thảo Nguyễn meeting of Thi Bui's friends in, 102; Thi Bui and, 100; work with presses to develop Vietnamese diasporic writers, 185

eating: communal aspects of, and meetings between interlocutors, 2; as reading, as theme in *The Cleaving,* 2; together, as act of care and love in Vietnamese culture, 2

Ecclesiastes, Scroll of, 79

economic justice, as prerequisite for narrative plenitude of works about Vietnamese, xiii

The Education of Little Tree (Carter), 194n6

Elliott, Dương Vân Mai: on agent as key to getting published, 118; on Americans' lack of interest in Vietnamese perspective on war, 118; on Americans' lack of knowledge about Việt Nam, 123–24; dialogue with Hayslip, 118–25; education of, 122; efforts to educate Americans about Vietnamese middle class, 124; family's migration to South Vietnam in 1954, 122; on Hayslip's *When Heaven and Earth Changed Places*, 118, 123; on increasing interest in books about Việt Nam and refugees, 119–20, 121; on pigeonholing of Vietnamese authors, 119–20, 121–22, 124; on refugee aesthetic among Vietnamese diasporic writers, 124–25; *The Sacred Willow*, 118, 120, 124; on target audience for her book, 122–23; translations of *Sacred Willow*, 120; on Vietnamese authors' difficulty getting published, 118; Viet Thanh Nguyen on, xi; works suppressed in Việt Nam, 120

Eng, David, 56–57

environmental destruction, slow violence of, 198n1

Espiritu, Yến Lê, 5

Everett, Percival, 149

expatriates (Việt Kiều), Phi on Vietnamese hatred of, 35

family, estrangement from: Che on, 45; Hieu Minh Nguyen on, 163–64; Huynh on, 162–63

family separations at US border, 36, 187

Famous All Over Town (Santiago), 194n6

feminism: influence on Hoa Nguyen's work, 112; influence on Nguyễn Phan Quế Mai's work, 111; Lan Cao and, 60; women diasporic Vietnamese writers as inherently feminist, 76

fetishism of Asian women, Doan Bui on, 28

France: anti-Asian racism in, 184, 201–2n18; Asian Americans' lack of identity platform in, 47; national fascination with Việt Nam, 117; paternalistic and romanticized view of Vietnamese, 117; Vietnamese community in, and anti-Asian racism, 184, 201–2n18; Vietnamese migrants' level of education, 115; Vietnamese migration to, before Vietnam War, 114–15

Full Metal Jacket (film), Lê's "sniper girl" and, 153, 155

"Future Ancestral Technologies" (Luger and Dunnill), 152

future collective political becoming for Vietnamese Americans: and aesthetic, politicized enactments of refusal, 152; and healing of self and land, 152; Indigenous views on, 152; Muñoz on, 151, 152; queer and BIPOC theorists as inspirations for, 152; and remembering outside of heteronormative, possessive individualistic family structures, 152–53; "survivance" and, 152

future free from death and fear, Vietnamese diasporic writers' imagining of, 10

Gandhi, Evyn Lê Espiritu, 198n2

Gates, Henry Louis, Jr., 46

Gay, Roxane, 202n1

Gaza, Israeli war in, 188

gaze of racist majority: books about, 192n6; and stereotypes of Asian Americans, 9. *See also* stereotypes

Germany, colonial projects and anti-Asian racism, 200–201n12

Global North literary landscape, impact of Vietnamese diasporic writers on, 3

Global Village Foundation, 119
Glück, Louise, 176
"good" Asian stereotype, 31, 75, 117, 187
Great Hunger of 1945, Nguyễn Phan Quế Mai poem on, 110–11

Hai Bà Trưng, 90, 196n16
Hàn Mặc Tử, 78
Hanson, Pauline, 201n13
Hartman, Saidiya, 39
hate crimes, anti-Asian, increase in, 27
Hayslip, Le Ly: on Americans' lack of interest in Vietnamese perspective on war, 118; on Americans' lack of knowledge about Việt Nam, 123; books banned in Việt Nam, 120; dialogue with Elliott, 118–25; donations to Việt Nam through Global Village Foundation, 119; on educating others about Việt Nam as goal of Vietnamese writers, 121; on her difficulty getting published, 118–19; on her flight from Việt Nam as refugee, 122; on her lack of education, 122; interest in ghosts and mediums, 120; movie version of *When Heaven and Earth*, 119, 123; as pioneering book by Vietnamese authors, 118–19; on refugee aesthetic among Vietnamese diasporic writers, 124; on Vietnamese Americans' teaching of Americans how to live together in the world, 123; Vietnamese community's dislike of communist sympathies of, 121, 125; on Vietnamese diasporic writers' responsibility to explain Vietnamese to younger generation, 125; Viet Thanh Nguyen on, xiii; *When Heaven and Earth Changed Places*, 118–19, 120, 123
hooks, bell, 9
human contact and communication, as theme in *The Cleaving*, 3

Hurston, Zora Heale, 194n6
Huynh, Matt: on audience reaction, drawing to elicit, 165; comic about family's experience in refugee camps, 168; on comics as visual poetry, 164; dialogue with Hieu Minh Nguyen, 153, 162–68; on drawing as safe space, 164; estrangement from family, 162–63; on fiction as representation of greater truth, 167; on hiding behind comics, 164–65; on his family's stories about Vietnam War, 168; on his goal in making art, 166; on his work as effort to create a recognizable image of himself, 165; on meaning in empty spaces in comics, 164; Viet Thanh Nguyen on, xiv; move from Australia, and issues of home and family, 163; on transforming of subject through art, 165–66

ideal American selves, Strom on projections of, 30
identity, new ideas of, through processing of trauma, 10
identity politics, as American phenomenon, 47
I Love Yous Are for White People (Lac Su), 9, 172
immigrants: connotations of term, 4; indeterminate time frame of status, 5
Indigenous people: anti-Indigenous racism in Australia, 182; discrimination against, in Canada, 182; on futurity as tactic to heal the land, 152; and "survivance", 152; United States's many wars against, 188; views on future collective political becoming for Vietnamese Americans, 152. *See also* Dunnill, Ginger; Luger, Cannupa Hanska
institutional racism, Phi on, 29–30

internalized racism, Phi on, 30
internalized stereotypes: and self-esteem, 9–10, 192–93n9; Vietnamese Australians' internalization of Australia as white nation, 143, 144
Iraq War, and US expansionist ambitions, 188
Israel: Vietnamese refugees settled in, 115; war against Gazans and Palestinians as racist imperialism, 188

Kapil, Bhanu, 12
Kaya Press, 185
Kearney, Douglas, 41
Kiarostami, Abbas, 43
Kim, Elaine, 74
Kingston, Maxine Hong, 9, 74
Knausgaard, Karl Ove, 92–93
Kupersmith, Violet: *Build Your House Around My Body,* 90; on burden of representation, 93; dialogue with Rosewood, 87–96; on evasion and subversion in her writing, 96; fairy tales as inspiration for, 88; *The Frangipani Hotel,* 90; on Hai Bà Trưng, 90; on her rebel DNA, 89–90; on her writing career as subversion of stereotypes, 88; on implications of an author's name, 92; monsters in works of, as indirect reference to Vietnam War, 93; on mother as disobedient woman, 89; on mother's concern about her work, 95; on mother's mixed marriage, family's shock at, 94; period living in Việt Nam, 88; on refugee trauma at heart of her books, 95–96; on struggle with Vietnamese-ness as "mixed" person, 93–94; subversion of heterosexual monogamous norms in work of, 90–91; and Vietnam War, disinclination to write about, 93; Viet Thanh Nguyen on, xiv; on wearing of different identities, 92; works by, as eerie rather than scary, 95; writing routine of, 96

Lại, Thanhhà: on childhood pressure to choose White or Black peer group, 67; current indifference to others' opinions about her, 66, 67; dialogue with Barry, 66–73; on differing tastes in literature, 72; on her childhood in Alabama, 66–67; interest in gender issues, 72–73; on pressure from Vietnamese community's expectations for women, 70–71, 73; on quality of writing *vs.* racialized authenticity, 69; on readers' interpretations of her stories, 72; refusal to be constrained by gendered and racialized authorial voice, 67, 68, 71–72; Vietnamese lineage, 66; Viet Thanh Nguyen on, xiii; work-in-progress about Texas cowboy, 67
Lakshmi, Padma, 103
Lam, Vincent: *Bloodletting and Miraculous Cures,* TV adaptation of, 62–63; as Canadian-born, 58; and Canadians' social expectations, decision to act in opposition to, 59, 60–61; childhood experiences of racism, 61; decision as racialized person to write alone, 62–64; dialogue with Cao, 58–65; as ethnic Chinese, 61; *The Headmaster's Wager,* 62; on intellectualization as defense against racism, 61–62; longing for Việt Nam, 58–59; parents' flight to Canada, 58; as physician, racism and, 63; Scotiabank Giller Prize won by, 62; on white Canadians' view of Vietnam War, 59; Viet Thanh Nguyen on, xiii; work as television writer, anti-Asian incident ending, 63
Laos, US war in, 188

Last Night I Dreamed of Peace (Đặng), 139
Lê, An-My, 155
Lê, Ngoc, 155
Lê, T. K.: "Afterlives" and "Afterlives II," 160–61; on conversation between her and Đoàn's poetry, 161; dialogue with Đoàn, 153, 155–61; on detail, excess focus on, 157; Đoàn on poetry of, 159–60; on Đoàn's *We Play a Game,* 155, 158, 160–61; "The Fisherwoman and the Fisherman," 158–59; on her life in suspension, 160; joy in poetry of, Đoàn on, 155; "sniper girl," 155, 161; telling of family's story, in hope of understanding family, 157–58; Viet Thanh Nguyen on, xii; on Vietnam War, US reshaping of story to justify its actions, 157–58, 160
Lee, Li-Young, 1–2, 7
Lê Lợi, 8
lê thị diễm thúy, 12, 75
Li, Lillian, 129
Lien, Tracey: *All That's Left Unsaid,* 144–45, 146–47, 148–49; on audiences' "colonialist reader's eye," 149; on author events, types of questions and comments at, 147; on authors of color, stereotypes about, 149; on authors' panel in "hometown" Cabramatta, 144–45; on childhood efforts to model herself on white Australians, 144; concerns about right to tell certain stories, 144–45; on cultural alienation as child in Australia, 143; desire to avoid being pigeon-holed as Asian/migrant writer, 146–47, 148–49; dialogue with Dao, 143–50; on difficulty of overcoming public image of Australia as white country, 147; ethnic background of, 145; on joy of writing, 150; on parallels between her life and Dao's, 143; on places that feel like home, 145; on public's lack of awareness about Vietnamese/Asian community in Australia, 143; recent years as US resident, 144
Linder, Valérie, 86
literature: importance in battle against racism, sexism, and imperialism, xi; Lại on differing tastes in, 72
Lorde, Audre, 173
loss, as pervasive in Vietnamese culture, 16
Lowe, Lisa, 74
Lực, Marcelino Lực: critique of West's romanticized vision of Communist revolution in Việt Nam, 141; current project on Vietnam War, 140–41; dialogue with Pham, 134–42; early childhood ambitions, 134–35; family of, discussed in graphic novels, 137; father of, as scholar who valued education, 137; on his brother's artistic talent, 140; on his brother's troubled life and suicide, 137; on his fascination with Việt Nam, 140; on his law training, 134; on his turn to art career, 137; on modern Việt Nam, as physically and politically unappealing, 141–42; mother of, as artistic type, 137; on parents' view of his art career, 139–40; Pham on high quality of graphic novels of, 136; as pre-1975 War migrant to France, 115; on Republic of Việt Nam, troubled history of, 135; *Saigon Calling—London 1963–75,* 137; study of English literature at the Sorbonne, 134; *Such a Lovely Little War—Saigon 1961–63,* 137; on Việt Nam as subject for his work, 140; Viet Thanh Nguyen on, xiv; on Western bias in reporting on North *vs.* South Vietnam, 135

Luger, Cannupa Hanska, 152
lullabies, Vietnamese, Hoa Nguyen and Nguyễn Phan Quế Mai on, 113
"The Master's Tools Will Never Dismantle the Master's House" (Lorde), 173
Les memoires de Sain Simon, influence on Doan Bui, 21
MeToo movement, 81, 197–98n17
middle-class Vietnamese, Elliot's *Sacred Willow* as effort to educate Americans about, 124
Midwest, US, racialization of Southeast Asians in, 31
Miranda, Lin-Manuel, 4
Möi, Anna: *The Butterfly's Venom,* 128, 129–30; on choice of language to write in, 129–30; dialogue with Pham, 126–33; on experience of return to Việt Nam, 126, 131; on her writing, necessary element of poetry in, 133; on multiple identities of diaspora Vietnamese, 130; parents' departure from Việt Nam, 128; on parts of her books' potentially offensive to Vietnamese government, 128–29; on Phan's *The Reeducation of Cherry Truong,* 126; as pre-1975 migrant to France, 115; *Riz Noir,* 128–29; on translations of her books, 128–29, 130; on Việt Nam today, censorship in, 132; Viet Thanh Nguyen on, xiv; on young Vietnamese in Việt Nam, daily lives of, 131, 132
Morrison, Tony, xiv, 179
movies: as high-impact but expensive medium, xii; influence on Đoàn, 156–57. *See also* Vietnam War movies
Muñoz, José Esteban, 151, 152, 173

narrative plenitude of works about Vietnamese: as goal, xiii, xiv–xv; movement toward, xiii–xiv; social and economic justice as prerequisite for, xiii
narrative scarcity of works about Vietnamese: as present reality, xiii; as symptom of structural inequality, xiii
Nelson, Maggie, 12
New York Times's racialized view of Truong, 51–52
Ngô Đình Diệm, overthrow of, 135
Nguyen, Beth (Bich) Minh: childhood hope of meeting children like herself, 26; childhood reading and story-writing, 25–26; on conversation with Doan Bui as comforting Vietnamese-only space, 25; dialogue with Doan Bui, 21–28; Doan Bui's knowledge of, through her books, 21; on increase in anti-Asian hate crimes, 27; influence on Doan Bui, 21, 22, 23; on life in white world, damage done by, 22; love of books as child, 22; on need for Vietnamese-only spaces, 25; *New Yorker* essay on changing her first name, 26–27; *Pioneer Girl,* 22; on racism and white supremacy as global problems, 27; reasons for writing, 22; on shame felt in white-run spaces, 25; on tiresomeness of always considering white people's feelings, 27; on Vietnamese food, value of learning to make, 24; Viet Thanh Nguyen on, xiii; on white role models in childhood, damage done by, 22; writing as effort to rethink, unsettle, and remake, 22
Nguyen, Diana Khoi: on animal behavior as way of understanding humans, 41–42; on Bergvall's *Drift,* 42–43; on Che's *Appocalips* project, 39, 41, 42–43; on Che's "Essay on Beauty," 43; on Che's *Fade In,* 39; on Che's

Split, 45; dialogue with Che, 11, 39–45; "Đổi Mới Series," 41–42; *Ghost of,* 40; as haunted by family past, 40, 41; on Kearney's Critical Karaoke, 51; on Kiarostami's *Close-Up,* 43; on multi-vectored works, 42–43; on multi-genre projects, 44–45; on Polley's *Stories We Tell,* 43; on similarities between her family and Che's, 43–44; time in video work of, Che on, 40; Viet Thanh Nguyen on, xii; on writing in persona, problematic aspects of, 39, 45

Nguyen, Hieu Minh: on audience's expectations for Vietnam War stories, 167–68; on coming out, and estrangement from family and Vietnamese culture, 163–64; dialogue with Huynh, 153, 162–68; estrangement from family, 162, 163–64; family of, as "chosen" family, 163; on family's memories of Vietnam War, 168; on forfeiting desire to be understood, as type of freedom, 164; on forgiving as privilege, 168; on insights on forgiveness gained from poetry, 165; on multiple interpretations of a poem, 166; on persistence of war trauma through generations, 168; on poetry as filter to "find your people," 166–67; on poetry as means of understanding his family and their history, 165; on poetry as shield from world, 163–64; on representation as widening, 167; on right to tell certain stories, 167; Viet Thanh Nguyen on, xiv; on writer's responsibility to tell family's story, 167

Nguyen, Hoa: on childhood in US, experiences of racism, 108; as child of Vietnamese mother and white father, 105; on complex structure of time, 112–13; dialogue with Nguyễn Phan Quế Mai, 105–13; departure from Việt Nam as young child, 105; on epigenetic transfer of trauma, 112; experience of, as "inflected" by refugee experience, 105; on feminism's influence on her work, 112; *Ficus Carica Sonnet,* 113; honoring of mother in poems, 109; mother's complete abandonment of Vietnamese identity, 108; poetry of, as effort to heal rupture from Vietnamese origins, 108–9; on recovery from trauma as underlying theme in her work, 112; *Red Juice: Poems* (1998–2008), 112; shamanistic connection with ancestors pursued through poetry, 108–10, 112; *A Thousand Times You Lose Your Treasure,* 109; on Vietnamese lullabies, 113; Viet Thanh Nguyen on, xiii; visit to Việt Nam, as powerful experience, 109; on writing that mimics structure of time, 110

Nguyen, Ly Thuy, on refugee futures, 152–53

Nguyễn, Philip: as cohost of "ÁCCENTED: Dialogues in Diaspora" series, 185; on COVID-19 pandemic, 170; feeling of friendship for Tran, 170; on his childhood in California, 171–72; on his work across the diaspora-verse through DVAN, 176; on latent inheritance of trauma, 171; on need to work for diaspora's better future, 178; process of reconnecting with the diasporic Vietnamese heritage, 172; on Su's *I Love Yous Are for White People,* 172; use of ethnic and Asian American studies to build bridge between family and broader community, 174; Viet Thanh Nguyen on, xiv; on Vietnamese show of love through action and not words, 172

Nguyễn, Thảo: dialogue with Thi Bui, 97–104; discovery of Vietnamese community beyond traditional one, 102; empathy of, Thi Bui on, 103; encounters with racism and sexism, 103; facility with language, Thi Bui on, 104; *Go Vote* music video, 100; meeting of Thi Bui at CAAM, 102; mostly white childhood friends, 101–2; on songwriting as communication, 104; on Thi Bui's *The Best We Could Do,* 104; turn to celebration of Vietnamese culture, 102–3; on Vietnamese history, gaps in his knowledge about, 104; Viet Thanh Nguyen on, xiv; *We the Common,* 97; work on electoral politics, 100, 102; work with California Coalition for Women Prisoners, 97

Nguyen, Vaan: on Bible as inspiration, 79; dialogue with Aubert-Nguyen, 77–86; on distance from everyday existence provided by poetry, 85; early influences on poetry of, 77; family's migration to Israel, 115; father's wish to arrange marriage for, 84; on her conversion to Judaism, 80–81; interest in spirituality, 85; on living between two different cultures, 81–82; "Mekong River," 82–83; poetry of, as map of her relationships with the world, 85; recent poems written in Việt Nam, about Việt Nam, 85; search for other Vietnamese people in Israel, 84; third book of poetry, subjects to be addressed in, 85; *The Truffle Eye,* 82; and Vietnamese poetry, recent interest in, 77–78; Viet Thanh Nguyen on, xiv; on visits to Việt Nam, 84

Nguyen, Viet Thanh: on authors' dislike of critics' and scholars' discussion of their books, 56–57; as cofounder of DVAN, 184; as cohost of "ÁCCENTED: Dialogues in Diaspora" series, 185; on current critical moment in US life, 52; and *diaCRITICS* magazine, 184; dialogue with Truong, 49–57; on equal opportunity to be mediocre as goal, 52; and gendered and racialized authorial voice, effort to move beyond, 51, 52–53; on increasing anger of Vietnamese American writers, 53; influence on Doan Bui, 27; on narrative plenitude of works about Vietnamese as goal, xiii, xiv–xv; on overthrow of Western racism, imperialism, and colonialism as goal, xiii–xiv, xv; on published Vietnamese diasporic writers as voice for the voiceless, 181; and Pulitzer Prize, opportunities opened by, 52; as scholar, and authority of her authorial voice, 49–50; *The Sympathizer,* difficulty finding publisher for, 56; on Truong's *Bitter in the Mouth,* 54; on Truong's *Book of Salt,* 50, 55; yearning to learn about Việt Nam, vii

Nguyễn Du, 78, 195n8

Nguyễn Phan Quế Mai: desire to write about unresolved issues among Vietnamese, 107–8; dialogue with Hoa Nguyen, 105–13; difficult childhood in postwar southern Việt Nam, 105–6; *Dust Child,* 111; on DVAN, importance of work, 108; on epigenetic transfer of trauma, 112; on feminism's influence on her work, 111; on flight of Southern Vietnamese and Chinese Vietnamese, 107; on Hoa Nguyen's *Ficus Carica Sonnet,* 113; on Hoa Nguyen's *A Thousand Times You Lose Your Treasure,* 109; impact of childhood on writing, 107;

The Mountains Sing, 112; on neighbors in Việt Nam sent to reeducation camps, 106; *The Poem I Can't Yet Name,* 110–11; poem on Great Hunger of 1945, 110–11; poems of, as writing back to colonialism and male gaze, 111; on poet's task, 109; *Rice Lullaby,* 113; shamanistic connection with ancestors pursued through poetry, 110–11, 112; on Southern Vietnamese resentment of Northern conquerors, 106, 107; talks with dead grandmothers, 112; Viet Thanh Nguyen on, xiv; on Vietnamese lullabies, 113
Nguyen Qui Duc, 194n6
Ninh, erin Khuê, 75
Nixon, Rob, 198n1

Okada, John, 9
Operation Desert Storm, and US expansionist ambitions, 188
Orderly Departure Program, 116
Ossoff, John, 100
outsider, feeling of being: Lam on, 62–64; refugees and, 60; Strom on, 30

Page Act of 1875, 199n6
Palestinians, Israeli war against, 188
parenting, Strom on goals of, 37
Pelaud, Isabelle Thuy, DVAN and, 184
person(s) of color: as authors, stereotyping of, 149; and Civil Rights Movement, 46; and community pressure, 75; in France, and objections to *réunions non-mixtes,* 24; gains of, as won through resistance and solidarity, 181; and outsider status, 62–64; percentage of population in Canada, 182; Phi on desire to be, 30–31; and pigeonholing by ethnicity, 47, 48, 50, 181; and shame in white spaces, 25; and "slaps in the dark," 103

Pham, Andrew X.: and authorial voice as gendered and racialized, 194n6; on blatant disregard for human rights in Việt Nam, 138; books banned in Việt Nam, 136, 138; *Catfish and Mandala,* 9, 139; current project based on grandmother's life, 138; dialogue with Lực, 134–42; on dubious existence of events not reported in the news, 139; early childhood ambitions, 134; early interest in art, 135–36; father of, as software engineer, 137–38; on gender transition and suicide on his sister, 136; on his childhood in Louisiana, 135; on Lực's graphic novels, 136; residence in Thailand, 136; on responsibility to represent Vietnamese Americans in his work, 139; self-immolation witnessed in Sài Gòn, 139; translation of Đặng's *Last Night I Dreamed of Peace,* 139; turn to career in writing, 136; on two Việt Nams, one inside him and one in real world, 138; on Việt Nam, as place he was "strongly advised" not to return to, 138; on Việt Nam as nearly-exhausted topic for his writing, 138–39; Viet Thanh Nguyen on influence of, xiii; visits to Việt Nam, 138
Phan, Aimee: on acceptable level of brutality in portrayals of trauma, 132–33; current project about Vietnamese who stayed in Vietnam, 131; dialogue with Möi, 126–33; on Lillian Li, 129; on Möi's *The Butterfly's Venom,* 129–30; on multiple identities of diaspora Vietnamese, 130–31; *The Reeducation of Cherry Truong,* 126–27; on refugees' fears of lost homeland, 131; on refugees' return to Việt Nam, complex issues

Phan, Aimee *(continued)*
  in, 126–27; on Vietnamese Americans' feeling of obligation to families in Việt Nam, 131–32; on Vietnamese refugee trauma as subject of her work, 132; Viet Thanh Nguyen on, xiii; *We Should Never Meet*, 132–33; on young Vietnamese in Việt Nam, 131
Phi, Bao: "Called (An Open Letter to Myself)," 29; on childhood in South Minneapolis, 29; childhood refuge in books, 30; on complicity in systems of harm, 37; on coolness/conformity, need to build alternatives to, 33, 37; on desire to be white or person of color, 30–31; dialogue with Strom, 11, 29–38; experiences of racism and cross-racial hostility, 29–30; on family separations at border, 36; on fatherhood's effect on his poetry, 33; on "good" Asian stereotype, 31; on his early slam and spoken-word poetry, 32–33; on his internalization of marginalized identity, 32–33; on internalized racism, 30; on physical experience of Vietnam War as baby, 29; recognition of collective consciousness of trauma, 35; on self-erasure to fit in, 30–31, 192–93n9; on separation from wife and child, trauma of, 35–36; *Sông I Sing*, 9, 29; on Vietnamese hatred of expatriates (Việt Kiều), 35; Viet Thanh Nguyen on, xiii; on visits to Việt Nam, 34, 35
Phillips, Carl, 174
Pinsky, Robert, 158
PiVOT [the Progressive Vietnamese American Organization], Thi Bui and, 100–101
police harassment, Phi on, 29–30
Polley, Sarah, 43

Proust, Marcel, 21
psychological injury from trauma: compounding of, by daily events, 8; as difficult to grasp and express, 10; impossibility of empirical measurement, 8; mask of coolness as response to, 11; as not resolvable in one lifetime, 10; resistance as response to, 11; as theme in Vietnamese diasporic literature, 8
publishers, pigeonholing of Vietnamese diaspora authors, 48, 117, 119–20, 121–22, 124

racial capitalism, and COVID-19 pandemic, 3
racism: experience of, as "being slapped in the dark," 103; as global problem, 27; microaggressions, psychological damage from, 9; severity of, 28; as still alive today, 181; Thảo Nguyễn's encounters with, 103
racism, anti-Asian: in Australia, 182–83, 201n13, 210n16; in Canada, 182; COVID-19 pandemic and, 3, 181–82; in France, 184, 201–2n18; in United States, 3, 108, 181–82, 199–200n6
racism, imperialism, and colonialism of Western countries, xi; overthrow of, as goal, xiii–xiv, xv; Vietnamese diasporic writers as marked by, xii–xiii; writing's importance in battle against, xi
radical solidarity: and Asian American movement, 186–87; as blend of identity and ideology, 186–87; danger of devolving into limited solidarity, 187–88; radical refusal required by, 187–88, 189; as required to fight war, racism, and imperialism, 188–89. *See also* Asian American solidarity; solidarity of people of color

Rankine, Claudia, 12, 57
reading as eating, as theme in *The Cleaving*, 2
reeducation camps, postwar, 106, 197n14
refugee(s): connotations of term, 4; Critical Refugee Studies Collective, 4; and "refugee reflex," 171; as term evoking US militarism and imperialism, 5; as term in *The Cleaving*, 4–5. *See also* Vietnamese refugees
representation, burden of, xii, xiii, 6, 9; effect on creativity, 47; as felt responsibility to correct inaccurate US ideas about Vietnamese, 116, 117; Pham on, 139; and revisiting of old and new wounds, 183–84; and right to tell certain stories, 145–46, 167; Rosewood on, 93. *See also* authority of authorial voice
Republic of Việt Nam, Lực on troubled history of, 135
resistance: gains by people of color won through, 181; as response to trauma, 11
Roots Asian American studies program, 99
Rosewood, Abbigail Nguyen: on an author's name, implications of, 91; on art as resistance to definition, 91; on artmaking as inherently disobedient, 87–88; on burden of representation, 93; on characteristics of Vietnamese *vs.* English languages, 92; dialogue with Kupersmith, 87–96; effort to subvert Vietnamese and American stereotypes of Asian women, 87; on fairy tales about breaking rules, 88–89; on fiction as catalyst for dialogue, 95; on fiercely claiming one's space, 91; focus on courage and truth in work, 87; on Hai Bà Trưng, 90; on her rebel DNA, 90; *If I Had Two Lives,* 90, 95; mother of, as disobedient women, 89; mother's life, in fairytale form, 89; on mother's reaction to her writing, 95; nameless characters in works of, 91, 92; on protecting the imagination, 91; on "pure bloods" as fictional concept, 94; and subversion of heterosexual monogamous norms, 90; use of child's point of view, 91; on Việt Nam as matriarchal society, 90; on Vietnamese artists' work, 94; and Vietnam War, disinclination to write about, 93; on wearing of different identities, 92; Viet Thanh Nguyen on, xiv; writing routine of, 96
Rostopchine, Sophie (La Comtesse de Ségur), 21

San José, California, Vietnamese refugee community in, viii
Santiago, Danny, 194n6
self-erasure of Asian Americans: Phi on, 30–31, 192–93n9; Strom on, 192–93n9
self-esteem, internalized stereotypes and, 9–10, 192–93n9
self-hate in Vietnamese literature, 9–10, 192–93n9
Seraph on the Suwanee (Hurston), 194n6
shamanistic connection with ancestors pursued through poetry: Hoa Nguyen on, 112; Nguyễn Phan Quế Mai on, 110–11, 112
shame felt in white-run spaces: Beth Nguyen on, 25; Doan Bui on, 24; racial stereotypes and, 52
social justice: Asian American writers' work toward, 9, 192n5; as prerequisite for narrative plenitude of works about Vietnamese, xiii

solidarity of people of color, 9, 192n5. *See also* Asian American solidarity
Sông I Sing (Phi), 9, 29
Song of Songs, 79–80
Southern Cross the Dog (Cheng), 69
stereotypes of Asian Americans: and gaze of racist majority, 9; "good" Asian stereotype, 31, 75, 117, 187; internalization of, and self-esteem, 9–10, 192–93n9; in US Midwest, 31
stereotypes of Asian American women: literary examples of, 74; women diasporic Vietnamese writers' writing against, 74, 76
stereotypes of authors of color, 149
stereotypes of Vietnamese American literature, 12–13
Stories We Tell (Polley), 43
Strom, Dao: childhood efforts to deny race, 30; on childhood in northern California mountains, 30; on childhood outsider status, 30; on collective consciousness of trauma, effects of, 35, 36; on commitment to honesty in her work, 33; on coolness/conformity, need to build alternatives to, 32, 37–38; on Danish stepfather, 30; dialogue with Phi, 11, 29–38; on family separations at border, 36; on her atypical family, 34; on her parenting goals, 37; on later-life embrace of Vietnamese roots, 30; on parents' lives in Việt Nam, 31; on Phi's "Called (An Open Letter to Myself)," 29; on projections of ideal American selves, 30; realization of disconnection from Vietnamese culture, 33–34; recognition of collective trauma, 35; and reconnection with Vietnamese heritage, 32; on self-erasure, 192–93n9; Viet Thanh Nguyen on, xiii; on visits to Việt Nam, 32, 33–34, 35; on wishing to be white, 30

structural inequality: and COVID-19 pandemic, 3; narrative scarcity of works about Vietnamese as symptom of, xiii; in Western countries, marked identities of Vietnamese diaspora as evidence of, xi
Su, Lac, 9, 172
symbols, as arbitrary, Vuong on, 17–18
systems of harm, Phi on complicity in, 37

television, as high-impact but expensive medium, x
Texas Tech University Press, 185
Thơ Mới [New Poetry]: Aubert-Nguyen's interest in, 78; defined, 195n8
Thúy, Kim: on beautiful sadness in Vuong's writing, 15–16; on Canadians' limited knowledge of Vietnam War, 13; dialogue with Vuong, 10–11, 12–20; *Em,* 20; on *em* (little sister or brother), deep personal meaning of, 20; *The Gangster We Are All Looking For,* 12–13, 76; on her writing process, 12–13; as inspiration for Vuong, 14; on licking stamps to get high, 13; on liminal space of creativity, 19–20; on maturity of Vuong's writing, 14; name recognition of, viii; and pressures on women writers of Vietnamese diaspora, 75; on strength of Vietnamese people, 16; on Việt Nam, experience of visits to, 18–19; on Vietnamese as present-tense-only language, 15; on Vietnamese people, strength of, 14–15; Viet Thanh Nguyen on, x; on Vietnamese sense of time, 15
time, Vietnamese sense of, 15
Tran, Barbara, 9
Tran, Paul: *All the Flowers Kneeling,* 172; current project about mother and her twin, 177; dialogue with

Philip Nguyễn and Minh Huynh Vu, 154, 169–78; on drive to discover future possibilities, 177; on emotional impulses as driver of formal imperatives, 173; on failed poetic investigations, 175–76; on family holiday dinners, 169; on future of Vietnamese writing, 177; goal of writing to produce knowledge about race, gender, imperialism, and etc., 171; "the Hydra" poetic form invented by, 172–73; inability to continue pretending, 171; on mother as twin, 177; on move to California, 169; "Orchard of Unknowing," 177; on Philip Nguyễn as sibling from another lifetime, 169; poems on possibility of loving and being loved, 175; on poetry as discovery and transformation of experience, 174–75; on poetry as enactment of experience, 173, 174, 175; on poetry as necessarily based on deep inward search, 174–75; on present life mingled with memories of past, 170–71; on pretending as first job of children of refugees, 169–70, 177; queer and diasporic critique of received forms as goal of, 173–74; "Scheherazade/Scheherazade," 175; second collection of poems about starting over, 174; Viet Thanh Nguyen on, xiv; "The Twin" new poetic form developed by, 177

trauma: collective, Phi and Strom on, 33, 35, 36; epigenetic transfer of, 14, 112; persistence through generations, 171; Phan on acceptable level of brutality in portrayals of, 132–33; recovery from, as theme in Hoa Nguyen's work, 112; of refugee, as central to Kupersmith's work, 95–96; of refugees, as theme in Phan's work, 132;

resistance as response to, 11; of war, persistence through generations, 168. *See also* psychological injury from trauma

Trump, Donald, on COVID-19 as "Chinese virus," 3

Trump administration: border policy, 187; and deportation of Southeast Asians, 98; and family separations at border, 36; Truong on, 53

Trưng Sisters, 8

Truong, Monique: and authorial voice as gendered and racialized, 49, 50–55, 194n6; *Bitter in the Mouth,* 54–55; *The Book of Salt,* 50, 53–54, 55; on current critical moment in US life, 52; on David Eng as target audience for her books, 56–57; dialogue with Viet Nguyen, 49–57; on literary scholars, writing for, 56; on *New York Times*'s racialized reception of *Bitter in the Mouth,* 54; on publishing process as brutal, 54; self-image as political writer, 53; Viet Thanh Nguyen on, xi; on Trump administration, 53

Truyện Kiều (Nguyễn Du), 78, 195n8

United Nations Convention Relating to the Status of Refugees (1951), 4

United States: anti-Asian racism in, 3, 108, 181–82, 199–200n6; campaign to ban teaching of race and racism, 27; characteristics of Vietnamese refugees in, 115; closing of borders, as affront to minority, immigrant, marginalized, and colonized peoples, 187–88; expansionist ambitions, 188; as force of war, racism, and colonization, 188–89; ignoring of Vietnamese refugees due to humiliation of losing war, 117; national fascination with Việt Nam, 117; oppressive white

United States *(continued)*
supremacist heteropatriarchy of, 151; past and ongoing genocide, slavery, and warmongering, 151; progress by people of color gained only through resistance and solidarity, 181; racism and sexism in, 199–200n6; Vuong on expectations for Vietnamese writers in, 13–14

Uvalde, Texas, school shooting, 202n1

Việt Nam: border war with China (1979), 107; censorship in, 120, 132, 136; centuries of war and foreign occupation, 8; creativity of young people in, 18; opening to markets and outside world in 1990s, 126, 197n14; Strom on parents' lives in, 31; as term, *vs.* Vietnam, ix, 191n2; Western countries intervention in, throughout twentieth century, 5

Việt Nam, American perception of: as different from that of Vietnamese Americans, vx; influence of Vietnam War on, ix, xi

Vietnam, as term *vs.* Việt Nam, ix, 191n2

Việt Nam, experience of visits to: Aubert-Nguyen on, 84–85; Hoa Nguyen on, 109; Kupersmith on, 88; Möi on, 126, 131; Pham on, 138; Phi on, 33, 35; Rosewood on, 94; Strom on, 32, 33–34; Thúy on, 18–19; Vaan Nguyen on, 84; Vuong on, 17–19

Việt Nam, postwar: Nguyễn Phan Quế Mai on life in, 106–7; persecution of South Vietnamese supporters of US, 115–16; programs allowing emigration of US loyalists, 116

Vietnamese American community: as fourth-largest Asian American group, 114; as largest Vietnamese population outside Việt Nam, xiii, 114; perception by some as foreigners, xi–xii. *See also* future collective political becoming for Vietnamese Americans

Vietnamese American literature: playfulness of, Vuong on, 12–13; stereotypes about, Vuong on, 12–13

Vietnamese culture: Hieu Minh Nguyen on estrangement from, 163–64; importance of food and language in, 34; legends of warriors and resistors in, 8

Vietnamese diaspora: as both cleaving from and cleaving to, 2; countries with largest Vietnamese populations, 114; cultural inheritances of, 153; definition of, 3; destination countries of, x–xi; diversity of individual characteristics and motives, 3–4; as embedded in settler colonial histories, 151; emotions entangled with, 4; and English as "master's tongue," x; finding basis for unity of, as goal of *The Cleaving* project, 186; in France, diversity of, 3; to France, before Vietnam War, 114–15; global number of, x; ideological cleavages within, 186; implications of varying terms used to describe, 4–5; many faces and facets of, 2; as method of analysis, 4; realization of disconnection from Vietnamese culture, 35; Vietnam War as prerequisite for, 186; younger generation's embrace of estrangement, 153

Vietnamese diasporic writers: changing of Global North literary landscape by, 3; characteristics of works by, 184; and choice of ignoring or being dominated by past, xiv; choice of writing as means of expression, xii; *diaCRITICS* magazine and, 184; disproportionate number published *vs.* whites, 181; diverse perspectives and interests of, 180; greater freedom to publish than Việt Nam residents, x–xi; increasing anger of, Viet Nguyen on, 53; increasing interest in, 183; in languages other than English, xii–xiv; layers of internal and external pressures faced by, 180, 199n3; liminal space of creativity in, Thúy and Vuong on, 19–20; as marked by white society's racism, sexism, and colonialism, xii–xiii; multiple identities, Möi and Pham on, 130–31; publishing in English, great increase in number of, ix; refusal of marginality, 179; unique challenge to create freely on their own terms, 179; views on publishing industry, 54, 69, 71, 118–19, 180; as voice for the voiceless, 181; Vuong on, 18; women and queen writers' ambivalence about family and community expectations, 180. *See also* publishers, pigeonholing of Vietnamese diaspora authors; representation, burden of; women diasporic Vietnamese writers

Vietnamese households, laughter in, 15

Vietnamese language: as present-tense-only language, 15; untranslatable phrases, Vuong on, 16–17

Vietnamese people, strength of, 14–15, 16

Vietnamese refugees: Cao on effects of experience as, 59, 60, 62; Coppola's use of, in *Apocalypse Now*, as violence, 42; demographic diversity of, 114; and emotional burden of having lost homeland, 117, 131; experience of, in Hoa Nguyen's work, 105; flight following Communist victory in Vietnam War, 5, 107, 115, 117; as forced from Việt Nam, 114; Hayslip on life as, 122; Huynh comic about family's experience in refugee camps, 168; increasing interest in books about, 119–20, 121; indeterminate time frame of status, 5; as initially unwelcome in US, 192n8; Nguyen, Ly Thuy on refugee futures, 152–53; Pham on refugees' fears of lost homeland, 131; raping of, 122; refugee aesthetic among Vietnamese diasporic writers, 124–25; return to Việt Nam, complex issues in, 126–27; strong attachment to Việt Nam, 114; as subject of Phan's work, 132; Tran on pretending as first job of children of, 169–70, 177; trauma of, in works of Kupersmith, 95–96; to US, characteristics of, 115; US ignoring of, due to humiliation of losing war, 117

Vietnam Veterans Memorial, failure to recognize non-American deaths, ix

Vietnam War: American memories of, in 1970s–80s, ix; Australia and, 182; Canada and, 182; deaths in, 114; histories' focus on plight of North Vietnamese *vs.* South Vietnamese, 116; influence on global perception of Việt Nam, viii; loss of, as American humiliation, 117, 197n10; media depiction of Vietnamese as inferior, 117; necessity of ongoing engagement with meaning of, 8–9; number of bombs dropped in, 114; as one of many US wars, 188; predominance of Marxist, antiwar perspectives in histories of, 116; as prerequisite for Vietnamese diaspora culture, 186; television coverage of, and US view of Vietnamese, 116–17; upcoming 50th anniversary of end of, 189; as US invasion of Việt Nam, x; US reshaping of story about, to justify its actions, Lê on, 157–58, 160; US withdrawal, and sense of betrayal in Vietnamese supporters of US, 115; Vuong on expectations for Vietnamese writers to write about, 13–14; white Canadians' view of, 59

Vietnam War movies: *Full Metal Jacket*, Lê's "sniper girl" and, 153, 155; objectification of Vietnamese people in, ix–x, 10, 116, 196n6; preoccupation with reviving lost manhood of American soldiers, 116. See also *Apocalypse Now* (Coppola)

Vizenor, Gerald, 152

Vu, Minh Huynh: on correspondence between Tran and Philip Nguyễn, 178; Viet Thanh Nguyen on, xiv; dialogue with Paul Tran and Philip Nguyễn, 154, 169–78

Vuong, Ocean: on beautiful sadness in Vietnamese culture, 16; on creativity of younger generation in Việt Nam, 18; dialogue with Kim Thúy, 10–11, 12–20; *On Earth We Are Briefly Gorgeous*, 17; on expectations for Vietnamese writers in US, 13–14; on laughter in Vietnamese households, 15; on liminal space of creativity, 19; maturity of prose, Thúy on, 14; name recognition of, viii; on playfulness of Vietnamese American literature, 12–13; on rules for writing, 12; on strength of Vietnamese people, 14, 15; on symbols as arbitrary, 17–18; Thúy as inspiration for, 14; Thúy on beautiful sadness in writing of, 15–16; on *The Gangster We Are All Looking For*, 12–13; on trauma's effect on DNA, 14; on untranslatable phrases in Vietnamese, 16–17; on Việt Nam, experience of visits to, 17–19; Viet Thanh Nguyen on, x; on Vietnamese sense of time, 15; on writing process, 17

war, racism, and imperialism of US, radical solidarity required to fight, 188–89

wars and violence: as traumas causing psychological injury, 8; in Vietnamese history, 8. See also psychological injury from trauma

Western canon, consuming to take in and take apart, 2

Western countries: bias in reporting on Vietnam War, Lực on, 135; racism, imperialism, and colonialism of, ix; romanticized vision of Communist dictatorships. Lực on, 141; as sometimes tolerant of Vietnamese, xi; structural inequality in, xiii

white supremacy: cis-heterosexist and patriarchal, as difficult to see, 9; COVID-19 pandemic and, 3; as global problem, Beth Nguyen on, 27; Hoa Nguyen's childhood experiences of, 108; Thi Bui on effects of, 102, 103–4

Wilder, Laura Ingalls, 22

The Woman Warrior (Kingston), 74

women diasporic Vietnamese writers: bitterness resulting from family pressures, 75; community pressures on, 70–71, 73, 75–76; family pressures on, 74–76; as inherently feminist, 76; types of works acceptable to publishers, 74; voyeuristic gaze of mainstream readers and, 75; writing against heterosexist and racist stereotypes of women, 74, 76; writing against white mainstream expectations, 75–76

Wong Kar-wai films, Đoàn on, 156–57

writing: importance in battle against racism, sexism, and imperialism, xi; joy of, 150; as low-cost medium of expression, xii. See also Vietnamese diasporic writers

Founded in 1893,
UNIVERSITY OF CALIFORNIA PRESS
publishes bold, progressive books and journals
on topics in the arts, humanities, social sciences,
and natural sciences—with a focus on social
justice issues—that inspire thought and action
among readers worldwide.

The UC PRESS FOUNDATION
raises funds to uphold the press's vital role
as an independent, nonprofit publisher, and
receives philanthropic support from a wide
range of individuals and institutions—and from
committed readers like you. To learn more, visit
ucpress.edu/supportus.